*Praise for Malcolm Mackay's Glasgow Trilogy*

'Gripping and vivid . . . Mackay succeeds magnificently'  *Guardian*

'Superb . . . Mackay is a true original, managing to conjure up a gripping new way of portraying city-noir . . . He's no longer a rising star. He's risen'  **Marcel Berlins, *The Times***

'Reviewers often groan at the hyperbole with which publishers adorn new novels, but with Malcolm Mackay it is justified . . . this is crime writing with ambition. The youthful Mackay has the command of a writer twice his age, and he has delivered a conclusion to his trilogy that is just as cohesive and forceful as his previous two books'  *Financial Times*

'Remarkable . . . the existing clan of Scottish writers may have to look to their laurels'  *Daily Express*

'Mackay ratchets up the tension like a master'  *Daily Telegraph*

'Brutal, witty and well-written . . . brilliant'  *Sunday Telegraph*

'An amazing novel, incredibly gripping from the first page to the last. A vivid portrait of the Glasgow underworld, it's completely hypnotic'  **Mark Billingham**

'A real revelation, a real find for me'  **Kate Mosse**

# THE SUDDEN ARRIVAL OF VIOLENCE

**Malcolm Mackay** was born and grew up in Stornoway, where he still lives. *The Necessary Death of Lewis Winter*, his much-lauded debut, was the first in the Glasgow Trilogy, set in the city's underworld. It won the Crime Thriller Book Club Best Read Award and was shortlisted for the CWA John Creasey New Blood Dagger Award for Best Crime Debut of the Year and the Scottish First Book of the Year Award. *How A Gunman Says Goodbye*, the second book in the series, won the Deanston Scottish Crime Book of the Year Award. *The Sudden Arrival of Violence* is the concluding part of the trilogy. Malcolm's fourth novel, *The Night the Rich Men Burned*, will be out soon.

Follow Malcolm @malcolm_mackay

# THE SUDDEN ARRIVAL OF VIOLENCE

MALCOLM MACKAY

PAN BOOKS

First published 2014 by Mantle

This paperback edition published 2014 by Pan Books
an imprint of Pan Macmillan, a division of Macmillan Publishers Limited
Pan Macmillan, 20 New Wharf Road, London N1 9RR
Basingstoke and Oxford
Associated companies throughout the world
www.panmacmillan.com

ISBN 978-1-4472-8649-3

1 3 5 7 9 8 6 4 2

A CIP catalogue record for this book is available from the British Library.

Typeset by Ellipsis Digital Limited, Glasgow
Printed and bound by CPI Group (UK) Ltd, Croydon, CR0 4YY

To Helen & Andrew

# CHARACTERS

**Calum MacLean** – So much talent, and he doesn't want to use it. Used his talent as a gunman on Frank, a man he cared about. Now he wants a different life.

**Peter Jamieson** – Too many distractions, too many betrayals. Now he needs to get back to what he does best, taking down enemies and making money through his criminal organization.

**John Young** – It was rough when Frank stabbed them in the back. Now they move forward, with Young the schemer as Jamieson's right-hand man.

**DI Michael Fisher** – Cases have slipped through his fingers. Possible informants falling away. People are starting to talk. Maybe he's not the hot talent in the city any more.

**William MacLean** – For years he's been worrying about Calum, his little brother. There's nothing he wouldn't do to help him escape his life as a gunman.

**Hugh 'Shug' Francis** – First lesson you learn when you run a criminal business is that you can't do it alone. Make the right deals, and everything can work your way.

**David 'Fizzy' Waters** – He's Shug's right-hand man, and he'd go to the ends of the Earth for him. But there are risks being taken and sacrifices made that don't sit well.

**Kenny McBride** – He's just a driver, but he got nervous. He went to Fisher and talked. But it doesn't have to be a big deal, so long as Jamieson never finds out.

**Shaun Hutton** – Shug's gunman, which is – so far – an easy thing to be. But he's always worked the right angles, stayed friends with the right people.

**George Daly** – You spend your life content to be menial muscle for Jamieson, but your talent won't let you be happy. Others want more, including the betrayal of friends.

**Deana Burke** – She loves Kenny, but he can be weak sometimes. She pushed him towards the police and is praying it doesn't come back to haunt her.

**Richard Hardy** – With decades of experience as an accountant, he knows how to work a book. Shug trusts him with all his financial affairs.

**Alex MacArthur** – You don't become one of the biggest gangsters in any city by standing still. You pick your opportunities, and look for profit in every corner.

**Nate Colgan** – Perhaps the most quietly intimidating man in the city. You pay him, he does the job and you don't ever expect to be friends.

**PC Joseph Higgins** – Does talking to Young make him bent? Well, he talks, but he does his best and, as his confidence grows, his best is getting better.

**PC Paul Greig** – The bigger the web you weave, the more likely you are to get yourself entangled. How long can anyone keep doing the things he does?

**Don Park** – Many people think he's MacArthur's natural successor. One of MacArthur's senior men, he clearly sees himself as the future.

**Barry Fairly** – One thing people in the criminal industry will always need is counterfeit IDs. A good counterfeiter like Barry can make a killing, so long as he doesn't make enemies.

**Frank MacLeod** – A legendary gunman, a father-figure for Jamieson. But he screwed up, and he wouldn't accept being retired. Jamieson had no choice but to order his killing.

**DC Ian Davies** – There's a real danger, if he keeps working in the same office as Fisher, that he's going to have to do some actual work soon.

**Emma Munro** – Her relationship with Calum could have gone somewhere, if she hadn't found out what he is. She found out because Young wanted her to, and she walked.

**Kirk Webster** – Nobody wants to employ a man like Kirk, but many people have to. He works for a phone company, which makes him a useful idiot.

**DCI Anthony Reid** – People are losing faith in Fisher, but it's Reid's opinion that matters. For now, he still believes in his most dogged officer.

**Elaine Francis** – She loves her husband, but she's watching Shug change. He's taking decisions that alter her life and their children's lives, and she can say nothing.

**Tommy Scott** – He had so much ambition when he started dealing for Shug. He thought he had the better of Frank, until Calum turned up and killed him.

**Andy 'Clueless' McClure** – Clueless always followed Tommy, even to the grave. Calum killed them both, rescued Frank and let Clueless take the blame for a murder-suicide.

**Lewis Winter** – He was Shug's first attempt at impacting on the drug trade. He was a bad attempt, and Calum had no trouble removing him on Jamieson's behalf.

**Glen Davidson** – Shug's second attempt. An ill-judged revenge effort to kill Calum, which ended with Davidson dead and Shug back at square one.

**PC Marcus Matheson** – Any young cop needs to catch the eye of the senior officers, make a good impression. Matheson's doing his best.

**Roy Bowles** – A little old man, so nice to everyone he meets. He's been selling guns to people like Calum for decades and is indirectly responsible for a lot of dead bodies.

**Des Collins** – One of Alex MacArthur's gunmen. A tough cookie, with a track record everyone knows about.

**Alan Bavidge** – He seemed like such a nice guy, but there was always a darkness there. He worked for Billy Patterson, which tells you plenty. Then someone killed him.

**Billy Patterson** – He runs a competent business. Debt collection, that sort of thing. Always been good at avoiding stepping on toes.

**Helen Harrison** – A likeable middle-aged lady, working for a charity she believes in. Their office is right across the hall from that nice Mr Hardy.

**Ashraf Dutta** – One thing he has in common with Shug is that he trusts Hardy with his finances. Mr Dutta has less to hide, and cares more about his accountant.

**PC Tom McIntyre** – When you've been a PC for nearly a decade you do get tired of the enthusiasm of your younger colleagues.

**Tony O'Connor** – The strength of Shug's car-ring comes from men like Tony. A longtime friend, an excellent steady hand to run a garage.

**Maurice 'Sly' Cooper** – He's been a mate of William MacLean for years. Everyone likes William; nobody knows anything about his brother.

**Morven Rae** – She was William's girlfriend for six years, and he still wouldn't marry her. She walked, and William doesn't like to talk about it, if you don't mind.

**Kevin Currie** – One of Jamieson's best earners, with his tax-free cigarettes and alcohol. The sort of self-assured guy that organizations need.

**Angus Lafferty** – Another vital cog for Jamieson. A drug importer, a key part of the process and a profitable man. Profitable makes you popular.

**DC Curtis Baird** – He doesn't strive for anonymity like DC Davies, but it's rather thrust upon him by Fisher's dominant attitude.

**Marty Jones** – Bearable only for the profits he makes from women and moneylending. Still trying to wriggle back into the good books after keeping more of those profits for himself than he should.

**Potty Cruickshank** – A second generation loan-shark, and one of the biggest sharks in the city, in every sense. Fat, fearsome and no friend to anyone he can't dominate and make money from.

**Bobby Wayne** – Runs a large warehouse in the city, which is a useful thing for people like Peter Jamieson who need places to move their product through.

**Greg Lacock** – A middle-aged, chubby, arrogant man who wrongly thought he could become a big player. He was Calum's first employer in the business.

**Alasdair Marston** – He owned William's garage before William did, and was a friend of Lacock's. He hired William, Lacock hired Calum.

**Stan Austin** – Was an old school-friend of William's, did some work for Lacock. One perceived slight later, and Lacock sent Calum round to use his fists.

**David Kirkpatrick** – He was, apparently, a threat to Lacock and his business. He was then the first person Calum was ever hired to kill.

**Charles Simpson** – A lawyer, and a good one. Good means expensive, and means that you have to be someone like Peter Jamieson to afford his services.

# 1

He's working later than intended. It's after seven o'clock in the evening now. Late enough to call it a good day's work. Putting documents away. All into their folders, placed neatly on the shelf. He'll be working on them again tomorrow. It's boring work, sure, but he long ago reconciled himself to that. He's been doing accounts for thirty-five years; you can reconcile yourself to anything in that time. Might be different if it was a bigger operation. Way back in time, when he'd had ambition, he thought he could build something exciting. Gave up on that. Richard Hardy is happy with what he has now. A one-man company. A little office in a small building where he looks after his select group of loyal customers. There are two offices downstairs; he doesn't see the people there much. A small charity has the office across the hall from his – something for the children of the very poor. Run by two middle-aged, well-meaning women. Richard used to have a secretary, but he had to let her go. Tough times. But he's surviving.

His customers are loyal because of the type of accountant he is. Reliable, solid, silent. Most of his clients are small-business owners, honest enough on the surface. They just want to catch a break now and then. It's hard for them, Richard understands that. Moving money around saves some of it for the client. There's nothing immoral about that, in his eyes. These people work hard; he helps them gain the fullest rewards. Surely the legal system has bigger things to worry about.

He's getting his coat from the peg on the back of the office door. Cold night out. He's not in any hurry. There's nobody waiting for him at home. His wife died twelve years ago now; they had no kids. More her choice than his. He didn't mind, not as long as she was there. Once she was gone, it got lonely. Would've been nice to have a family then. Twelve-hour working days eat away at the loneliness. His accounts have become his children. That thought makes him feel sad and pathetic.

Locking the office door carefully behind him. It's a nice area these days. Wasn't so quiet when he first got the office, but they've cleaned up around here in the last two decades. Never had a break-in, but you can't be too careful. He has a client who develops property and rents it out. Some might call him a slum landlord, but Richard's always thought that was unfair. People on very low incomes need somewhere to live, and they can hardly expect the Ritz. Anyway, this fellow had a string of break-ins at his office. The police figured it was something to do with his work, a disgruntled someone or other. They warned people connected with his business to be careful, Richard included. Really, though, what can you do? If people want to smash their way in, they will.

He's the last one out of the building. No lights on anywhere else. The front door locks automatically behind him – you have to be buzzed in or have a key. There's a little courtyard at the front of the building, with parking for a select few who use the surrounding buildings. He's been around long enough to claim one of the spots. There are only two other cars there right now. One's always there. Must be a company car that nobody takes home. The other one he doesn't recognize. Ordinary-looking black saloon. He's taking his mobile out of his pocket to check for messages: anyone wanting some late-night advice, which might require their file. He's over beside his own car before he realizes there are two people inside the black saloon. Two men, it looks like, sitting there in the dark. As he unlocks his car, the passenger door of the other car is opening. A young man's getting out, looking across at him. Looks well dressed. Dark coat, dark trousers, smart shoes. He's walking briskly across, while the driver gets out to join him.

'Excuse me,' the young man's saying, 'Richard Hardy?'

'Yes,' Richard's saying, a little uncertain. He has his car door half-open. He's ready to drop in, if this turns out to be some nut, or some thug looking for information about one of his clients.

'My name's Detective Sergeant Lawrence Mullen. This is

Detective Constable Edward Russell.' He's pulling his little wallet out of his pocket, holding it out for Richard to look at.

Richard's nodding. 'Okay. How may I help you?'

'We need you to come with us to the station to answer a few questions about one of your clients.'

'The station? Am I being arrested?'

'No, no, not at all. There are documents we would like you to see. Confirm they belong to one of your clients. You're a witness, nothing more.' Saying it with a reassuring smile.

'Can I ask who it is you're investigating?'

'I don't think it's wise to discuss that out here on the pavement,' the cop is saying, looking briefly around for show.

Common sense says you don't argue with the police. Being questioned may be damaging for his business, but it would be worse to cause a scene. Being arrested could be fatal for his business. A little bit of a panic. He's dropped the mobile onto the driver's seat of his car. He's closing the car door, locking it and following the young cop across to his car. Then wishing he'd put the mobile in his pocket. Might need to call a lawyer. Too polite to ask if he can go back and get it. Too nervous to say anything.

'We'll try not to keep you long,' the cop's saying, sounding a little disinterested. 'We'll drop you back here when we're done.' He seems nice.

Richard's getting into the back of the car. Detective Mullen is sitting beside him, the older one back in the driving seat. Starting the car. No great rush to it. The policemen both seem relaxed, and that's relaxing Richard. The initial shock replaced by natural nerves. Richard's not the sort of person who finds himself in the company of the police often.

'Am I in any sort of trouble?' Richard's asking. It's been a couple of minutes of silence. He feels the need to say something.

'Oh no,' Mullen's saying with an impatient shake of his head. 'You might have information that's useful to us. One of your clients. We'll not question you under caution. If you'd feel more comfortable with a lawyer present, then you can call one when we reach the station. It's entirely up to you.'

He's paying Richard no attention. Looking out the window, then looking straight ahead. The driver, he seems more interested. Richard's seen him looking back in the mirror a few times. The driver, DC Russell, is starting to look nervous. Making Richard feel as though there's more to this. Like maybe he *is* in trouble. Okay, he's turned a blind eye to a few things. There are things he's hidden away that should have been left in the open. Never pretended he was an angel. But, come on, that's hardly a big deal, is it? He's done nothing that he ought to be ashamed of, he's damned sure of that.

'Could you at least tell me what this relates to?' he's asking Mullen. He needs to hear something reassuring. Anything.

'We're investigating the way in which one of your clients

makes his money. We believe he uses his legitimate business as a front for criminal activities. We just want to ask you a few questions. You're under no suspicion. If anything,' Mullen's saying, 'you're a victim, too.'

The initial shock masked it. Now it's seeping through. The feeling that something isn't right. The cop who couldn't care less and his nervous driver. These two want to ask him about a client. Want to ask about his money. So why take him away from the office? Richard is sneaking a look at Mullen. So relaxed, that one. Surely if there's something they need to find out, they would have stayed at the office. They would want him to look things up. Go through his files. Check figures. That's what he does. Can't do it from the station. Surely they're going about this the wrong way. He wants to say something. Wants to tell the cop they might be better doing this back where they started. Looking at Mullen again. That disinterested look doesn't seem reassuring any more.

# 2

He's had a vague awareness of their surroundings as they've been driving. Familiar streets, so he hasn't paid much attention. Now he's starting to look. To focus on where they're going. This isn't into the city centre. This is north. This is away from the built-up areas. It doesn't seem to make an awful lot of sense. He's looking around sharply.

Mullen's glancing at him. 'Won't be long now.'

Richard's sitting back in the seat. Pointless to complain. This is something too big for him to fight against. His life has always been about the confidence of others. Other people take command. He facilitates. It worked for him. Not a perfect life, sure, but better than many. Sit back and let other people play their games. Stay quiet. Stay friendly.

They've left the city behind. Richard isn't saying anything. This might not be as bad as it looks. As bad as it feels. Maybe they just want information. They might knock him around a little. Or just take him to the scene of a crime and ask some questions. Yeah, that could be it. Certainly nothing to gain from complaining. Rarely is. Quiet and friendly. Let them do as they please, and walk away from this. Neither of them has said a word for a while now. The silence is becoming uncomfortable again. Threatening even. Richard feels a need to say something, just for the sake of politeness. It's how he handles clients. Never let things get too cold. Keep them talking. Not these fellows – they're not interested in anything he has to say. Not yet, anyway.

They've avoided the main roads. Richard's noticed that. Maybe this is the route they have to take to get where they're going. Certainly not something he's going to mention. Not the sort of thing these guys would want to discuss with him. Richard's taking another look at Mullen. 'DS Mullen' is what he said. He looks a little young to be a Detective Sergeant. Means he has a higher rank than the one driving, who's obviously older. Richard's had clients over the years who've told him a few scare stories about the police. They are willing to use scare tactics if they think it'll get a response. This must be what their scare tactics look like. Scary, he'll give them that.

Still going. Still on minor roads, very little traffic. Richard doesn't recognize where they are. Well out of the city now, that's for sure. Looks like the countryside. His hands are beginning to shake. Not sure why. Not sure what's changed. He keeps telling himself that it'll be fine. These things don't happen to people like him. Why should they? Everything will be fine, if he just keeps quiet and doesn't cause any bother. Tell them what they want to know. Doesn't matter who it incriminates; tell them whatever they need to hear. All you can do is be honest. When they have what they want, they'll let you go.

Turning to glance at Mullen. A cold look shot back at him. The young cop's attitude has changed. More unpleasant than before. Just you wait, young man. When this is done, there will be complaints. People like you always get their comeuppance. Starting to realize why he's become so much more nervous. The driver is slowing. Looking for something. Looking for a turn-off. Only country lanes to turn onto around here.

'That's it, on your right,' Mullen's saying to the driver. Speaking quietly. He doesn't sound nervous.

The driver's slowing and turning carefully. No lights on the road ahead. Feels bumpy. Not much of a road at all. More of a track. What could there be around here that has anything to do with Richard's business? Stay calm. Don't let them see that you're nervous. That'll only annoy them, and there's nothing to gain from that. Trees on either side of them. The car's crawling along the track. Been going for a few minutes now. Pitch-black. No sign of lights ahead. They must be into some sort of woodland. A part of the world that Richard Hardy could not be less familiar with. This is making no sense at all. Richard's looking at Mullen. Mullen's not looking back. He's just staring ahead, into the darkness.

The car's slowing almost to a stop. There's a building there. Looks like a barn, but Richard only caught a glimpse in

9

the headlights. The car's stopping beside it, reversing. Turning to face the other way.

'No, a little further,' Mullen's saying.

The driver's moving the car a fraction to the right.

'That's it,' Mullen's saying now. Satisfied they're in the exact place. Exact place for what?

The driver's switched the engine off, but left the headlights on. Shining off into the trees. Ahead of them a circle of flat land beside the barn where they've parked, and trees all around. Now the driver, DC Russell, is getting out of the car. Doesn't seem to be doing so with any great enthusiasm. He's closed his door, left the two of them alone in the back. Russell's walking round behind the car. Richard's turning to look. Russell's opening the boot.

'Your client, Hugh Francis,' Mullen's saying quietly. It's a slight struggle to hear him. Russell's clattering about in there, taking things out of the boot that sound heavy. Something rustling, something else dropped on the ground.

'Mr Francis, yes, the garage owner,' Richard's saying enthusiastically. Such a nice young man, Shug Francis. Always treated Richard well, always been loyal. Richard does his books for him. Handles his payroll. Has more employees than he ought to, and Richard hides that for him. Not a big deal.

'What can you tell me about his financial records?'

'Well, er, I don't know. This would be easier back at the

office with his records in front of me.' Pausing, considering. 'There have been times when, I guess you could say, I've wondered about one or two things. Some of the money he brings in, where it comes from. Why he has quite so many employees. Nothing blatant. Nothing significant, I wouldn't have said.' Pausing again. That didn't sound like enough. He needs to offer them more to keep them happy. 'Of course I'd be willing to show you the complete accounts.'

Mullen hasn't said anything. Just a raising of eyebrows, and Richard knows what it means. Knows the cop is saying that looking at the books means nothing. Means the police know that Richard's been subtly adjusting the figures to make Francis Autos look more legitimate than it really is.

'I admit that I've . . . ensured that, er, Shug's books add up. Perhaps I've broken the law. I accept that. I've needed to make sure that the figures add up. I basically handle his pay-roll. I needed to make the figures work for the number of employees he has.' Talking more quickly as the sentences go on.

Mullen's nodding, as if he knows all this already. It's because he knows it that he's here. He knows that for the last few years Richard has been making sure that all Shug's people get paid each month.

There's a thump behind them. The boot closing. Richard's catching a glimpse of DC Russell walking past the car with a large bundle under his arm. Hard to see what it is. He's walking in front of the car now. Dropping the bundle on the ground. It looks blue. He's pulling something out. Also blue. Looks like a sheet of tarpaulin. He's spreading it out carefully, about halfway between the trees and the car. Now he's picking up the rest of the bundle and walking across to the trees. He's only gone about three or four feet into them. Still in view of the car. Richard and Mullen both watch him. Each seems as concerned as the other. Watching him lay out the rest of the tarpaulin. Carefully taking out the contents that had been wrapped within it. Two shovels. Something white. Looks like a towel. Russell starting to dig. Richard's watching. He can no longer hide the fact that his hands are shaking.

Mullen's moving his head left and right. Trying to get a better view of his colleague digging. A sigh. Mullen's getting out of the car. Walking round the other side, opening Richard's door. 'Come on – out,' he's saying. Still talking quietly.

Richard's doing as he's told. Always doing what he's told. That's his life. Looking across to Russell. He's hacking at the turf with his shovel, trying to roll up lines of it and place the turf on the tarpaulin beside him. Mullen's glancing across at his colleague. There's a roll of the eyes and a tsk of the tongue. He's clearly not impressed; obviously feels he could do the job better himself. Must be why he's the senior one.

'What's he . . .' Richard begins to ask and then stops himself. If they want him to know, they'll tell him. It's not his place to ask questions. He's not even sure he wants to know.

He can feel Mullen reach out and touch his arm. A glance at Mullen's hand. A moment of confusion. Mullen appears to have some sort of glove on. The sort of thin, clear glove the cleaners use when they're working in his office. Must have put them on since he got out of the car. He's pushing Richard gently forward. Leading him to the sheet of tarpaulin that Russell has placed in the middle of the clearing.

They're both standing in silence. Watching Russell dig away at the ground beneath him, putting all the dirt on the plastic sheet. Grunting as he digs. Not a man who's used to this sort of labour. He's sweating heavily; even in this strange light you can see that. Slowing down all the time. Every now and then Richard can hear a little sigh of exasperation escape from Mullen. Subtle, but the only other noise is coming from Russell. The exasperation comes every time Russell makes a mess, misses the tarpaulin with a little mud, that sort of thing. Tiring arms flinging the mud around. Richard's turned to look at Mullen a couple of times. Saw him look at his watch once. Other than that, he's just watching Russell. Watching carefully, waiting for something. Presumably waiting for him to finish digging. Richard doesn't want to think about the digging. Not entirely sure what it's all about. Might be digging something up. There's a little voice in the back of his mind scoffing at him. Telling him it's entirely obvious what Russell's digging. It's your grave, old man.

Richard's starting to cry. Can't help it. Not able to kid himself any longer. This is it. This is the end. What a remarkably stupid way for his life to end. Can't stop thinking how absurd it all is. He's not the sort of person who should have an ending like this. It makes no sense. Part of him just wants to laugh at the whole thing. Can't laugh when he's crying this hard, though. Completely uncontrollable. Tears are streaming down his face, his shoulders are rocking, he's grunting repeatedly. He can see through the blur of tears that Russell's stopped. The cop leaning forward, hands on hips. Coughing, spitting. A sigh from Mullen. Just the sound of his own panic now. A gesture from Mullen – Richard can't see what. Russell's digging again, with more vigour this time. Louder, though, grunting with every movement. A touch on Richard's back.

'Sit down,' Mullen's saying, still so quiet. That calmness. God, that calmness is shocking now. Sickening.

Mullen's pressed him down. Richard's sitting on the tarp, leaning forward. He doesn't want to look at Russell any more. It's cruel that they've made him. Callous. Making him watch a man dig his grave. Why should he try to be nice to them? Why do what he thinks they want him to do? From now on, he'll do as he pleases. He'll cry. He'll lean forward. He'll look away from what will be his final resting place. And for what? Because of Shug Francis, apparently. Such a nice young man. Always ready with a smile. Always asking after Richard's health, making sure he's content. Yes, there were questions about his business. He was up to all sorts, that boy. But this? How is this fair punishment for the work Richard did? He made numbers add up that shouldn't. Is that so bad? Another moment of realization. This isn't to punish him. This is to punish Shug Francis. That, somehow, makes it even worse. Dying just to inconvenience someone else.

Russell's still digging. Slowed right down again. Mullen's still standing next to Richard. How long have they been like this? Five minutes. Ten, perhaps. More, actually. He's lost sense of time.

'Bring across that towel,' Mullen's saying. A little louder than before, talking to Russell.

Russell climbs out of his hole and walks slowly across with the white towel. 'It's deep enough,' he's saying as he passes it across to Mullen. You can hear he's exhausted. Leaning forward, hands on hips again.

'No, it isn't; another couple of feet,' Mullen's saying. That cold, hard voice. The sort people don't argue with. The sort Russell doesn't argue with. He's going back to dig.

Richard can feel something press on the back of his head. He's reaching up a hand.

'No, leave it,' Mullen's saying. 'Lean forward.'

There's a moment of confusion. Richard isn't sure what's happening. Something on the back of his head, pressing him down. Then nothing.

# 3

They're back outside. Glad to be out. Into the car, driving away. Should be a moment of celebration. It isn't. Shug's not saying anything. He knows exactly what Fizzy's going to say. He doesn't want to hear it. He's going to hear it anyway.

'You just gave it all away,' Fizzy's saying. 'For what, huh? For what? So that things can carry on exactly the same – that's what. If you'd gone to Jamieson and done a deal, you could have ended the threat. You'd still have lost just about every-thing, but there wouldn't be anyone trying to kill us any more. All you've done is make matters worse. You've given everything away and pissed off Jamieson even more.'

He keeps saying 'you' instead of 'we'. Shug's noticed that. Twenty years David 'Fizzy' Waters has been best friend to Shug Francis, and now it's suddenly 'you' and not 'we'. Started as kids messing around with cars together. Turned it into a string of garages and the only effective car-theft ring in the city. Profitable business. Profitable car-ring. But not prof-itable enough. Shug wants more, and that's why they had this meeting. Meeting with a leading figure in the drug trade to talk about attacking another leading figure in the drug trade.

'We're going to beat him,' Shug's saying. Talking about

Peter Jamieson, a man they've been failing to beat for months. They've attacked him, attacked his people. Trying to take over Jamieson's patch. Jamieson always too powerful, smart or lucky to be harmed.

'We're not going to beat him,' Fizzy's shouting, incredulous. 'Listen to yourself, man. If Jamieson does get beat, it won't be by us. It'll be by MacArthur and his mob. We get the risk of leading the charge. We'll get the glory, the man says. Fuck's sake! Glory? We get the glory and he gets the rewards. Is that all you want, glory? Well, whoop-dee-fucking-doo. I'll make sure they write it on your gravestone. "He had glory."'

They both know Alex MacArthur doesn't do things out of the goodness of his heart. You don't lead one of the biggest criminal organizations in the city because of the goodness of your heart. You don't last the decades at the top that MacArthur has because of the goodness of your heart. Quite the reverse. MacArthur has a brutal love of money and power. That's what persuades him to accept the deal on offer. The chance to make some money and attack Peter Jamieson at the same time. Jamieson a rival to MacArthur. Shug attacking Jamieson. My enemies' enemy is my profitable friend. Shug's too desperate to see the obvious truth.

Everyone thinks of Shug Francis as this happy-go-lucky kind of guy. Mostly that's true. But he has his moments. Fizzy's seen him when he's in a huff. Shug doesn't go into a rage, scream and bawl and get it out of his system. He sulks, and it can take a while to leave him. He can hide it from most people. People who don't know him like Fizzy does. It can make Shug reckless. Happened last about three years ago. An old man had been doing forged documents for them since they started the car-ring. He ditched them, went to work for someone else. Not doing vehicle documents; doing bank statements and the like instead. They were ditched for a two-bit con racket because it was easier work. Shug was furious, demanded that the old man come back and work for them. He told Shug where to get lost. Treated Shug like the car business was a joke. Shug sulked for a few days, and then hired some gorilla to deliver a message. Didn't kill the old boy, but it was still a stupid thing to do. Everyone knew who was behind it. Reckless. Unnecessary.

They're back at Shug's house now. Along the corridor and into what he calls his playroom. Office, really. There's no real tension between them, even in this moment of disagreement. They know each other too well, trust each other too much. But they do disagree. Fizzy is still trying to chip away at him.

'You need to end this. Find a way of backing out. Something that leaves you with a business.'

Shug's shaking his head and slumping onto the couch. 'It's done now. Pull out now and we piss off MacArthur, which would be even worse.' Took a lot of work to set up the meeting. MacArthur playing coy. Multiple meetings between contacts. Always dealing with Don Park, one of MacArthur's senior men. It was PC Paul Greig who did most of the work for Shug. Another one Shug knows he shouldn't trust. Greig's a cop, after all. A man playing all sides at once, who still gets pissed off if you imply he's bent. But he negotiated well: a 20 per cent cut of Shug's car-ring and garages for MacArthur's support in destroying Peter Jamieson. A fifty-fifty split of the proceeds from Jamieson's network.

Fizzy's running both hands down his face. This is madness. Madness born of stubbornness. They were never going to get out of this with everything intact. There's a price to pay for failure in the criminal industry. It's typically a high one. Escaping Jamieson would have meant paying him off with a share of both the legit business and the car-ring. Could have been done. Jamieson's a businessman, first and foremost. It just meant accepting that Jamieson had won.

'You show weakness and those bastards will rip you apart anyway,' Shug's saying. He sounds depressed. Fizzy can take the credit for that. Spoiling what should be a hopeful moment. 'We let Jamieson in and he'll have the whole business within two years. He'll force us out. Make our lives a misery. How does that help us?'

He's right. Fizzy knows it. A man like Jamieson doesn't forgive and forget, not even for the right price. It's about prestige. About PR. Someone challenges you, attacks your business. You accept peace with them and start working with them, just because you're making money from it. Other people see that. Other people think it's worth attacking you, because they can buy you off later, if things don't go their way. It creates a sliver of vulnerability that others will seek to exploit. A man like Jamieson can't have people think that attacking him comes with a safety net. So, yeah, Jamieson would take the deal. Then he would carefully destroy Shug and Fizzy and anyone else linked to them. Anyone watching would know that there are no get-out clauses in a fight with Peter Jamieson.

'So selling out to him destroys the business. Doing it this way just means the bugger kills us.'

'Not if we get to him first,' Shug's saying.

'Uh-uh, not us – MacArthur. MacArthur gets to him first. He gets all the reward. Then he does to us what Jamieson would have done anyway.'

Shug's shaking his head. 'I don't think so,' he's saying. Speaking quietly, thoughtfully. 'See, Jamieson can't be seen letting us off the hook. Same time, MacArthur can't be seen to hurt someone who's done him a service. Then nobody wants to work for him.'

It's a theory, but not one Fizzy's sure of. He's shaking his head. 'Nah, I don't think so. He doesn't need people to see him rewarding us. Didn't he say that he wanted us to be the face of this? He's going to be in the background, out of sight. So people think we took down Jamieson. Then people think we've tied up with MacArthur afterwards. He can do what he wants. Treat us how he likes. So it's him destroying us, instead of Jamieson.'

The naivety of the amateur. That's what Shug thinks of Fizzy. He forgives his friend, but it's annoying. There are too many people working in the background for MacArthur to stab him in the back after the event. People like Greig. He works with a lot of criminals, but he's still a cop. He still makes arrests. He commits to Shug, and it sends a message. Shug is a guy on the rise. Greig wants to be close to him. And say MacArthur does screw them over after they're finished with Jamieson. What does that say about Don Park? One of MacArthur's own senior men. He organized this. He set up the meeting they just came from at the engineering-company office. It would trash Park's reputation within the MacArthur organization. MacArthur couldn't do that to him. It would cause a split in his own business. See, Fizzy doesn't think of these things. He still has the mindset of the small business. He needs time to grow. Or maybe this is too big for him.

Shug's frowning, and sighing. 'I don't want to talk about this any more. We have a lot to plan. There's going to be some serious action. New stuff for us, and we have to be ready for that.'

'Jesus, Shug, will you listen to yourself! Being led to the edge of the cliff by these fucking gangsters, and you're just going along with it.' Fizzy's raised his voice. Frustration is getting the better of him.

Shug's glaring back at him. 'You keep your voice down. You want the whole bloody street to hear? Just you remember something, Fizzy. This is my business. It was me who set it up. It was me who got this running the way it is. If I want to gamble with it, then I will gamble with it. You were along for the ride. You've always been useful, you've always been there. Don't go thinking that this is your business, though. It ain't. It's mine.'

There's tension between them now. Real, angry, dangerous tension. Something completely new, and something Fizzy doesn't know how to react to. He can't remember this happening before. How long have they been friends? More than twenty years now. Never had a moment like this. Been tense times with other people in the business, and they've always been forced out. Shug wouldn't allow them to stick around after falling out with them. He was always convinced those differences would resurface at some point, become an issue again. Is that what this is? Is this the beginning of Shug trying to force him out? Bloody hell, no. It can't be. Twenty years of being best friends, practically brothers. Since they were kids. This can't be what it feels like. This can't be the end.

Fizzy's getting up. Not saying a word. Anything either one of them says now is only going to make things worse. The tension's too thick. Anything would sound like an insult, like provocation. Sure, they need to talk this through. Need to sort it out before any moves are made. But this atmosphere – damn, he just doesn't know how to handle it. He's walking towards the door, glancing back at Shug. Shug isn't even looking at him. He's just looking at the floor. Letting Fizzy go because there's nothing left to say. Fizzy's opening the door and he's out into the corridor, half-hoping that Shug will call him back. Half-expecting it, if we're being honest. But there's nothing; just silence. A silence that says this relationship has changed, maybe forever.

# 4

It was an unpleasant kill for Calum MacLean. Whole thing feels wrong. Counter-intuitive. Dressing up as a cop and picking the guy up in the city in the evening. Taking this long with the whole damn thing. Depending on Kenny McBride to dig the grave properly, something he has spectacularly failed to do. Kenny's a good driver, but that's all he is. And now he's stopped digging, just because Calum's pulled the trigger. Now is when he should be hurrying up. Not how Calum would have done it, if he was freelance. But he isn't, any more. He doesn't get to decide. Peter Jamieson does.

'Keep digging,' Calum's saying quietly, 'I have this.'

He's using the towel on the back of the head to stop the blood-spray. He doesn't want one drop going further than the tarpaulin that Richard Hardy will be wrapped and buried in. They need to move fast. Make the assumption that someone heard the gunshot and that you're racing against the clock.

Unlikely anyone heard it, though. Calum picked the location for that reason. This has been his go-to location for a burial in bad circumstances for a while. Long way from the road, away from any occupied buildings. He was keeping it as his place to use for a daytime killing, on the assumption that such a killing might occur. This isn't daytime, but it is still unusual and worthy of this precaution. He came out here and found the place on the first visit. Came back two weeks later and checked the barn, made sure it wasn't in use. Didn't look like it, but you have to know. He broke in, which involved nothing more than shouldering the rotten side door, and looked around. Big holes in the roof, and completely empty. Not in use. A safe place, if such a thing exists. At least the location's right.

Nothing else about this night is right. Calum's pressing the towel down against the wound, not letting the blood flow out. Holding it tight as he presses the old man down into the tarp and rolls him gently onto his side. Going through his pockets. Car keys, a wallet and a few coins. No mobile. Calum noted the fidgety fingers letting it drop onto the driver's seat of the car back at the office. An ageing man in a nervous hurry to help the police. The wallet and keys Calum takes, the coins he leaves. He's lifting the tarp up and wrapping it around Hardy from both sides, creating the burial sheet. Hopeful he's done enough to make sure that no blood escapes before Richard Hardy's put in the ground. The tarp will serve another purpose, now that Kenny's proven his incompetence as a gravedigger. It should keep the smell in for longer. It really doesn't look like a deep grave, which it should be. Shallow graves are for the unprofessional.

'Right, that'll do,' Calum's saying to Kenny. There's a last lazy swipe of the shovel from the driver, and now he's placing it on top of the mud pile he's created. Clambering out of the grave, not watching where he's going. Stumbling, exhausted. He has no sense of caution. No sense that even muddy boot prints could be a giveaway. Someone walks a dog through the area, past the barn; sees the boot prints, realizes they're fresh. They go over and poke around, see the disturbed ground where Kenny hacked the turf. It could happen. But Calum won't criticize Kenny. Not to his face, anyway. He's a driver. He chauffeurs Peter Jamieson, their boss, around. He delivers stuff. This is way out of his league. He was obviously shocked when John Young, Jamieson's right-hand man, told him he'd be working the job with Calum. A little horrified. He's done it, though. Done it to the best of his ability, such as it is. He probably hasn't seen a hit up close before. Hasn't been involved in something this tense. That excuses his nerves.

Kenny's plodding across towards Calum and the body. Looking to Calum for guidance. Calum has to lead the way. He's the one who's been here before. The one who knows how this works. He also appears to be completely at ease. No obvious nerves. No sweating, no shaking, no quivering voice. Seems like it's no big deal for him.

'You take the legs,' Calum's saying.

Kenny's reaching down, grabbing the tarp in his hands.

He's starting to drag it a little. Then he's startled by the raised voice.

'No,' Calum's saying, louder than intended. 'Don't drag. You'll leave a mark. Lift it up; carry it clear of the ground.'

Kenny's doing what he's told. Struggling to lift, the sweat running off him. But being obedient. What else can you do in this position? He's conflicted, and it probably shows. He needs to do a good job, because he doesn't want a bad report going back to Jamieson. Last thing he needs is to lose his job, especially now that they're moving against Shug Francis. At the same time he doesn't want to do such a good job that this becomes a regular thing. Please, God, let this be a one-off.

They're lifting Hardy up now, carrying him across to the grave. Placing him down at the graveside. Calum's starting to sweat a little now. Not used to manual labour. Burials like this aren't common. Most of his jobs have been gun and run. This is how it's going to be from now on. When you're the lead gunman for a major organization there's a lot of cleaning up. His last kill had a burial too, but he doesn't want to think about that now. Kenny's moving to lift the body again – Calum's stopping him.

'No, get in the hole.'

'What for?' Kenny's asking.

They've been through this before. Calum explained the whole thing to him last night, but Kenny's ignored a lot of it. You have to dig the grave carefully at the top, to remove obvious traces. You have to dig the rest quickly, to reduce the amount of time spent at the barn. Reduce the time between the victim realizing what's happening and the kill. You have to make sure that you leave no mark away from the hole. And you have to bury carefully.

'We have to position him in a way that takes up as little space as possible. You know this,' Calum's saying, exasperated. He told Kenny last night. You make the body as small as possible. You pack the soil around it as tight as possible. That way, when you roll the turf back on top, it should look just like it did before you got there. It won't, because the turf will be a mess. Hopefully it'll knit together before the soil pushes up. A small mound will form, but you hope that by then the turf will heal and it'll look natural. It's why you always try to bury on bumpy ground. Calum explained all this last night, and he doesn't like having to say it again. Not now. A good sidekick doesn't need a second set of instructions.

'Fine,' Kenny's saying. He's dropping carefully back into the hole. Ready for Calum to pass the body down.

Getting a grip of a dead weight wrapped in slippery material is a nightmare. This isn't going to be dignified. Lifting Hardy, and taking a little baby-step to the edge of the grave. Ready to pass him down to Kenny, who has the easy part here anyway. He can just drop Richard and shove him into a corner.

'I'm going to get mud on my clothes,' Kenny's saying now.

Bloody hell! They've been through this, too. 'You're going to get rid of every stitch you're wearing,' Calum's saying, with a wheeze.

Kenny has a loose grip of the body, but it's firmer than Calum's. Calum's let go, Kenny's holding the body for all of half a second, pulling it backwards and letting it drop with a thump onto the soil. There's a moment of relief for both of them. Familiar for Calum; a new experience for Kenny. It always comes when the body is in the grave. It's that sense that you've broken the back of the challenge you faced. The hardest part done.

Kenny's making a meal of moving the body. All he has to do is shove it over to the corner. The grave's four feet deep at most. It's almost circular, and not a fine example of Scottish engineering. There's already a dent where part of one wall has fallen in. Calum's shaking his head, preparing himself for the next part. Kenny's oblivious to this. Trying to shove the lump inside the tarpaulin with his boot. Shoulders and arms burning from the effort of digging. Sliding the body across to the closest resemblance to a corner that this grave has. It's the deepest point. He thinks he's done.

'No,' Calum's saying. 'On his side. Push him right up against the wall. Flat as possible.'

Kenny's sighing, but not complaining. He's the junior man. The junior man doesn't complain. He gets on with the job, no matter how bad. Get this done, go home and forget about it. That's what he keeps telling himself. It's a one-off. Doesn't matter if you hate it. You'll never have to do it again.

He's right – he'll never have to do it again. As Kenny's bending over, shoving the body against the wall, Calum is taking his gun again from his inside coat pocket. He's standing at the edge of the grave, just above Kenny. Calum's dropping down to his haunches. Watching. Waiting for the right moment. Kenny is ducking slightly again, pressing the tarpaulin as tight to the body as possible. Now. Calum's extending an arm. Kenny's head is almost at knee height. An easy shot into the temple. Louder this time. Much more likely to be blood-spray. That's the risk. Watching Kenny slump forward, face into the wall of mud. Calum dropping down beside him, pulling Kenny's body from the wall. Laying him out and rolling him onto his side. Checking every pocket, making sure they're as empty as Kenny was instructed to keep them. Pushing the body up against Hardy's. Pulling the edge of Hardy's tarp around Kenny. It needed a deeper grave for two bodies. Kenny should have seen this coming. Should have realized. This is what happens to a grass.

# 5

He's out of the grave, filling it in. Not as quickly as he'd like. Always so cautious, always trying to do the perfect job. Patting the soil down with the spade every chance he gets. All the time worrying that someone could be on the way. You have to work fast, and Calum's working as fast as he reasonably can. Stopping to look at his watch. Twenty minutes to nine. Pausing. He doesn't know if that's good or bad. The job's taking longer than he'd like, but he guessed that would be the case. He'll be back in the city in less than an hour, he hopes. Going about the cleaning-up process with people still out on the streets – that can't be good.

Throwing in another spade full of mud. Reaching down and patting it. He's started by filling in around Kenny and Hardy, making sure they're kept firmly in place. Now he's filling up the rest of the empty space in the too-wide, too-shallow grave. And now, with the sweat starting to trickle down his back in an annoying manner, he's dropping the mud on top of the bodies. He's immune to the effects now. Once upon a time he might have been moved by the thought of burying a man he knows. Didn't know Kenny well, but saw him around the club a lot, always said hello. Kenny was a grass. He created this ending for himself when he started talking to the police. There's no sympathy. You do the job, and you keep your focus.

Calum's not used to this intensity of work. He's done burials, of course, but usually with a second pair of hands. He does the killing, and they're happy to do the spadework. Most people will do anything to avoid being the one who pulls the trigger. The lackey of choice to accompany him on this job turned out to be Kenny, for reasons that were never explained to the driver himself. Jamieson called Calum into his office. Went through the job proposal in all its unfortunate glory. Killing the moneyman was no big deal. Usually Calum would have asked for George Daly, a Jamieson employee, to come along with him on the job. He's forgiven George for ruining his relationship with Emma. It wouldn't have been George's idea to interfere. Would have been Jamieson's. Or, more likely, Young's. Protecting their investment in their number-one gunman. Get rid of the girl who's become a part of his life. A good gunman needs to be isolated. He doesn't hate George for scaring her away. He just hates the life he has to live.

Stop thinking about it. For God's sake, keep your focus. There's so much to do. Tonight will be busy; the next few days will be busy. Concentrate on getting the soil into the awkward little gaps between the bodies and the wall of the grave. Use every available inch of space. Filling in fast, arms starting to burn. The sweat's running off him now. Forcing him to accept that the donkeywork that's so often done by others isn't as easy as it looks. This is going to take longer than anticipated. How the hell does George fill these things in so fast? He's been working at this for more than ten minutes and Calum's only just covered the bodies. Another five minutes to fill it up completely. It looks okay, though. Not much of a mound, if any at all. Certainly nothing that'll be out of place in this bumpy area.

Now the turf at the top. What a bloody mess Kenny made of it. Jesus, look at it! His last job, and Kenny fucked it up. In a typical burial you have four or five strips of turf, usually three or four feet long. Done well, you can be left with only a couple of strips, carefully rolled up and then rolled back out again when you're re-laying them. Depends on the turf. Kenny, in his infinite wonder, has managed to hack it into at least twenty pieces. No time to stop and count. Calum could almost believe that Kenny had done it on purpose. Pick out the pieces; push them in hard against the undisturbed turf at the edge. Work your way across from one side to the other. Pushing them in as tight as possible, sometimes tucking a piece under the edge of its neighbour. Make sure every piece is returned, and that the final picture is as close to its original state as possible. Calum's stepping back and looking at his work. Not good. Thank you very much, the late Kenny McBride. It's an obvious patchwork. It will knit together in time. Maybe quite quickly. The hope is that nobody stumbles across it before it does. It's not perfect, and that's going to nag at Calum.

Too much work to do to stand and worry. It's done. He's throwing his own and Kenny's shovels into the tarpaulin that was used to collect the dug-up mud. Rolling it up, shovels inside. Lifting it carefully and checking the ground underneath. Well, they got that bit right at least. There's no telltale thin film of mud on the ground beside the grave. Without the tarpaulin they would never have got every speck back into the grave. It would be all too obvious that someone had been digging here. Calum's now carrying the tarpaulin sheet back to the car. Opening the boot and throwing the tarp in. Ready to leave. Always a good feeling to leave the scene of a burial. Tonight's different, for all sorts of reasons. Tonight Calum's stopping beside the driver's door and looking across to the trees. The headlights illuminating the scene. Taking it all in.

Pulling slowly away. Don't go screeching and skidding and creating tyre marks. Driving slowly and carefully along the narrow lane, back to the road. Wouldn't it be just his luck to drive the bloody thing into a ditch and get stuck there? What a story that would be to tell his fellow inmates when he's serving life. Got caught on the way out. Didn't see the edge of the road. Oh, how they'd laugh. Looking at the clock on the dashboard. One minute past nine. Still no idea if that's good or bad. He knows it's bad that he's working at this hour. Knows that a job shouldn't be carried out when the world around you is still awake and alert. No choice. Needed to pick Hardy up at an hour that would convince him to get into the car. You turn up at his house at two in the morning and he might refuse. They would have had to put together a fake warrant. First rule: keep everything as simple as possible.

Driving back into the city. Taking a different route, but still trying to keep away from the main roads. His first target is the only one he scouted yesterday. It was all at such short notice. Not for the job itself, but for Calum's own plans. If he can just get this right, it could change everything. The first job is getting rid of the tarp, shovels and Hardy's identifiable belongings. Then the car. He scouted a location for ditching the tarp. Supposed to go back to a garden shed that Jamieson uses – a random house in a random street that happens to be owned by a Jamieson man. A trusted man. The man would wait a couple of days and safely ditch whatever little surprises he happens to find in his shed. He's not warned in advance, so he'll be expecting nothing. That's a good thing; Calum can't have someone wondering if the job's been done. Can't have anyone asking questions. Not yet. Not for a while. So he's parking up on a building site he found yesterday afternoon. Harder than it used to be to find a good building site. Nobody around. Opening the boot, placing the wallet and car keys with the shovels inside the rolled-up tarp. Taking out the tarp. Another look round, and he's hurling it into a half-filled skip. More building-material detritus will be thrown on top of it, and it will all be carted away.

Now the car. This is easier. This is the old routine. Driving east to his brother's garage. His older brother William has a majority share in a garage from which Calum borrows cars for jobs. People bring a car in to be fixed; William lets Calum borrow it for a few hours. Rarely more than that. William asks no questions. He knows enough to realize that knowing more would be dangerous. Calum's own car is parked on the street outside the garage. There's a parking space three cars down from it. Calum's driving slowly, taking a careful look up and down the street. Nobody in view. Calum once asked his brother if there were CCTV cameras on the street. William laughed. There aren't many businesses on this street any more. Nobody is going to pay for that. Nobody wants it. William's is not the only business with little things to hide.

Stepping out of the car and onto the street. The keys are in the visor, he's closing the door. He doesn't want to be seen with the car. The car might become the key to any police investigation. They might work out that it was used in the disappearance of two men. They might appeal for anyone who saw it this night. Dropping into his own car. Familiarity. Wonderful, comforting familiarity. Pulling down the visor, the keys dropping into his lap. You take nothing with you on a job, not even your car keys. Starting up and pulling away.

Driving back to his flat and parking two streets away. A flat that's never felt like home. That never will. If he could, he would never go back. Doesn't have that luxury. One last visit.

He's touching the front of his coat, feeling the shape of the gun. Should have got rid of it. On any other night, any other job, he would. But this isn't any other job. This, he intends, will be his last.

# 6

Peter Jamieson's been sitting in his office for the last couple of hours. The one point in a big job when there's nothing he can do. You plan it. You deal with the aftermath. The job itself is for others. Calum and Kenny were sent to do a job that will never be spoken of. That shameless little bastard Kenny. Still makes Jamieson's blood boil to think of it. Talking to the police and still turning up here every day, pretending to be a loyal employee. Telling tales to the enemy. Shit! Jamieson trusted Kenny. Thought he was a solid guy. Not too bright, not too impressive, but solid. You just don't know. First Frank MacLeod, now this. As soon as John Young came to him with the revelation, Jamieson knew what he was going to do. Two birds with one stone. Kenny would pay the price; but he needs to put Kenny out of his mind for now. There are other things to deal with.

Jamieson's behind his desk, as he always is. Young's sitting on the couch to Jamieson's left, where he always is. Just the two of them. The office is above Jamieson's nightclub. Soundproofed, but imperfectly. You can still feel the little thumps of the music below. Usually ignorable, but annoying on a night like tonight. A night of action. A night when you need to be switched on. Things can, and do, go wrong. Have gone wrong recently. Tonight should change that. Tonight, and the next few days, should change it all.

'We should have done this months ago,' Jamieson's saying to his right-hand man. 'No matter the bullshit that was going on.'

Young's nodding. 'Maybe. Less risk now, though. Doing it now means doing it right. Doing it perfect. Couldn't guarantee that before.'

Jamieson's nodding, and tapping the desk with his forefinger. Glancing across at Young and suddenly laughing. This is it! This is what it's all about. The action, the thrill, the risk. This is what they're in it for.

'I've set up a meeting with that goofy prick, Kirk,' Young's saying.

Jamieson's frowning. There are plenty of goofy pricks to choose from, and this particular name doesn't ring a bell. 'Who?'

'Fellow works for the phone company. I'll get him to set up a few fake calls. Put them in the records. Shug to a gunman, gunman to Shug. I'll use Des Collins as the gunman. He's technically freelance. It'll look legit.'

They've discussed this already. The phone calls are just a little extra. Jamieson doesn't think they're necessary, but Young likes this sort of thing. His chance to be nice and busy.

'I still don't think you should be meeting him. It's a risk. He'll blab. You should send someone else to do it.'

'It's fine,' Young's saying with a shrug. 'The kid doesn't know shit from chocolate. He can grass all he wants – I have deniability.'

Fine, the calls are a bonus. But the job is important. People will notice that Kenny's gone. Not least the cop he was grassing to. Someone has to take the blame. For that and for Hardy. Shug is linked to Hardy. The police will check Shug's phone records. They'll find he made calls to a known gunman, Des Collins. Suddenly the police aren't even considering Peter Jamieson for the crime any more. Shug's link to Hardy would have set the police on that trail anyway. Still, you can never have too much evidence against your enemies. Collins does most of his work for Alex MacArthur. So the police start sniffing around old MacArthur. They won't do anything, but sniffing around weakens him. Then things get interesting. Jamieson puts the Shug battle behind him. Victory achieved. A risk, but one every organization has to take if it wants to grow.

This is where John Young's speciality really comes into play. The planning and scheming. Playing people along. Reading the movements of others before they make them. He loves it. Always has. Always where his strength lay. Young was the planner. Jamieson the man of action. Action gets you to the very top. Planning gets you second in command. They're both comfortable with that.

'Marty's been sniffing around a lot as well,' Young's saying. An amused glance across the room to Jamieson. He knows what reaction this is going to get.

'Tell him to fuck off. Tell him to make sure he pays me what I'm owed from him, the bastard.'

Young's smiling. 'I've told him that often enough. He's trying to ingratiate himself. Get back in the good books. There's nothing he won't do to win you round.'

Jamieson shudders. 'Tell him he'd be wise to keep his distance for now. He tried to rob me of my cut. If he didn't make so much damn money, I would have dealt with him before now.'

Young's smiling again. Marty Jones is a lot of things. He's a pimp, for one thing. A loan-shark, too. Has his fingers in all sorts of pies, as it happens. Has a knack for making good money, fast. It's the one thing that keeps him popular.

Jamieson's sneaking a glance at his watch. The main job of the night should be done by now. He's waiting for a phone call. Not from Calum. That won't come. This is something else. Something separate. So much going on.

'You know they arrested Potty Cruickshank,' he says.

'Good,' Young's saying with no interest. He heard this news a week ago. Cruickshank's another loan-shark. Another scumbag. One of the very worst. No friend to the Jamieson organization.

'I hear that Cruickshank has Paul Greig in his pocket. Then I hear that the evidence to arrest him can only have come from Greig.'

Young's looking across the room. Frowning. 'I know not to trust Greig. He's not on anyone's side. Cruickshank should have known that. One of the good things about Shug trusting him. Greig's only on his own side. He still filters things back to his superiors. It's why they put up with him.'

Jamieson's sighing. They shouldn't be anywhere near the likes of Greig. Too much risk.

The phone's ringing. Jamieson looks at the display. Looks across to Young and nods his head. This is the call he's been waiting for. As Jamieson says hello, Young's getting up to leave. He could stay and listen, just doesn't see the need. Jamieson will tell him everything he needs to know about the conversation. In the meantime there are other things to get along with. Meetings to arrange. There's a little part of him, a tiny part, that wishes he could do some of the dirty work. Young thinks about men like Calum, and Frank MacLeod. Okay, Frank was a traitor. Nothing to be envious about there. But the life he lived. The thrills he had. Something you just can't get by making phone calls. The sort of thrill that Calum MacLean is getting right now. That's another one he'll have to keep an eye on. Question marks about Calum's commitment. Still. Shit, he likes a challenge, but it used to be easier than this.

Young has a little office downstairs that he almost never uses. The fact that it's downstairs is one reason. The fact that it isn't soundproofed is another. The racket tonight. Jesus, you can't hear yourself think! Sounds like someone battering a dog with a bag of spanners. And they call it music. He was going to make a call, but now he won't bother. Now he's just killing ten minutes. Waiting until he knows that Jamieson's finished on the phone. It irks a little. Just a little. Young does so much work to set these things up; Jamieson handles the key call. That means he gets all the credit for this. Not a problem. Not really. Young's used to it. It's fine, it's just – it would be nice for him to be able to close out a job, not just plan it. Less than ten minutes. Fuck it, this music is giving him a headache. He's going back upstairs. Through the snooker room and along the corridor to Jamieson's office. Inside, and seeing that Jamieson's finished his call. Young gives him a questioning nod.

'Everything's on,' Jamieson's saying. 'As expected.'

# 7

He didn't tell her what it was, but he didn't need to. He was scared of the job.

'If you don't think you can do it, then tell them,' she said to him last night, but Kenny just shook his head.

'It's not that I can't do it. I can. It's a driving job. Just another driving job. Really, don't worry about it. It's a bit different from what I'm used to, that's all. Just a different sort of driving job. As long as I'm careful . . .' he trailed off. 'And I won't be alone; I'll be with good people.' He said that as if he meant it. As if he was confident of the quality of his companions, whoever they would be.

Deana didn't say anything else about it. Now she wishes she had, no matter how uncomfortable the subsequent conversation would have been.

It was late, that's her excuse. Kenny came back from the club at close to midnight. She was already in bed; he was undressing as he told her that he had a big job tomorrow, and then a couple of days off afterwards. He never explained why he was getting a couple of days off. He hinted that it was because the job was so big. Maybe the sort of thing that requires you to keep your head down. He'd never had anything like that before. Not in his life. She knows him well enough to know he'll struggle. He doesn't cope well under pressure; it's why she's always been able to dominate the relationship. Now it's twenty-four hours later. She's lying in bed again, looking at the clock. Half past midnight. He told her he'd be home by eleven. Probably earlier. He's been late before, plenty of times. Much later than this. But this feels different, and she thinks she knows why.

Deana encouraged Kenny to go to the police. It was the right thing to do. No matter what's happened, it was the right thing to do. He told her everything. Too much. If he'd kept some of his worries to himself, then he'd never have set up the meeting with DI Fisher. Kenny didn't have the guts to do it himself. He needed a push, so Deana pushed. He was worried about Jamieson taking so long to deal with Shug Francis. Worried it was a sign of weakness. If Jamieson's organization was picked apart, where would that leave Kenny? He's just a driver, nothing else. Ten a penny. Who-ever took over Jamieson's patch wouldn't need him, they'd have plenty of drivers of their own. He'd have no work. Worse still, no protection. Sure, people take over an organization and want to keep the old employees happy. They keep as many as possible on the books. They offer protection. But that generosity is for people who matter. It rarely finds its way down the food chain to drivers.

Kenny was worried sick. Convinced that Jamieson was

tripping over too many small distractions. Sure that Shug was getting the upper hand, or at least showing others how vulnerable Jamieson really was. If Shug didn't get him, then someone else soon would. He told Deana all this, and she told him what to do. Go to the police. Give them little bits of information – nothing that can incriminate Kenny. In exchange they offer you a little protection, if Jamieson's world implodes. Better than nothing. Only safety net you can get. So he set up the meeting, went and saw the cop. Three times now. It seemed easy. Seemed to go well. There was no suggestion that anyone had found out. He was actually getting used to being a grass. Losing his fear of it.

Now this job. Something that unnerved him. Something out of the blue. You might say she's reading too much into it, but it's past two o'clock in the morning now, and he's still not home. It was obviously something big, this job. Now much as she loves Kenny – in a comfortable, unfaithful sort of way – she knows he's not a man for the big occasion. Hard to believe that people as smart as Peter Jamieson and John Young don't know it, too. But they sent him. Desperation? Could be, but Kenny seemed to think they were getting on top of things. He kept suggesting the organization was back on track. No whiff of weakness to be had. So they deliberately sent him on a job they knew he wasn't the best person for. Well, that's not like them at all. Kenny's come home on umpteen occasions and told her how careful they are about recruitment. Told her tales of picking up new employees. Tales of the lengths that are gone to, making sure the right person does the right job. They don't suddenly get sloppy.

Half past two and Kenny's still not home. Deana's out of bed and downstairs. Just walking back and forth in the living room. Going over to the window and sitting on the ledge, looking out into the street. Waiting for a car to pull up. Beginning to worry about what car it will be. Let's say for a minute that this wasn't Jamieson setting Kenny up. That this wasn't his punishment for talking to the police. Let's say instead that they went along on this job, and something's gone wrong. They've been caught. Maybe the car that pulls up at the house will be a police car. Come to tell her that Kenny's buried under a mountain of shit, and would she mind coming to the station to discuss what she knows about his life. Not beyond the realms of possibility. Put that on the back burner for now. For now, the fear is that Jamieson knows, and tonight was punishment time.

She's gone back to bed. Calmed down a little. So he's late. Very late. That's not a first, now is it? He's been late plenty of times. This is a bigger job than usual. A more intense challenge. Maybe there's a very different aftermath to these things. If Kenny was involved in something big, then it's fair to assume that the clean-up will be bigger, too. She's convinced herself, at ten past three in the morning, that this is just the natural consequence of a bigger job. There are

47

women who go through this every night. Women tied to men who do big jobs on a regular basis. Deana's met a few of them over the years. Some of them look like they don't have a care in the world. Some look exhausted. That's how she tells the difference between the ones who really love their men and the ones who don't.

Kenny's not the first man in the business that she's been in a relationship with, but most of the others were down the chain, too. Low-rank people of no consequence, the sort who don't get big jobs. She's been with a couple of guys higher up, but only briefly. One was a long time ago, when she was a teenager. It was a fun thing for both of them; went nowhere. The other was since she met Kenny. Since they moved in together. Theirs is a curious sort of relationship. Each trusts the other to be untrustworthy. Each knows the other isn't entirely faithful, but they care about each other's feelings. There's nothing open about it. They have no kids, a decent income and a good time together. They've come to love each other. It's not the sort of love that people get giddy about, just the type that lasts.

She met a guy outside a restaurant. She'd been out with friends; she was calling a taxi to get home. Kenny was working, probably late. This guy approached and asked her if he could give her a lift. Nice-looking guy, a little younger than Deana, but she wasn't going to tell him that. She was thirty-three then, thirty-four now. This guy was mid- to late twenties, could have passed for younger. She'd seen him before. He'd seen her. Something relating to Kenny's work. Something at the club, she thought. Or maybe somewhere else. His name was Alan Bavidge. He worked for a man called Billy Patterson, a man with a growing reputation. Patterson has an organization of his own, but it deals in the murky end of things. He's managed to grow in the shadows, not stepping on toes. Stayed out of most parts of the drug trade. His business revolves around moneylending and the security business. Being with Bavidge was an eye-opener for Deana.

She spent five weeks with him. Sweet, handsome guy, smart too. She worked him around Kenny. He was fun, but she knew Alan wouldn't last. Five weeks together, and he stood her up four times. All because of the work he did. He was high up in Patterson's organization. He never told her exactly what he did, he wasn't a talker like Kenny, but she's good enough at maths to put two and two together. Alan did nasty things, no doubt. Beatings – maybe more. At first she was annoyed about being stood up, but his apologies were genuine. He had a tense and weary look when he eventually showed up, which you don't get just because you're late. He'd been working. He would keep that tension for hours, sometimes days. They went their separate ways. Kenny was getting irksome; he'd figured someone else was on his scene. Neither she nor Alan was committed to the relationship. They parted on good terms. Alan wasn't the sort of man anyone could have a relationship with. Too many nights standing at the living-room window, wondering if he would make it home that night.

Strange thing was, when she found out Alan was dead she didn't feel anything. Not sad, not emotional in any way. It always seemed inevitable. He was the sort of man who lived to die young. Killed by someone as yet unknown. His body found in an alleyway behind a row of shops. A place he had no business being in. Who knows what he suffered? What he was suffering even when she was with him. She found it hard to care. Alan knew what he was involved in. He knew the risks and he faced them head-on. That was the impression she had of him.

Kenny is the total opposite. Only vaguely aware of the dangers, unwilling to face them. Such a good man. She can't bear to think of him suffering. Another glance at the clock. Ten to four. Come on, Kenny, where the hell are you? She's drifting off to sleep. She's waking with a start now. Looking at the clock. Five past eight and Kenny's still not home.

# 8

Calum's taking almost nothing. Purposely leaving anything they would expect him to take. He has to give them doubt. They have to believe that he might have died last night, same as Kenny and the moneyman. Maybe something went wrong, and all three of them are lying dead in a forest somewhere. That thought will scare the crap out of them. They'll go looking for the body. Good. Look for something you can never find. That'll prove a useful distraction for Calum. He wants Jamieson and Young to have as many distractions as possible. The second they suspect what he's actually up to, they will hunt him down like a dog. He will become their absolute priority, at the expense of all other things. He has to be long gone by then.

He won't be notifying anyone that he's leaving the flat. That's obvious. A man who's possibly died the previous night doesn't then notify people of his departure. He will disappear. Not just from Young and Jamieson, but from everyone. Well, not quite everyone, because he needs a little help here. Can't do this alone. Things have to be organized, and quickly. The first is the departure from the flat. He has to show them what they expect to see. Let's make no bones about it: they will come round to the flat. Calum has no doubt that they have a spare key. They've never told him they do, but Jamieson provided the flat. They won't own it – they're smarter than that. They don't want people knowing that Calum's their employee, so they won't do anything as crass as put him in their own property. Still, they'll have taken every precaution. After all, they had a key to Frank MacLeod's house when they sent Calum to kill him. His own predecessor. The man he's trying to avoid becoming.

They'll expect him to have left his mobile behind, so that's been untouched since he put it on the kitchen table last night. He'll leave it where it is. He won't buy a new one until he's out of the city. His wallet he's leaving on the counter in the kitchen. Don't pile all your belongings up beside one another – makes it look like you've left them to be found. Put them where others would expect to find them. A wallet tossed casually onto the counter. The mobile checked for messages before he left, placed on the table, ready for him to check again on his return. Living up to their expectations. His passport is in the drawer of the desk in the living room. Won't take them long to find that. His driver's licence is there with it, his cheque book too. The driver's licence is the only one he had to stop and think about. He'll be getting a new one anyway, but where would they expect it to be? They might think he would have it in his car. No. Maybe someone with lower standards, but not Calum. They know he wouldn't have it anywhere near him on the night of a job. Leave it where it is.

He's been thinking about running for weeks. Months, truthfully, but it was an idle thought to begin with. Then it became a plan. Not a lot he could do in advance. Not when he didn't know when the chance would come. It's here now. One thing he has prepared are clothes. Not much, but he has what he needs. Clothes and a bag. Went out and bought them with cash. Not all at once. A few different shops, over the course of a week. Assume that Jamieson's organization will be able to access your bank details. If they see you were spending money in clothes shops in advance of disappearing, they might start to wonder. Why does a fellow who rarely buys new clothes suddenly splurge? A few items of clothing and a bag, hidden in the bottom of his wardrobe. Never worn before, ready for departure.

He's done the same thing with money. He won't empty his account. Leave something there, just in case Jamieson has access. So you take out a little more than you need each time you go to a cash machine. You need fifty quid, so you take out a hundred. He's been doing that for five weeks now. It's not a perfect system. More money than usual goes out, and someone with a sharp eye will spot it. The hope is that no one with a sharp eye will look. Hope that Young and Jamieson will only glance at his account and see that there's still plenty of money there. No large transfer of money. If they don't look for a spending pattern, they won't see anything of note. So he has more than six hundred and fifty pounds in a wad, wrapped in three elastic bands. That's going into the bottom of the bag.

It's a funny feeling when you know you're leaving a place for the last time. He never had the chance to feel this way about his old flat. That one he left in a hurry, after Shug Francis sent Glen Davidson round to stab him in the night. Calum is still very much alive. Glen Davidson is not. He breathed his last on the kitchen floor of Calum's old flat. A place that felt like home. And then he could never go back. He and George got rid of the body, but you can't take the risk of returning. You can't go back to a place where you killed a man. If that place happens to be your home, then you never go home. He'd lived in that flat for eight years. He knew every little piece of it and felt so comfortable there. He had his routines. Everything was in its rightful place. The last time he left it, he left with both hands slashed open. He had dishcloths wrapped round them, trying to carry his share of the weight as he and George Daly took Davidson's body down to the van. He never went back. This is different. No sense of leaving home. Just leaving a flat. Not coming back, and wouldn't care to, even if he had the option, thank you very much.

He has the bag of new clothing and nothing else. Well, the clothes he was wearing last night, but he needs to ditch those. And the gun. That's still in the inside pocket of his coat. He needs to ditch that, too. He knows it. Should have done it sooner. Unprofessional to have it so long after using it. It's a comfort, though. In the wake of any job you have the threat of arrest. That's something he's accustomed to, after ten years of killing people for a living. That threat is old hat. There's a new one this time, never before experienced. The threat of his own employers. They aren't going to arrest him. They aren't going to make sure he has a lawyer present at the time of punishment. They're going to do what they do to anyone who tries to walk away without permission. Anyone who knows too much. They'll put a bullet in him. The gun's comforting, but too much of a risk. He'll find a random bin and ditch it. Usually he would return it to the person he bought it from and get some of his money back, but no one must know that he's alive.

Out the door, locking it. He'll chuck the keys along with the clothing. Down the stairs and out through the front door, looking carefully up and down the street. Nothing out of place. No car that he doesn't recognize. Calum's stopping at the top of the three steps outside the front door. Pretending to fiddle about with something in his bag. Using the seconds to look carefully. Is there anyone peering out a window who can see him? Anyone slinking down in the driver's seat of a car, trying to hide from him? Can't see anyone.

Down the steps and along the street. Moving quickly, but not so fast that it would grab the attention of the casual observer. Round the corner and along the next street. Every now and again checking behind him. Not too often – that would be conspicuous. Mustn't look like a man who's checking behind him. Onto the street where he left his car last night. Starting it up and driving away. So far, so good; but so far was the easy part. Now he needs the help of others. He's going to see his big brother.

# 9

The phone call is made by one of the women who work across the hall. They think it odd that Hardy hasn't turned up for work. They can't remember him taking a day off in all the time they've shared the top floor of the building. They didn't report it straight away. You don't, do you? You don't rush to call the police just because someone doesn't turn up for their work. Could be any number of reasons. Maybe Richard Hardy is sick. Been a bit of flu going around, after all. So they do nothing, until a client turns up looking for him. An Asian businessman who visits regularly. Been visiting for years, seems to be an important client for Mr Hardy. They buzz him into the building. The man's knocking on the office door, obviously unsure whether or not to leave. His accountant's never stood him up before. It's so unlike Hardy.

One of the women has come out into the hall and is talking to him now. Asking whether Mr Hardy cancelled their meeting or not.

'No, he didn't. I'm very surprised at him,' the business-man's saying.

'I don't want to overreact,' the woman's saying, 'but he's never missed a day before. We both said it when we got here. We both said: He's not here, and that's not like him at all.'

'I have his mobile telephone number,' the businessman's saying, putting his briefcase down and taking his own phone from his pocket. Calling, but getting no answer. People don't like to make a fuss. The businessman and the woman are agreeing that they'll leave it until lunchtime before they take it any further.

The businessman's down the stairs and out the front door when he stops in his tracks. Isn't that Richard's car? Sure looks like it. Might not be, but that's the sort of car he drives. A pause. He's taking his phone out of his pocket and trying again. This is concerning. Holding the phone to his ear, leaning against the car he thinks is Hardy's. Sounds like the ring is echoing. That's weird. It's coming from inside the car. It *is* Richard's car. That's his phone on the seat, the display lighting up as the businessman rings it. Well now, this is beginning to look like something worth being nervous about. Richard would never go off without his mobile. Goodness, he would never go off without his car. A man of his age, how far would he get? No, this is definitely unusual. He's been buzzed back in now and he's knocking on the charity-office door. He's talking with the women.

At this point, because none of them know Richard's home number, they call the police. The woman calls. Helen Harrison, her name is, if you're interested. PC Joseph Higgins is interested, for about ten seconds. When he hears the missing person has been missing for a couple of hours and has only missed one appointment, he is less bothered. Pretty blasé about the whole thing, in fact. The car's outside. The woman's confirmed that Hardy usually gets to the office before them. So Hardy gets here. Decides to nip along to a shop to pick up something. Maybe falls over. Maybe takes a turn. Maybe some emergency comes up. A respectable, ageing guy like Hardy, it's usually health-related. He's gone somewhere and had some kind of episode. Probably in a hospital as we speak, being told that he needs to lower his blood pressure, take a holiday. No big deal.

Left his mobile in the car. Not a lot they can do, truth be told. As far as these people know, the man's been gone two hours. No search party needed for that. He's finding out Hardy's address.

'We'll pop round,' PC Higgins is saying, nodding to his silent, disinterested colleague. 'If he's there, we'll tell him to call you. If not, we'll ask around, make sure people know to keep an eye out for him. Not much more we can do, though. Right now he's only late for work, not technically missing.'

Higgins is good at polite. Not particularly good at interested. The woman knows he's going through the motions, but what more can you expect at this early stage? Police these days. Hard to feel safe when they won't go to any lengths to look for a good man like Richard Hardy.

Higgins and his colleague, PC Tom McIntyre, are making their way to Hardy's address. It's a quiet Tuesday morning, this is something to do. Something harmless, which gives them an excuse to avoid bigger investigations. That's how McIntyre sees it. Not Higgins. His instinct and ambition see a case like this as a waste of time. It's a quiet morning, though. Uncharacteristically nice weather, too. A little drive out to the suburbs. Nice little area where Hardy made his home. Finding a parking place along the street and walking up to his front gate. A plain but neat front garden. Detached house, sort of area mostly populated by the middle-aged and upwards. There's a driveway and a garage. No car in the drive, garage locked up.

Before they've even reached the door they can see something's amiss.

'Newspaper,' McIntyre's saying, pointing at the end of a rolled-up newspaper sticking out of the letterbox.

'I can see that,' Higgins is saying, looking at his colleague with a frown. They shouldn't be lumbering him with people like McIntyre. Higgins is twenty-six, McIntyre in his early thirties. If McIntyre had talent and ambition, he'd be higher up the chain by now. He's become lazy, just looking to avoid work. The sort of person who holds younger cops like Higgins back. Ringing the doorbell and waiting. Nothing. Knocking on the door and waiting. Nothing.

'We'll check with the neighbours, see if they know

whether he was home last night,' Higgins is saying. A thought's forming in his head, thanks to that newspaper. Let's say he didn't leave the car at the office this morning and go somewhere. Let's just say, for argument's sake, that the car's been there since last night. Now he's been missing for fifteen hours, and it starts to look interesting.

First door they knock on is opened by a grey-haired old lady. Big surprise.

'Hello, dear,' Higgins is saying, doing his best at insincere friendly. 'We're looking for your neighbour, Mr Hardy. He doesn't appear to be at home.'

'No, he's not,' she's saying, nodding her head in the way people do when they know something you don't. Particularly people who aren't used to knowing something you don't. 'And I'll tell you something else,' she's saying, revelling in her moment. 'He wasn't back last night. Didn't come home.'

'You're sure about that?' Higgins is asking.

'Of course I'm sure. I hear him, every night. He comes back and parks his car in the garage, and he slams that garage door shut. Every night, slams it shut. And he leaves his outside light on until he goes to bed after ten. Every night, that light blaring in through our windows at the side of the house. Not last night, though. Wasn't a light in the house last night.'

Okay, so now he's a missing person. A proper, actual missing person, rather than some old fart late for work. It's a myth that a person has to be missing for twenty-four hours before the police get concerned. They get concerned at the point when a person's disappearance seems concerning, logically enough. Might be sooner than twenty-four hours. In some cases a person has to be gone much longer. Here's a reliable fellow who didn't get home from work last night. Didn't turn up for work in the morning. Completely out of character. Now it's worth calling it in to the station. They're back in the car, Higgins radioing in a report and a description. It's the fact that he left his car behind that gets Higgins. You don't go off the grid for hours and leave your car parked at your office. And with his mobile inside it. That's another funny little act worth noting.

Back at Hardy's office. The client with a missed appointment has gone. Has a life of his own to get on with. The two women from the charity office are still hanging around, having more fun than they've had in years. They call the janitor for Higgins, and he unlocks the office door. Hardy locked up, but didn't leave in his car. No sign of disturbance in the office. First thought is that wherever Hardy went, he went willingly. Locked up and left. His car locked, too; Higgins tried the door handle on the way in. A thought occurs, and he's kicking himself. Not literally, of course. He doesn't want to say it. Doesn't want to accept that he might have blundered. He's about to ask the question of one of the women, when he gets a message on the radio. No Richard Hardy admitted to any local hospital or the reported victim of a crime. He's looking at Helen, the charity worker, who's trying hard not to look thrilled.

'Do you know if perhaps Mr Hardy had a girlfriend or partner of any sort?'

She's about to say no, and then she's pausing. They'd never considered it. He's an old man, a widower. It seems so unlikely, but if you can't disprove it, it becomes a possibility.

Everyone feels a bit embarrassed. McIntyre's smirking just enough for his colleague to notice. Helen's gone toddling back into her own office to share the wonderfully salacious new theory with her colleague. Higgins is taking a stroll round the office, looking at the files on the shelves, in the hope of seeing something notable. Hope realized: two of the first four names he sees written in block capitals on the side of the bulky files are familiar. Men known to the police. Nothing major, but people of dubious repute. It's the sixth name that stops him in his tracks. He's standing there staring at it. Francis Autos. There's a row of big thick files, one for each of the last seven years. Shug Francis. Higgins is pulling down the file for this year.

'Hey,' McIntyre's saying, 'don't get into that. Let's go.'

Higgins is ignoring him. Shug-bloody-Francis. And it's everything: employee payment details, tax forms, the whole nine yards. Even if Hardy isn't missing, this is a chance. Higgins is on the radio to the station. DI Fisher will want to be all over this.

# 10

They've been sitting looking at each other for the last ten minutes. Every now and then William will shake his head. Sometimes he'll ask Calum to repeat himself. Then another shake of the head. Calum got here early. Waited for William to come home from work. That was lunchtime. Calum's given William a brief rundown of what he wants to do. The bullet points, if you'll pardon the pun.

'Okay, fine, give me the details then,' William's saying.

And Calum's smiling, because he knew his brother would say that. He's asking a lot of William, and he knows it, but he also knows his big brother won't let him down. Just by asking for the detail William's committing himself to this. As Calum knew he would. It's dangerous for William, but he's always wanted his brother to get out of the business. He'll accept the risk.

It was the one thing in all of this that Calum agonized over. Sure, he regrets that he won't see his mother again, but there's no danger for her in that. It's the risks William will take on his behalf that made Calum stop and think. Is there a way of doing this that doesn't put his brother in danger? Short answer is no. In a perfect world Calum would have had everything prepared months ago. It's not a perfect world, rather obviously. He could prepare things like the clothes, but for the fake identity and the bank accounts he had to wait. Do those things months before your escape opportunity comes along and you're asking for trouble. Someone finds out you've purchased the ID and wants to know why. Only reason you need the ID is to do a runner. You can't explain it away. A good gunman doesn't do business with counterfeiters. You do no business with any criminal you don't absolutely have to. So that had to wait.

'I needed to wait until I had a job,' Calum's telling William. 'I had one last night.'

William's grimacing, slightly raising a hand. 'Don't tell me what I don't need to hear.' It's one thing to know what your little brother does for a living. Quite another to hear him describe it. William already knew there was a job. He didn't want to know more when he lent Calum the car; doesn't want to know more now.

'So I had a job. I know that Peter Jamieson and John Young won't expect to hear from me or see me for as much as a week. They won't get pissy if they don't hear from me for a fortnight. So I maybe have that long to get away. Put some distance between me and them.'

'Good,' William's saying, nodding his head. He knows what this is. This is the good news before the work starts. The little hook to convince him it's all going to work out, before

Calum reveals the mountain of preparation and risk. 'I'm guessing you've worked out the detail then,' William continues. 'Tell me what we need to do, in order.'

Calum's nodding. This would be so much harder if William didn't know the business. If he was too stupid to work out what happens next. Calum's always thought of himself as the more intelligent of the two. The more cerebral. That doesn't make William dumb. William went to work in a garage when he was eighteen. By twenty-four he had a share in the business. A small one, but he made it work for him. Now, at thirty-two, he runs the place. Owns most of it, although not quite all. Yes, he's occasionally side-stepped legality in pursuit of profit, but he's always been smart enough to get away with it. Smart enough to make no enemies. That's been key. That ends today. If Jamieson finds out that William helped Calum escape, then William makes one big enemy.

'First thing we need to do is get rid of my car,' Calum's saying. 'Respray and retag, break it down for parts – whatever. I need to make a little bit of money out of it. They'd expect it to be missing. They don't know that I use you for the cars, although they might guess. Obviously you deny it if they ask. So the car needs to disappear.'

William's nodding, thinking. 'How much cash you got?'

'About six hundred.'

William's frowning now. 'Won't get far on that. Six

hundred quid? All right, listen. Breaking it down might be safer, but I think you should go for a dressing-up. A good spray and tag, and nobody knows it was yours. I can get it a new logbook. Sell it. Car like that, you could get, maybe, a grand and a half after costs. Might be a bit less if we're selling in a hurry. Gives you more to run with.'

Calum's nodding. 'As long as it's safe. Safety first. That needs to be the first thing,' he's saying. 'After that, I need a new identity. I know a guy who can come up with a new passport and driver's licence in good time, if the money's right. I can't go and see him about it,' Calum continues, with a bit of a shrug. A 'you know what that means' kind of shrug.

'I can go see him,' William's saying. A pause. 'I know a guy: does fake service histories and whatnot for cars. I know he does driver's licences too. I could have a word with him.'

Calum's shaking his head. He chose his man carefully. Any counterfeiter who lasts is a good counterfeiter. But a driver's licence and a passport are two different things. These new biometric passports require a speciality. They also need the passport to be falsely registered – something his chosen man can do for him. Same with the driver's licence, but that's easier.

'We'll stick with the guy I've chosen. He should be fine. I'll tell you what I need.'

'I'll go see him tomorrow then. You have enough time for all this?' William's asking.

'I hope so,' Calum's saying quietly. 'The counterfeiter will already have IDs he can use. They set these things up and hold the IDs for years before they sell them. Gives them a history.'

'Is this one of those dead-baby things?' William's asking with another frown.

'Might be a stolen ID, might just be made up. I will need to set up a bank account in the new name, but that'll be a piece of piss. Then I'll need to book tickets to get myself out of here.'

'You'll need his ID before you can get through an airport,' William's saying. 'If you're not leaving Britain, you could always just drive.'

'Nah,' Calum's saying. 'I will have to leave at some point. Jamieson has connections with people all over the country. He could find me anywhere in Britain.'

'He could find you anywhere,' William's warning.

'He could. But he won't.'

Another moment of silence between them. Quiet in the house. William lives alone. He's never married, although he was with a girl called Morven for years. Six years, maybe a little more. Then it all fell apart, in no time at all. Calum never knew why. Knew William didn't want to talk about it, so didn't ask. Been a couple of girls since, but William hasn't settled. The elder brother's the one to break the silence. Has to be. He has the right to ask; Calum only has the right to answer.

'So you going to London or what?'

'Probably. Just to begin with. Then on somewhere else. I'll see how the land lies. See where I can go.'

'You got any idea where you'll end up?'

'I have an idea,' Calum's nodding, and saying no more. It's not an idea he'll share with William. Not yet. Safer for his brother to know as little as possible. William understands that.

'So does this have something to do with that wee firecracker you were knocking about with? The one who came and called me all sorts of terribly insulting things at the garage?' William's asking with a smile, teasing but genuinely interested.

The firecracker's name is Emma. Calum hasn't seen her since the day she walked out of his flat nearly two months ago. She asked him to walk away from this life, and he told her he couldn't. Which was true, at the time. He doesn't know where she is now. He does know he'll never see her again. He can't, when he's using a new identity.

'It is and it isn't,' Calum's shrugging. 'It's not about her personally. It's about having someone like her. Having that kind of life. I can't have it. Not if I stay. Only way all that can be mine is if I make a break. So that's what I'm doing.'

'Hell of a risk for a life you might not enjoy.'

'I don't enjoy this one much, so it's a risk worth taking.'

William's sitting in his armchair, nodding his head. The conversation's become morose. Failing lives. Might as well get that one last miserable question out of the way.

'What about Ma?'

Calum's sighing. 'I don't want to have to do this to her, but I don't have a choice. I can't go see her. People will ask her about me, and I can't have her place me in the city any time after last night.'

'Fuck's sake, Calum, you can't let her think you're dead. She nearly fell apart when Da died. What's this going to do to her?'

'Well, what do you want me to do? Go round and tell her the truth. Hey, Ma, guess what: I need to flee the city because I killed a bunch of people! What would that do to her?'

William's rubbing his forehead. 'We'll come up with something. I won't have you dying on her, poor old cow. You're her blue-eyed boy. We'll find a way to keep her content.'

Now William's gone out for a couple of hours. He was due to meet some friends to play five-a-side football. Does it every Tuesday after work. He wanted to cancel; Calum said no. You go and you act normal. Nobody thinks there's anything going on. You do nothing that raises an eyebrow. So he's gone. Agreed to send a text to Calum's mobile. He'll send a couple more, and make a few calls in the next few days. Calling a phone he knows is lying on Calum's kitchen table. Keeping up appearances. Calum knows how this will work. William's upset because his little brother is going away. Because there's risk involved. He's not bothered about the risk to himself. It's Calum he's frightened for. Calum's the one who could be killed for walking away from a man like Peter Jamieson. But tomorrow William will be bustling with energy. Ready to face the challenge. Ready to go and see the counterfeiter. Play his part. It's a reassuring thought. Comforting to have someone else's enthusiasm to feed off.

# 11

Richard David Hardy. A sixty-one-year-old widower. A professional accountant all his working life. A regular at his local church. A hard-working individual. A gentleman. An intellectual. And one crooked little son of a bitch. That was DI Michael Fisher's first instinct after a quick glance around the office, and he's not finding anything to prove him wrong. He's carefully writing out the list of clients mentioned on file. Of the eleven so far, there are only two names he doesn't recognize. The nine others are all names that have crossed his path at one time or another. In Fisher's experience, it is fair to judge a man by the company he keeps. To be honest, none of these men are in the top rank. None of them are serious players. They're all low- to middle-grade criminals. Schemers and crooks of various varieties, but nobody Fisher would work up a sweat to arrest. Not worth it. None of them worth it but one. Hugh 'Shug' Francis.

That file's caught his attention. He's flicking through it now. Sitting at Hardy's desk, the office door open. Higgins and McIntyre are still around. The two women across the hall have developed a habit of leaving and returning to their office. All so that they can peek in through the office door and see what Fisher's doing. They'll see nothing interesting. What they'll see is the sort of thing that gets a conviction. Flicking through pages of numbers, trying to work out what should be there and what shouldn't. There's plenty. Hardy keeps details. There seems to be info on every deal Shug's done, every employee he keeps. It'll take an expert to unpick it all. Work out what Hardy changes, to make the numbers add up. Something must have been changed. There are people listed here who must be involved exclusively in criminal work for Shug. Money brought in through criminal work, and then hidden amongst the honest cash.

Fisher's closing the book. Take a step back and consider everything you have. Hardy's gone missing. Car's outside with his mobile in it. Didn't make it home last night. Made it as far as his car – that's why the mobile's there. So someone picks him up outside work. No reports of someone being forced into a car last night, so let's say he goes willingly. You go willingly with someone you know. Who, that Hardy knows, would turn up at the end of the day and pick him up in the car park, rather than book an appointment? Someone with malicious intent, obviously. Someone with a lot to hide. Someone who's concerned that Mr Hardy is no longer the best person to hide his secrets. Wouldn't be any of the low-level crooks. They aren't capable. Wouldn't be willing, either. They just want things hidden away. No, it has to be someone growing. Or someone trying to grow. Someone very much like Shug Francis.

It's not exactly a case, but it's a workable theory to be getting on with. Could be that Mr Hardy will walk through the door and ask what all the fuss is about. Could be that Shug has taken him, to talk: tell Hardy what he's going to do for Shug now. Then he lets him go. Not likely. Not with a guy like Hardy. If he's been taken, it's to be killed. You don't grab someone like him off the street just to give them a warning, or to force new instructions upon them. Nah, you grab them to get rid of them. Can't release someone like Hardy and trust him to follow instructions. Someone who perhaps doesn't understand the consequences. Someone who thinks the police can protect him. No. If they took Hardy, they took him to kill him. He'll be dead already. That should give Fisher the power he needs to get all this paperwork investigated.

Needs to find out more about Hardy. Find out how close he was to his clients. One in particular. Find out if he had any debts. If he was fiddling around with women he should have avoided. Long shot, but it could catch you out. You go racing after Shug, and find out Hardy had three mistresses and a mountain of gambling debts – they'll be laughing at you for months. First, prove that there could have been no other motive. Then go for Shug. Until then, he needs to keep this quiet. Higgins he trusts. That boy's been useful before. Smart and honest, willing to work. McIntyre, on the other hand . . . Going to have to be more careful with him. Those two old biddies across the hall aren't to be trusted, either. Nothing Fisher can do to stop them blethering away to their leathery-skinned, turkey-necked peers. Witnesses – they really are insufferable!

Fisher's going out into the hall. Higgins and McIntyre are both there.

'Don't need two of you,' he's saying. 'Higgins, you stay here, you can help me bag some of this. You,' he's saying to the other one, 'can go and find something else to do.' That means: go and do anything that doesn't have you under my feet. Sod who you're supposed to be working with – I don't want you here.

McIntyre's nodding. Looking a little downcast, but that's for show. This gives him the opportunity to dawdle his way back to the station. Fisher's given him the chance to piss away the next hour or so. McIntyre's not the sort of man to waste such an opportunity.

Higgins, on the other hand, is walking briskly into the office, eager to help. He knows Fisher's the sort of guy who could get him interesting cases. Maybe even push a promotion his way. The sort of cop who can hold your career in his hands.

'Close that bloody door,' Fisher's saying with a frown. He can hear the door across the hall opening again. He might be more patient with the women if they were useful. They have no idea about Hardy's clients. No idea about Hardy twisting the numbers in his accounts. No idea about his home life. Bloody useless.

'The women across the hall identified the man who came today as Ashraf Dutta,' Higgins is saying. 'His family have been known to the police for some time.'

'They have,' Fisher's nodding. 'His son and nephew had some piss-poor little racket selling fags. They're nothing. Neither is the old man. He's not who we're looking for. He would hardly come here and place himself at the scene.'

'If he had an appointment he might think he had to be seen keeping it. And maybe it wasn't him who ordered it. Maybe it was the younger ones.'

'No,' Fisher's saying firmly. Higgins is pissed off because he didn't recognize the witness when he had him at the scene. He wasn't paying attention because he didn't think it was important. That was a mistake, and he wants to take the frustration out on the witness. 'This,' Fisher's continuing, 'is where we're going to find what we're looking for.' He's gesturing to the pile of files. Not specifically at Shug's, but it is at the top, and Higgins is too sharp not to notice.

'Okay,' Higgins is nodding. 'What can I do?'

'I want you to go through every drawer in this office. Every folder. Every slip of paper. Let's find anything that's obviously out of place. Anything we get before the experts take over will buy us a head start. I'm going to let them know that we need the finance unit to look through all this. When you're done here, you're going back to Hardy's house. Get inside, rummage about. Find anything interesting. Might be a better chance of getting personal info there.'

There's plenty else to do, and a lot of it will be boring. Doesn't matter. This feels good. Feels like one of those sneaky little chances that you can grab hold of. Fisher's lost a couple of chances lately. Good ones. This feels different already. Hardy wasn't in the industry, not properly. Better chance that he slipped up. A chance that this could lead to big arrests. This does feel good.

# 12

It's long enough. Been hanging around the house all day waiting for him, but nothing. It's nearly five o'clock in the afternoon now. Deana's nerves can't take any more of this. She has to do something. The only thing that ever calms her nerves is action. Sitting here waiting for the phone to ring or a knock to come to the door, that's not helping. But what? She can't just go out and look for him. Where the hell do you start? He could have gone anywhere. Might not even have been in the city. Jamieson has contacts and business all over the place. Little stuff mostly, but getting his foot in the door in new markets all the time. Kenny's told her all about it. Jamieson has work all over the country; he could send Kenny anywhere. No, looking for him herself is a non-starter.

She could go to the club. She would, too, if she didn't much fancy surviving past the end of the day. As it is, she's rather attached to this living lark, so rattling that cage is out. If Kenny's been killed, then it's surely by Jamieson. They found out. Fine, they found out that Kenny was a grass, and they killed him. That was the risk Kenny took. Or maybe not. Maybe Kenny went out on an actual job and was jumped. Maybe Jamieson doesn't know about it. Kenny always says that when people go on a big job, they don't go back to the club. They stay underground for a few days. Let the heat die down. Maybe they think Kenny's doing that right now. He was supposed to have a couple of days off. Maybe they'd be horrified to find out that he hasn't come back. No. Jesus, stop kidding yourself, woman. You're smarter than this. You know the business better than this. Jamieson found out. Or, more likely, that creepy little shit John Young found out.

So there's nothing she can do for herself. Not without getting into more shit than she has any hope of wading through. Makes her feel pretty hopeless. Can't go to Jamieson. Best-case scenario, he pats her on the head and tells her not to worry. These guys don't tend to lean towards best-case scenarios. So that's out. And it leaves her with one option. One bad, filthy and almost certainly useless option. But it's the only one she has. It's the option that probably killed Kenny. She's sitting on the window ledge in the living room, looking out onto the road. No cars. Nobody coming to tell her what happened. No Kenny. She could do nothing. Most would, in her situation. A woman who's lived in the industry knows that you do nothing. Your man doesn't come home, you stay silent. Don't report him missing. Don't raise the alarm. Accept that he took the risk and lost. Move on. Thirty-four isn't old. She's still attractive, and she knows it. No kids, so no baggage to scare a man away. She could easily start again.

But she won't. Not yet. For one simple and curious reason. She owes Kenny better. All the cheating, all the arguments – they were regrettable. But it was still a great relationship. He was weak, he wasn't burdened by great intelligence, he wasn't entirely faithful to her either, but he loved her in his way, and she loved him for it. Now that he's gone, and she's quite convinced now that he has, who else will stand up for him? Who else is there to find out what happened to him? To make sure there's justice. Kenny's father's dead. His mother's alive, but Kenny hadn't seen her in years. He has a sister, but God alone knows where she is. He had friends too, but none of them will step up. They know who Kenny worked for. They know the possible consequences of making a fuss. If Deana doesn't do it, nobody will. Only she will stand up for the dead.

One of Kenny's other failures: very predictable. A man with a mediocre memory, who keeps a little notepad badly hidden in his bedside cabinet. Not hard to work out what sort of thing is going to be in there. Phone numbers and addresses. You can see in the first couple of pages where he's tried to code it. Badly. A is one, B is two, and so on. He gave up on his coding effort quickly. Terrible handwriting, but she can recognize the names and numbers. She's shaking her head as she flicks through another page. He was just a driver. Didn't have the talent to be anything more than that. Just a driver. She shouldn't have pushed him towards the police.

But he brought it up. His nerves . . . Forget that. The fifth page is the last with anything on it. DF and a number. Detective Fisher. Kenny was Fisher's contact, and he may be dead because of it.

Downstairs, sitting comfortably. Time to begin. There was an office number in black ink. Then, below it in blue, a mobile number added later. She's calling the mobile, so Fisher should answer. Maybe he'll recognize Kenny's home number, maybe not. It's ringing.

'Hello,' says the emphatically and deliberately bored voice on the other end. A cop who wants his contact to know that he doesn't matter.

'Hello, Detective,' she's saying. A pause, and silence. 'You don't know me. My name's Deana Burke. I'm Kenny McBride's partner.'

More silence. Doesn't matter how cool the smug arsehole wants to play it, he knows who Kenny is. Kenny was his contact inside the Jamieson organization, and no detective forgets something like that.

'Uh-huh,' he's saying. 'And what can I do for you?'

'Kenny didn't come home last night.'

There's a chortle. 'Okay, I'm pretty sure that's something you can discuss with him when you see him. I hardly think that's a police matter.'

'I'm fairly sure he's been murdered.'

That bought a little more silence. She's not going to

break it this time. His turn. That one sentence, and the fact that she's calling him, has to tell him everything he needs to know.

'How can you be sure of that?' Fisher's asking. 'The man stays out one night and you have him in the grave already.' Speaking almost in a whisper now.

'I know that he went out on a job last night. I know it was a bigger job than he's ever done before. I know he was terrified about it. I think it was a set-up. He should be back by now. Should have been back last night. But he isn't. I think they found out about him contacting you.'

That has the wheels turning. She can hear Fisher sighing, buying himself a few seconds while he considers it.

'Listen, Miss Burke, I think you're making a pretty big leap here. You're assuming something terrible has happened. It could be nothing. Kenny works a job where he's not going to have regular hours. Maybe he's left you, you thought of that? I need something that at least looks like evidence before I can assume a crime has happened.'

She wants to shout at him. Tell him it's all his fucking fault. What kind of detective gets a good contact like Kenny and then does nothing to protect him? But that's not going to get her anywhere, and she's smart enough to know it. She mustn't give him the opportunity to turn his back on this. Turn his back on Kenny.

'I know that Kenny was your contact. Now I think Peter

Jamieson knows it, too. We both know that's dangerous,' she's saying. 'But I don't much care about how dangerous it is. How dangerous it is to you or to me. I'm not going to let them get away with this. I will do something about it. Maybe I'll go to Jamieson, demand answers.'

'Well, I hardly think that's going to do you a lot of good,' Fisher's saying. Sounding fed up now. She's pushing him a little too hard, and she realizes it. This isn't a man to be intimidated.

'Listen,' he's saying to her. 'I will look into it. I'll make sure that, if Kenny's out there somewhere, we spot him. I won't take him in or anything. Unless you want us to. Do you want to report him missing?'

'Of course I don't,' she's saying. This is getting tetchy. Fisher accusing her of being stupid enough to put her name to a missing person's report. 'If I wanted to report him missing, I wouldn't be calling you, would I?'

'Fine. I will keep a lookout. And please don't do anything stupid. The most likely outcome is that Kenny's been stuck somewhere on this job he's doing. Just keep your head and, if I find anything, I'll be in touch.'

He's hung up. Kenny was right about him – Fisher is a piece of shit. Arrogant. Thinks he's better than the people he deals with. He's right about one thing, though. Deana has to keep her head.

# 13

He got the meeting with Kirk out of the way yesterday. Fake phone calls set up. Thank Christ for that! That means today is for meetings with competent people. Already had the first one. That provided an interesting name. Apparently Deana Burke has been talking to the police. Silly girl. That was a good first meeting, with a good contact. Another one now. Not really a contact. An employee. George Daly. George is a good boy. A talent. Hard not to think of him as a waster, though. So much talent, but he won't step up. Young's been trying to persuade George to take on more responsibility. Wanted him to become a gunman, in fact. George wasn't having it. George is allergic to responsibility. Another reason Young wants him to take more of it. Someone smart enough to see the danger of power is exactly the sort of person who should have it. But George is stubborn. So Young's trying a different approach. Gently reducing the amount of muscle-work George does. Replacing it with seemingly small jobs. Things that don't look, on the surface, to be important. Build it up. Eventually he will make George important.

A knock on the front door. Young's been here for the last twenty minutes. A quiet little flat, hidden away in a quiet part of the city. A good place to meet contacts. Been useful, but they've been using it too long. Time to put it on the market. Young's found an alternative, but he'll miss this place. Had a great run here. They'll lose money on it. The market isn't where it was when they bought. Doesn't matter. This place has paid for itself a dozen times over. Information is always the most valuable currency. This place has delivered on that front. But neighbours will start to ask questions. An empty flat in a good area. What's happening with it? People don't like seeing a place like that empty. Makes them nervous. So you sell, and go through the same routine somewhere else. Buy the flat, keep it empty, use it for a few months. Then move on. Young thought about putting someone in this place, just to keep it. But no. Contacts much prefer coming to a sparsely furnished place that nobody lives in. The comfort of the contact matters most. Gets you more information.

Young's answering the door to George, gesturing for him to come in. George hasn't been here before. No need for such secrecy with someone who works for the organization, but Young has another meeting here in a little while. George is walking through to the living room. Sitting where Young gestures him to sit.

'So what's the news?' Young's asking. He's had George out on the streets. Dealing with contacts. Gathering information. George must see that this is more responsibility. But he does it, because he can't argue.

'They've started an investigation into the disappearance of Richard Hardy,' George is saying. Getting straight to the point. 'Don't know yet which way it's going.'

Hardly a surprise. People will be talking about it. Shug's accountant goes missing, it's not going to take long for the information to start leaking out. Young's wondering if Shug knows. He doesn't seem very well connected, and the people who matter won't rush to tell him.

'What about Shug? What are his moves?'

'Predictable, so far,' George is saying. 'I know he got in touch with Angus Lafferty, but that won't go anywhere. Shug's trying to be friendly to start with. Win people round. Hinting about the backing he has. Didn't come straight out and say it, not to Angus anyway.'

Young's nodding. Makes sense. Shug will look to move fast. Make moves against only the most senior men. Lafferty is Jamieson's largest importer. A key man.

'I also had a word with wee Bobby Wayne. He's nervous. Reckons someone was sniffing around his warehouse last night. Broke in. He says he doesn't know if they took anything, but I think that's bullshit. They took something, he just doesn't want to admit what it was. Something he shouldn't have had, probably.'

Young's nodding again. Bobby Wayne is smaller than Lafferty, but valuable. Runs a warehouse through which a lot of things flow. Jamieson gets his cut. Wayne runs a well-oiled machine. Useful for Shug.

'What's your opinion of all this?' Young's asking George.

George is frowning. Doesn't want to be drawn into this. 'I think it's no big deal that Shug approached Lafferty. That was obvious from the start. I think the Wayne one is more important. If that was Shug, then he's moving broadly. Getting a lot of people talking. Makes us look weak. I don't know. Just my opinion. You get people talking, and people believe what they hear.'

Young's smiling. George is far too smart to be muscle. Shug's moving against all the senior people, not just some. Charm some, intimidate others. Looking to cause a little panic. Jamieson looks like he's lost control. Shug looks like he's gained it. Smart move, if you have the people to back it up with.

'Thanks, George. Keep your ear to the ground. Keep listening.'

George has left. Young's sitting alone in the flat, considering their position. So the moneyman's dead, and Kenny-fucking-McBride has fallen off the face of the Earth with him. Young's thinking that Calum MacLean is a little bit special. Every job he's done for Jamieson has had complications, and he's handled them all brilliantly. They really should give him a rest – been using him more than is reasonable. Won't happen, though; plenty more work on the horizon. Young's up and walking to the window, glancing out. Nothing to see here. Never is in this flat. Quiet area, that's the point. Another meeting this morning before he heads to the club. A cop. This is a routine meeting. Well, as routine as these things get.

That's the knock on the door now. Fifteen minutes late. A contact Young neither likes nor trusts. One he uses as little as possible, but one who is useful. PC Paul Greig, standing in the corridor, looking as casual as you like. Not a care in the world, this one. Coming to meet a criminal, and oh so calm about it. Wrapped up in a complicated turf war, and not the least bit concerned. Young's opening the door, nodding for him to come in. Greig was the first police contact he cultivated. An achievement in itself. Would be nice if he'd turned out to be an achievement to be proud of.

'How are things?' Young's asking.

'Complicated,' Greig's shrugging. 'As usual.'

Aye, Young's thinking, complicated because that's how you make it. How you like it.

'Any news?' Young's asking. Greig won't have anything Young doesn't already know. Greig's role in helping Shug is over. He helped negotiate with Don Park. Helped get Shug his meeting with MacArthur. Greig needs to be careful not to think he's become terribly important because of that. He's dangerous enough already, without thinking he matters.

'Not really,' Greig's shrugging. 'I know the meeting's happened between Shug and MacArthur. I know that Shug was up bright and early this morning. Calling around, looking to get things moving. Started yesterday, I think. He's not wasting time. Seems to be moving about as fast as possible.'

Young's nodding. Interesting. Not because of the basic information – that was obvious. Of course Shug's moving fast. It's the only chance he has. Go slow and die. But it's interesting that Greig knows. Shows that he's already had a discussion this morning. Probably not with Shug. Probably with Don Park, MacArthur's right-hand man. Which suggests that Park is dumb enough to trust Greig.

'Heard something else this morning as well,' Greig's saying. 'Something interesting, I think, anyway. Seems like Shug's had a falling-out with his right-hand man. That Fizzy guy. They've been friends since school. Fizzy's been key to Shug's business. Word is, Fizzy was against the MacArthur deal. Could leave Fizzy on the outside.'

Okay. Young's often critical of Greig, but this is actually interesting stuff. Potentially valuable, if used right. Fizzy on the outside. It's a maybe, but it's a start. A man not used to being in danger. They could make a lot from this.

'Thank you, Paul,' Young's saying as he's walking Greig to the door. Been a long time since he said that to him. Greig's shrugging, taking it casual. He already knew that info would be important to Young. He always knows what matters and what doesn't.

Greig's gone and Young's alone in the flat again. Always

good to see the back of the little bastard. They might not have time to make a profit from Fizzy. Depends how things play out with Shug. Seems to be moving nicely. Perfect, even. Shug spilling his guts to Park, Park to Greig, and Greig to Young. All flowing in the right direction. But it's tenuous. Could all fall apart in an instant. Going to need a lot of attention to keep everything going their way. There's plenty to worry about, but it's not worry that's coursing through Young now. It's excitement. It's all cranking up. Shug making his moves, walking into the trap. The police starting to pay attention. Need to make sure they pay attention to the right things. He's waited ten minutes. That'll do. Young's up and making for the door. Making for the club to see Jamieson.

# 14

Calum talked him through what to say. Doesn't help. Doesn't make this any easier. William's still going to meet a crook he doesn't trust, to buy material that could get him arrested. Or worse. If Jamieson finds out that William helped Calum escape, there will be greater consequences than prison. That thought runs through his head as he's driving to the counterfeiter's house. It's not a thought that lasts long. Replaced by thoughts of Calum. For the last – what is it now? – nearly a decade, William's watched his brother's life with worry. Terror, even. Wanting him to get out. Well, Calum's getting out. Can't do it alone. Someone has to be there to help him out the door, and who else can he trust? This is a duty. William was there when this started. Partly his fault. This is a responsibility. In fact, this is a pleasure. William's smiling, thinking about his brother. Every late-night phone call has caused a flash of panic for William. Someone calling to say they found his brother's body. To say he's been arrested. No more of those fears. This is a price worth paying.

There's still the problem of their mother. Calum won't go to say goodbye, and William can understand that. It's for her own good. She can't know something that might get her into trouble. Spin her a yarn, and hope nobody else goes to the police to report him missing.

'Who else would?' Calum asked. 'If you or Ma don't do it, nobody will.'

William raised an eyebrow, but didn't go any further. Pretty damning indictment of his brother's social life. William's never really thought about it before, but that must be because of the job. Calum was always quiet, but he was a nice guy. The isolation comes from hiding, and the hiding is because of his work. Something else his job has ruined. So there are no friends to report him gone. His employers aren't going to raise the alarm. William will keep his mouth shut. That just leaves their mother. She'll accept a story. She'll take William's word for it. He just has to get the story right.

That's out of his mind now. He's pulling onto the street where the counterfeiter lives. William's been on this street before, recognizes a house on the corner where he went to a party. That was a couple of years ago, but he has a good memory for parties. Parties and cars. What else is there? Nice area. The counterfeiter lives further along the street on the right-hand side. Trees on the street – always a good sign. Bad areas don't get foliage. There's parking at the side of the road, if he can find a gap. Stopping the car, taking a deep breath. This is the big moment for William. There will be more to do, but this is the one job that he absolutely has to get right, all by himself. Find a distraction. He's calling the garage, asking how they're getting along with Calum's car. William wants it sprayed, tagged and sold within three days. One of the two mechanics he employs is telling him that they're working on it right now. Doesn't sound impressed that William is checking up.

Stop wasting time. Time is the one thing you don't have. Barry Fairly is the counterfeiter's name, apparently. William's never heard of him. Calum has, seems to think he's the best in the business. But they can't afford to look like they're in a hurry. William wasn't going to argue with that. Last thing you do is look desperate. Didn't need Calum to warn him. You look desperate, and a counterfeiter starts to worry. Starts to think he can't trust you to keep him out of trouble. You play by his rules, and you play casual. William's stepping out of the car, checking his pockets. A small wad of cash. This bastard's going to account for a big lump of the cash Calum has available to him. Something else for William to worry about. A little passport photo. A printed sheet with the required details. It's all he needs.

Up the steps to the front door. More steps than he realized. Ringing the doorbell. Barry doesn't know to expect him. You don't phone ahead. You go round and ask if he'll help. If he will, he takes the job. If not, you go away and don't come back. If he takes the job, then this and the collection will be the only points of contact. The collection will not happen at the house. The collection is the other thing William has to get right. William's standing two steps down, holding onto the railing. The door's opening. A stout middle-aged woman is looking down at him. She doesn't look impressed with what she's seeing, which seems a bit rich.

'Yes?' she's saying.

'I'm looking for Barry,' William's saying. Remembering Calum's orders. Keep it polite. Tell Barry you want to see him about his hobby. Tell him you have a garage. 'I'm here to see him about his hobby.'

'Hold on there,' she's saying.

She's closed the door in his face, which suggests the politeness is a one-way street. She's obviously waddled off down the corridor to see if Barry wants to meet this new arrival. It's more than a minute and a half later when the door opens again. Same stout little woman.

'What's your name?'

'William,' he's saying.

'Hold on there.' She's closed the door again, and William's still standing on the doorstep. Feels pretty conspicuous to him, but if that's how they want to play it. Another two minutes have gone by. Doesn't feel like this is going well. The door opening. This time a man. Still closer to obesity than is advisable, still short in the arse, but definitely not the woman. Curly, sandy hair and glasses meet the description of Barry Fairly that Calum gave William.

'You are?' the man's saying, looking down through his

glasses. He sounds annoyed. That'll be with the wife he sent to find out who was at the door, and who came back with no useful information.

'William MacLean. I have a garage on the east side. I heard you might be able to help me,' he's saying quietly. 'With your hobby.'

The man's nodding. Calum had told him to mention the garage. That'll get him in the front door, at least. If you stand on the steps saying you want a passport for someone else you could spook him. Certainly make him wary. He hears 'garage' and he thinks it's car stuff. That'll get William inside. Good money supplying garages. The man's giving a single nod for William to follow him.

Front door shut behind them. These are big houses, but old. Narrow corridors, lots of small rooms, gloomy. They're along a corridor, through a kitchen, into a utility room and out into the back garden. William's getting a little concerned, but now he's seeing the large shed at the bottom of the garden. Door open.

Into the shed. There's a heater opposite the door. A radio on a shelf. A power supply coming from the house. There's a comfy chair, and a desk against the single window. On the desk is a single sheet of paper, with a closed folder beside it. Work, obviously. William can catch a glimpse of a couple of things pushed out of view under the desk. One will be a laminator. He can smell that it's been used in the last few minutes. Under the folders he can see what looks like a laptop. Barry hiding a sophisticated operation behind the shoddy appearance of a garden shed.

'So you have a garage, huh?' Barry's asking him.

'I do.'

'So what are you looking for, book or licence?'

William's a little taken aback. Didn't even ask for the name of the garage. Didn't ask for any proof of ID. Doesn't seem to be very cautious. Maybe he already knows who William is from the name. Calum says he's the best for passports.

'Licence,' William's saying casually. 'While we're at it, I thought you could do me a passport as well. I heard you were good at them.'

That's got a look from Barry. He doesn't seem to like the combination of driving licence and passport.

'Did you now? And why does a guy with a garage need a passport along with a driving licence?'

William's shrugging. 'He doesn't. But he thought he might as well kill two birds with one stone, you know. Reduces the risk, I figured.'

Barry's nodding a little, looking up at William. William has what people like to call an open face. He looks friendly, the sort of guy you can trust. 'Thing is,' Barry's saying, 'it's not like I know you. Not like I know I can trust you.'

'I don't know you, either,' William's saying, 'but I'm willing to risk it. I know you have a good reputation. You'll find mine is solid. Besides, this goes well, I might need more licences and log books.'

Greed. That's what it's all about. You don't find out that you're good at counterfeiting by accident. You find out you're good because you give it a shot. And you give it a shot because you want easy money. The prospect of another garage coming to him is more temptation than a simple man can resist.

'Well, things are changing in the car business in this city,' Barry's saying with a knowing nod. He heard about Shug. Heard about him trying his hand at harder work. If it succeeds, he'll leave his humble car business behind. If it fails, he's out of the business anyway. It's a golden opportunity for anyone who isn't already his counterfeiter. 'I've got a bit of a backlog,' Barry's saying. He's not a good liar, but you have to try, don't you?

'I don't want this taking long,' William's saying. 'An opportunity kind of fell into my lap here. I've been thinking about switching. Things going on, you know how it is. Changes. Anyway, I need it quick as you can do it.'

Barry's made a series of noises that are supposed to make it sound like he's thinking. Make it sound as though he's contemplating some great sacrifice. William doesn't think someone would literally huff and puff at such a prospect, but he's not here to argue.

'I could have it by the start of next week, but it'll cost you,' Barry's saying. 'There's a lot that I would have to put aside to help you out here.'

William does have some previous experience of counterfeiting. No emergencies, to be sure. No rush jobs. Calum seemed to have an idea of what would happen. Said that Barry would try to screw him out of all sorts of money. Try to delay it as much as possible. That way he can charge for taking all that time, but instead work on other things.

William's shaking his head. Firmly, but with that open and fair expression he does so well. 'No can do. Need it sooner than that, or I lose a job. Pointless if you take that long. I need it in twenty-four hours.'

Barry's not going to let this one get away. He's guessing that MacLean is testing him here. He's good at what he does, but one day is asking a bit much.

'The licence I can have by tomorrow,' he's nodding. 'Passport, maybe on Friday. I'll need the right info from you today. I'll need to get some info from my people at the passport office as well,' he's saying, trying to make himself sound terribly important. Like he has people. 'You got a picture, preferred details?'

'Got a picture,' William's saying, taking the photo and sheet of paper from his pocket. 'Some details, but I want you to come up with a safe ID.' The address is William's own, for now. Calum will change that as soon as he finds somewhere to live. Barry's looking at the sheet, nodding at the details. Saying nothing about the false ID. Easy for him, he has plenty in reserve. Suspicious, but he didn't get where he is by asking questions. No good counterfeiter asks too many questions.

'Going for a passport and licence for the same guy?' Barry's asking. 'What about a National Insurance card?' Looking to create a little extra work.

'Nah,' William's saying dismissively. 'Not needed.' Calum might get a fake card at some point, but not yet. Only thing he's likely to need that for is legit work, and he's nowhere near that stage yet.

Now William's passing across the passport photo. This is the moment. The picture of Calum is a couple of years old, but still recognizably him. It could pass for William, if your eyesight wasn't up to much. If Barry knows what Calum looks like, then he'll recognize him. Bound to. Recognize that this is more of a risk than he wants to be involved in. Calum's convinced that Barry's never seen him. Might have heard of him, but probably not. Barry's looking at the photo. Pausing. Glancing up at William. He's seen a similarity, but he knows better than to comment on it. You don't chase business away. It usually runs of its own accord.

'Right. Two days it'll take me. Leave a number with me and I'll call you when it's ready. Tell you where to pick it up. Okay? Let's call it four hundred up front, four hundred on delivery.'

William's pausing, then scoffing. Don't let him know you're desperate. He'll know if you let him overcharge you. 'Let's call it two up front, two on delivery. We can talk about a set price for the future if this goes well.'

He seems like a nice guy, does Barry Fairly. William knows better than to trust him. He's back in his car, two hundred pounds down and the agreement in place. This is when it starts to get nervy. They're relying on someone else, and William doesn't like that. If it was just himself and Calum, everything would be fine. Trusting other people – that's the thing. Two days of waiting. Hoping you can trust this guy. If they can't, Calum could be finished. William's getting angry as he's driving home. Angry at Barry for a crime not yet committed. If that Barry stabs them in the back, by God, William will return. Back to that shitty little shed to rip it and its inhabitant apart. Okay, that might not be true, but he won't let it go unpunished. For now, it's home again. Back to Calum and the weird atmosphere. It feels like they should be cherishing every moment. Making the most of what could be their last few days together. They can't. Can't go outside. Can't be seen or heard. Not much to talk about that doesn't work its way back to killing people and running away.

# 15

Peter Jamieson doesn't get out much. The consequences of importance. There was a time when it was different. Back when they started, Peter was the one who pounded the streets. He was the one with menace, because he was the one who could hurt you. Young was his sidekick. The smart guy you didn't need to be afraid of. That changed with power. It got to a point where Jamieson couldn't safely do the things he used to. He misses very few of those things, to be fair. Being the tough guy? Huh, leave that to the meatheads. Plenty of those around. And now Young has the menace to scare people anyway. Not because he's got any tougher; he hasn't. It's because people know he has power behind him, and there's nothing quite as intimidating as power. All of that power still belongs to Jamieson. Take him away and Young's back to being the smartarse weakling.

Jamieson's sitting in his office, watching TV. Half-watching, in fact. Paying a little attention to the local news, but contemplating other things. Got a text from Young saying he would be late in. No problem to Jamieson. He's not what you would call a morning person. Work's been heavy lately; he could do with taking a weekend to himself. It'll have to wait. Big plans ahead. Very big. Career-defining. Get this thing with Shug just right and it sets up the next few years. No mention on the news of missing persons, so he's switching the TV off. No mention in the local press, either. Young was confident this wouldn't go big. Hardy had nobody to care if he went missing. Kenny only has his girlfriend, and she's been around long enough to know better. In normal circumstances Jamieson would be reassured. His instincts tell him it'll be fine. But his instincts told him Kenny was a good guy. People keep saying you have good instincts for the business, and eventually you get to believe them. Dangerous thing, believing others.

Young's coming into the office now. Looking a little flustered, a little fed up. That's not like him. Means there's something to discuss. You spend more than two decades working by someone's side and you learn what every expression means. Over time, both of these men have learned how to go expressionless. That's valuable, too. You show no expression to an outsider and they have no way of knowing your mood. Young's sitting down with a thump on the couch, looking across at Jamieson.

'Had a couple of meetings already this morning,' he's saying.

He's trying to look like this is some terrible struggle for him. Jamieson isn't buying it. John Young likes to be busy. Everyone knows it. 'What's the problem?'

Young's puffing out his cheeks. 'Met with George and a couple of contacts. Separately, obviously. Good news is: Shug seems to be going the predictable route. Trying to make quick moves. He's going broad, though. Targeting everyone with a name. I've been thinking. He knows about Calum. Knows that he works for us. He might make Calum a target again.'

Jamieson's scowling, but it isn't a huge surprise. There was always a chance that Shug would target Calum, especially if he knows that Frank MacLeod isn't around any more.

'Okay,' Jamieson's saying. 'Well, we have to decide if we need to contact Calum or not. Give him a warning.'

Young's pausing, thinking about it. 'I don't think so. A day and a half after he takes out two targets? Better for us, and him, if we keep quiet right now. Thing is,' he's saying, and bobbing the foot of his crossed leg up and down while he thinks, 'he's made one move against Calum and failed. Shug hasn't mentioned Calum to anyone, far as I know.' He's shrugging. 'Certainly hasn't gone big on making it public.'

'We can't rely on it staying that way,' Jamieson's saying with a shake of his head. Going with his instincts. 'If this goes our way, then Shug's in all kinds of trouble. He'll sing. Bound to. He's too legit not to. He'll mention Calum.'

'Yeah,' Young's nodding, 'but I might be onto something that could help us with that. I think we can get to Fizzy Waters. If we have him on board, it could make Shug sweet in the long term. Depending on whether we get a chance to play him properly. All depends on timing,' Young's saying, 'but why rush into warnings that spook people.'

Hard to argue with that. Jamieson's never been convinced of Calum's loyalty. But he keeps doing the jobs he's given, and keeps doing them well. Still, they've worked hard to make him feel comfortable with them. Sought to be good employers. He's a young man who likes a lot of space, likes to be left alone. Fine, they've left him alone. Never put him under any unnecessary pressure. But it's those instincts again. Young got this wrong before. Got it wrong with Calum. Had the chance to move him before Shug sent Glen Davidson to kill the boy. Worked out in the end, so Young got off the hook. Calum killed Davidson instead, which was a stroke of luck. But you can't rely on Calum getting himself out of bother again. They need to be alert. Be ready to help Calum. Play this one cautious.

'So that's Shug. What other news did you have?' Jamieson's asking. There's something else. All this Shug talk will have come from Greig, but Young mentioned two contacts. That means he met the young lad he has such high hopes for.

'My other contact had a bit of news. Fisher's taken the bait on Hardy. Looking into his links with Shug, which is a start. If Calum was up to scratch, then we're off to a good start. Thing is, Fisher had a phone call. Came from Deana Burke.'

'Deana Burke?'

'She's Kenny McBride's girlfriend, partner – whatever you want to call it. She knew Kenny was Fisher's contact. Kenny told her he was going on a job. When he didn't come back, she called Fisher. We're going to have to do something about her.'

Jamieson's frowning and tapping the desk with his fore-finger. Kenny, you weak little bastard. Even in death you're a fucking nuisance. What kind of professional tells his girl-friend that he's a police contact? She wasn't even his wife, for Christ's sake. So he tells her he's a grass. Must have given her Fisher's number as well. Bloody hell! Then he makes a point of telling her he's going on a job. Shit, how much detail?

'What did he tell her about the job?'

'Doesn't seem to be any detail there,' Young's telling him with a reassuring tone. 'No mention of what the job was. No mention of who else was on the job. As far as I know, anyway. If she'd said something, then Fisher would be all over it already. He's not; he's still working on Hardy.'

'Doesn't mean she doesn't know. Just means she hasn't said anything yet. I wouldn't put it past Kenny to have blurted out everything.'

'Which is why we have to decide what we're going to do about her,' Young's saying.

Killing her is off the table. Not an option. There's a moral reason – if you want to look hard for it. It's way in the background, but it's there. Jamieson has qualms about killing

105

someone just because they're trying to find out what happened to a loved one. Sure, it's annoying, when she should know better. And yes, if she becomes dangerous, then he'll have no second thoughts about removing her. But, right now, all she's doing is trying to find out what happened to her man. That's gutsy, and rather admirable. Jamieson likes a strong woman. The other reason, the one that dominates, is that it's not professional. Her man goes missing, she complains and then she goes missing too. You don't think that would get the police all excited? Course it would. So you don't go down that road. And they only have one gunman right now, Calum. That's going to change soon, if all goes well, but right now it's Calum, and Calum alone. No way Jamieson's sending him to do another job so soon. So that leaves him looking at other options.

It has to be something that lets her know just how Jamieson feels about this. Something that gets the message across. But nothing that will draw the police to the scene. Nothing that harms her physically. She's been around the business, so that informs the decision. Someone from the outside and you would have to use a lighter touch. Any pressure could send them running to the cops.

'This Burke woman, how tough is she?'

Young's shrugging. 'Hard to say. Been around the block. Been with one or two serious people, so she knows what can happen. Don't know about tough. The one she settled down with was Kenny. He was about as far from tough as you can get and still be in this business.'

'Mm.' Getting thoughtful. Getting pissed off. They shouldn't be in this position. Kenny should have kept his gob shut.

'Right,' Jamieson's saying decisively. 'Call Nate Colgan. Get him in here. I'll send him round. He can have a conversation with her. Nothing physical. Just a chat. If she doesn't get that message, then she's a dumb bitch and deserves whatever happens to her afterwards.' He finishes with a little thump on the table.

'Fair enough,' Young's saying. 'But what if she doesn't get it? Where do we go after this?'

'Wherever we have to,' Jamieson's saying. Colgan will do the job. A smart guy, and as scary as all hell. Nate Colgan scares everyone, including his employers. It's why he never lasts. Which is another good reason to use him. Nobody knows that Colgan has been working almost exclusively for Jamieson these last couple of months. He approached one of Jamieson's men with favourable terms on some gear he'd been stuck with. Been using him since. Colgan's freelance, though; anyone could hire him to intimidate this woman. No reason it should blow back on Jamieson.

As Young's making the call to Colgan, his mind is racing. There's an opportunity here. If DI Fisher and his lot are going to start poking about after Kenny, then there ought to be something for them to find. Something nicely distracting. Something that keeps them running merrily in the direction they're already going. Towards Shug. It's not how he would like to do it, but if you have to come up with policy on the hoof, then you might as well make it comprehensive. This could be useful. He might not be able to invent anything that definitely links Shug to Kenny, but something that raises suspicion is easy. Of course, if Deana Burke gets the message to back off, then this plot is pointless. And the fact is: most people get the message when Nate Colgan delivers.

# 16

It's two hours later, just ticking into the afternoon. Deana's got some shopping, got a coffee. Going to go see her friend Claire in the late afternoon. Claire has a little shop of her own, has given Deana a few hours' work in the past. Going to need a few more now. Kenny didn't have any great savings. Wasn't like he earned that much. Good money for what he did, but not enough for her to live on now. She has his bank card in her pocket. Took two hundred out at the cash machine. Not sure what'll happen to his money, now that he's disappeared. The police might take it. She hears of that happening more and more. If they prove he got it for committing crimes, they might take it all. Better to get some of it out of the account and into her pocket.

She's not dumb, and the guy following her isn't subtle. Doesn't seem like he's trying to be subtle. He went round the block twice while she was standing at the bus stop. Now he's in the traffic not far behind the bus. Slim chance that he's following either of the two elderly women who got on the bus at the same stop as her. Cops don't follow you like that. If they have something to say, they say it. If they follow you, it's because they don't want you to see. This guy wants her to see him. Which makes this a warning. Not hard to guess where that warning is coming from. She keeps looking behind her, and the car keeps following. No point in trying to escape it. No point in trying to be smart about this. Just go home. See what happens.

Getting off the bus. Watching the car go past. A man driving. Looks like he's pushing middle age. Looks big. The car's gone down the road and turned at the corner. Gone out of view. He'll be back, she knows it. He's going round the block again. She's up the street and turning left. A short walk, crossing the road and turning right onto their street. Their street – that's a laugh. The house is in Kenny's name. Nothing to do with her, legally at least. Homeless and with no money. This is going to be fun. She's stopping. Just for a second, now she's moving again. It's there. At the other end of the street, parked near the corner. The car, with the driver still in it. She can make him out. Sitting, watching her. Bold as you like. Expressionless, it looks like. She doesn't recognize the face, not at this distance anyway. She's turning into the front garden. Key in the door. Getting nervous now. Bag of shopping on the step. Door open, picking up the shopping, getting inside.

There are those few minutes of panic, when any nightmare scenario seems possible. Then the calm, and the logic. If he intended to harm her, he would not have gone for visibility. This guy wants her to know he's there. This isn't some kind of attack. This is just a warning. Letting her know they can get to her at any time. That they can follow her around and make things awkward for her. Right, good, so we can forget about dying today. He'll sit out there like an idiot, and tomorrow he'll be gone. A warning doesn't last forever. They'll have other people for him to be all big and scary to. A man like Peter Jamieson isn't going to waste an employee on her for long. It's a warning for her to keep her mouth shut about Kenny. A pause. How much do they know? Is this some sort of general warning? She should know he's dead now, so they're preaching the value of silence. Or do they know she's spoken to the police? If it's the latter . . . Oh, shit! A knock on the front door.

She's considering not answering. Considering it long enough for him to knock a second time. What's the point? A guy like that could get in here without her opening the door for him. She's at the door. Pulling it ajar.

'Yes?'

'Deana Burke?'

'Yes.'

'You and I need to talk.'

He says it in a tone that doesn't allow for disagreement. A tall man, broad. Younger than she thought at first. Might only be her own age, and handsome too. Has the sort of dark and slightly lined look that tells her he'll age well. But that look isn't appealing. Handsome, yes, but cold. He looks like a man who gets angry often and with meaning. Angry at the world, and willing to hurt everything in it.

'You'd better come in,' she's saying. Saying it because she couldn't stop him if she wanted to. And because everyone has a little streak of self-destruction in them, which pulls danger close rather than pushing it away.

He's sitting on the chair in the living room. The one Kenny used to sit on to watch TV. God, he could be lazy sometimes. Deana's sitting on the couch. Her usual place. Might as well be comfortable.

'So, what do you want?' she's asking. This could go any-where. A man like this, as cold as he is. You can't read him. Can't know what's going through his head. This feels like a warning, he wouldn't be so public otherwise, but it could be a brutal warning. There are men in the business who don't know where to draw the line. Deana's glancing at the living-room door. Nope, couldn't make a run for the front door from here and get away.

'I know that your boyfriend went out a couple of nights ago and didn't come back,' the man's saying. Low, flat voice, like he's bored with this already. 'You've probably worked out that he's not coming back. You need to learn to keep that to yourself.'

That's it. A bored man telling her to forget about Kenny. Like this is going to be enough warning.

'You're telling me to just forget about him?' she's asking incredulously.

'Can't be that hard,' he's saying quietly.

Arrogant bastard. 'You think you're so tough and scary, don't you? People like Peter Jamieson think they can just run over the top of people like Kenny. Throw them away, like they're trash. Well, I'll tell you . . .' And she's stopping. Stopping because this guy is smiling at her. The smile of a man who knows something she doesn't. 'Something amusing?' she's asking, just about ready to lose control.

He's shrugging. 'That's your problem. Old-fashioned thinking. You think Peter Jamieson got rid of your man?' Shrugging again. 'Think what you like. If Jamieson's the man you want to hate, then you can rest assured, his punishment is coming. Jamieson has enemies, and they're coming for him.' That irritating knowing smile again.

Now she's stuck. All her rage directed at Peter Jamieson. Then this smug git comes into her house and tells her she's aiming at the wrong target. It's shut her up, which the man seems to appreciate. He's getting up.

'That's supposed to convince me, is it?' Deana's saying. Getting her voice back. Her anger back. 'You say it, so it must be true.'

The man's pausing, looking down at her. Smart eyes. 'You don't know who I am?'

She's shrugging.

'My name's Nate Colgan. I used to do some work for Jamieson. Not any more. I can see the change coming.'

Now she's looking at him. Now she's frightened. Nate Colgan.

'I won't keep you any longer, I'm sure you're busy,' he's saying sarcastically. 'You needn't worry yourself, you're under no threat. You'll soon see this unpleasantness over. We'll overlook you running to the police this time. We can be generous like that. Just make sure there isn't a second time, okay.' He's making for the door, not even glancing back at her.

Deana's listening to the door closing, then a pause, then the front gate banging shut. He's gone. The infamous Nate Colgan. She's heard the stories about him. Everyone in the business has. The man the scary people are scared of. She knows she should be scared of him, too.

But right now it's not fear, it's anger. The more she thinks, the angrier she gets; the more people she's angry with. If Colgan isn't working for Peter Jamieson, then he's working for Shug Francis. Has to be. Kenny told her all about Shug's attempts to muscle in on Jamieson's market. Told her about Jamieson's failure to deal with it. So Shug wants to hit some-one close to Jamieson. Someone Jamieson will notice is gone. So he goes for the easy one first. The driver. That's so cheap. Even Deana knows what the reaction will be. Everyone in the industry will just think Shug's pathetic. Going for a driver?

Fuck's sake, they're ten a penny. Kenny used to say it himself. You have to go after someone that matters if you want people to take you seriously. Maybe Jamieson can be an ally. That would be a relief. Then she would have more friends than she'd realized. More people with the ability to get things done.

Not like that prick Fisher. Another arrogant bastard. Is he any better than the one who just left? Someone else who thinks Kenny was trash. A pause. Remembering the words. 'We'll overlook you running to the police this time.' That's what Colgan said. Just about the last thing he said before he left. As if he was doing her a huge favour. He was, in a way. The moron. Told her that they know she's gone to Fisher. It couldn't be Fisher himself, could it? No, no way. Kenny talked a little about him. Told her the kind of cop he was. Tough, surly, but definitely honest. Everyone said so. Got a hard-on for gangland stuff. Just because people think he's honest, doesn't mean he is. She knows enough of the business to realize that there are many strings wound around places you wouldn't expect. People entangled in dark corners. It's a shock. In minutes, her enemy and her ally have swapped places.

It was never going to take long, and here it is. The shock replaced by more anger. An explosion of it. She's off up the stairs, shoving open the bedroom door. Into the drawer of her bedside cabinet and pulling out the notebook. Flicking through the pages a little too fast, crumpling the corners. Finding the number and looking round for the phone. Where the hell is that phone? She wants to make this call right away. Needs to make it before her anger subsides. Might not be the smartest thing to do, but her anger will turn bitter and linger if she doesn't. She's found the phone. Shit! Pushing the buttons too fast, hit the wrong one. Button with the red phone logo to hang up, and trying again. This time she has it. This time it's ringing. Come on, pick up. Don't dodge this one. You haven't earned the right to escape this wrath.

# 17

Fisher's about to leave the office. Go and kick a few pseudo-cops up the arse. They got the files from Hardy's office late yesterday afternoon. How much more time can they possibly need? He's not looking for every fucking detail. Enough to make an arrest or three would be quite enough. They like to be slow about it. Meticulous, they call it. Getting every detail, so everything stands up nicely in court. Which is fine, don't get Fisher wrong. He wants everything done to the best standard. What he doesn't like is people using that as an excuse to drag their heels. Go and see what they have. He told them to work the Shug file first. That one matters most immediately. The others will be bullshit. Petty stuff for fiddling the taxman. The Shug file is the one that gets people killed.

His phone's ringing. Bloody thing, always ringing when he's about to go. Never rings when he has nothing better to do. Mind you, it isn't often that he has nothing better to do. The telephone brings nothing but bad news. Even from within the station. People come up to the office if it's something positive. He's picking it up. Might as well. Gives the financial unit a few more minutes to have something ready for him.

'Hello.'

'You bastard.'

We'll be honest here and admit that's not the first time Fisher's been greeted with those words. Nor the most aggressive. Not even in the top five. Still, you don't expect it when you put the phone to your ear. It's a female voice, which narrows it down a little. Still could be one of many. Wife, lover or mother of someone he's arrested and put away. They're sometimes a ferocious bunch. More so than their men, actually.

The first thing he's doing is sighing, so this woman understands that her insult is nothing new to him. Let her know that she hasn't shocked him. Now that he's done that, he's moving on to a snide comment. Put her in her place.

'And you are?'

'Hah,' she's laughing, but it's a hard little laugh. 'I bet you don't recognize me. One day after I call you, and you've forgotten me already.'

'Deana Burke,' Fisher's saying. Not with any enthusiasm. She's a pest and she's about to throw a bucket of abuse over him.

'Yeah, Deana Burke. Not the first time since we last spoke that you've used my name either, is it, Detective? You've been gabbing my name around all over the place. To some interesting little friends of yours. I bet your bosses would be interested, anyway.'

'I'm sorry, I haven't a clue what you're talking about,' he's saying. If it sounds genuine, it's because it is. What he wants to say is that she sounds like she's out of her fucking mind, and he has better things to do than listen to her. The policy-makers frown on that sort of response, though.

He's halfway towards hanging up when his brain catches up with his instinct and stops him.

'What do you mean talking to interesting friends? Who do you think I've been talking to?'

'I had a visit from one of your friend's employees. A charmless bastard who came into my house and told me to keep my gob shut.' She's not going to name names. Not when the name is Nate Colgan.

Hard to argue with that, Fisher's thinking. 'Wait, wait. Slow down. Someone broke into your house and told you what?'

'Nobody broke in. He came to the door.'

'And you let him in?'

'Yes, I let him in,' she's saying, her voice starting to rise back towards a shout. 'What was I supposed to do, push him out the fucking gate? The guy was twice my size. A mean-looking bastard. The kind of mean-looking bastard that knocks little women like me around for fun.'

Fisher's letting her breathe. Letting the conversation calm a little before he continues.

'So this guy comes in and tells you what, exactly?'

'Tells me to keep it shut – I just told you,' Deana's saying, exasperated. 'Told me they would forgive me for talking to your lot. That things were happening, and it would soon be over. If I keep away from the police from now on, I'll be left alone. They know I talked to you. You told them, you bastard. You told them. I can't believe it. They know I talked to the police, and you're the only cop I ever talked to in my life. Now they're sending people round to intimidate me. Because of you, Detective, because of you. Kenny's blood's already on your hands. Mine next, is it? Not that you care. You went and told them as soon as I was off the phone to you. You phoned up Shug Francis and told your wee pal that I was a danger. Oh, you are some piece of work.'

She is crying a little bit by the time she reaches the end of the rant. Doesn't matter. Fisher lets her carry on. Do her some good to get it out of her system. Do him some good to listen to her. Shug Francis. Unbelievable! Shug Francis already knows that the police are looking for Kenny, because of Deana's call. Which means someone told him. Someone from within this station. Easy to find out that the police are looking for Kenny. Hard to find out that it was Deana who reported it. Impossible, unless it came from the station.

'He said he worked for Shug Francis?' he's asking, after a few seconds.

'He didn't say it,' she's saying. Quiet now. Anger all used up. 'He said he worked for someone that was about to destroy

Peter Jamieson. Which means Shug Francis, in case you lot haven't been paying attention.'

'Uh-huh,' Fisher's saying. He has been paying attention. Better than Deana, it would seem. Shug isn't going to destroy Jamieson, doesn't have the ability. Not soon. Not ever. Has the ability to kill his driver, though. Cheap move like that might be right up his street.

'Right, listen to me, Deana, this is important,' he's saying. He doesn't mean to sound superior this time, but it's hard not to. She's emotional, annoying and badly informed. 'We need to talk face-to-face. I need to know who this person was, and I need to know every detail of what he said. I did not tell Shug Francis, or anyone else, about this. Frankly, I'm offended that you think otherwise. But we'll gloss over that for now. Right now we need to make sure you're safe and that we can find out what exactly has happened to Kenny.'

Another harsh laugh from the other end of the phone. 'You think I'm going to come and meet you? You think I could ever trust you after this? You must be off your head. No way. Never. If you're such an honest and decent guy, then you have to prove it first. You find out what happened to Kenny. You can go and do whatever you do, but don't expect any-thing from me. From now on I'll do what's best for me and Kenny.'

She's hung up. No point phoning back, she won't answer. That last sentence. Saying she would do what was best for her and Kenny. Jesus, that sounded almost like a threat, the way she said it. Fisher's shaking his head as he puts the phone down. One of those bitches who think they can take on the world. Go stick her nose into this mess and get herself hurt. His concern for her lasts all of two seconds. His thoughts have raced somewhere else. Somewhere darker. Someone in this station leaked that Deana Burke reported Kenny missing. Could have been an accident. A stupid fuck-up. But he doesn't believe that. Brain-dead and detestable as some plods round here are, they all know better than to name a witness. Nope, this was deliberate. Instinct runs to Paul Greig, pointing at him enthusiastically. Brain is pulling it back again. Talk to Higgins first. Fisher gave him the order and left it with him. Hear what he has to say. Then blame Greig.

Takes half an hour to get Higgins. He's out on the street somewhere. Fisher doesn't know what he's up to, but he's on his way back to the station now. Should be here, helping Fisher. He's not getting the officers he wants for this investigation. The DCI reckons the number-crunchers can handle most of the work; all Fisher gets to handle are the arrests. The Hardy disappearance isn't getting enough support, either. Not enough proof that it has anything to do with organized crime. Going to need more. Kenny McBride: that could be the link that pulls everything together. Would give Fisher the size of investigation that he needs. Two linked disappearances. Linked by the suspect. Linked by Shug.

Here comes Higgins. Walking into the office in his uniform and across to Fisher's desk. A nod to DC Davies. Higgins has more confidence around the detectives than he used to. That's a good thing. He's a talent, and he'll end up with a desk of his own in here one day.

'Kenny McBride,' Fisher's saying.

'Nobody's seen him,' Higgins is answering. 'I put the word out but . . . nothing.'

'When you put the word out, what detail did you give?'

'What do you mean?'

'Did you tell anyone who reported him missing?'

'No, course not. I didn't even say he'd been reported,' Higgins is saying, a little defensively. 'I said if anyone spotted him to report it back to the station. No arrest, just report. I hardly gave any detail at all.'

Fisher's nodding. Shug gets rid of Kenny. Someone tells him the police are looking for him. Maybe he puts two and two together. Fisher told only Higgins about Deana. Higgins told the station to keep their eyes open. Someone told Shug the police were looking. Someone is guilty of a leak.

'Okay,' Fisher's saying, putting an end to it.

'Something the matter?' Higgins is asking uncertainly. 'Did I do something wrong?'

'No, no,' Fisher's saying. He hates cops who are always looking for reassurance. The hand-holders. Higgins isn't one of them. Not yet anyway. 'Nothing wrong. Word got out that we're looking for Kenny. Shug Francis sent a man round to Deana Burke's house to tell her to keep her mouth shut. Threatening visit.'

'Shug Francis?' Higgins is putting a hand up towards his mouth. Rubbing his chin and thinking. 'Shug Francis?'

'Yeah, so?'

'So I heard something about Shug Francis. I mean, I don't know. It might be nothing. A rumour. Came from a legit source, close to but on the outside of the industry. Doesn't tell me much, but it's usually reliable when he does. I heard that Shug was getting close to Alex MacArthur. Trying to get help before he goes after Peter Jamieson. I only got that this morning, so I don't know how recent it is, but I trust the source.'

Now it's starting to add up. Shug goes running to MacArthur. That sly old bastard. You had to wonder how long it would take before he tried to cash in on all this. Has there been any trouble in the city in the last thirty years that MacArthur hasn't tried to make money from? So Shug goes running for cover. Must have offered MacArthur a big cut of his business to make it happen. First thing MacArthur is going to say is that they need to consolidate. Time to bring your books over to our accountants. Can't have that old fart running around with all your old secrets now, can we? A very predictable conversation. And, of course, Shug agrees, because he can't afford not to. So Hardy's a target with no defence. But Shug wants something in return. He gets rid of his own moneyman, but he can't leave it at that. A clean-up job makes him look like he's bending over for MacArthur. So a hit against Jamieson. Pick an easy target, because you don't know how to get rid of the tough ones. The driver. And now we have Kenny and Hardy, together in one investigation. One big investigation.

'I'll let you know when there's more,' Fisher's saying. 'I think this investigation is about to grow. Keep an eye out for Kenny, though,' he's saying as an afterthought. You keep looking, even if you don't expect to find. It's just polite.

Higgins has gone, off to do his pounding-the-beat thing. Shug Francis. Not the biggest target in the city, not by a long way. Still important. Getting more important by the day, it would seem. Getting either bold or desperate. Both are dangerous. Two possible murders to tie him up with. A link to MacArthur could be all kinds of useful, if confirmed. It won't be confirmed, obviously. Fisher knows that already. A man like MacArthur doesn't survive this long without being careful. But Shug? He's not careful. He wouldn't be throwing himself at Alex MacArthur otherwise.

And Greig. Still Greig. Who else? Someone took this to Shug. Someone told him there was a search out for Kenny. He got a little antsy and sent his man round to put the pressure on the woman. The sort of rookie mistake he would make. And it came from Greig, the leak. Had to. The man standing beside the criminals, facing away from his own colleagues. There are some in the station who think it's fine. Not a problem. You need people who are close to the criminals. How else do you learn? But this is different. So close he's putting people's lives at risk? Come on, even in this station nobody could justify that. It's poison like Greig that destroys a police force. There is no greater threat than the threat from within the force.

# 18

William doesn't need to knock, he has a key. So does Calum. So does the next-door neighbour. At one point they had to tell their mother to stop handing out keys to all and sundry. She's a very trusting woman. Right now, that's a good thing and a bad thing. Good that she might just believe the cock-and-bull story William's about to throw at her. Bad that she might just spread the word around. Calum's convinced this is a bad idea. Told William so. Told him in no uncertain terms. Put on that cold and angry face he does. It obviously intimidates other people, but it doesn't work with William. When you've seen someone running around the house with no clothes on as a child, the intimidation factor dims.

'She'll tell her friends,' Calum was saying before William left the flat. 'She'll tell them, and they'll tell their families, and word will eventually get back to Jamieson. I'm telling you, it will.'

He has a point. This city is a village, when it comes to gossip. Three degrees of separation, at the most. Their mother gossips to a friend, who gossips to a friend, who gossips to someone working for Jamieson. Inevitable that it gets back to him.

'Would be better if you just didn't tell her anything,' Calum said.

'Better for you, not better for her,' William answered. Putting his foot down on this one. Playing the role of big brother. It's okay for Calum, he'll be long gone. Doesn't seem to have occurred to him that William will be the last person left to look after their mother. Their father dead; Calum running. All the responsibility falling to William. He'll accept that. Do his duty as a son. But he's not going to make this any harder for their mother than he has to. Thank goodness she's trusting. More willing to believe a positive lie than face the negative truth.

'Hey, Ma. It's William,' he's shouting. She's a woman of routine. He knows she'll be at home. Wednesday morning she does some old ladies' dance class. Friday morning she does her weekly shop. Thursday morning, she's at home. She tells Calum and William all about her life when they go round to visit. They nod along in all the right places, and forget what they heard the minute they leave the house.

'William,' she's saying with a wary smile. 'What brings you here?' She's alert to a problem. Not expecting her eldest at half past ten on a midweek morning. Not expecting an unannounced visit. William's always been the one she suspected of being up to no good. She loves him. He's a charmer. But he was in trouble at school, and his mouth has always been too big. She worries that he hangs around with the wrong people.

Calum, on the other hand, was the quiet one. Never any bother.

'That's a charming greeting, that is,' William's grinning. 'A guy can't even come round and visit his decrepit old Ma any more.'

'Less of that,' she's saying. Her guard down a little now. William seems to be in a good mood, but that's never been a great indicator of anything with him. She still wants to know what he's doing at the house at this hour of the morning.

'Och, Ma, you're so suspicious. I was picking up a car, coming past this way on my way back to the garage. I thought I'd come round and see you. See how you're getting along. Am I invited round for lunch this Sunday?'

She's smiling. He has such a charming way of scrounging. Got that from his father, God rest him. 'You're invited, if you want to come. You're always welcome, my boy. Invite your little brother round as well. It'll be nice to have us all together.'

That's what he expected to hear from her. She always wants them all together. He wanted her to introduce Calum into the conversation. It'll seem like less of a big deal that way.

'Ah, well, Calum won't be here this Sunday,' he's saying, forcing his cheekiest smile. 'But I can't tell you why.'

'You can't tell me why? There isn't anything wrong, is there?' A mother's reaction.

William's laughing. 'No, Ma, there's nothing wrong. Listen, if I tell you, you have to promise not to let on to Calum when you see him next. Okay? Keep this between you and me.'

'Okay.'

'Calum's down in London just now. Going to be down there for a few more days, at least. Thing is, he's got himself a wee girlfriend. She's from here, but she got a job down there. And, like a lovesick puppy, my wee brother went running off after her.'

Oh, she likes that. William knew she would. It's been a big concern for her that neither of her boys is married. She thought William would get married to that nice Morven and give her grandchildren, but it all fell apart. She still doesn't know why. How can you spend six years with a woman and not marry her? And there's been no sign at all of Calum settling down with a nice girl. She's clapped her hands together and she's grinning.

'He's away off after her? So it must be serious then? Who is she? What job does she have down there?'

'Whoa, slow down. I've only met the woman a couple of times. Not for long, either time,' he's saying with a smile. 'Seems pretty enough. I don't know. More his type than mine.'

'I don't mean what does she look like. You're such a man. I mean what sort of girl is she? Is she respectable?'

Questions about the girl means she accepts that the girl exists. She won't dig too deep. Not as long as she's hearing what she wants to hear. Which means William has to come up with some convincing detail.

'Her name's Emma,' he's saying, conjuring up an image from the recent past. That little brunette who came to the garage to call him a liar. Correctly, but still . . . 'She has a degree,' he's saying, knowing that that will impress their mother. 'She got a job with a research company down in London. Not like scientific research – you know, the good kind. Nah, it's political research, whatever that is. Probably those people that phone up and want to ask you how you voted. Bloody annoying. She's been down in London for a few weeks. Calum's been itching to get down there and see her. I don't know, seems like he's taking it seriously. I haven't seen him this serious before anyway.'

'Now that is fantastic,' she's saying. She likes the idea of a respectable daughter-in-law. 'Is she from a good family?' She can be strangely snobbish when she wants to be, their mother. Not sure why.

'I don't know her family at all,' he's saying with a smile and a shrug. William never thought his family had much to be snobbish about.

He's been here half an hour now. Long enough. Made casual chit-chat, the conversation constantly coming back to Calum.

'I don't suppose you'll be hearing from him for a while anyway,' William's saying. 'Not just because of the girl, either, although she's got most of his attention. Us plebs are off the radar. I had to bloody chase him up just to say hello. But he won't be calling. Lost his phone – idiot!'

'Now, don't call him that. He's no idiot. Is it one of the little mobile phones he lost?'

'Yep. It got real mobile on him. He'll have to get another one. Put all the new numbers on it. He was complaining about it. Anyway, I'd best be off to the garage. I'll be round about midday on Sunday.'

'Well, I'm pleased about Calum. Although if she's going to be staying down there, I suppose there's a chance that he might stay there with her. I wouldn't want to see him leave the city, but I want him to be happy. You know, William, it's a sign. If your little brother has a girlfriend, then don't you think it's about time you do too?'

He's made a rod for his own back with this lie. She's been on at him about getting a girlfriend for a while. Keeps reminding him that he's not as young as he used to be. Like he's ancient at thirty-two. He's back at the flat now. Calum's sitting where William left him. Still looking lost in thought.

'She bought it. When you get in touch with her, tell her your girlfriend's name is Emma. Tell her she has a degree and that she works for a political research company. Other than that, you can say whatever the hell you want.'

'Very original,' Calum's smiling wryly. 'However did you think of that?'

'Aye well, you'll have to call her eventually. Give it a few weeks. Then let her know you're okay and not coming back.'

Calum's nodding. That's not the problem. Once he's settled somewhere, he can call. Might have another new identity by then. He can get a cheap pay-as-you-go phone just to use for calls to his mother.

The problem is Jamieson and Young. He's worried about how far they'll go. They will want to find out what happened to him. Nobody likes a mystery. Not in this industry. They will go to great lengths to find out what they want to know. If they find out that Calum's mother is talking about her son as though he's alive and well and living in London, then they will send someone round to talk to her. They'll try to be subtle at first, but only at first. When the time comes for them to demand information, they will demand it from anyone. An old widow included. They're not above knocking her around.

'I still think it would be better if she thought I was dead. Or just didn't know what happened to me.'

William's shaking his head. 'They're not going to do anything to her,' he's saying quietly. Sitting opposite his brother and looking him in the eye. 'Let's say they do go round and talk to her. They'll sweet-talk her. Find out that I know more than she does. Then they'll come to me. I'm the one taking the risk here, not her.'

And Calum's nodding, because he knows that as well. William is taking the risk, and it's a dangerous one. They'll turn nasty a lot quicker with William than they will with their mother.

# 19

Everything's gone smoothly so far. It should be a nice feeling, shouldn't it? Young isn't so sure. Sitting in the club, flicking through newspapers. Seeing nothing relevant. A manoeuvre this complicated should come with more bumps in the road. There should be little difficulties to overcome. Things he didn't expect or plan for. So far, only this Fizzy thing. That's not a difficulty. That's an opportunity. Deana Burke – but that's sorted. Jamieson isn't here with him. He's at a meeting. A lunch meeting, which he found terribly amusing. Like the guy he's meeting is so busy he has to eat and talk at the same time. He and their current major importer, Angus Lafferty, going to meet with a smaller importer to see if they can strike a deal. Exclusivity. The market's getting tougher, so you want as many importers tied to you as possible. Frankly, Young's just delighted that they've reached a point where they can focus on growth again. Doesn't matter if they don't do a deal over lunch, a meeting is a step forward.

They allowed themselves to become far too distracted by Shug, but that's about to end. And they were distracted by Frank, but that was unavoidable. Their top gunman. A friend to Peter. And as soon as they had to retire him, he went to the police. They had to remove him. There was no alternative, but it was hard on Peter. Now it feels like they're putting all that behind them. Getting back onto the schedule Young had plotted out for them months ago. And it's all going so well. The accountant and Kenny gone. The Shug set-up going perfectly. The police walking blindly into an investigation that's going to lead them wherever Jamieson and Young choose to send them. That's what makes it all a little uncomfortable. Something this big shouldn't be this easy. Yes, it's well planned and carefully executed by good professionals, but that's not usually enough. The only time things go this well is when someone else is setting you up for a massive fall.

A knock at the door. Young shouting for the person to enter. The barman. It used to be Kenny who came and told them there was a visitor, but now it's the miserable guy behind the bar. Jamieson still hasn't hired another driver. Still not sure that he will.

'There's a woman here to see you,' the barman's saying. Just his head sticking in the door. 'Says her name's Deana Burke, says you know who she is.'

And here it is. The bump in the road he's been waiting for. There's a mix of feelings. Annoyance, for one. Silly bitch should know better than to turn up at the club looking for answers. She'll have had her encounter with Nate Colgan. Be interesting to see what she took away from it. That's another feeling right there: interest. Keen to see if he can use her as part of the set-up. To see how best he can overcome the challenge she'll present. And there's relief. He's been waiting for something to go wrong. If this is the worst of it, well, he'll take that.

'Show her in,' he's saying to the barman. Going to need to learn that fellow's name if he's going to make a habit of sticking his head round the door.

In she comes. A good-looking woman, which takes Young slightly by surprise. He's seen her before, but it was a while ago and he didn't really notice her then. She was some bird on the arm of a driver. How is that worth his attention? Deana's dressed for the role of the widow now, but still making sure eyes turn her way. The grieving widow who knows she'll have to get back on the horse sooner rather than later, or learn to face poverty. Black skirt, black top, both a little tighter than you might expect from someone wanting to play shy. Hair tied back to show her pretty face. She's alone, which is good. She has a bag big enough to conceal something dangerous in, which isn't so good.

'Deana,' he's saying, and standing up. 'John Young. You're Kenny's partner, aren't you? Nothing wrong, I hope.'

She's looking at him. A hard look. 'Perhaps you can tell me,' she's saying. 'I came here to ask you if you know where Kenny is. I haven't seen him in three days.'

There's a tone of challenge in the voice, but it's slight. She's trying to play this clever. She doesn't trust these people much, not yet. She wants to see what the reaction is before she goes into any detail. If he manages to convince her that he's as pissed off as she is, then he can have all the detail he wants. She can't trust Fisher to get to the bottom of this. His station seems to be riddled with corruption, whether he's behind it or not. Besides, he's restricted by the law. Peter Jamieson and John Young are not. If someone's hit one of their men, they will have to do something about it. She likes that thought.

'If I know where Kenny is?' Young's saying with polite puzzlement. 'I don't. We haven't seen Kenny for a few days either, but I know he was given time off, so, you know, we weren't expecting him. When did you last see him?'

'He went to do a job for you on Monday night, right? I saw him before he went. Not since. Nobody's seen him since.'

Now it's all about the careful judgement of people. Judge Kenny and judge Deana. Judge their relationship to work out how much she knows. How much would he have told her? He was weak. Scared too, that's why he went to the police. People don't go for any other reason. It's not a moral choice. Their bottle crashes and they look for safety. Deana, on the other hand, has the guts to turn up here. She's gone to the police, she's been confronted by Nate, and yet here she is. So she has far more balls than Kenny ever did. A weak man in a relationship with a strong woman is going to spill his guts. You have to assume that he told her everything. So she knows as much about that job as Kenny did before he went. Not that much, to be honest, but enough. They kept a lot from him, but the little Kenny knew was still dangerous. She also knows that Kenny was talking to Fisher. She suspects that Jamieson was behind the killing. Or she did.

Young's sitting down. Making a show of his thoughtfulness. 'Erm,' he's saying, as though suddenly aware of her, 'please, take a seat.' There's a chair in front of the desk and another against the wall opposite. She's taking the one from in front of the desk and placing it opposite Young. She's sitting and looking at him, waiting for him to make the next move. Putting him under a little pressure, but not too much. If this was Shug's doing, then she can't afford to alienate this guy as well.

'You haven't seen him since the night of the job,' he's saying quietly. Not a question, a statement. 'Well, the job was done. That's the thing. The job was done, and the person who was working it with him is fine. I'll have to check to be certain, but I think he said that when Kenny dropped him off, Kenny was on his way home. We'd told him to take a few days off, so . . .' he trails off. 'I don't know what to say.' Knitting his brow, a slightly angry look. Frustrated that he doesn't know what's going on.

He seems genuine. He seems annoyed, and that's good. Time to make him more annoyed, and make him more determined to find out what happened.

'I had a visitor yesterday. I don't know who he was. Came to my house. Told me not to make any noise about Kenny going missing. My impression was that he was working for Shug Francis. He seemed to suggest that Kenny was just the first. That Shug is going to take out Jamieson.' Still not mentioning Colgan by name. Why invite that trouble?

Young's head picked up sharply at the mention of Shug. Now he's glaring at her. Considering what she said, it looks like. Now he's looking down at the floor and shaking his head. 'Shug's already tried to hit one of our people before,' he's saying quietly, making it sound like an admission he doesn't want to make. 'Someone . . . not senior.' A polite way of saying someone as irrelevant as Kenny. 'It didn't go at all well for Shug's man. We figured he'd backed off. We knew he'd make a move against me and Peter. Desperation. He's close to the brink, he knows it. We thought everyone else was out of the firing line.'

She's waiting for something more. He's told her what he thought was going to happen, and that's no practical use to her. She needs him to tell her what he's going to do next.

'I think you'll be safe,' he's saying to her. 'If they went for Kenny, then it was to get at us. You have no part to play in that.' It feels like he's telling her what he thinks she wants to hear. That's what it's supposed to feel like. Now the hook. 'You can rest assured, Deana, we'll provide you with any protection you feel you need. And we will not let this go un-punished. We will strike back.'

This is what she came here to hear. Young knows it. He played his part, now he's delivering the words that will keep her happy.

'If you say I won't be a target, then I don't need protection,' she's saying. 'But I want to know that you will find out what happened. I want you to keep me informed about what you're doing. You owe Kenny that much.'

Thank the good Lord for Jamieson's lunch meeting. The first importer they've ever met who thought these things were fashionable and appropriate. If not for him, Jamieson would have been here to hear that last comment. He would almost certainly not have reacted the way Young's reacting right now. Nodding stiffly. 'You're right,' he's saying. It sounds to him like he managed to get the words out without seeming bitter. The idea that they owe that traitorous bastard any-thing is an insult. But he's playing a part. Playing it well. So he keeps playing. 'We're already doing things to put a stop to Shug Francis – that goes without saying. We will get him. And we will make sure he knows that some of it's for Kenny.'

She's nodding. 'When will I hear from you?'

'Well,' he's saying, puffing out his cheeks. 'I'll have to speak to Peter. We have Kenny's number, so if we can reach you there, we'll be in touch.'

Buying a little time. He wants to use Deana Burke as profitably as possible. That'll take some thought. Some discussion. He's showing her to the door.

'Hard to believe,' he's saying. 'Poor Kenny. We'll try and find out, you know, where it happened. Where he is now. If you want to know, we'll tell you. If not, well, that's up to you.'

'I'd like to know,' she's saying. 'And I want to be kept informed. That's not an idle request, Mr Young. If I'm not kept involved, I will be back.'

'Of course,' Young's nodding. 'Your loss is much greater than ours, I understand that. I'll make sure you're very much a part of this.'

She's gone, thank God. Time to sit and think. Nate Colgan played his part well. No surprise there. She's convinced it's Shug. If she speaks to Fisher again, it'll be with the right message. Oh, this could work out very nicely. The little challenges you don't expect. How you handle them is everything.

# 20

Been drinking for a while now. It's given him clarity. Shug isn't much of a drinker, it tends not to help, but this is different. Today it's settled him. He's been thinking about Fizzy and nothing else. Fizzy has become a danger. He doesn't want to be a part of this. He made that clear. So he's a dead-weight. If he's not willing to be a part of this, then he's just a guy who knows too much. A guy who isn't contributing. You can't have people who don't contribute. You sure as hell can't have them at senior level. He could offer Fizzy a pay-off, but that would look weak. Fizzy would probably turn it down. Even with a pay-off, he'd be on the outside. It doesn't remove the danger, just pushes it further away. That's not enough. Fizzy should be a friend. But he doesn't seem to want that any more. Well, if he doesn't want to be a friend, he becomes an enemy. Fizzy has no one but himself to blame for that.

Shug's finishing off the last of the half-bottle and slumping back in the couch. Plotting the next move.

The easy thing to do would be to call up Don Park. He would organize everything, make it all work. But it would look weak. Would look like Shug can't handle this himself. It's an internal matter. Would be different if he was making a move against someone from another organization. But he's not. He's moving against one of his own. He ought to be able to handle that by himself. Ought to be able to clean up his own shit. He would consider MacArthur weak if he couldn't handle his own people. So Shug will do it himself. Damned right he will. Feeling pretty good about it, actually. This is a chance to make a clean break with the past. Get rid of one of the small-time thinkers who held him back for so long. Most of all, it's the chance to show Alex MacArthur that he can handle this sort of thing himself. Organize it. Get it done quickly. Then be nonchalant about it. Let MacArthur think that it's no big deal to him. That'll make a good impression.

Picking up the phone. Calling Shaun Hutton, his gunman. See, that's something else that'll impress MacArthur – the fact that he has a quality gunman of his own. Everyone wants one of them. So he's carefully calling Hutton. Hutton answering, saying hello.

'Shaun, it's Shug, come round to the house, right away.' Picked his words carefully, his tone even more so. Doesn't realize how slow he was talking. Doesn't realize that he's obviously the wrong side of a bottle. Now he's slumping back and thinking about the job. Shouldn't be hard to hit Fizzy. Get him at his house. It'll need a burial. Yeah, make him disappear. No need to use it to send a message. Should be easy. Work out nice and neat. As long as Hutton does a proper job, then this is a fast way to make a good impression.

But now he's thinking about Fizzy. All the things they did together. The friendship they had. Known Fizzy longer than he's known his own wife. Been through everything with him. Truth is, Fizzy knows more about Shug than Elaine does. Fizzy's been there through the worst of times. Helped Shug so much. Did so much tough work that nobody else in their right mind would have done. It was often Fizzy who did the riskiest stuff, when you think about it. Fizzy who went and had meetings with garage owners down south. Persuaded them to do deals with the car-ring. That took a lot of guts. Took a lot of loyalty. It was Fizzy taking the biggest risk, Shug getting the biggest reward. Man, there were some good times there too. Some real fun, messing around with the cars. It was a good little group they had, in the old days. That group's dissolving anyway. It's mostly just been Shug and Fizzy in the last few months. Now it's just Shug. The natural evolution of the business.

The doorbell ringing. Someone coming along the corridor. The big frame of Shaun Hutton coming through the door. Big lad, tall and broad. Too big to be a gunman, Shug's thinking. A gunman's supposed to be silent and blend into the background. Never mind.

'Come in, sit down. I have a job for you. I need to get it done right away.'

Hutton's sitting on the desk chair opposite the couch. Nodding to Shug. 'Who's the job?'

'Fizzy.' Said with more force than he intended. Trying to make it sound like he's being decisive and that the personal relationship doesn't matter to him. 'I want Fizzy gone. He's on the outside now, and he's dangerous. Might make moves against us. It needs doing. Get it done quick. Make it a clean job. Get rid of the body. Might make people think that he's run off or something. I don't want there to be any trace. People don't need to know that it was me who did it. Or, anyway, the people that matter will know. Nobody else.'

Hutton's nodding quietly. Saying nothing. Shug's drunk, obviously. Rambling, telling him things that don't need to be said. A hit against Fizzy would be very easy. It's a bad sign, though. It's not a break with the pathetic past, from where Hutton's sitting. It's a clear sign that Shug isn't capable of taking his own people with him when his organization grows. Think about it: Fizzy isn't the only person from the past who knows incriminating things about Shug. Anyone who ever worked for his car-ring does. Is he going to go round killing them all? Hutton won't say any of that, though. Not his place. Not his plan.

'Okay. I know where he lives. I'll make sure it's clean.'

'Should be easy at his house,' Shug's going on. 'His girlfriend won't be there. Her father's dying of cancer in Dundee, so she's up there staying with her sister. That's a bonus, eh?'

'Aye,' Hutton's nodding, and getting to his feet. 'That'll make things easier.'

Hutton's out of the house and into his car. Contemplating what he just heard. Shug's weak. Throwing his weight around to try and look strong. Always means you're weak. Easy to see which way the wind is blowing. As if Hutton didn't already know. He's been planning this for a while. He and John Young, planning it together. Now has to be the time. If not now, then when? He's well away from Shug's house before he pulls over and gets his mobile out. Dialling the number Young gave him, waiting for an answer. Young's a smart operator. Kept giving Hutton little jobs over the years to keep him sweet. Never hired him full-time, but bought a little loyalty.

'Hello.'

'Hi, George, it's Shaun Hutton. We need to meet. Urgent.'

No pause at all. 'Same flat as before. I'll be there in fifteen minutes.' Hanging up. No need for long conversations. They're the sort that get you into trouble.

Hutton would be happier if he was meeting Young personally, but that's out. Too much risk at a time like this. Got to keep as much separation as possible. So Hutton's going to meet one of Young's people. Fellow called George Daly. Smart little cookie, by all accounts. They met before, a few weeks ago. George is essentially Hutton's handler. Seems weird to Hutton, but that's how Young wants to play it. Makes sense really, if you think about it. If Young and Hutton get spotted together then everyone knows Hutton's stabbing

Shug in the back. Hutton and George are seen together and it could mean anything. Could be that George is feeding info to Hutton, rather than the other way round. Lets you keep control of the situation. Hutton's at the flat, sure that he hasn't been followed. Grotty little place. Grotty little area. Hutton assumes this is what all the flats they use as meeting places look like. He hasn't seen the better ones. Won't, either, until he crosses over to work for them full-time.

George is five minutes later than expected. Apologies for the delay. They're sitting in the kitchen because there's less damp there than in the living room. Less being relative. You can still smell it. See the black patches on the top of the walls and in the corners.

'Shug called me to his house,' Hutton's saying, 'about an hour ago. Little over that. Told me that he wants me to do a job on Fizzy Waters.'

'His right-hand man?'

'Yeah.'

'Why?'

'Says Fizzy's on the outside. Must want to move on, leave him behind. Except that he doesn't want to leave him behind. Wants to get rid of him altogether. Wants it done quick, too. I don't know. Seems to me like the guy's losing it.'

'Doesn't he know what it'll look like if he wipes out his best mate?' George is asking. Genuinely shocked that Shug could be this stupid.

'Nah,' Hutton's saying, and waving a dismissive hand. 'He doesn't know how the business works. Not really. He's making it up as he goes along. Bugger doesn't have a clue.'

George will talk to Jamieson and Young about it. Report to them, find out what they want done. They tell George, George tells Hutton. Then Hutton does what he's told. If they want Fizzy dead too, then Fizzy's a dead man. Might be useful for them to let Shug make a mug of himself. Be seen to make very public mistakes. Hopefully not. As he makes his way back home, Hutton's hoping that his future employers want a different outcome. Don't let Shug have his own way. Hutton can hardly think of a worse job. A man losing control of his business, hitting the bottle, lashing out at his friends. The odds of this ending in disaster are pretty damned obvious. Hutton doesn't want to be anywhere near Shug when it all starts to implode. If he's lashing out at lifetime friends, what's he going to do to a man like Hutton? The sooner he makes the crossover to Jamieson's organization, the better.

# 21

A knock on the door. Loud, demanding. Deana Burke is sitting bolt upright in bed. Looking at the clock. Five minutes past eleven. It won't be someone she wants to see. Creeping to the window and looking down onto the street. There's a red car parked two doors down that she doesn't recognize. Can't see anyone. She's wearing a thin slip, so she's grabbing a dressing gown from the wardrobe. Putting slippers on, thinking it's a good idea in case she has to run outside. Run in slippers. Yeah, that'll get you far. She's cursing herself. She should be ready for the worst. She should have to hand everything she needs for a quick exit. So some thug tells you that Shug doesn't see you as a target. That doesn't mean you stop thinking for yourself. Plan. Plan for everything.

She's standing at the top of the stairs. Another knock. Just as loud second time around. She hasn't switched a light on. They can't know for certain that she's home. Unless they've been watching the house. Of course they bloody have. They'll have been watching it for hours. They'll have seen the lights on. They'll know she hasn't left, just gone to bed. She knows this is how they do it. Can't remember now who told her. Not Kenny. Another boyfriend, years ago. She said something about people breaking doors down or sneaking in with lock-picks. Someone or other laughed and said no, gunmen mostly just ring the doorbell. You answer and they shoot. The gun's going to make a noise anyway. Better it makes a noise when you're standing on the doorstep ready to run, than upstairs in a dark house you don't know. This person banging on her door could have the gun out already. Ready to fire on her the second she opens it. She never asked what happens when the person doesn't answer.

Out the back. No. They'll have that covered. This isn't some halfwit organization. They got rid of Kenny. They've won round Nate Colgan. They're lashing out at Peter Jamieson. They know better than to leave the back door unguarded. Face it – that's what you do. You hold your head up and you face it. Like when Colgan turned up for Shug, she answered the door because the alternative was to hide in terror. That's not her. She won't let them turn her into that sort of person. She's marching down the stairs – and marching is the word – flicking on two light switches at the bottom. One for the stairs, one for the hallway at the front door. It's overkill, but she wants the place lit up. She wants people to see. She's grabbing the door handle. Twisting the lock and yanking open the door. The man on the step has taken a sudden step backwards. Surprised by her aggression. She's about to say something quite unladylike when she sees who it is. Now she's saying something worse.

'Bloody hell, what the fuck are you doing knocking on my door like that at this hour? I nearly had a heart attack.'

'I'm sorry,' DI Fisher's saying, putting up a calming hand. 'I didn't mean to startle you. I knew you were in bed, so I had to knock loud.'

'How the hell did you know I was in bed?'

'I've been watching the house for the last couple of hours,' he's saying. 'Checking up. You said someone came and threatened you. I wanted to see if they were watching you. See if they were keeping tabs. Might be that you're a target too, no matter what anyone says. So I've been out here for the last couple of hours. Further down the street. I saw the lights going off in the house. Figured if they were going to change shifts, it would be then. Nothing. There's nobody watching you.'

'I don't recognize that red car,' she's saying, nodding out towards the street. It's a surly comeback, wanting to shoot a hole in his argument because he rattled her.

'That's mine,' he's saying. 'I moved it up the street just now. Listen, Deana, can I come in? We still need to talk.'

They don't need to talk. That's what Deana's thinking. But she knows you don't send a copper away. You play along and let them say and do whatever makes them happy. She's stepping aside and letting him pass. Glancing out into the street as she does so. What if one of Shug's men *is* watching? She's closing the door and turning to face him. Fisher's standing politely in the hallway, waiting for her to decide where the conversation will take place. Politeness doesn't seem a natural fit for him, from everything Kenny said. She's seen pictures of the cop. Kenny pointed him out in a couple of newspaper articles. He looks older in real life. Shorter, less imposing. He does look tough, though, and Kenny said he was. Looks like he's struggling with his politeness.

Deana's decided that they're going to have this conversation in the kitchen. Better to have a light on at the back of the house than the front, she's figuring. Fisher's sitting at the table. She hasn't offered him a cup of tea, and she won't. Nothing that encourages him to stay. He isn't going to do anything for her. He's not capable. She's put all her eggs in Peter Jamieson's basket, and she's content with that. If anyone's going to make sure Kenny's killers see justice, it'll be Jamieson. She's making sure her dressing gown is pulled firmly shut. No hint of skin. Only a face with no make-up. Nothing that would make him want to stay.

'Have you had any trouble since?' Fisher's asking. Opening the conversation, trying to keep it friendly. Hard to keep it friendly. He hates this woman. Can't put it any simpler than that. She's every bit as bad as Kenny. She knew everything he was up to. She turned a blind eye, because she liked the life it paid for. These gangster tarts make him sick. But he is better at hiding it than he was.

She can see the effort. The strain it puts on him just to

make conversation. But she can't see the loathing, or at least doesn't recognize it. She just thinks he's an arrogant, anti-social prick.

'No trouble since,' she's saying with a shrug. 'The thug who was here said there wouldn't be. So long as I don't talk to you, so thank you very much for coming.'

'We need to have a conversation that you can't hang up on,' he's saying. 'I can't find the people who took Kenny until I know what you know. I'm working on the assumption that Kenny is dead. I think that's the common-sense approach to take. But I also have another missing person to try and find. Have you heard the name Richard Hardy?'

Thinking about it. 'Doesn't ring any bells. Is he involved?'

'I don't know for sure,' Fisher's saying. 'He disappeared the same night Kenny did. Might have been a victim of the same manoeuvres. I'm just trying to get a clear picture.'

Never heard of Hardy. Feels like Fisher's clutching at straws here. What does he expect to hear from her? If there was something worth hearing, she would have said it already. She's beginning to suspect that Fisher has nothing to go on.

'The job he did the night he went missing,' Fisher's saying. 'He told you he had a job. What did he tell you about it?'

'Nothing really,' she's saying. Relieved that she's on safe ground here. Kenny didn't go into much detail. He told her it was a big job. Told her he was nervous about it. Nothing else. 'He didn't say what it was. Just said it was a big job. Bigger than usual for him. I mean, he was a driver. That's all. He drove Peter Jamieson home at night. That was it. He was never involved in anything that mattered.'

Fisher's nodding. There's some truth in that. But sometimes you need a driver for a big job. Hell of a coincidence if he's working a big job for Jamieson and is then picked up by Shug. Everything else makes sense but that. Shug getting into bed with MacArthur. Getting rid of the man who knows all his financial secrets. Making a hit against Jamieson, just to show that he can. That all adds up. It's this job of Kenny's – it would be an obvious set-up by Jamieson. Tell your driver you have a big job for him. Get him somewhere secluded and kill him. Punishment for being a grass. That was the risk Kenny took.

'But this was a bigger-than-usual job. He told you that,' Fisher's going on. 'He must have said something else. I mean, presumably he didn't go on this job alone. It can't have been a driver-only job. He must have been driving someone. Did he hint who he was going with? More importantly, where they were going? I need to know where to look.'

How much does she tell him? She doesn't want Fisher to know that she's talking to John Young. That'll get him back on his high horse.

'He did say there would be someone with him. Someone he trusted. Didn't say anything about what it was or where it would be.'

Fisher's sighing. 'You believe that Shug was behind this and not Jamieson?' he's asking her. A sincere question. Not trying to get at anything, genuinely interested.

A little shrug. 'I believe it. I don't think they know that Kenny was talking to you. I, er . . . John Young called. I went to the club. He asked if I knew where Kenny was. We discussed it. Discussed it a little. I didn't tell him everything, obviously. I'm sure they don't know. They think it was Shug. I'm convinced of that.'

Fisher's grimacing. 'Jesus!' he's muttering, and shaking his head. This was always going to mean war, but it's moving faster than he expected.

Jamieson will strike against Shug. Has to. If Shug's taken out one of Jamieson's men, then he has to be seen to hit back. Fisher's hope was that he could get an arrest made before retaliation. That could take the wind out of some sails, cool people down. Leave them without a target. But not if they know already.

'What did Young say to you? Exactly what?'

'Just that,' she's saying. 'He wanted to know if I'd seen Kenny. Said that Kenny was the only one missing. I guess they heard a rumour or something. I think I confirmed what they were expecting.'

Fisher's getting up. He's heard all he's going to hear. He's not prepared to assume that Jamieson is innocent in this.

Not yet. But it's all pointing to Shug now. He's out the front door and into the night. Knowing that he needs more. He has two or three days at the most to make an arrest, or there will be more blood.

# 22

It's getting uncomfortable. Neither of them would ever say it. They're brothers. Calum and William should be able to deal with this. William gets it. He knows that Calum can't just run. He needs to have everything in place first. Say he runs to London. Tries to get all the things he needs for a new ID when he arrives. That'll take a while. He doesn't know where to go, for a start. So by the time he has everything, Jamieson knows he's run. Sends someone after him. They catch him. They've got him bang to rights. They won't forgive and forget. Stay in the city; get everything organized more quickly. Then disappear completely. If they catch you in the meantime? Well, you never left the city. You were at your brother's house. Lying low after a job. Gives Calum a chance to tell them what they want to hear.

All of which is fine, until you live it. The sheer intensity of it. Every sound a scare. A knock on the door while they're having breakfast. Calum running into the spare bedroom. William going nervously to the door. Terrified at first. Then angry at his own fear. Defiant by the time he's opening the door and seeing his friend, Maurice 'Sly' Cooper.

'William,' Sly's saying. 'I was starting to think you had fallen off the world. Where you been?'

Pausing before he answers. Not thinking about himself, but thinking about Calum. People must be talking. Talking about the fact that William hasn't been out much. Not his usual, social self. Been to work, but mostly ignoring his friends. Keeping appointments, but making no new ones. 'I've been here. Busy, you know. Work stuff.'

Sly comes in, stays five minutes and leaves. He'll have got the message that he wasn't entirely welcome. He'll go back and tell their mutual friends that something's definitely going on with William. And they'll speculate. Things can't go on this way.

'He's gone,' William's saying to Calum. Calum coming out of the spare room and looking at his brother. Seeing the tension in him. There's going to be another day of this.

'Maybe I can find somewhere else to stay for the night,' Calum's saying. 'Wouldn't be any great hardship for me. Bed-and-breakfast. Maybe find an empty flat somewhere. It would be safer.'

'No,' William's saying with force. 'I won't have that. No way. You stay here until it's time. It wouldn't be safer to go somewhere else. Not now – you know that. More chance of someone seeing you. You'd be throwing away everything you've done so far. You're nearly out, Calum. Nearly out of that business. You're not going to do anything to let them catch you now.'

Can't argue with his brother. Doesn't want to. Going somewhere else is inviting failure. He has to stick it out here. No matter how unpleasant it becomes. The phone rings. They both look up sharply. William's laughing and walking across to it. Trying to take away some of the tension. Calum's watching. Listening. William agreeing with someone. Checking his watch and saying it'll be fine. Skipping across to the table and getting a pen. Writing something down on the front page of a newspaper. Then hanging up.

'That was Barry Fairly; he's got your stuff. Wants me to go pick it up right away.'

Calum's nodding. This is good news. Progress. But also a worry. Anything could happen here. Could easily be a set-up. 'You know where to go?' he's asking.

'Yeah, he gave me an address. Some office. I know the street, I'll find the building.'

William's gone to get a coat and the rest of the payment. Calum's standing by the front door. William's smart, but he still needs instruction. Even if he doesn't like hearing it, he needs it.

'Listen,' Calum's saying when his brother reaches the front door. 'When you get there, park a little away from the building. Check every car on the street. If there's anyone out of place, just leave. Come back here. When you get inside, if there's anyone other than Fairly, leave. Even if it's just him, collect the stuff, hand over the money, get out. Nothing else. Fairly tries to get you talking, ignore him.'

William's raising a hand and smiling. 'Don't worry. I'm going to be more cautious than I've ever been. Captain Cautious. In and out like lightning. They won't see me for dust. I'll be a blur of dodgy ID and bank notes. Okay?' Seems like a joke, but serious.

'You stick to that,' Calum's saying.

It's an ordinary little street. William's driving down it for the second time. Found somewhere to park a few doors down from the office Fairly named. Office above a gadget shop. Plenty of little shops on the street. Well-populated area. That's reassuring. Maybe it's supposed to be. He looked in every car on his first approach. Now walking slowly along the wrong side of the street, looking for anything out of place. Nobody sitting in a car waiting. Nobody hanging around a doorway or alleyway. If someone's hiding, then they're doing a fine job. Just shoppers, all disinterested in William. Across the street and up to the door. Not the door to the gadget shop, a plain door to the right of it. Pressing a buzzer and waiting. A buzz for a reply. William pushing open the door, finding himself at the bottom of dimly lit stairs. Starting to get pretty damned nervous now. This is the sort of thing Calum does regularly. This is his life. That's what William's thinking as he walks up the stairs. Walking into the unknown.

A plain door at the top of the stairs. No markings. An office, Fairly said. An office that doesn't advertise, obviously. Standing outside staring at a blank door isn't going to get him anywhere. William's pushing the door open. An office inside. Three desks. A bunch of filing cabinets. Computers on the desk, but there's something odd about the place. Takes William a few seconds to realize. There's nothing lying around that could identify what work they do here. There are times, in the garage, when he's been careful to keep some documents out of view. Cars he shouldn't be handling, that sort of thing. This is obviously a whole company of things worth hiding. Probably loan-sharking, something like that. Which isn't reassuring. Not even Barry Fairly sitting alone at one of the desks is reassuring. He's the only one here, but there's a door behind him and another to his right. Anyone could be in there. Anyone could come up the stairs behind William and block him in. This is not a time to relax.

'Don't worry,' Barry's saying, 'this place is safe. I do some work for the guy who owns it. He lets me use it now and then. It's fine.'

Now it sounds like Barry's trying too hard to reassure him. William's getting paranoid. 'You have the stuff?' he's asking.

'I do,' Barry's saying, tapping a plastic bag on the desk. 'You have the money?'

'I do,' William's saying. Taking a wad of notes from his pocket. Taking a few steps across to the desk where Barry's sitting. Putting the two hundred pounds down beside the bag. Doing his best to look confident. Not an easy trick. He's picking up the bag and opening it. Yes, he remembers what Calum said. Get it and get out, quick as you can. But he's not going to get outside and find that he has a couple of pieces of cardboard in there. He has to know that he's getting what he came for. Pulling out a passport. Looks convincing. Driver's licence the same.

'There's a printout in there with a few details about the ID. Stuff that isn't on the passport or licence. Parents' names. That sort of thing,' Barry's saying.

'Looks good to me,' William's nodding, dropping them back into the bag. 'I'm sure we can do more business in the future. A lot more.'

Out the door and down the stairs. Going a little faster than his sense of pride says is proper. Never mind that. Out the front door and onto the street. Crashing into someone. Dropping the bag. William taking a step back, getting ready to throw a punch. Ready to run. To do anything that keeps him alive.

'Whoa, look out there, fellow,' a short guy in his thirties is saying. 'I didn't see you.' He's looking at William with bemusement now, seeing the intensity of his reaction.

'Sorry,' William's saying. Pulling himself together. 'I was in such a rush. My fault.' Saying it with a smile. The man stepping back out of William's way. Walking on down the street, glancing back over his shoulder as he goes. William's reaching down and picking up the bag. Looking up and down the street. Nobody suspicious. Nobody paying him any attention, other than the guy he crashed into. Walking briskly back to his car. By the time he reaches it he's so glad to be there that he doesn't even check for threats. Just gets in, starts up and drives.

'Here you go, Donald Tompkin – everything you need to fuck off with.' A relieved grin on William's face as he drops the bag on the kitchen table.

'No problems?' Calum's asking.

'Nope.'

'And you weren't followed?'

'Nope,' William's saying, and wishing he'd checked.

Calum's taking the passport and driver's licence out of the bag. They look good. Perfect, in fact. As good as he hoped Barry Fairly could manage. Just about the last piece of the puzzle. Just needs to set up bank accounts in his new ID and use them to pay for his plane ticket.

'Thanks, William,' he's saying with a smile. 'You've done brilliantly. And that's the last thing I'll ask of you.' A fact that's a relief to both men.

# 23

The man keeps walking down the street. Looking behind him all the time. Watching the guy pick up the stuff he dropped and scurry off down the street. So this was the guy Fairly was meeting. They're not usually complete saps. Fairly's just about the best counterfeiter in the business. His clientele usually know how to carry themselves without drawing attention. Without drawing suspicion. Not this one. Must be new at this. Better not scare him. Marty's walking away until he's sure Fairly's client can't see him any more. Now he's stopping, turning and walking back the way he came. That extra little walk down the street was a favour for Fairly. Don't scare his clients. Don't give him anything to complain about. Fairly is useful. Very useful, sometimes. His passports work like a charm. Best you can get, other than the real thing.

In the door and up the stairs. It's his office above the gadget shop. Doesn't use it a lot, but he needs it. He lends people money. Short-term loans, long-term customers. It continues to amaze and amuse, how stupid people can be. And Marty just keeps taking advantage. Because Marty's smart like that. He sees people's weaknesses, and he makes money from it. Cash and women. Those are the two that make the most money. Marty's involved in all sorts of other things, but those two are golden. The moneylending is harder. It's a bitch, truth be known. See, there's always more women. Some of them let you down. Some go work for someone else, but there's always more. The moneylending? Jesus, that's shark-infested waters. Brutal. As bad as it gets. Some of the biggest thugs are lurking in this part of the industry. Marty wouldn't be involved at all if he didn't have Jamieson's protection. And he's in danger of throwing that away.

Fairly's still in the office, looking all gormless as usual. Smart guy, but he doesn't get involved in the brutal side of things. He doesn't live it, like Marty. Shit, nobody lives it like Marty, Marty's thinking to himself.

'Was that your guy I saw stumbling out of here a couple of minutes ago?' Marty's asking. Making polite conversation. He wants Fairly out of here. Got a couple of his guys coming round with money they've collected this morning. Tough guys. Better Fairly doesn't see them.

'Yep, that was him.'

'Didn't seem like one of your usual. Looked nervous as hell to me.'

Fairly's shrugging. People like Marty think it makes them seem tough if they pretend they never get nervous. That's bullshit. Marty's probably shitting himself right now. Word going around is that Marty and his brother are in Jamieson's bad books. Throwing private parties at the brother's nightclub, not cutting Jamieson in on his share. Stupid, greedy bastard. Yet he thinks he's the tough one. Huh!

'Things are changing,' Fairly's saying as he gets up from his seat. 'Especially in the car trade. Opening up. He's a new one. William MacLean, got a garage on the east side.'

There's a pause. Fairly's starting to head for the door, about to say goodbye. Marty's standing in the middle of the room, his brain trying to find a gear that lets it move forward. Still trying. There it is.

'You say William MacLean?'

'Uh-huh.'

'Got a garage in the east?'

'That's what I said.'

Marty's holding up a hand. Telling Fairly to stop while he thinks. Fairly's sighing, but he's doing as he's told. Marty pays well. He's a little shit, but if Barry was prone to judging people, he wouldn't be in this business.

'You have a copy of the stuff you did for him?' Marty's asking.

Fairly's looking at Marty with a frown now. You don't stick your nose into someone else's business. Even Marty has to know something as simple as that.

Fairly's turning to walk for the door. Marty's darting in front of him. Blocking the way out, but with his hands up, pleadingly.

'Look, Barry. This is important. That William MacLean –

there might be more to this. Trust me. I might be about to do you the biggest fucking favour anyone ever did you. No word of a lie. Let me see a copy. If I'm wrong, I'm wrong. Who cares? If I'm right, I'll be saving your bacon here, mate. Saving it.'

That wheedling tone. Fairly would love to tell him to shove it, but he can't. Self-preservation. He's going back across to the table, unbuttoning the pocket on his jacket. Taking out the rough copy he made. That he always makes. Because you never know.

Marty's standing over the table, looking down at the picture. Puffing out his cheeks.

'Well?' Fairly's asking. Annoyed, impatient.

'This is . . .' Marty's lost for words. He wants to say that this is a brilliant opportunity. That this could get him right back into Peter Jamieson's good books. But that's not what he's going to say to Fairly. 'This is important. Listen to me, Barry, yeah? Listen. Right. I need to keep this. Just for a wee while. Go home, I'll call you. I need to set up a meeting. You'll need to be there. This is important. I'm not kidding you here.'

Fairly's left the office. Marty's sitting at the desk, looking at the copy of the passport in front of him. He knows the face. Not a recent photo, but he knows the face. How to profit most. Go for the long-term. That's always the answer. Especially when you're hanging on, like Marty is. This could solve a lot of problems. He's picking up the phone. Calling Young. No answer. Shit! Probably ignoring him. They're still pissed off. Fine, be like that. There's another way. Calling Kevin Currie. Explaining a little, holding back enough. He needs to have something to take to the meeting with him. Marty knows how to play these games. Currie doesn't like it. He wants everything. Sure he does. He wants to be able to pass on all the information himself. Gain more of the credit for it. Marty's pissed off that he's having to go through Currie anyway. Currie's a senior man with Young and Jamieson. Makes them a lot of money with booze and fags. They trust him. Shouldn't be this way. Young should just answer his damn phone.

Two big bastards have just come into the office. Marty's gesturing at them to get out. He's still on the phone to Currie. Going to try Young again. The two thugs are going out. Not looking too impressed. Marty isn't an easy man to work for. They've heard the rumours about a fallout with Jamieson as well. They're worried. Not going to take being pushed around for much longer. Not unless they hear more positive stories about Marty's protection. Marty's finished with Currie. Calling Young again. Again the call ignored. Little bastard!

Marty could just go to the club. One of them is bound to be there. No. Don't turn up without warning. They won't like that. He has to play this one by the book. Go in there with information that'll floor them. They won't like the info he brings. Too smart to shoot the messenger, though. This'll make them see how useful Marty and his connections can be.

# 24

Late night last night. Early morning this morning. The meeting with Deana Burke has pushed Fisher back towards Shug. That's what he wanted. He didn't want to know that he was running out of time, sure, but he wanted to know that he was running in the right direction. Shug had Hardy killed as part of his deal with MacArthur. Alex MacArthur would have insisted on it. Oh, how sweet it would be to get MacArthur too. Can't get him directly, but might get lucky via Shug. If he can get solid charges against Shug. Have him in an interview room, get him nervous and get him talking. With a hardened operator, you get nothing. But Shug Francis isn't a hardened operator. He's nice and soft. Fiddling around with stolen motors doesn't harden you for life at this level. There are a lot of very naive low-level criminals. They think what they do makes them tough. Makes them ready for anything. They have no idea.

Didn't get a lot of sleep last night. Too much thinking. Working out the best angle for attack. No longer thinking about the best way to arrest Shug and get a solid case. Now thinking about the fastest way. If Fisher delays, Peter Jamieson takes the decision out of his hands. Then he has to target Jamieson, and that's not likely to get him anywhere. Not now, anyway. He had Kenny, and that could have led to something. He nearly had Frank MacLeod. Got this close. Then, nothing. Frank disappears off the face of the planet. Two possible reasons. The less likely is that he ran. The more likely is that Peter Jamieson had his former gunman killed. Silenced, if you want to look at it that way. Now Kenny's gone, and Jamieson didn't have to do a thing about it. Shug, in his stupidity, has taken away an avenue of destruction for Jamieson. Doesn't even know that he's done his enemy a favour.

Right now Fisher's hoping Shug will do another enemy a favour. He's sitting along the street from the house. Car facing the other way, watching his mirrors. Far enough away that nobody in the house will see him in the car. Also far enough away that he has a poor view. Poor is better than none. He's waiting for Shug to leave. To drive somewhere in one of his chintzy sports cars. Lead Fisher to a new point of investigation. Find someone that Fisher can lean on. Just give them some new information. All they've been drawing are blanks. You deal with people like Jamieson and MacArthur and they leave you nothing to play with. A guy like Shug leaves plenty. Makes enough mistakes. Maybe that stops now – he's living up to MacArthur's standards. Or maybe they just need to watch Shug a little more closely.

Watching the house and waiting. Watching the clock ticking down. How long will Jamieson wait? He'll want Shug crushed. It'll happen soon, and leave Fisher with nothing. Worse than nothing. His entire investigation a source of ridicule for others. That's if his efforts in recent months haven't already become a joke in the station. Failure piled upon failure. Young cops losing their respect and fear of him. He needs something. Now he's watching closely. His thoughts are interrupted by movement at Shug's front door. A woman coming out, going to a car in the driveway. Taking something from it and going back into the house. That'll be the wife. Elaine. She'll become a target for Fisher, if he can't find anything better. Usually wiser to ignore the fierce women of the underworld. They don't crack. But she's not like them. She could be soft too. Give it another couple of days. Find something concrete, or go for her.

It's nearly eight o'clock in the morning when a car pulls up further down the street from Shug's house. Looks like the driver's in a hurry. A man getting out, small, close to middle-aged. Hard to spot facial features at this range. Should have brought a camera. Could have turned in the seat and zoomed him. He's walking quickly up to the front door. Ringing the doorbell and waiting. Standing with his back to Fisher. Little bastard, whoever you are. The door's opening and the man's going inside. Now Fisher's sitting and waiting. Making a judgement. Who do you follow? Sit tight and mark Shug, or pick up the newcomer? Not an easy one to make. The newcomer could be important, or he could be a complete waste of time. At least with Shug you know you're tailing a man who matters. You're tailing your principal target.

The man's been inside all of five minutes when the front door's opening again. Fisher's sliding down a little in the seat, looking in his mirror. Still can't get a good view of the man as he comes out. Make the judgement. Someone inside for that long is not going to be important. He could lead to someone important. Could be that Shug's given him something to deliver. But not likely. Probably just some pathetic little shit that runs errands for the boss. Pick up his shopping, that sort of thing. Let him go. Watch the house; follow Shug when he comes out. If he comes out. He used to be very active. Used to spend a lot of time at the garages. Used to go to races every weekend. Even bought his own track-day race car. Was going to spend a lot of time with that. Word is he's stopped all that. Fisher heard from another cop that in the last two months Shug's hardly visited any of his own garages and never goes racing. The lifestyle change of a man with a lot to worry about.

The little man's across the front lawn and down to the road. Getting into his car and coming this way. Fisher's sliding all the way down now, out of sight. The car's going past. Just as Fisher begins to straighten back up, he has a flash of recognition. Not much. He's only seen the back and some of the side of the driver's face. Enough to change his judgement. You see something in a split second that gives you an opening. He could be wrong. He could be making another blunder. Wouldn't be the first recently. But if he's right, this could pull everything together. He's starting the car, but staying where he is. Letting the driver get out of view. He's likely to be paranoid, looking for a tail. Fisher's going to have to be careful. A glance in his rear-view mirror to see if there's anything behind him that might grab his interest. No sign of movement from Shug's house. Good. Concentrate on the driver.

Staying in the Goldilocks zone. Some police drivers are good at it. Fisher's been in a car with a police driver tailing a robbery suspect. Suspect didn't know he was being followed. Fisher knew he was moving the weapons they'd used on the job the day before. The driver had to keep a perfect distance, without ever losing the target. He played it flawlessly. Never got too close. Never fell too far back. Worked the traffic like you wouldn't believe. Amazing how a good driver can manipulate the traffic around him. Fisher's not that good, and he knows it. So he's playing cautious. Hanging a little further back than he should. Risking losing the target rather than getting too close and giving the game away. Trying to make sure he only catches glimpses of a car going through the morning traffic. So easy to lose him. Couple of times he did lose him. Got bogged down in traffic or stopped at lights while the target pulled away ahead. Got back in touch by luck rather than design.

Now it's all swinging in Fisher's favour. All because he's worked out where the target is going. Armed with that info, there's no need to keep him in view. Let him get ahead if he wants. Fisher's even taking a slightly different route, so that he'll arrive at the destination from a different direction. Make sure the target doesn't know Fisher was following him. Now he's in a comfort zone, and actually enjoying the drive. Who cares about the morning traffic when you know there's good news waiting at the end of the journey? Nearly there now. Coming round the corner and onto what should be the last street. Seeing the target car coming the other way along the street and turning off. Turning into the car park, as expected. Fisher isn't rushing to get there. No need. He's turning off the street and pulling into the car park. Slowing down and pulling into his usual spot.

He can see the door of the target car opening. Fisher isn't out of his car yet. He can see the driver getting out. Short man, thin, approaching middle age. It's so obvious now. Couldn't see it from a distance, but here it's easy. The dark hair, the scar on one cheek. PC Paul Greig. Just finished visiting one of his scumbag criminal mates and now on his way to work. About to head into the changing rooms and put on his uniform. The uniform in which he's supposed to protect the public from people like Shug Francis. The uniform he so routinely disgraces. Fisher's getting out of the car. Greig's walking across the car park. As Fisher's pressing the button on his keys to lock the car, he's raising his eyes. Eye contact with Greig. The temptation is to smile and say hello. Now that he has the bastard by the balls, he doesn't feel the hatred so much any more. He only hates the fact that Greig gets away with it. That will soon change. But no. No smile, no hello. Just looking back down at the keys, stony-faced. Don't let Greig know that anything has changed between them.

He's been sitting at his desk for the best part of an hour. The plods have brought a few things to him – nothing that matters right now. The financial boffins have put together a list of discrepancies in Hardy's books. All relating to Shug, to begin with. Interesting stuff. List as long as your arm. Took some effort to pick it all apart. It'll all go on the charge sheet. It would be a failure if it were all that went on the sheet. He wants more. The disappearances of Hardy and Kenny. The meeting with Greig. There's so much that he could throw at a man like Shug Francis. The more he throws, the more he might get back. Fisher's willing to do deals. Cut some of the charges for information that matters. But he needs more charges. How long now before Jamieson moves? Can't be long. Jamieson will try to hit hard, Fisher thinks. Unaware that he is the mechanism Jamieson is using to strike. Rushing to beat himself to the punch. He's smiling, though. For the first time in months it feels as though an investigation is coming towards him rather than getting away.

# 25

God, it's early. Way too early. George is staring at the ceiling. Contemplating the day ahead. Contemplating all that can go wrong. That's a lot to think about. Going to need a coffee first. Twenty minutes later: showered, dressed and downing as much caffeine as one cup can hold. Got to meet Hutton at nine. Not much to clear up, but there's no such thing as too much preparation. One of the things he picked up from Calum. It's preparation that decides whether you succeed or fail. So meet Hutton, run through everything Jamieson said. Make sure Hutton knows what he's doing. Make sure he knows not to do the job on Fizzy. That was a surprise. George thought they'd be delighted to see Shug make such a stupid mistake, but instead they came up with a better idea. A more profitable one. It was Jamieson who told George about it last night, but it sounds a lot like a John Young idea.

John Young. It's funny, but George hates the man now. No good reason to. All the things George doesn't like about his life are his own fault. He knows it. It's just that Young epitomizes all the mistakes George has made. Probably because Young's the one that gives the orders. Young told him to ruin Calum's relationship with that girl Emma. So George did it.

His own fault. He keeps doing these jobs and doing them well. No matter how often he tells Young that he doesn't want any more responsibility, he keeps getting more responsibility. And here we are again. A job with responsibility. George will be meeting someone who matters, having a discussion that matters. Something he can't believe he'll be any good at. It's not killing someone. That's something. He's drawn a line in the sand there, and so far has never crossed it. But this will be another step towards becoming the one thing George doesn't want to be. Important.

There aren't many people like George Daly in the business. Smart muscle. He goes round and beats people up, intimidates them. He's the warning Peter Jamieson sends to people who owe him money. Usually pathetic souls that anyone with the ability to stay upright could batter. It's easy, mindless work. It's mostly carried out by mindless people. Halfwit thugs that Jamieson can hire and fire without consideration. But George is different. He's smart, tough and a likeable guy. That draws attention. Means he gets all the challenging muscle-jobs. Means that Young and Jamieson want him to start doing more serious work. Take on more responsibility. Back up a gunman like Calum. Go and do a job like today's. George doesn't want that. He's not just smart. He's smart enough to know that ambition is poison. That responsibility is a curse. In this business, the best thing you can be is irrelevant.

Out of the flat and heading for his car. Looking up and down the street. A simple precaution. George doesn't live in fear of death. If you stay away from the killing, it tends to stay away from you. But he has beaten up a lot of people in his working life. Some who are just stupid enough to think revenge might be a good idea. He's had a couple of people come after him over the years. Looking to get even. Looking to show the people around them that they're still tough. It's a certain type of person you have to worry about. The pathetic junkies are no threat. They're living day to day. They have no concept of revenge for historical acts. It's small-time dealers, the wannabes. They borrow money from Jamieson, or take stock from him with the promise of a cut of the profits. When Jamieson doesn't get the money he's due, he sends George round to serve a warning. You beat up some little bastard who thinks he's a big tough gangster. He's humiliated, so he looks for revenge. Happened twice. Both times they tried to deliver the beating themselves. Forgetting that George is a professional. Beating is what he does. A second humiliation taught them to give up. There's nobody here today, so he's into the car.

The first meeting is with Hutton at the same flat as yesterday. No trouble getting there. Hutton's waiting. Looks nervous. Strange, George didn't expect him to be like this. Thought he would be the same as Calum, all cold and relaxed. Guess they must all behave differently. No shame in nerves.

'Job's off,' George is saying, and watching the nerves settle. 'Jamieson's going to try and play this a different way. Wants to try and set something up with Fizzy. No hit, though. Word from Jamieson's own mouth is that you should ignore Shug from now on. If he calls, blank it. Sit tight until you hear from me or John Young. I don't think you'll be doing anything else for Shug now.'

Hutton's trying to hide his relief, but not quite managing. Not from someone as skilled at spotting it as George. 'That's fine,' Hutton's saying, playing it cool. 'I'll wait for one of you to get in touch. Ignore anyone else.'

'One last thing,' George is saying as Hutton's getting up. 'I'm on my way round to meet with Fizzy Waters. Can you give me some directions?'

George knows the city well. Not obsessive about learning the back streets and new-build areas like some. Gunmen, for example. For them it could be a matter of life or death. Capture or escape. For George, knowing the city is a matter of convenience. Only rarely does he have to do a job in a hurry. The kind of people he intimidates aren't going anywhere. He's going to Fizzy's house now. Knows the area, and Hutton gave him directions to the house. Some people are good at giving directions. Hutton isn't one of them. Said all the wrong landmarks to look out for. George thinks he knows where the street is; he thinks wrong. He doesn't want to switch on his satnav to find out where to go. Another lesson learned from

Calum. When you're doing a job, be paranoid about technology. It can tell tales on you. It takes him twenty minutes of driving up and down random streets in the area to find the right one.

Out of the car and up to the front door. Hoping that nobody saw him driving around like an idiot. You see someone driving that way and you remember them. George doesn't want to be remembered. Ringing the doorbell and waiting. Fizzy might not be at home. If he has any sense, then he won't even be in the city. Run a mile, you fool. But Shug told Hutton he'd be there. Seemed sure Fizzy would stay. So that's the most reliable info George has to work with. Someone coming to the door. Opening it. Don't be a woman. Apparently his girlfriend isn't in the city, so that should help. It's a man. Fizzy. Staring down at the young man he doesn't recognize. George, all curly hair and easy smiles.

'Hi, Mr Waters, my name's George. Listen, I know this is difficult, but we need to talk. Better not to do it out on the doorstep. I work for Peter Jamieson.'

The tone was the key. Easy for those words to sound like a threat. Easy for any mention of Peter Jamieson to be taken the wrong way. But George aimed for sympathetic and friendly in his tone, and he nailed it. Fizzy's nodding. Opening the door all the way. Too trusting, George is thinking. That's what comes from only working in the car business all these years. George could be anyone. Could be working for

Shug. Could have been sent round to test Fizzy's loyalty. Fizzy's lucky that he's not going to learn the hard way.

George is inside. The first hurdle over. He's not carrying, so if this turns nasty, it's going to be tough for him. He has to assume that Fizzy's armed. Assume it, even though it's unlikely. Fizzy is in his own home, which has to comfort him as well. No reason why this should turn nasty, but you never know. Don't assume you know what goes through the head of another person. Fizzy's smart, but inexperienced. If he realizes he's on the outside, he should be desperate for help. This should be an easy conversation. Should be.

Fizzy's led him through to the family room at the back of the house. Houses round here are bigger than they look from the front. George is impressed, a little jealous. Shows how well Fizzy was doing from the car-ring. Enough to buy a place like this. There was good money in what they were doing. Shows how stupid they were to want more. There's a lot of people like that. Made stupid by greed and ambition.

'I shouldn't need to tell you what the situation is here,' George is saying as he sits down. 'You know that Shug's throwing away everything. He's tied himself to MacArthur, but MacArthur's setting him up. MacArthur's been feeding info to Peter for weeks now. Looking to get rid of Shug and take his business, so he's hoping Peter will take Shug out. He actually called Peter the night you had your big meeting with

MacArthur. I'm guessing you're not surprised by that,' he's saying, watching Fizzy's expression.

'No. Not really. Sounds about right.'

'You should also know,' George is saying, and looking at the floor. Pick the right words. Don't make it sound melodramatic. Sometimes the truth can be made to sound like a lie. Tread carefully. 'Shug called up Shaun Hutton last night. Told him he wanted rid of you. Said you were a danger to him – a threat. I don't know what went on between you and Shug, but he seems to want rid of you.'

Fizzy's sitting there, just staring straight ahead. No shock. No immediate emotion. 'Okay.'

'Now, you don't need to worry,' George is assuring him. 'Well, you do need to worry a little bit, but not about Hutton. He's not going to carry out the job, that's been made sure of.' Keep that bit vague. Fizzy doesn't need to know that Hutton's crossed over until he follows him. 'You may still need to worry about Shug, though. Once he has it in his head to kill you, it's not easy to turn that around. In this business, when someone thinks of you as an enemy there's usually no way back.'

Keep talking. Fizzy's clammed up, but that's fine. He's not arguing against what George is saying, which is enough. 'I'm not going to pretend that Peter's sent me here out of the goodness of his heart. He hasn't. Shug pissed him off. Shug's going to go down, you know that? MacArthur's setting

184

him up for a big fall. If he lives long enough, he's looking at big time. You need to be as far away from him as possible when that happens. Anyway, Peter Jamieson has bigger things to worry about. Shug was a nuisance, but MacArthur is more than that. He's sizing up Peter, looking to make a move against him. Everyone knows it, Peter included. He's not going to let that happen. Peter's going to undercut MacArthur in this wee game. See, MacArthur wants all of Shug's business. Peter reckons he can get it instead. If he does, he needs someone to run it. Someone credible. Someone with the know-how. That's where you come in. In exchange, you get the full benefits and protection of a senior person in the Jamieson organization.'

It would look amateurish to leap to an answer, so Fizzy's taking his time. Doesn't really need to. What else is he going to say but yes? Jamieson's offer is the only one on the table. The bastard probably knows it. He can stay loyal to Shug, but that'll get him precisely nowhere. Not now. Shug wants him dead. He'd like to pretend that the order probably came from MacArthur, but it's only pretending. It came from Shug. George is right, the friendship is over. Fizzy has to look after himself now.

'If your man can get control of the business and keep me safe, then I'll run it for him. I'll want to do it a certain way, keep it out of the drug trade.'

George is putting a hand up and nodding. 'There'll be no

crossover, I can guarantee that. Most of all they want the legit business.'

Fizzy's nodding. 'Fine. They get control of it. Keep me safe. Shug goes down, and I'll run the business for Jamieson.'

# 26

They haven't lived together since they were kids. More than thirteen years since William moved out of the family home. Now they're together, knowing it might be for the last time. Calum's on the laptop, sitting on the couch. Looking for flights to London. Today, preferably. Willing to wait until tomorrow if there are no seats. Not from Glasgow: he'll drive across to Edinburgh and fly down from there. Glasgow would make things too easy for anyone who wanted to chase.

'I don't want to leave it any later than early tomorrow,' Calum's saying. 'If people start digging around, it won't take them long to find out something's up.'

'Who's going to dig around? No reason for people to look,' William's saying.

'There's risk,' Calum's shrugging. 'Barry Fairly, for one.'

'Nah,' William's saying. 'He knows what side his bread is buttered.'

William's right. Counterfeiters aren't stupid. Takes smarts to get where they are. They know not to ask questions. They have a keen sense for maintaining deniability. But there are other risks. Jamieson getting twitchy and looking for Calum.

An emergency job comes along that only Calum can do for them; they go looking and don't find him. Or the police. Always possible that they come looking for him, too. Not likely, though. He's been careful. And even if there was an emergency, Jamieson would draft in a freelancer this close to the Hardy and Kenny hit. Calum knows he should feel safe, but he doesn't. Sitting around the flat, watching the clock tick. Waiting for his chance to get away. That chance is coming, and coming fast.

So he'll book flights. The money will come out of a bank account he set up this morning. It's in William's name, opened using Calum's money. Opening the account was no bother at all. He'll use it to pay for this flight, and then close it. Calum will open another to pay for his flight out of London. Then another for accommodation, wherever he ends up after that. By the time he settles down and starts to build a new life for himself, he'll be onto his fifth or sixth new account. The first two or three in William's name, before he switches to his false ID. He hasn't told William, because William hasn't asked, but the intention is to find another new ID when he settles. Donald Tompkin will be a travel name. Hopefully, when he settles somewhere, he'll be able to find another counterfeiter, another false ID. Another link in an ever-growing chain leading away from his old life.

There's another reason he hasn't told William. Something he doesn't want to discuss. Or even think about, if we're being honest here. Focus on getting away. On freeing himself from the life he'll leave behind. So what will he walk into? What will his new life be? There's only one thing he knows how to do well. Kill people. He knows how to scout a target. Knows how to do the job. Knows how to get away. He's good at it. Spent years thinking about it, planning each job, learning every detail. His biggest challenge will be avoiding that career from now on. Making sure he doesn't weaken, and take a job somewhere. Wouldn't be hard. Every city has its own criminal industry. Every criminal industry needs talented gunmen. The pay is good; the work is easy, if you have the skill for it. Wouldn't be hard to meet the right people. Not if you know what you're looking for. And his first day in a new city, he'll look for a counterfeiter.

That thought's been running through Calum's head all day. No seats available tonight. Too late to get an available seat on an afternoon flight. Wouldn't get to Edinburgh in time. Booking a morning flight for tomorrow. Then thinking about what he's flying towards. What job will he do? Anything that pays money, probably. Not exactly weighed down by moral quandaries about raising cash. No, stop that train of thought right now. Stay away from the criminal stuff. Easy money, but a slippery slope. You start down it and before long you're back where you started. Killing people, making enemies and living a life of isolation. The whole point of this is to get away from all that. It'll be a legal job. Legal money. You live that life and you can have all the things this life has denied you. You can meet anyone you want. Have a social life. Have a relationship that goes somewhere. Keep that ambition in mind. Put up with the boredom of a nine-to-five. Suffer the tedium of mind-numbing work. Ignore the thrill-seeker inside you. Ignore the lazy bastard who only wants to work a few days every few months. Ignore the perfectionist who wants to do what he's good at. Focus on the ambition of a normal life; ignore anything that stands in the way.

He and William have had an argument about money already. Not a furious row. Just William trying to be the big brother. Worries about Calum's financial situation. He started by trying to persuade Calum to empty his old account.

'No, they might be able to get access to my account. They have contacts working in banks that can check these things. Bank staff they pay off. Probably not every bank, but I can't risk it. I don't want them seeing anything out of place. They have to doubt that I'm even alive.'

William gave up on that line of attack. Moved onto what he considered safer ground. The car. It's been resprayed, retagged. There's nothing on it that could identify it as having been Calum's. Now it's time to put it up for sale.

'That might take a wee while,' William's saying. 'It's in good nick, but the market isn't exactly booming right now. I'll sell it,' he's saying, 'and I'll get a decent price for it, but not before you go. So, if you're going to be farting about, changing accounts and whatnot, I should give you the money up front. You know, so that you have it with you now, when you need it.'

He's not what you would call cunning, is he? A man concerned about his brother's financial situation, suddenly offering a large amount of cash up front. He does have a point, though. By the time he sells the car, William might have no idea what account to put the proceeds into. It is more convenient to do it this way, but it makes Calum uncomfortable. He knows exactly what William will do. He'll put far more money into the account than he'll ever make from selling the car. He loves Calum, and he wants his brother's new life to succeed. He feels responsible for introducing him to the old life. And he is the big brother. Doesn't matter what Calum's done in his life, it's still hard to argue against the guy who grew up across the hall from you. The guy you secretly wanted to emulate.

'How about you put half the money into the account now, and the other half you'll owe me when you've sold it. I'll drop you a line, tell you where to put the money.'

William's looking at him, a mixture of incredulous and offended. 'How does that help? This ain't a regular job here. You're family. I'll put it in now. Then, when I sell it, I just keep the money for myself. Hell, I might even make a profit on you.'

Calum's smiling now. 'You think you can make a profit, huh? So how much are you going to give me for it, and how much do you think you can make back on the sale?' he's asking. He's filled out his false details for the flight while talking, clicking confirm to pay.

William's putting on the face and tone he uses when he's being dishonest with a customer. It won't work with Calum, but it's worth a shot. He's usually overcharging someone, not undercharging them. This is new. 'Well,' he's saying, trying to work out how much extra he can give Calum without starting an argument. 'I reckon I can give you about three grand. I'll make somewhere around that.'

'Really?' Calum's saying. 'You remember how much you said I would get for it when I showed up here on Tuesday? A grand and a half, if I'm lucky. And there was mention of costs. Now it's three grand and no mention of costs.'

William's getting a little pissed off now. He doesn't like Calum acting all superior. 'All right, fine – you want to play it that way, let's play it that way. You'll be lucky to get a grand and a half for that car,' he's saying with aggression, his voice rising. 'It cost me about three hundred just to make the fucking thing safe, so that's a grand and two hundred. But I'll tell you something, if I decide I'm putting three grand into that fucking account, then I'm putting three grand into that fucking account. I don't see you doing anything about it, either, Mr Invisible. You'll take what I give you, and one day you might just be bloody grateful for it.' There's a pause. William still angry, Calum looking sheepish. 'If you want to be a total dick about it,' William's continuing more quietly, 'then when you get yourself set up somewhere you can owe it me back. Okay?'

Calum's nodding, putting the laptop to one side. 'Look, I didn't mean it that way. I am grateful. I just don't want you being out of pocket on my behalf. And I don't want you being in a position where you're not able to explain what you did with that money. I'll take it, and I will be grateful for it. And, if I'm able, I'll pay it back, because that's the kind of total dick I am.' That got a laugh, and it's taken the heat out of the conversation.

William's standing at the window now, looking out at the rain. He has a cup of tea in his hand. Sandwich finished, ready to put in an appearance at the garage. Been slacking off. Needs to show his face, make sure nobody mentions a change in his routine.

'You think they're out there somewhere looking for you?' William's asking. First time he's mentioned the people who might be looking. Thinks about them a lot, though.

'No,' Calum's saying. 'Not yet. They wouldn't expect to hear from me yet. They won't think anything's wrong. Not for another week at least.' And they'll be distracted. Very distracted. They'll be setting up Shug by now. They'll be moving against him. Calum knows the general plan. Setting up the cop to do their work for them. They'll be too busy moving against their enemies to check on their friends.

# 27

A lot of people want to meet Peter Jamieson. Not surprising. Nothing new. Hardly any of them get to. Not unless they're already known to him. It's John Young's job to do the filtering. The top people – the ones they know are important – get Jamieson. Very few of those. Then there's the next level down. Interesting people they haven't met before. People who might have something worth hearing. They get to meet Young. There's a few of them, but not many. Three or four a week, tops. Of whom maybe half go on to have a meeting with Jamieson. The vast majority of people who want to meet him fall at the first hurdle. They want a meeting with the boss. They're not interesting enough to warrant a meeting with his right-hand man. Usually more than twenty of those a week. They have to make do with talking to someone much lower down the chain. Like it or lump it.

On a week like this one, nobody gets to see the boss. Jamieson's busy, you'll have noticed. Young, too. He's still taking a glance at a few names. Couple of people wanting a meeting who have been in touch in the last couple of days. Usually these people go to someone lower down. That person passes the message up the chain. Some guy who thinks he has a good business opportunity. Don't they all. Jesus, the amount of shitty ideas that Young has to wade through. Fantasists, mostly. A busy week like this, there's no way he's finding time to meet this guy. Kick it back down the chain. Other one's interesting, though. Barry Fairly. Been in contact with Marty Jones. Marty called one of Jamieson's senior men, Kevin Currie. Currie, a very profitable tax-free cigarette and booze seller, has marked it urgent. Says Fairly has possible info relating to an employee. Won't say who. Fairly does counterfeit ID. That makes him interesting. The fact that it comes from Currie matters, too. He's an independent thinker. Handles most of this stuff himself. Always pays his percentage to Jamieson, grows his business well. For him to suggest this is urgent means it's urgent.

Young's made the call to Currie. Currie's delivered a warning. Marty Jones is sniffing around this one. Not just reporting it, but wants to be a part of it. Young sighed, but accepted it. Told Currie to find Marty and Fairly and send them round to the club. Be interesting to know who's been going round buying ID. Could be some idiot of no value. Or some idiot of value who's prone to doing stupid things. But Currie's a good judge. And Fairly seems like a solid member of the industry. Marty's a fucking nuisance, but that doesn't mean he's wrong. It's only an hour later when the barman's sticking his head round the door. Christ, still haven't learned his name. See, this is why so many people think Young's not very nice. Too impersonal. If it was Jamieson, he would have learned the name ages ago.

'Couple of fellows here to see you. Barry Fairly and Marty Jones.'

'Send them in, thanks,' Young's saying. Making a point of adding the thanks. It would be nice to be as well liked as Jamieson. All the staff think Jamieson's terrific. A charmer. Generous and likeable. They're all good at showing that they don't think of Young in the same way.

Fairly's coming into the office. Looks uncertain. Coming over to Young with a hand outstretched. Shaking enthusiastically. Sweaty hand, but Young won't mention that. Unimpressive-looking man. Won't mention that, either. Marty's behind him all the way. Shifty-looking bastard. Always too confident. A quick shake of his dry hand.

'Take a couple of chairs across,' Young's saying, and sitting on the couch.

They're doing as they're told. Fairly seems nervous. You'd think a man of his reputation would be used to meetings like this, coming to see a man like Young. Fairly's known in the business. Respected for his art. Done a lot of work for a lot of people. He's brought the chair across and he's sitting opposite the couch. Hands on his knees, looking straight ahead at Young. They all do this. Sit there staring at Young. Waiting for him to say something. They make an appointment because they have something to say, but they expect Young to start the conversation. Mostly afraid of saying anything without permission. Even people with Fairly's experience fall prey to the fictional bullshit. Don't speak unless spoken to. The big bad gangster might blow a fuse if you do. As though nut jobs who can't stand other people talking to them are going to last in this business. No such issue with Marty. He's sitting next to Fairly, and he's talking already.

'I think you'll want to see this, John,' he's saying with confidence.

Young's looking across at him. He doesn't like Marty talking to him like they're best friends. They're not. Never have been, never will be. Even when Marty was in the good books, he was suffered rather than enjoyed. 'Go on.'

'See, I let Barry here use one of my offices for some of his work. People collecting stuff, that sort of thing,' Marty's saying. Not explaining what Fairly does, because Young will already know. Young already knows most things. 'And I bump into this guy leaving the office this morning. I go in. I ask Barry about him. Barry tells me who he is. I ask to see the copy, get a look at the picture. I see it, and straight away I'm on the phone to you. Straight away, John. There was no answer. But I knew this was important, so I made the effort to get in touch with you through Kevin.'

Marty's stopped. He's looking at Young with a smile. Waiting to be told what a good job he's done. Young's grimacing. Leaning forward on the couch and looking down at the floor.

'You still haven't told me what the hell this is about. Barry, is it?'

'Yes,' Fairly's saying. Still looking terrified of the whole thing.

'Who came to you?'

'Fellow called William MacLean. See, the garage business is changing, and I need to make sure I'm up to speed with that. So, well, this fellow has a garage. Came looking for documents. Didn't seem like a big deal. He has a garage. Wouldn't have let him across the threshold otherwise. It seemed, you know, legit.'

Marty spotted it. No look of recognition when Barry mentioned William's name. 'I've got a copy of the passport he had done,' Marty's saying, taking it triumphantly from his pocket.

Marty's passed him rough copies of the passport and driver's licence. What matters is the picture. Young's looking at it. It's Calum. Not Calum as he is now. Photo must be two or three years old. Definitely Calum, though. Or Donald Tompkin, as the passport says. Young isn't saying anything. Sitting on the couch, holding onto the passport a little too tight. Thinking about it. There are reasons why men in the business pick up a fake ID. Sometimes you want it for a job. Not a passport, though. Driver's licence maybe, not a passport. Maybe Calum just wants to go abroad. Go on holiday.

Not unreasonable. Maybe he's paranoid about being on the police radar, so he wants to go under the radar. Nah. There are people in the business who are stupid enough for that explanation. People who go to ridiculous lengths just for something as irrelevant as a holiday. Not Calum. Too smart. He'd just holiday at home.

Thinking, and thinking some more. But there's nothing to think about. There's only one explanation. It's leaping up and smacking him in the face. Jamieson said it. He called it right. Calum isn't happy with them. Hasn't settled. He's had a run of tough jobs. Too many in quick succession. He wants out. He's running. No other conclusion. Their only gunman is running. Young's suddenly remembering that Marty Jones and Barry Fairly are sitting opposite him, gawping.

'Okay, that's fine,' Young's saying. Standing up to lead them to the door. 'Good of you to come, but I did already know about this. It's for a job, so it's hush-hush. But thanks for coming anyway, I won't forget.' And he won't forget. Won't forget that Fairly had this information for two days and had no intention of doing anything with it. 'You've done well, Marty,' Young's saying, as he begins to close the door behind them. Pains him to say it, but it's true. Marty's fluked his way back into the good books. Now, Young needs to get in touch with Jamieson urgently.

# 28

It hasn't been a long conversation. As short as the urgency demanded. Jamieson almost ran into the office to join Young.

'We're sure it's Calum?' he's asking. Pointless question.

'Here's the copy.'

Jamieson's looking at it. Frowning. He knew. That's what's pissing him off right now. He knew Calum wasn't happy. Knew he wasn't comfortable being part of an organization. His instincts told him they needed to do more to keep the boy happy. Persuade him that this is where he wants to be. Frank was comfortable; no interest in working alone. That made it easy for Jamieson. No persuasion necessary. Calum only knew the life of a freelancer when he came to work for them. There was always a chance it wouldn't work. As long as Jamieson spotted the problem first, he could do something about it. And he did spot it. Knew it all along. And he did nothing.

'How long's he had these?' Jamieson's asking. The question that matters most.

'His brother picked them up this morning. So, I don't know – a few hours. Could be long gone by now.'

Jamieson's nodding. Considering. Standing in Calum's

shoes, what would he do? Probably get out of the city today. Even if it's not far. Maybe Edinburgh, leave the country from there. That would make sense. How fast could he go? Could be gone already. The brother's the key. He's obviously been helping Calum. He organized the ID. Calum wouldn't use anyone else. His brother, and his brother alone. So Calum will be staying with him.

'We need to go to the brother,' Jamieson's saying. 'Send someone to watch his house. Don't go in. Not yet. Not until we know. If the brother has a garage, then he might be there. Worth checking that, too. Who do we have that can find out if a plane ticket was bought in this name?' he's asking. 'This Donald Tompkin.' Spitting out the name with contempt.

Young's considering it all. 'I'll send someone to watch the house. I'll go round to the garage myself, if the brother's there. Might be worth me having a conversation with him. Make it friendly to start; see if I can't persuade him to spill his guts. Maybe take someone with me.'

Jamieson's sighing. This is Young wanting to go round and beat the shit out of William. This is anger getting in the way of judgement.

'See if we can find out where Calum is first,' Jamieson's saying. 'There might be a chance for me to have a conversation with him. And the tickets – find out about the tickets.'

Young's nodding. 'Best bet will be a police contact. I'll get in touch with the reliable one. I'll see what he can find out. I'll check Calum's flat. I'll get someone round to the brother's house. That's the main thing.'

'Mm,' Jamieson's saying. Not the main thing for him. Main thing for him is that he might be about to lose another gunman. That just leaves Hutton. A man he knows nothing about professionally. His only experience of Hutton is as a man who's proven very adept at avoiding his work.

Young's out of the office, phone to his ear. The excitement of the moment. The anger of betrayal. All clouding his judgement a little. Get someone subtle to watch the brother's house. Calling George. He can hear the crushing disappointment in George's voice.

'Watch William's house? Why? What's he done? Maybe you should speak to Calum first.'

'It's Calum I want you to look for. Don't go in. Don't let them know you're there. Just keep your eyes open for any sign of him.'

'Calum,' George is saying. Not saying no. Can't say no. Not an option. But obviously reluctant. Willing to let Young hear his reluctance. Let the boss know that he doesn't believe in this job. That George trusts Calum. An empty gesture, but he'll still do it.

Young's opening a locked drawer in his own, little-used office downstairs. Finding the bunch of keys, and finding the one to Calum's flat. A pair of gloves from a box in the store-room. Out of the club and into the car. Driving round to the flat. Already knowing what he'll find. Still worth looking, when it's this easy. He can let himself in and look around. Parking, and going up the stairs to Calum's front door. There's nobody around. He's knocking on the door, just to be on the safe side. No answer. Of course there's no answer. Pulling on the gloves and slipping the key into the lock. Quickly inside and closing the door. Absolute care. One way or another, Calum's disappearing. Either the disappearance he wants, or the one Jamieson will order for him. A neighbour might report him gone. The police start sniffing around. They find out that a neighbour spotted a man coming to the flat days after Calum disappeared. This man had a key. That would get the police excited. Young needs to be invisible.

Flat looks normal. No sign of trouble. No furniture over-turned or drawers emptied. Looks like a flat that someone expects to return to. There's a mobile phone on the table. A little green light flashing on it. Presumably to say that there are missed messages. How long ago did he run? He did the job. Young knows that. Jesus, it was that night! Must have been. He used the Hardy and Kenny killings as a cover for his escape. Cold son of a bitch. Led them out there, did the job and then came back to his brother's. Knowing that Jamieson wouldn't expect to hear from him for at least a week. Smart bastard. A wallet in the kitchen, on the counter. Okay, that's convincing. Calum knew what he was doing when he went. Into the bedroom. Pulling open the wardrobe door. Looks full. Doesn't mean anything. He could be using his brother's clothes. His brother could have gone out and bought him new clothes. Back into the living room. Over to the writing desk. Pulling it open. There's a passport in there. A cheque book. Back out into the kitchen, opening the wallet. Two bank cards. Some cash.

Standing in the middle of the room, looking at the letters on the floor inside the front door. If Calum's run, then he's done it well. Covered every track. If only he didn't need new ID, he would have got away with it. But it is convincing. Convincing enough to make Young stop and wonder. Maybe he isn't running. Maybe he's dead. Maybe he went and did the job and died in the process. Maybe it's not Calum who's up to something. Maybe it's his brother. The brother finds out that Calum's dead and comes up with some dumb plan to cash in. No. They're not that sort. William wouldn't do it. This is Calum running. Can't be anything else. Out of the flat and down to the car. Calling George.

'Any sign of life at the brother's place?'

'No, nothing,' George is saying. 'Only been here for about twenty minutes, though.'

Could be somewhere else. No, if Calum's still in the city, then he's at his brother's house. Wouldn't risk going anywhere else. That's if he's still here.

Driving to William's garage. Doesn't know what he'll say to the brother. There's no time for pleasantries. Jamieson says he wants to talk to Calum, if there's a chance. Wishful thinking. Not going to happen. Young needs to find out what's happening. If the brother won't tell him willingly, then Young will make it happen. This is too much of a rush for the softly-softly approach. Pulling into the street where William's garage is. Finding a parking space. Walking along the street and into the garage. A couple of guys working on one car. They seem quite befuddled by it. Neither fits the description of William MacLean. One too young, one too old. No sign of anyone in the office towards the back.

'I'm looking for William MacLean. He about?' Young's asking. Keep it casual. Don't give them a reason to panic.

'Nah, you just missed him. He's away,' the older mechanic's saying. 'I help?'

Young's looking at his watch. 'Half-four. He always knock off at half-four?'

The older man's shrugging. 'No, he's a grafter,' he's saying defensively. He likes his boss. 'He nipped off early today.'

'Been nipping off a lot this week,' the younger one's saying, and shutting up when he sees the look his elder colleague is giving him.

Young didn't hang around. Just missed William. That could mean just about anything in mechanic-speak. Last time Young took his car in, they said the MOT wouldn't cost much. Two days and six hundred quid in repairs. His phone's ringing as he's walking back to his car.

'That's William just turned up at his house,' George is saying. Not sounding impressed at all. Here's another one who isn't happy in his work, Young's thinking. Another one they might have to keep an eye on.

'Keep watching the place,' Young's saying. 'Let me know if anyone else turns up or leaves.' Hanging up. Thinking. If Calum's in the city, then he's in that house with his brother. Leave George there for now. Young has one more avenue to run down.

# 29

They're sitting in silence. Not awkward silences any more, just silence. Brothers with nothing left to say. There are nerves there. Nerves and guilt and a whole load of other things. Plenty they could say, but don't want to. Going through the motions. Calum's watching TV. He knows that, months from now, when he's settled somewhere else and can't speak to William, he'll regret this. Regret that he didn't say any of the things that are going through his mind. But that regret won't prompt him to say it now. Say that he loves his brother. Tell William how grateful he is for this. For all the support he's got from him over the years. Tell him not to feel guilty. Nah, he'd never say that one. He knows that a lot of William's fear for Calum comes from the guilt. Maybe William doesn't even know it himself. So Calum won't say anything about it.

Must be more than eleven years ago now. William had been working at the garage for about a year. Just a mechanic, learning his way. No ownership then. But he knew enough to know that his boss was a crook. A lot of shifty types hanging around. William didn't make anything of it. No skin off his nose. He fixed cars. Occasionally sprayed them. Once in a blue moon he'd be given a car that needed a complete over-haul. Change every identifying feature. It's a job. It pays. He asked no questions, so knew nothing incriminating. Now and again Calum would come down to the garage, pick William up from work. He'd hang around, chat to the people there. Didn't bother William. So Calum talked to a bunch of scumbags. So what? He could do that anywhere. Not like he was all that close to his little brother at the time anyway.

It was a guy called Greg Lacock. Middle-aged guy. Chubby, but thought he was God's gift. Anyway, he was hanging around the garage a lot back then. He and the owner, Alasdair Marston, were chummy. Used to go to a lot of the same parties. They liked the good life. So one time, driving home, Calum announces that Lacock's offered him a job.

'Crappy stuff, but it might lead to more,' Calum said. William didn't argue. Lacock was a dealer, everyone knew it. The jobs would be shitty stuff. Driving him around, that sort of thing. If Lacock was willing to pay Calum for it, so be it. If William had said something then. If he had objected. Well, you can't see the future. You can't know where these things will lead.

It started out menial. Driving. Picking things up. Then it started to get more serious. Gradually. Lacock was growing. A lot of people didn't take him seriously, which was a mistake. A party boy with a big mouth. A guy in his forties who'd never amounted to anything. There was nothing to take seriously.

But there was more to him than mouth. He was working away, keeping his movements quiet. And he grew. And he became serious. Calum saw it all close up. Mentioned it to William a couple of times. William took almost no notice. Then there was a guy called Stan Austin. William had known him since school. Austin did some work for Lacock. Hard to remember now what it was he did that pissed Lacock off. Didn't steal from him. Just did some work for someone else to make a little extra cash. Something trivial like that. Lacock wasn't having it. Seemed to think it was a matter of respect. He sent someone round to beat Austin up. They did a thorough job.

A couple of days after he got out of hospital, Austin went round to the garage to see William. Seemed like a social visit. It wasn't. It was a warning. Get your little brother under control. He was the one who had beat up Austin. William didn't believe it at first. Calum was never tough. Never a fighter.

'He's a cold bastard is what he is,' Austin told him. 'Get him sorted, or he's gonna end up six feet under. Lacock's nuts. Someone will put a stop to him real soon. He'll drag everyone down with him.'

So William, having just moved out, went back to the family home to have a word with Calum. A warning. Calum was quiet. He denied it, but not with nearly enough vigour. William knew. His little brother was muscle. What a laugh!

Calum wasn't tough enough for muscle. William told him so. Told him he was biting off more than he could chew.

Then it was David Kirkpatrick. Calum remembers the night. Lacock calling him up, telling him to come round to his house. Telling him that Kirkpatrick was going to wipe them out. Put them all behind bars. Kirkpatrick was a dealer. Another scumbag.

'He's got us all in the shit. We have to stop him talking. You have to stop him, Calum. You'll go down with me. You don't want that. We have to get him.'

Calum sat there calmly. 'Okay' was all he said. He knew what Lacock was asking him to do. It didn't seem like a particularly big step.

'Good boy,' Lacock grinned. He was relieved – you could see it written all over him. He was scared of Kirkpatrick. He was probably lying about the reason why, but he was honestly scared. He provided Calum with a knife. Told him where Kirkpatrick was. He was getting pissed in some shitty pub. Follow him. Do the job. Get it done that night. No messing around. Best way to do it, so Lacock said.

The area around the pub was quiet. Calum couldn't go in. Couldn't be seen close to Kirkpatrick on the night. So he stood outside. Across a little car park and behind a wall. Crouching down every time a car went past. It was pissing with rain, all night. Easy to remember those details. The wetness. Watching people come and go from the pub. Never

Kirkpatrick. It was twenty past twelve when he came out. Calum always remembers that. Twenty past twelve. Kirkpatrick and two other guys. One of them said goodbye to the other two. Staggered off across the road and weaved his way along the pavement and out of sight. Kirkpatrick and the other fellow were making their way in the other direction. Calum watched them go. Waited. Nobody else on the street. Only the occasional car. Pick your moment. Follow Kirkpatrick until he's alone. What if he's not alone? Calum didn't even know if Kirkpatrick was married. Where he lived. Who he lived with. He was starting to realize how dangerous his ignorance was. You should not be learning on the job.

He stepped out from behind the wall. Let them get just out of sight, then caught them up. They were talking loudly. He can still remember that. Couldn't hear what they were saying. Just the voices. Two drunk men, talking merrily in the night. A taxi came along the street. The other guy waved it down. It stopped. Calum could see the other guy trying to persuade Kirkpatrick to get in with him. Kirkpatrick refusing. His mate got in, the taxi pulled away. Calum had to keep walking. Getting dangerously close to Kirkpatrick now. The taxi driver must have seen him as he pulled away and moved down the street. The mate was too pissed, but the driver must have seen. Kept it to himself, if he did. It was just Kirkpatrick and Calum on the street now. Hard to remember what buildings were around them. Closed shops. Brick walls. Dark and silent.

No houses, he remembers that. Kirkpatrick slowing down. Making a sort of growling noise. Looking left and right. Seeing a wide alleyway between two buildings. Lurching sideways towards it. Kirkpatrick going too slow. Calum with no choice but to walk right past him.

Slowing and looking back over his shoulder. Kirkpatrick disappearing into the alleyway. Shit, what's he up to? Calum wasn't in control of the situation. Not at all. He reached into his pocket, felt the handle of the knife. Turning back. Nobody else on the street. No cars. Maybe Kirkpatrick isn't that drunk after all. Maybe he's lying in wait, a gun in his hand. Nope. Standing facing the wall. Fumbling with his trousers. Didn't hear Calum approach behind him. Stood there, pissing happily against the wall. Calum walked silently up behind him. No hesitation. Get it done. Knife out of pocket. Almost slapping it into Kirkpatrick. A second time, into the back. Kirkpatrick slumped forward. Hit the wall. Fell forward. Ungainly. A mess of sodden limbs, crumpled against the wall. He has to be dead. Calum raising the knife. Into the side of the neck. If that's not enough, too bad. A need to leave. A desire to run. But he didn't. Knife back into the pocket. Walking out of the alleyway and along the street. Back to Lacock's house, then home.

There was so much wrong with it. With the hit. With the situation. So many mistakes. It was luck alone that kept Calum safe. Luck and a little bit of judgement. That night he saw Lacock's desperation. Saw him out of control. Never did another job for him. Went off the radar. A month later, Lacock was in jail. Charged with supplying class-A drugs. They figured him for the Kirkpatrick hit, but they couldn't prove it. Lacock never spoke about it. He went away for six years anyway. William crossed his fingers and hoped that was the end of it. Because he knew. He knew Calum had murdered Kirkpatrick. It had to be him. Lacock had nobody else to do it for him. It was Calum. Time passed, and it seemed like Calum was out of the business. Then a few rumours. Calum was doing work for people. Freelance. Good at what he does. And William went back to worrying.

But the guilt was there. Calum met Lacock at the garage. William had multiple chances to warn Calum off. To force him to back out. Ignored all of them because he didn't care enough. Didn't see the trouble coming. Misjudged his brother. Thought he was too good a human being to be caught up in that sort of thing. And he still feels the guilt, because he never did anything about it. Let it go on for years. Now there's a chance to help, and there's nothing he won't do for Calum. Nothing he won't do to help him get away. William will never come straight out and say it. He's sitting down opposite Calum with a cup of tea. Saying nothing at all. You don't speak about these things. You keep it all to yourself. You hope that the other person is smart enough to work it out for themselves. And Calum is. He knows. It doesn't need to be said. Should he say something to William? Tell him there's nothing to be guilty about. They were all Calum's choices. Nah. William's smart enough to know that, too.

# 30

Sending a text: *Come to flat NOW*. Hoping that his contact will see it and turn up in good time. Hoping he has his phone with him, wherever he is. Young's going straight to the flat. Parking along the street and going up. He'll be there first, waiting as usual. Thinking he ought to call Jamieson. And tell him what? No progress. No sign of Calum. He doesn't need to know that. Call him when you have something to say. Young's sitting with his head in his hands. He'll go back to the club after this meeting, because there's nowhere else to go. Nothing else he can do. You spend so long trying to pull strings, and one little thing screws it all up. Spent so long setting up this thing with Shug and MacArthur. It was perfect. Fisher doing all the hard work for them. Taking Shug out of the picture. Setting up a run at MacArthur. It was delayed by Frank. Now it could be ruined by Calum.

It's less than twenty minutes later when there's a knock on the door. Young's up and walking to the door. Looking through the peephole. PC Joseph Higgins. He looks nervous. He should. Young can't remember ever making an emergency call to the young cop. That'll unsettle the boy. If he works out what's happening, then he'll be much more unsettled. Calum running could spark any kind of trouble. A running gunman gets talkative, and that's dangerous for anyone with even the lightest connection to the organization. Young's opening the door, nodding for Higgins to come in. The cop's moving quickly. Trying not to look intimidated by this call, and failing. Going and taking his usual seat in the living room. Young's walking in behind him. Trying not to look exhausted by the whole bloody mess, and failing. Higgins can see it in him, and that makes the nerves worse.

'I came as soon as I got your message,' Higgins is saying. Trying to start on a positive.

'Good,' Young is nodding. 'Now, this might not be much of a big deal,' he's saying, aiming for casual and missing, 'but it is time-sensitive. That's what the hurry's about. I hate to have to drag you into this, but you're the only person I can trust to do this properly. It's not a complicated job. And there shouldn't be much risk for you, I don't think. But I can assure you, I won't forget this help from you.' Young thinking about the latest bullshit business venture he's sucked Higgins senior into. Get the father into debt, bail him out, keep the son grateful. Knowing that Higgins junior is thinking of the same thing.

'Okay' is all Higgins is saying in response.

'I just need you to find out if someone's left the country or not. See if they've booked an air ticket or train ticket. We're trying to get in touch with someone, and we can't find them. Running out of time, to be honest with you.'

Higgins is nodding. He knows he can check. Easy enough. All he needs is a reason why.

'Who's the person?'

'Donald Tompkin,' Young's saying. 'May have left the city in the last couple of hours, or may be leaving in the next twenty-four.'

Higgins is frowning slightly. Never heard of this Tompkin guy. Thought he'd recognize the name. A known criminal. Then he could pretend at the station that he's heard rumours about this guy being a target. Say that he's looking for him. If the guy then turns up dead, he can say he thought the fellow was in trouble. Didn't think it was anything as bad as that. Might look a little iffy that he was investigating the name alone, but explainable. Harder to explain when it's a name unknown to the police.

'Donald Tompkin. Don't know him,' Higgins is saying. Won't push it further than that. If Young doesn't want to say who he is, then Higgins won't ask. 'I can check for him, though.'

Higgins is getting up to leave. Young wants this done in a hurry, so you look like you're in a hurry. He's reached the front door, and he's stopping. Well, damn it all, doesn't he at least have the right to ask? This is his career. His safety. He's entitled to one question. One reasonable question. He's going back into the living room.

'Is there any danger that this Tompkin guy is going to turn up dead?' he's asking.

Young's looking at him. Couple of months ago, the boy wouldn't have dared. Would have just taken his instruction and carried it out. He's changing. Maturing maybe. Or getting harder. Bound to happen eventually. He's becoming used to being a contact. Starting to think he's entitled to ask questions. How long does it take them to become as hard as Paul Greig?

'There is absolutely no prospect of Donald Tompkin turning up dead,' Young's saying. 'It's not like that at all. You don't have to worry.'

Higgins has gone. Said he'd call in the next couple of hours. Young told him the truth about Tompkin. A man who doesn't exist can't turn up dead. A man who doesn't exist can still ruin your career. Can ruin everything, if he wants to. Young's giving Higgins a head start. Trying to think of something else he can do. Calling George.

'Anything?'

'Nothing. Nobody's come out since William went in.' A pause. 'Would it not be better for someone to go in there and find out what's going on?'

Stupid question, born of impatience. Born of loyalty to Calum. Young's getting frustrated. 'Just sit where you are and keep your eyes open. Anyone goes in or out, you tell me. No pissing about here.' Hanging up. Getting out of the flat and driving to the club. Relief to be in the car, focusing on the drive. Focus on anything that isn't this colossal fuck-up.

Up the stairs and through the snooker room. A room Jamieson has spent very little time in recently. Along the corridor and into the office. Jamieson sitting at his desk. Reading something, looking up at Young as he comes in. Young walking across the room and sitting on the couch.

'Any news?' Jamieson's asking.

'None useful. Brother left work early, went home. He's at the house now. It's being watched. Apparently the brother's been taking a lot of time off this week. I've got someone checking travel details for Donald Tompkin. I'm sure he hasn't gone yet. Sure of it.'

Jamieson's saying nothing. Shouldn't be sure of anything. Not yet. Not when they're in danger of falling into a river of shit. Calum's been a smart little bastard. Setting up his escape just after a job. Knows they won't be expecting to hear from him. This job in particular. Knows how distracted they're going to be. Such a shame. Smart and cold like that – he could have been brilliant.

They've been in near-total silence as they wait for Young's mobile to ring. It's dark outside. The club will be filling up. It's Friday night, so it'll be heaving with people down there. A long night and a loud one. People oblivious to what's going on above them. Wouldn't care anyway. As long as it doesn't get in their way. People just want to have a good time and be left alone. That's one valuable lesson Jamieson's learned over the years. Let people have their way and leave them to it, and they'll have nothing bad to say about you. It's been two hours since Young got back to the office. Nothing. This is taking longer than it should. Maybe Higgins has run into trouble. Jamieson's glancing across at Young, who's pretending to read a paper. How well does Young know these contacts of his? He thinks he can trust this Higgins character. Jamieson's never met the boy. Stop that. Stop thinking that way right now. You lose trust in your right-hand man and it's all fucked. There's enough people to doubt right now. John Young ain't one of them.

It's nearly ten o'clock when Young's mobile starts to ring. He's looking at the screen. Looking across to Jamieson and nodding before he answers.

'Hello. Uh-huh. Okay. That's excellent.' And hanging up. Keep the conversation as short as possible. 'Donald Tompkin is still with us. Has a plane ticket to London for tomorrow. Leaving from Edinburgh airport.'

Jamieson's frowning. 'Could be in Edinburgh already.'

'Nah,' Young's saying. 'He won't have left his brother's house. Not since the night he killed Kenny and Hardy. He'll be hiding there. Won't want anyone to see him. Won't take the risk. I'll bet his brother will give him a lift across to Edinburgh tomorrow. Flight's in the afternoon.' You can hear the enthusiasm in Young's voice. He feels as though they're back in control.

Jamieson's sitting at his desk and he's thinking. Plotting. Go with your gut. That's what he's always done. It got him a long way. Started to doubt his instinct lately. Started to doubt himself. Frank's fault. And Kenny's, to a lesser extent. You let people get close to you, and they let you down. How can you trust yourself after that? Because you have to, is the short and simplistic answer. His gut tells him that Calum's finished. Common sense tells him the same thing. So it's unanimous. They have to find Calum. And they have to kill him. There's no other way out. No other punishment will do. They can't take him back. That's what Jamieson had hoped for, but he can see now it's not going to happen. Once a gunman tries to get away, you have to stop them altogether. He tries once, and he'll try again. He's not happy now, and he's never going to be. So Jamieson knows exactly what they're going to do.

'We need to get him out of the house and away from his brother,' Jamieson's saying. 'Going to have to do it tomorrow morning.'

# 31

William's leaving the house early. Going to head in to the garage and spend an hour or two there. Should probably be with his brother, but it's too tense. Besides, he's going to drive Calum across to Edinburgh later this morning. There'll be plenty of time for goodbyes then. Calum has said they'll stay in touch. Might be a while before he's able, but he'll make it happen.

'When I've settled somewhere, established my new ID, I'll be in touch. I'm not going to suddenly forget that you're my brother,' Calum told him. Won't forget what William's done for him, either. Didn't say that. Didn't need to.

Nice to be out of the house, William's thinking now. Nice to get to the garage and focus on work for a little while. Make sure that nothing indescribably stupid has happened in his absence. He's driving away from the house. Didn't stop and check for any sign he was being followed. Getting blasé about it now.

If he'd stopped to look, he might have seen George. Exhausted George, sitting in the car. He fell asleep last night. Should have been watching the house, and he fell asleep for more than two hours. Unprofessional. But he is only human.

He's calling Young now, telling him that William's left the house by himself.

'Should I follow him?'

A long pause. The long pause of a bad decision being made. 'No. Stay where you are. Keep an eye out for Calum. If he leaves the house, then you follow him. Otherwise, stay where you are.' It wasn't supposed to be this way. It was going to be George who followed William. George who delivered William's punishment. But Young's changed his mind. A lack of trust. George is too close to Calum. Wouldn't deliver the punishment that must be delivered. He'd let William off the hook. William MacLean knew what he was doing. Knew the risk he was taking. Now he has to pay for that.

Young's calling Shaun Hutton. Hutton is still going to deliver Calum's punishment. The only man they have who can. First, he's going to deal with William. Young's telling him what to do. Where to draw the line. Hutton doesn't sound enthusiastic. Thinks this sort of thing beneath him. He's a gunman, not muscle. Maybe Young should have gone with George after all. No, too late.

'Go round to his garage,' Young's saying. 'He might be there. If not, let us know.'

Was that the right move? Jamieson will be pissed off. He wanted George to handle the brother. Jamieson likes George. Thinks he has talent, which he does. Been making a point of getting George involved, meeting personally with him.

Thinks the lad has brains, which he does. But none of that matters if you don't have trust. George is too close to Calum.

Hutton's sitting outside the garage. He's seen the man he thinks is William. It's turning into a lovely day. Bright sunshine. Sent round to punish a guy in the daylight. Yeah, like that's ever a good idea. This whole Jamieson organization is starting to seem like a mess. Feels like they only have shitty jobs for a man to do. Maybe crossing over was a mistake. Maybe he should just have ducked out. Lie low for a while, then find work freelance. Too late. Can't get off a horse halfway through a race. Not without taking a painful tumble. So he's watching William MacLean. Coming out of the garage and looking at a car parked on the street. Trying to look under it. Looking at a sheet of paper he has in his hand. Seems like something doesn't add up. Shaking his head slightly and going back into the garage. No sign of anyone else. Saturday morning. The other mechanics won't be there. Just the boss coming in for a little work. Close those garage doors and it'll be just the two of them.

William's been in there a while. Still no sign of anyone else. Hutton's getting out of his car. No time like the present. Young told him to be quick about it. Locking the car and walking up to the entrance. Feels weird, doing a job in the daytime. Out in the open like this. Not a hit, which justifies the lack of caution. Still doesn't feel right. He's stepping inside the large doors, looking around. Gloomy in here.

Nobody moving about. One car up on the ramp on the right-hand side of the garage, another two parked close together at the back. There's what looks like a little cabin at the back, windows overlooking the garage floor. A light on there. Hutton's tall enough to see the top of someone's head, sitting at the desk in the office. That would be our target. Hutton's turning and pulling shut the garage doors. They slide across. Slow and loud, but he's reached the point where stealth doesn't matter.

William doesn't think anything of the scraping noise. Heard it a million times before. Hardly registers that it's the garage doors closing. It's the reduction in sunlight. Always dark at the back of the garage, that's why he needs the light on all the time. Still, you notice when the little sunlight there is disappears. He's craning his neck to look out the window and into the garage. He can see a figure closing the doors, but not who it is. He's getting up, angry at first, then nervous. Could be a cop. William's coming down the few wooden steps to the garage floor. Walking towards the man who's approaching him. William's about to say something. Something that shows his annoyance, but not something that pisses off a cop. Play nice. If they ask about Calum, play dumb. The man's reached him. Big fellow. The only light is coming from the office. Just enough to see the man. Just enough to see that he isn't a cop.

It's obvious to Hutton that William doesn't know who he

is. Recognition is one of the things you learn to look for. Hutton's bigger than William, which will help. Doesn't know the surroundings so well, which won't. Means he has to make the first move. Press home that size advantage as early as possible.

'What do you want?' William's asking.

He's expecting an answer. You play on the expectations of others. That's why Hutton's lashing out. A firm punch. Not all his weight behind him. Wants to knock William on his arse, doesn't want to break his hand in the process. William's going over hard. Didn't see it coming – that's the point. Now Hutton wants to finish this fast. Keep him down. Looking around for weapons. Nothing nearby. All the tools carefully packed away on the other side of the garage. Never mind. Getting him down early makes a weapon unnecessary.

Doesn't even know what William's done. Never done a beating before. Still feeling the tension of crossing over. Got caught with a loser in Shug. Now crossed over to what feels like a struggling organization. Feeling concerned about his future. He punishes the brother, and he'll have to handle Calum as well. Like he's the only person Jamieson has. What sort of organization only has one guy to do all this? Put all those concerns together and it might explain what's happening now. Might explain the state of Hutton's mind. Taking a step closer to William. William's moving as though to get up. Slowly, on his knees and elbows. Head still bowed to the floor. Hutton towering over him, fists clenched. Waiting for William to raise his head. Seconds passing. William finally raising his head. Now Hutton's moving. Moving while his anger is high. Moving before he can think better of it.

Kicking William. Kicking him repeatedly. Going for the head. Kicking with all his weight. Eight times. Nine times. Ten. Stopping. Panting a little. Not in great shape. Glaring down at William in the gloom. No movement from him. Lying on his side. Impossible to see his face. His reaction. Hutton missed with a bunch of those kicks. Just glancing blows. But he caught at least half of them hard. Hutton's bending over, looking for a response. A rasping breath from William. Catches Hutton by surprise. Makes him take a step backwards. It sounds like a provocation. Any sound puncturing this silence does. Hutton kicking him in the stomach. Then again, and again. Stopping now, and taking a step backwards. No sound coming from William. No movement.

Hutton can't get a good look at him in this light. Can't see the damage. Boy's not moving, though, so that means stop. The punishment given. The message sent. Hutton's never done muscle-work in his life. Every part of this felt bad. Reckless. Too close. Too personal. Another look around the garage, taking a few steps towards the office at the back. Nobody there. Fine, now leave. Out towards the doors. Pulling one slightly open, stepping out. Nobody on the street. Nobody to see him leave. Pulling the door shut behind him.

Makes the garage look like it's all closed up. Saturday morning. Believable. Nobody's going to go poking around in there for a while. Not until William crawls his way out. If he does. Now Hutton's worrying that he went too far. It was a message, not a hit.

Hutton's along to his car. Opening the door, dropping into the driver's seat. Looking down and seeing blood on his brown hiking boot. William's, obviously. Must have burst a nose or a lip. No big deal. Plenty of bust noses in this city. Driving away. Finding it a little difficult to focus. Nervous. That's weird. More nervous driving away from this job than he ever is driving away from a hit. Fear doesn't come from the scale of the crime, it comes from the quality. He's back home when he calls Young. 'It's done,' Hutton's telling him. Waiting to hear that he can relax.

'Good. Sit tight, stay where I can get in touch with you. You might have a big job very soon. Next twenty-four hours.' And Young's hung up.

Hutton's slumping into a chair. Another job in twenty-four hours. Calling it a big one. Sounds like the Calum hit. Two jobs in a day. Crossing over really does feel like a big mistake now.

# 32

This was Young's idea. Jamieson doesn't want to meet Deana Burke. A traitor's woman. A woman who knew what her man was up to. Frankly, she has no right asking for their help. Jamieson thinks she has a brass neck you couldn't mark with a fucking blowtorch. But he can see the benefit of playing her. Young's got her set up nicely. She's in contact with Fisher, and Young and Nate Colgan have persuaded her that Shug was responsible for what happened to Kenny. So they play her and she helps them get what they want. Blindly feeding misinformation back to Fisher. But it doesn't mean he's going to enjoy this. She's due at the club in ten minutes. He called her, spoke to her. Told her how concerned he was. Concerned about what happened to Kenny. About what might happen to her. Told her he wanted to do whatever he could to help. Asked her to come round. Said he thought it might benefit them both to talk face-to-face.

He's taking a small glass of whiskey. Just a small one. It'll help him to control his temper with her. When she comes in here and starts playing the grieving widow. Starts saying what a tragedy it was. At some point she'll say what a good man Kenny was, and Jamieson will have to agree. Pouring a second glass. Going to need it. Can't say what a good man Kenny was without sounding sarcastic. Not stone-cold sober anyway. Not in this mood. Might have been able to, if it wasn't for Calum. Another little bastard. Couple of glasses might not be enough. No more – if he takes a third he'll get a dirty look from John Young. Make sure he can speak soberly. She has to find him convincing. He has to be the tough but tender boss of a major organization. Has to convince her he's a man to listen to. Persuade her, so that you don't have to force her.

She's early. Of course she is. Kenny's woman was never going to be anything less than a royal pain in the arse. Young's gone downstairs to meet her at the door, bring her up. Show her some sympathy. He's good at that sort of thing. He'll be leading her through the snooker room, down the corridor to the office. She'll be getting herself ready for a performance. That's what it is, Jamieson thinks. A performance. She can't really care this much. Or can she? Maybe she actually did love the back-stabbing little piece of shit. More fool her, if she did. But she probably didn't. Young's gone through her back-story with Jamieson. The guys she was with before Kenny. All in the business. No, not love. Convenience. She wanted a man in the business. Someone making reasonable money. Someone who could give her a comfortable life. She just picked the wrong someone this time.

The office door's opening. Young holding it open for

Deana Burke to enter. She's wearing a tight black skirt, thin grey cardigan over a black top. With her dark hair tied back and minimal make-up, she's making a good job of looking bereft. Also making a good job of looking appealing. Jamieson's on his feet and walking towards her. How the hell Kenny McBride managed to get this woman to live with him is anyone's guess. She looks hard, but pretty. Thirty-four, Young said she was. Looks a little younger. Doesn't look girlish, but that's a good thing. She must be a complete idiot. That's what Jamieson's thinking to himself as he's walking towards her. No way a woman like her in a business like this goes with a guy like Kenny unless she's plain dumb. She could do so much better. If she was smart, she would know that.

He's reaching down a little and hugging her. Not tight, doesn't want her to think he's making a play. Taking a step back.

'Deana. It's good to see you. I wish it were under different circumstances. Please, come and sit down. There's a lot we should talk about.'

She's walking across to the couch with him. Trying to look demure, but making a piss-poor job of it. She has too much self-confidence to look retiring.

'I was glad you called,' she's saying. 'It's important to me that I know what happened to Kenny. And it's important to me that I know something is done about it.'

Quite a harsh voice, but she sounds bright. Kenny must have been a man of hidden talents.

'And that's what I want to talk to you about. I know this must be incredibly difficult for you. I think you probably know now that Kenny's dead,' he's saying, looking her straight in the eye. 'It can be hard to accept that without a body. Without a funeral. But we know from contacts that Shug organized the killing. We can't confirm the killing. Only the killer could do that, and we haven't got to him yet. But we can assume it happened. With that in mind, we now have to move on quickly and aggressively. And I believe you can help us there.'

She likes what she's hearing. Likes the tone. He's laying the business detail out for her. Not holding back on the fact that Kenny is dead. Not trying to spread false hope. But he's offering her the revenge she craves.

'And I want to help.' Say nothing more. Don't throw yourself at the situation. People like Jamieson will use you if you let them. They'll push you further than you want to go. She won't get emotional either, because that's not who she is.

'We haven't got to the killer yet,' Jamieson's saying, 'but we believe we know who he is. I don't know if you've heard of Des Collins?'

She's thinking about it. Trying to remember if Kenny ever mentioned such a person. 'No, I don't think so.'

'Well, he's a gunman. We believe he's the gunman who killed Kenny.'

He's letting that sit for a few seconds. Let the name of Des Collins settle in her consciousness before he mentions anyone else. And Jamieson's still trying to figure out her motivations. Maybe it *is* justice, of a sort. Hard to see how she thinks she can make any money out of this – unless she's just that smart. Jesus, surely not. If she is, then she's a remarkable woman. If she worked out what Jamieson and Young would try to do and played them. Let them have their way, knowing a financial offer would eventually be part of it. Let them feed info through her. Nah, she couldn't have worked that out. And if she had, she still wouldn't take the risk. Not after what Kenny did. But it's a hell of a thought, isn't it? That she worked out what they would do before they knew it themselves. Played along, waiting patiently for the pay-off that's about to be offered for the help she's given them.

'Kenny didn't mention that anyone was in touch with him, did he?' Jamieson's asking. 'Anyone that might have been working for Shug. Pretending they were someone else.'

'Not that I know,' she's saying with a shake of the head. 'Why? Was someone?'

'We don't know, but it might have been something they did. We've found it very difficult to work out where they picked Kenny up that night. Somewhere between him dropping off . . . his colleague, and getting home. You see, they did a job that night. Not a big one, in all honesty. Just starting something. It needed a driver who knew the area. It wasn't an especially big deal in itself, but the target was bigger than usual. You see, Shug has an alliance with Alex MacArthur. You've heard of MacArthur?'

'Yes, of course.' Everyone's heard of MacArthur.

'Well, Shug's gone under his wing for protection. The job Kenny was working on that night was pretty insignificant, except for that the fact that it was against MacArthur. Well, Shug and MacArthur.'

He said it in such a contrite way. Impossible for her not to realize what he's implying. Saying that Shug killed Kenny because of that job. That it wasn't random. They didn't just go for him because he worked for Jamieson. They went for him because of that specific job Jamieson sent him on. She's nodding slightly, not realizing she's doing it. It makes more sense. Makes it more certain, somehow.

'So what happens next?' she's asking.

'Collins has gone to ground,' Jamieson's saying. 'Gunmen do, after a job. Our job is to find him. When we do, well, you can probably work the rest out. We will punish him for what he did. But he's only part of this. Shug and MacArthur, they can't go to ground. They have to be visible or they lose everything. That's where you can play a role. I want you to go to the police and report Kenny missing. We already know there's a detective looking for him – guy called Fisher.

235

Try and talk to him, if you can. Point him in the direction of Collins. He'll find his own way to Shug and MacArthur from there. The police pressure on them will give us our opportunity.'

Young's sitting on the chair three feet away, stifling a smile. Jamieson is good. Damned good. He can go long spells without seemingly making any impact on the running of his own organization. Then the time comes for someone to step up. To deliver something difficult. He's always the man for the job. Always. He was so convincing about Fisher. Has been so convincing about Kenny. Good actors are dangerous. Now comes the money part.

'Listen, Deana, I want to talk to you about something sensitive,' Jamieson's saying. 'More so.' Said with a smile, a hand gently across the back of her hand to stop her getting up. She thought this was over. 'I know losing Kenny must have been a shock to you. I can't even imagine how you're coping so well. But there is going to be an issue with money. I know that you and he weren't married, and I'm concerned that might complicate things for you. I know you'll be reluctant, but I want you to accept a payment from us. Not a loan, and not charity. Don't think of it like that. Kenny was working for us. If he hadn't been, he would still be alive today. That's worth something to me. And it's important to me that you accept it.'

She's gone now. Sashaying out of the office. They didn't discuss numbers, but she accepted the offer. She put up a little token resistance at first, as good form dictates. But she took it. She was always going to take it. She won't get the money until after her meeting with Fisher. It's payment for telling Fisher what Jamieson wants him to hear, and she must know it. Young's coming back into the office after escorting her out.

'Went well, I thought,' he's saying when the door's shut. 'She'll definitely take Collins and MacArthur to Fisher.'

'Uh-huh,' Jamieson's nodding. Not looking terribly convinced.

'What's up?'

'She's a lot smarter than she's let on. Letting people think of her as the wee woman, out for revenge. It's bullshit. She might not think we killed Kenny, but she knows not to trust us. Oh, she's sharp enough. We need to watch her closely.'

'Not for long,' Young's saying. 'We're nearly done. Shug will be done inside the day. We're halfway through this Calum thing. It's going to work out fine.'

Jamieson's looking at him, raising an eyebrow. Saying nothing. If you have nothing polite to say, say nothing.

# 33

He has his single bag packed and sitting on the kitchen table. Been sitting there for the last forty-five minutes. William should have been back half an hour ago. Pick Calum up, drive him across to Edinburgh. Calum's printed out his boarding pass. It's in the side pocket of the bag. All he needs is his brother to drive him across. Sitting there, tapping the table. He phoned his brother's mobile twice, got no response. Called the garage, and no answer. Doesn't have his own mobile to use, only the house phone. Can't text him. Maybe William's driving. On his way back to the house, can't pull over and answer his phone. That's no excuse for how late he is. He knows what time he needed to be home. He said it himself when he went out. Calum doesn't want to think the worst, but there isn't much room for anything else.

Calling the garage one last time. Nothing. Calling William's mobile one last time. Nothing. Now his attitude is changing. Assume the worst. Treat everything from this point onwards as a job. Get that focus. They know – Jamieson and Young have found out. They've done something to William. Maybe just holding him. Or maybe beating him. Maybe even killing him. A flash of anger. Targeting William, just to get at

Calum. To lure him out. Calum's moving over to the window, looking out into the street. No sign of anyone there, but someone will be there. Someone watching and waiting. Waiting for the message that William's been punished. When they know the older brother isn't coming back, they'll go in and get Calum. They'll use Hutton. There's nobody else. Hutton will be nervous. He knows how dangerous Calum will be. Knows what happened to the last man who tried to kill him.

One more phone call. Calling a taxi firm he knows has no connection to Jamieson. Telling them where to pick him up and where he wants to go. Looking at his watch. He wanted to get to the airport early. Get through security and settle down on the other side. He could get the taxi to take him all the way through to Edinburgh. Would cost a fortune, but he could get away. They're not going to force a taxi off the road. They're not going to try to hit him in an airport, with all the security there. This could be his one chance at a getaway. When you know they're on to you, run. That's obvious. Don't consider anything else. Just run. If you stay around, chances are they get you. Put yourself first. Be selfish. Take the one chance you have to get away. If they have William, then that's too bad for William. He knew the risks.

A car blowing the horn outside. Calum over to the window, looking out. A taxi, driver craning his neck to see the front door. Calum's picking up his bag, slipping the strap over his head. Pausing, just briefly. Flee the city. Leave his brother in all sorts of trouble. Or go to the garage and check. If he finds nothing there, then he'll have to go to the airport anyway. No time to hang around. He's sighing. This shouldn't be a difficult decision. He should put his brother first. But he never has before. Never put anyone other than himself first. The joy of being a gunman. The isolation justifies selfishness. He's at the front door, pulling it open to let the driver see that he's there. Stepping out and stopping. He's making it look like he's locking the door, but he doesn't have a key. He's looking up and down the street. Can't see anything obviously out of place. He will, though. When the taxi starts moving, he'll see anyone who follows, because he'll know what to look for.

He's dropping into the back of the taxi.

'East end, is it, mate?' the driver's asking him.

A pause. This is the chance to change your mind. To leave William to his fate and go your own way. But he can't. He might be selfish, but he's still William's brother. The least he owes William is to go to the garage and check. 'That's right,' Calum's saying. The car's pulling out and getting to the end of the street. Calum's looking back over his shoulder. There's a car at the other end of the road. He can just see it as the taxi starts to turn. Its nose is edging out from its parking spot. The watcher, following. Calum's making a point of not looking over his shoulder too often. Don't spook the driver. Get to the garage; decide your next move from there. Another thought.

They're luring you to the garage. Hold the brother, so that the target comes looking. It's a good place to carry out a hit. No. They would only know that Calum's waiting for William if William told them so. And he wouldn't tell. Not ever.

Driving through the city. Occasional backward glances, making sure the following car is still there. Could be a gunman tracking him. Could just be a watcher, gathering information for the gunman. The gunman will be Hutton. Has to be. Calum's thinking. Thinking that he's tempted to go round to Barry Fairly's house and punish him for his disloyalty. It must have been him. He grassed. You know what happens to a grass. So Jamieson and Young know the new ID. Can they find out what plane ticket he has booked in that name? Course they can. So they know when he plans to leave. They know his brother's been helping him. Easy to guess that William's going to take him to the airport. Lure him to the garage.

Another look over his shoulder. Car's still there, but it's a long way back in the traffic. Can't make out the driver from here. Doesn't recognize the car. It'll be a company car. Designed to be unrecognizable. Thinking again. They won't be luring him to the garage, because they couldn't rely on him to turn up. They know what sort of person he is. Or, they should. They must know that he would be prepared to leave his brother and run.

They're close now. Calum can recognize some of the buildings.

'Next left,' he's telling the driver, 'the garage is halfway along on the left-hand side.' Make a judgement. Tell the driver to wait, or let him go. Might as well let him go. If William's there and there's nothing wrong, he can get a lift from his brother. If it's a set-up, then the driver isn't going to be any use. He'll drive away at the first sign of trouble, preferably without Calum aboard. He's pulling up outside the garage now. Calum's looking up and down the street. He can see William's car, parked right in front of the entrance. That looks like a lure. He's fishing in his pocket, getting money out for the driver. Stepping out of the car, looking along the street again. Nobody parked there that he wouldn't expect to see. Not a lot of action on the street. Never is. Few businesses left here. Little activity. Looking at the doors of the garage. Pulled tight shut. That's not right. Obviously not right. If William was working in there, as his car suggests he was, then the doors should be open, at least a little.

There are two ways of playing the situation that Calum's in. The subtle way, and the sledgehammer way. From where Calum's standing, the subtle way looks like a waste of time. They know he's running and they're making moves against him. They must know that he'll work out what they're up to. Playing subtle achieves nothing. Can't trick them, when they know more than he does. So you go down the sledgehammer route. You go aggressive, confrontational, none too subtle. You let them know that they're in a bloody great big fight. Let the bastards know that if they want to take you down, they're going to have to work for it. Few people can play that part well. Most aren't intimidating enough. Calum is one of the few who is. They know how dangerous he can be. They will fear him. And he will give them good reason to.

Watching the blue car coming along the street. He's hanging back beside William's car, not letting the driver get a good look at him. Now he's running. Out onto the street, into the path of the other car. He won't give them time to run him over; the car's still far enough away for Calum to pull back. But they will know that he's spotted them. And he will see who the driver is. Know your enemy. Nothing more important than that. He's expecting the car to accelerate, but it isn't. It's slowing down, the driver watching Calum. Fear, but friendship too. Calum's staring at him. It's George. Standing on the road in this quiet industrial area. Watching his friend follow him. His friend setting a trap. If George is following him, then surely Hutton's inside. Waiting for the prey to turn up like a simple-minded weakling. Walking in and letting them kill him. He's getting angry with George. He doesn't expect much from his friends, not in this business. But he hoped for more than this. And as the car creeps forward, Calum isn't moving. Too pissed off. Too defiant.

George is pulling over to the side of the road. He's not going to run Calum down. Knows better than to pick a fight with Calum MacLean. That's not a fight George has any prospect of winning. Not that he couldn't beat Calum up. Of course he could – that's where George's prowess lies. But he wouldn't go any further than that. He would beat Calum, but he would never kill him. George isn't naive. He knows that, if he had to, Calum would kill him and not give it a second thought. There's a line in the sand that George is unwilling to cross. Calum has no lines; no moral boundaries. He can switch those thoughts and emotions off. Accordingly, he can always survive. George cannot. So George is pulling over and switching off the engine. Getting out of the car and taking a few steps towards Calum. Raising his hands. Calum will know that George isn't armed. George can't be so sure about Calum.

'So what is this,' Calum's asking, 'a set-up? You got Hutton in there waiting for me?'

'No,' George is saying, shaking his head. 'This isn't anything. I swear, Calum. I was sent to watch your brother's house. I was told you were in there, and to report if you moved. That was it. I don't know what else is going on. I wish I fucking did. I don't even know what I'm following you for, but I know it's serious. The hell is going on here, Cal?'

Sounds genuine. Doesn't mean this isn't a set-up, just that George doesn't know about it. That would be a smart move. Keep George in the dark. Too close to the target to be trusted with the truth. 'I'm leaving,' Calum's saying. 'They know. William's been helping me, and now I can't find him.'

'You're leaving?' George is saying. There's real shock there. He understands what that means. Understands the consequences.

Calum's ignoring him. Walking to the door, pulling it slightly open and then stepping quickly back. No sound from inside. Stepping back to the door. George standing watching him, unsure what he should do.

'I'll go in first,' he's saying suddenly. Calum's turning and looking at him. About to say something and stopping, because George is marching towards the door. No arguments, George is going in first. Stepping up to the door, glancing quickly in. Can't see much in the gloom. Ducking inside, out of view. No movement. George knows what to look for. He's stalked about in the darkness before. Don't look for shapes. Look for movements and look for colours. Any movement is a threat. Any colour that stands out. Silver is usually a good one, but not so much in a garage. And listen. Always listen. Can't see or hear anything that shouldn't be there. Place seems empty. He can hear Calum step in behind him. The flick of a light switch and the place is transformed.

'Oh Jesus, Calum, get over here.'

# 34

He had another phone call from Don Park about an hour ago. That was good. Calmed him a little. Shug's been getting worried. Things aren't happening. This needs to be fast or the chance passes him by. Don told him to stop worrying. Things are happening. They should have the info for a set-up on John Young in the next forty-eight hours. Takes a little time to get these things organized. Made Shug feel a little daft, if we're being honest. He's been worrying too much. Needs to calm down.

He called Greig in yesterday morning and gave him a dressing-down. Taking too long to come up with details. Accused Greig of not trying. Told him there would be a price for his disloyalty. Meant it, too. Don calmed him down. That's because he's a pro. He and MacArthur have too much invested in this to back out now. Things always start slow as you gather info. But moves are being made against top people in the Jamieson organization. Greig's different. He's not pulling his weight. Chickening out. Or trying to switch sides. Either way, there will be a price to pay.

Now Shug's phone's ringing again. Mobile this time. Looking at the screen. Tony O'Connor. Runs one of the garages on the south side. Good guy. Runs the garage well. This'll be a call about something trivial. Tony might be good at what he does, but what he does doesn't matter to Shug right now. He's answering anyway. If he doesn't deal with it now, Tony will keep calling.

'Yeah, Tony,' he's saying. Sounding a little exasperated. Usually better at hiding it.

'Hi, Shug. Listen, I just heard something that's got me worried. Got a couple of the boys here worried, too. I called Fizzy, but his phone rang through to voicemail. Called his house and there was no one there. I don't like to bother you, but . . .'

'But?' More exasperation. If this is a call about Fizzy being hard to find, then he will really lose his temper.

Tony's spotted the annoyance in Shug. Unusual and obvious. Going more carefully now. 'Someone came into the garage talking about Richard Hardy. Said he's gone missing. Said the police are treating it as possible murder. Been gone for days. Now I don't know, might be bollocks. But the guy who told me's mother is neighbour to some old bird who works across the hall from Hardy. Said the police have been all over the place. He hasn't been seen for days. I know he does our books. See, thing is, I need my pay at the end of the month. I got bills, Shug.'

Silence. Thoughts running through his head. If Hardy's gone AWOL, then the boys won't be paid on time. Hardy releases the money. Checks who's been hired and fired. Who's done what. It's all in the records from the individual garages, but he's the one who goes through them. Hides the discrepancies. No Hardy, no wages.

'Yeah, listen, it's not a big deal,' Shug's saying, pulling himself together after a brief delay. He has to send the right message here. Can't have panic in the ranks. 'I know where Hardy is. It's not a big deal. Don't worry about it. But, Tony, keep it under your hat. I don't want people pissing their pants for no reason, okay.'

'Sure, sure, as long as you know what's going on, Shug. I was just a bit concerned, that's all. We all got mortgages and stuff, you know.' Like Shug's so detached from reality.

'Don't worry.'

Conversation over. Learned two things from it. One is that Tony has money troubles. Doesn't much care about that. There was a day he would have cared. Tony's a friend. A trusted guy. Good worker. In the past, Shug would have gone round to the garage and spoken to Tony. Got the truth from him and helped him out financially. Not now. Now Tony's a part of the small-time past. Now he doesn't matter.

The second thing he learned from the conversation matters to him. Matters a lot. Hardy's gone. Where the hell has Hardy gone? Gone for days. Treated as murder. Jamieson – has to be. Who else would target Shug's moneyman? There's no other logical answer. Jamieson's gone after his money-

248

man. Waited till the end of the month. Killed him off and left Shug with a bunch of employees getting no pay. Shit! The police. They'll be all over Hardy's office. Old bastard had all the details there: every last trick he pulled to help Shug. If they're half as smart as they think they are, the police will be able to unravel his entire business. He's up and walking round in a circle. He needs help. Can't handle this one alone. Calling Don Park. Waiting and waiting. Shit, can't get through. Said he'd be busy for the rest of the day. Getting more things set up.

Standing in the middle of the room and taking a deep breath. Okay. Priority: get information. The stuff that matters. Find out what the police know. How far along are they with their investigation? Find out if they have charges ready for anyone. Now he wishes he hadn't shouted at Greig. Going to have to go to him. Doesn't know any other coppers. Fizzy always said they should get another one. Someone more reliable. Someone they can trust. Well, Fizzy should have done that then, shouldn't he? Second in command and he did fuck-all about it. Now all they have is Greig. Shug's calling him. Gone straight through to voicemail. Bastard! Dodging calls. He's chicken shit, that's what it is. He took on the responsibility of working for Shug and now he can't handle it. He'll pay for it. He bloody will.

Now where does he turn? Trying Don again. Still nothing. Not unexpected. He's doing important work. Besides, might be wrong to call him. Makes it look like Shug can't handle this sort of thing for himself. Makes him look incapable. A man who built the only meaningful car-ring in the city. Who has a large, legit business. Of course he can handle this himself. He just needs to think. Think – come on! It shouldn't be this hard. And he's lashing out. Kicking the couch, for all the good it does. Now stopping and thinking. If you can't use Greig, who do you use? Maybe the police angle is the wrong way to go. Maybe the Jamieson angle is better. Who does he have that would know anything about Jamieson? Ha, that's a laugh. Nobody. Not a soul. Don would, but he's out of the picture today. Hutton maybe? No. Knows nothing, and he's busy with Fizzy. Who knows about Hardy? Fizzy.

Calling Fizzy's mobile. It's ringing and ringing before switching to voicemail. Calling the house. Ringing and ringing. Tony said he tried and couldn't get through. So Fizzy isn't answering to anyone. Could be dead already. Might be that Hutton's got to him. That's the risk you take when you move against an enemy – you get them too fast. Get them when they're still useful to you. Or Fizzy could be in hiding. Ignoring calls from Shug, because he's running. Running to whom? Might go to Jamieson. That makes getting rid of him all the more important. Maybe that's who Greig's running to as well. And Shug's smiling, because this is starting to add up. Greig and Fizzy both running for cover. Weaklings, running to a big man to protect them. Well, they'll both pay the price for that.

He needs to find out if Hutton's done the job yet. Needs to tell him what job is coming next.

Calling Hutton. He should answer the phone to his boss. Even if it's against protocol, he should answer. Straight through to voicemail. Oh, come on. Hutton too? That's just too much. Way too much. No coincidence here. Not a chance. Hutton's in on it. He's a part of this. All of them crossing to Jamieson. A gunman – that makes matters much more dangerous than Shug anticipated. Calling Don again. Never mind how it looks, this is too important. Don Park is one of MacArthur's main men. He can sort this out. He has the power and the connections. Ringing, but no answer. And now he's realizing how big the problem could be. Don Park could be a part of it. Alex MacArthur. It's not Jamieson they've run to, it's MacArthur. Shug's isolated. Completely alone against Jamieson. All because of MacArthur. Now he's throwing the phone against the wall. Kicking the chair and the computer desk and the couch again. Wanting to lash out, because he wants to see someone else suffer as much as he's suffering right now.

# 35

They've spent days on it, and they're coming up short. Not on the money side. There will be a multitude of charges against many of Richard Hardy's clients. Most of them don't matter a bit to Fisher. Ragtag bunch of arseholes and no-hopers. The one who matters is Shug Francis. There will be charges against him, too, but the ones that matter aren't among them. Charging him for financial crimes isn't enough. Doesn't send the right message. Might have seemed clever at one point, when Shug was smaller. Now Fisher wants murder charges. Doesn't have them. He's convinced that Shug killed Hardy. Convinced he killed Kenny McBride as well. You need more. You have to be able to prove beyond reasonable doubt. Show motive and opportunity. Show that there is no alternative. Plenty of motive. Plenty of opportunity. There are alternatives, but they're becoming less convincing. Peter Jamieson is the obvious one. No evidence there. Jesus, it just takes one clincher.

The office is quiet around him. The evening shift has come in now. They were warned on their way in: Fisher's in a foul mood. They knew his good mood wouldn't last. The guy's been losing it these last few months. Hasn't closed a single case. People are starting to talk about him. I mean, he was always difficult to handle. Always bad-tempered, always snooty towards those he thinks below him. Which is most of them, for one reason or another. But the guy got results. Worked his fingers to the bone. Still puts the work in, just isn't getting anywhere. This whole Shug Francis thing has got right up his nose. And the Scott and McClure case. Shit! Seemed like he just gave up on that one. A drug dealer and his mate, shot dead in Scott's flat. It was closed as murder suicide, but there was more to it. Fisher suspected, but he didn't push. It does happen to some cops – burnout. You push yourself harder and harder; always trying to go one better than your last result. You go off a cliff. That's what they're saying about Fisher now. But they're working silently, not giving him anything to be extra pissed off about. He's been here all day, working on this case. That'll mean he's wound up real tight.

The double door on the far side of the room is swinging open. Higgins. One of Fisher's little pet plods. Fisher won't explode on him. Not unless pushed. Higgins is heading straight for Fisher. Hardly a glance at the rest of them. These plods know the route to the top. Get well in with the DI, and he'll push you up the ladder. That was the case a year ago. Maybe not now. Not when the DI's getting a reputation as a man who can't close. Then you don't want to be any-where near him. He can hold you back rather than push you forward. There are a few in the station who would like to see Fisher become toxic. Fisher's looking up from his desk. Less interested in Higgins than the folder he has in his hands. Fisher didn't ask for anything. Must be something interesting. Actually, shouldn't Higgins be at home? He was on the dayshift. Someone else putting in hours beyond contractual obligation. Good lad.

Higgins has stopped at Fisher's desk. Putting the thin folder down with a flourish and leaning forward.

'Phone records. Records for Shug for the last couple of weeks. Check a couple of nights before Hardy and McBride went missing. Evening. Short call on his mobile.'

There's excitement in his voice. Fisher's looking down the sheet. A five-minute call to Derek Collins. Derek Collins – he knows that name. Another one of the murdering bastards who should be rotting in jail. Collins has done time twice. Never for murder. Never for long. He's a killer, though. Fisher knows it. Flicking to the next sheet. Collins: the corresponding incoming call. Then nothing. The two of them keeping their distance. This is it. This is what Fisher has been waiting for. Something so simple. So basic. Shug not learning his lessons. Not learning how to cover his tracks.

It's an hour later, and Fisher has everyone moving around. Most of them aren't doing anything useful, but he has them looking busy. Fact is, there's not an awful lot for them to do, but the energy is flowing outwards from Fisher.

He has a couple of them going looking for CCTV. Find out where Des Collins was on the night. See if they can find him moving around. It would be wonderful if they could place him at, or near, Hardy's office. As long as they can't place him anywhere else in the relevant period. That'll do as a starter. Makes Collins the likely killer. Makes Shug the man who ordered it. Makes sense. He has another cop trying to locate Collins. Not to arrest him. Not yet. You don't bring him in until you have everything you need to nail the bastard to the floor. But you need to know where he is. Make sure he doesn't run. Dopey bugger might even incriminate himself more while you watch. Don't need anyone to find out where Shug is. Get someone to confirm that he's at home. His right-hand man as well. He'll be in the dock, too. Oh, Fisher's going to round up every bloody one of them.

'Doesn't Collins work for Alex MacArthur?' one of the DCs is asking.

What's the DC's name again? Shit, Fisher can't remember. Big fellow, greying hair. Never mind. Not much of a cop anyway. 'Yes, he does,' Fisher's saying. 'Done jobs for other people, but he seems to have settled in with MacArthur. A few people have placed him close to Donald Park.'

'Okay. I thought that was it,' the cop's saying.

He looks nervous. A few of them will. Cowards. Plenty of them around. Scared of taking on MacArthur. If it's just Shug, then they're fine. They've always thought of him as small.

MacArthur they've always thought was big. A man with influence all over the city. A man who could make a cop's life difficult. For that reason, some will be wary of taking him on. Thing is, if you always back off, never challenge the scum, he'll grow and grow. Grow so big that he really becomes impossible to take down. They won't get MacArthur himself with this investigation. That's too much to hope for. But they'll get Collins and Shug, two men known to be on his side. And that chips away at MacArthur's credibility.

Everyone making an effort to look busy. Doesn't take much for Higgins to slip away unnoticed. Just downstairs. If Fisher wants him, then he can call down. Unlikely he'll bother. He has plenty of people upstairs to do the work. There probably won't be an arrest tonight. That's not Fisher's style. Meticulous. He'll want to make sure everything's neatly sewn up before the arrests. He usually would, anyway. Might go a different route with this. He needs an arrest. Higgins knows it as well as anyone. Been months since Fisher did something to disrupt the criminal industry. He used to be a pest for them. He's become an irrelevance. An arrest. A charge. A conviction. Get Shug put away, and it makes a statement. Get Collins put away, and it makes an impact. Shug's higher-profile. Collins, being MacArthur's gunman, will worry more people inside MacArthur's organization. Make them afraid. Just what Fisher wants.

Higgins is sitting in the corner of the changing rooms. His

shift ended hours ago. He's entitled to be lounging around if he likes. Hell, he should be at home by now. He's being careful. Making sure nobody's around. Nobody's likely to come in. Everyone working this shift has been in and changed; many have already gone out on the streets. He's taking out his mobile. Calling a number committed to memory, never to SIM card.

'I thought you might like to know that there's evidence linking Shug Francis to Des Collins. Should be arrests in the next forty-eight hours. I'll let you know more when I have it.'

'Good, thank you,' Young's saying on the other end, and hanging up.

The phone's asking Higgins if he wants to save the number and create a new contact. He's pressing No. Deleting the call from his call log. Hoping that Young will use his contacts to delete the call from official records. Taking a deep breath. Changing out of his uniform. Going home for sleep he really needs.

# 36

The plane to London is long gone. Hours ago. Calum wasn't on it. He's sitting in the hospital. Out in a corridor, with George sitting beside him. The last few hours are a blur. He remembers George calling him across to the side of the garage. Seeing William lying on the floor. Lying still. Lying on his side. Couldn't see him breathing. His eyes shut. Blood running down the side of his face. Not a lot of it. Coming from a cut on his head. Trickles from his nose and mouth. There was a bubble coming from the left nostril. That was what Calum noticed. What he remembers. A little bubble expanding and bursting as William breathed slowly out. That was when he knew his brother was still alive. It was a moment of relief. When he almost forgot what had been done to William. Didn't forget for long.

George had suggested they take William to the hospital in his car. Calum said no. Leave him. Don't move him until the paramedics get here. That's what Calum said, not necessarily what he was thinking. He was thinking that he still didn't trust George. Not 100 per cent. Didn't want his dying brother going off in a car with a man who can't be trusted. George called the paramedics from the garage phone. Didn't want an emergency call on his mobile. Calum knelt beside William. Told him it was going to be okay. Told him that he would be patched up and back in trouble in no time. Didn't get a response. When George was in the office, making the call, Calum told William something else. Told him there would be revenge. Didn't know if he meant it at the time – just felt like the sort of thing he should say. Someone beats your brother unconscious; you make big noises about revenge. Anything that might provoke a reaction from William. Nothing did.

The ambulance was there inside five minutes. Two paramedics, running in and crouching beside William. Calum already knew it was serious. Didn't need them to point it out. They did anyway. They made all sorts of ominous noises. Rushed William to the ambulance. Calum got in with him. George went to his own car. Followed to the hospital. They've been sitting in a corridor ever since, waiting for an update. Sitting in silence. A doctor approaching them. George is getting up, giving Calum some privacy. Walking along the corridor towards the corner. What a mess! Shouldn't be this way. Someone's fucked up, and someone's going to have to pay the price for that. It's not always the guy who fucks up who pays. Shit, they might blame him for it. Blame the guy who was nearby. Have to be seen to punish someone, preferably someone who doesn't matter to them. George is looking back along the corridor. Looking at Calum. The hard expression. Getting harder all the time. Bad news.

'If you have any family who would want to see him, you should get in touch with them right away,' the doctor's saying. They don't think William's going to make it through the night. Gather the family now – that's the instruction.

'I will,' Calum's nodding. The doctor's looking at him, pausing. He wants to say something about how William acquired these injuries, but he can't. It's the police's job anyway, and they'll be here real soon. Someone called them. The boy is going to die because of head trauma. Looks like he took a battering. May have been kicked. William MacLean was unlucky. The beating he took wasn't the worst the doctor's seen. Others have taken worse and survived. But sometimes it only takes one solid blow. One trauma and the damage is too much. One kick to the head can do it, and William took multiple kicks. The doctor's leaving the younger brother. He seems like the sort who prefers being alone.

Calum's looking along the corridor at George. George coming back along to him. Sitting next to him.

'Not good, is it?' George is asking.

'He won't last the night,' Calum's saying. There's a hard tone in his voice. Not mournful, not emotional in any way. There's a pause. 'I'm going to call my mother, tell her to get a taxi here. Before I do, I want you to tell me what you know.'

'What I know?'

'Who beat up William? Who was working on this? Did you know it was going to happen?'

George is pausing. Stammering. Scared of the questions. Calum's telling him to take sides. Something he absolutely doesn't want to do. 'I don't know who did it,' he's saying honestly. 'I know that Shaun Hutton's been involved lately. I don't know . . . I don't see why they would send him to do this, though. They shouldn't have. They should have sent me.' Strange thing to say. That he wishes they'd sent him to beat up William instead. But he means it. William would be fine now, if they had. Nursing a couple of cuts and bruises. Cursing George. No more than that.

There are a few other things Calum has to know before he contacts his mother. 'Did you call Young on the way here?' he's asking George.

'Young? No. I just followed the ambulance.'

Calum's looking at him. Questioning. Threatening. 'I need to know what Young and Jamieson know.'

'I called Young when you left the flat, told him you were on the move. He told me to call when I knew where you were. I didn't think to call him since. I mean, Jesus, when I saw William I just wanted to get him to a hospital, you know.'

He sounds genuine. George isn't a good liar; Calum would spot if this were untrue. So Jamieson doesn't know that Calum's at the hospital. Doesn't know where George is, either. This could play to his advantage.

There are plans formulating in the back of his mind.

Things he can do. Things he must do. None of them easy. Hard choices. But that's all they've left him with, so it's their own fault. Glancing at George. He could use him. No, leave him. Don't make his life any harder. Hell, if you want to be any sort of a friend at all, then you should be trying to help him out. He's in trouble, whether he realizes it or not. If Jamieson finds out that he came to the hospital without alerting them, then he's going to wonder what side of the fence George is on. If Jamieson reaches the conclusion that George was colluding with Calum, then George's life is in danger. He seems oblivious. Just concerned about Calum and William. So think about the things you need to do. Plan every movement. Plan every conversation. Make sure you control the flow of information. Nothing's more important than that right now. Jamieson doesn't know where Calum is. Where George is. Keep him in the dark, and he has a chance.

George is watching. He can see the look on Calum's face. He knows what's happening here. Calum knows that he's next. They've killed his brother just for helping him. They're going to kill him, too. So he's working out what to do. And George's heart is racing. You shouldn't be here. You're risking your life by being here. They'll think you helped Calum. What else was he supposed to do? If they'd bloody well told him what was going on. But oh no, they had to hold their little secrets tight. Tell him to do this, that and the next thing and not even give him a warning. They never said William was a

262

target. Didn't even say why Calum was. Shit! Jamieson might be his boss, but the boss deserves a kick up the arse. You can't tell people to do important jobs and not keep them informed. They push and push George to do more and more, but still treat him like crap. They deserve this punishment.

'Have you got any change on you?' Calum's asking. 'I'm going to call my mother from the pay phone.'

George has lent him a couple of quid, watched him walk along the corridor. He can see the nearest pay phone from here. No danger of Calum running. He's safe in the hospital. They're not going to hit him in here. Can't hit him until they know where he is, anyway. Calum's standing with the receiver to his ear. Talking to someone. A sad smile. His happy mother saying hello. Now Calum speaking. Explaining. How do you tell your mother that her boy is dying? Does she have any clue what sort of life her youngest son lives? How will she react, if she knows William's dying because of Calum? George is watching. Wondering if Calum is thinking the same thing. What do those thoughts do to a man? Doesn't matter that Calum is as cold as he is, he's still human. This has to affect him. Change him. Surely it makes him even more dangerous.

# 37

He's lying asleep when the phone starts ringing. It's only six o'clock in the morning. He'd been planning to let Elaine make the kids breakfast. Get them ready for school and out the door. Sleep until ten. He doesn't feel like doing anything. Let the world fall apart if it wants. He'll be under the duvet. Stuck his head up long enough to check his phone. No calls. Nobody wants to talk to Shug Francis. Sure, they all wanted to talk when there was something in it for them. You find out who your friends are when the pressure's on. No contact from Don Park, despite all the missed calls. Nothing from Shaun Hutton. Nothing from Fizzy. He won't be dead, just ignoring the calls. Hutton's not going to have done the job, not if he's working for MacArthur. There are no friends. Not even the ones you pulled up with you.

He thought about calling Don Park again. He must know what's going on. If anyone could confirm or deny, it would be Don. But if Shug's wrong about them working to isolate him, then he looks stupid. If Don has something to say, he'll call. But that's not why Shug hasn't picked up the phone. It's because he already knows what'll happen. He's worked it all out in his mind. Everyone's involved in this. Everyone has plotted against him. If he calls Don, he won't get an answer. He'll ignore him, because Don's working against him. Doesn't want to talk to the man he's ruining. Doesn't have the balls for it. You think someone's impressive; you think they're professional. Then they turn round and screw you. This is what happens when you trust. You give people a chance to rip you off and they will. Anyone. Lifetime friends. New friends. Right now, he wouldn't trust his own wife.

Reaching out and picking up the phone. Hasn't bothered to look at the display.

'Hello.'

'Shug, is that you?'

The rough, rasping voice. Old and rather weak-sounding. Sounding needlessly aggressive. Alex MacArthur. Couldn't be anyone else. 'It is.' That's all Shug's saying. Just about all he trusts himself to say. Don't accuse the old man of anything. Don't give him the chance to lose his temper with you. There are legendary stories of him losing his rag. None recent. They say he's mellowed in his dotage. Bollocks! Dangerous as ever. Just better at hiding it.

'This is Alex MacArthur. Is now a good time to talk?' Straight to the point.

'It is. Would it be better to meet face-to-face?' Shug's asking. This question matters. Face-to-face would mean MacArthur's not afraid of a bad reaction.

'No, we should do this now,' MacArthur's saying.

Shug knows. Doesn't need to hear it. Barely listening any more. Watching Elaine get up and leave the room, because she knows this is business. Knows she isn't meant to listen in.

'We have a problem,' MacArthur's saying. 'I've been hearing all sorts about you. Things you've been up to. Killing off targets without clearing it with me. Christ knows what you thought you were doing. Why the fuck did you want to draw attention to us? You got all sorts of nonsense going on. Police all over you. We had a deal, and you've pissed all over it, Shug. I can't be a part of this any more.'

Shug's scoffing. A bitter laugh. 'Really? You can't be a part of this because you think I've broken the agreement? Don't think I don't know what's going on here.'

'Doesn't seem like you have a fucking clue,' MacArthur's saying, and coughing. 'You been running around acting like some Hollywood gangster. Killing people off. Getting all this police attention. I thought you were smarter than this, boy. That's why I went along with this. I thought you knew better. Fellow with a legitimate business like yours – I thought you were smart. Well, you don't have an ounce of common sense. Not a fucking ounce.'

Shug's sitting up in bed, holding the phone to his ear. Hasn't said anything in ten seconds. Just staring ahead at the wardrobe opposite. Staring into space.

'Hello?' MacArthur's saying. He isn't finished yet.

'You've made your point,' Shug's saying. 'You might even

get your way. You might be able to screw me, but you'll pay for it in the end. You mark my words. You'll get what's coming to you eventually. Everyone does.' It sounds empty even to Shug.

'Yeah, well, you listen to me now. You've run around trying to act like a big man. Trying to make people think they should fear you. Well, there are people you should fear. You threaten me, and I'll bloody well give you something to be scared of. But I'll tell you something else. You still have Peter Jamieson to be scared of. He won't be happy until he's crushed you, boy. He's a dangerous bastard. There's evidence against him, you know. He's not as smart as he thinks he is. You might still be able to bring him down.'

It's just too much to listen to. This old bastard is trying to destroy him, but he still wants a favour. Thinks that Shug is going to do something for him. I break your back, you scratch mine. Trying to persuade Shug to take evidence against Jamieson. Knowing that Shug's in all kinds of trouble. Knowing that he'll end up in police company. Hoping that Shug will grass up Jamieson at the same time. Shug's putting the phone down. Makes him sick to listen to that old man wheezing. Thinking he can persuade Shug to do whatever he wants. There's nothing else to lose. MacArthur has no leverage left. Shug's just sitting there. Another twenty seconds passing. The phone ringing again. A man like MacArthur doesn't give up that easily. He's used to using people. Used to getting his own way. Shug's picking up the phone, dropping it back down again to hang up and picking it up again. Leaving it off the hook.

Remember when it used to be easy? Wasn't that long ago. The legit business was good. The car-ring was profitable and untouchable. Took a lot of work. Some risk. But they had a system that worked. They were generous towards the big organizations. Made sure they kept them all onside. Shug was good at that. None of the big ones made a run at his business. A few smaller ones did, but Shug had enough money to buy protection. Most of the people who tried to muscle in on the car-ring were aligned to big organizations. People lower down the chain who thought they could overpower a bunch of car geeks. Most were dealt with by talking to the big organization under whose umbrella they were operating. They were slapped down. Shug paid a kickback. Problem solved. Everything goes back to normal. Nothing to worry about from the police. The car-ring was never a priority. Police didn't even care much. Investigating something like a car-ring would cost a fortune. The reward would be to take Shug's men off the street, leave a vacuum. Would take the best part of a fortnight for someone to set up a replacement. Probably someone who worked for Shug and knew how to do it. Police couldn't be sure that the new ring would be so non-violent. Better the devil you know.

And it still wasn't enough. A strong business. Good money

from the car-ring, well hidden in the legit accounts. So hard to get a system that works, but he had one. A legit business big enough to absorb the finances from a criminal enterprise. Everyone making money. A loyal little bunch of employees. Good people. Or it seemed like it, anyway. But other people were making more money. Not doing anything complicated. Didn't seem to be doing anything that Shug couldn't do. Someone suggests that, as he's moving cars around the country for sale, why not put something in them? Make a little extra cash. No great risk – great reward. Shug held back. Moving stuff around steps on toes. No great risk from the police, sure. But great risk from people who think you're working against them. So if you're going to do it, you can't go in half-hearted. There's real money. If you do it well, you make a fortune. A killing, even.

That's the problem with things being easy. You think it's going to stay that way. You think that if you can put together a car-ring, then you can put together a drugs network. Control it top to bottom. You become used to that level of control when you have an untouchable operation. So you plot. You organize. You employ. You identify the weakness in others. Identify the target and the mechanisms you can use to bring it down. Take the target's share of the market. Then move on to the next. The next one always being slightly bigger than the last. Keep working it that way until you get to the top. Of course, Shug knew it would be more dangerous. There are no gunmen in the car trade. At least not that he knows. But he never thought it would be this way. So destructive. Pretty much from day one. And everything he tried blew up in his face. Left him looking weak and stupid. Left him with nothing. All those friends. The perfect system. The easy money. Worthless.

# 38

His mother's hardly said anything since she got here. Been hours now. She can't get her head around it. How could this happen to William? George has stayed. All night. Just sitting in silence, ready to help when he can. Hasn't made any attempt to contact Young. Still letting Calum have control. Still sitting in the corridor. They operated on William, trying to relieve pressure on the brain. Didn't go well. Nothing more they can do. They've invited Calum and his mother in to sit with William now. The final hour.

George is staying out in the corridor. Not his place to go in. He's thinking about leaving. He's entitled. No friend could begrudge him taking this opportunity to protect himself. But he's not. He's staying. Still thinking that this is at least partly his fault. Calum probably wanted out, after what happened with Emma. Okay, all the stuff with Frank MacLeod and Glen Davidson probably played a big part. But that's the job. Calum always handled the job. It's the personal stuff that would prompt him to run. And that was George's doing.

Calum and his mother are sitting in silence. Looking at William, lying in the hospital bed hooked up to a machine.

It's a strange sensation for their mother. You take away the tubes and, apart from a broken nose and cut lip, William looks fine. Calum's seen the patch of hair that was shaved away before they operated. That's where the damage is. Where he was kicked. He's seen enough dead people. Seen some who looked like they hadn't been touched. It just feels strange that it's William now. Seen so many that he didn't care about. Frank was different, too – seeing a man he liked lying dead. Burying him. But this is worse. Frank was part of the business. William doesn't deserve this. This is Calum's fault. If it weren't for the work Calum does, William would be fine.

The police have visited. Spoke to Calum and George in the corridor. Calum did most of the talking. George was just the friend who went to the garage with him. Calum said he couldn't understand it. Didn't know of anyone who would want to hurt his brother. The cops nodded along. A bored-looking detective asking a few questions. At the moment, from the police perspective, this could be anything. Money. A fight over a woman. They can't even guess at it. Eventually the name will filter around the service. Someone will point out that Calum MacLean is connected to Jamieson. Then people will get excited. Then the police will start swarming. Calum wants to control that. Doesn't want them anywhere near his brother yet. Not until he's dead. When William is gone, and Calum's done his brotherly duty, then things can change.

The machine's making a noise. Doesn't look like there's any change in William, but they know. A nurse is coming in. Sympathizing. Calum's looking after his mother. She's crying, and he's doing what he can to help her. Which is very little, because he knows this is going to get a lot worse for her before it gets any better. He's going to have to sit her down and have a talk. Have a conversation that might just destroy her. He's spent hours thinking about it. Trying to come up with an alternative that would spare her. There is none. It has to be the hard approach. Be cold. Hurt her. There's no other way. For now, he has his arm around her. They're still in the room with William. The medical staff have left them. Giving them a moment of peace. A chance to say goodbye.

They're out in the corridor. Judge the moment. Calum's looking at his watch. Ten past eight. William's been dead for thirty minutes. Their mother doesn't want to move. Just wants to sit. Shock, probably. George is lingering in the corridor, waiting to find out what happens next. Calum's ready to tell.

'George, will you go wait for me at the front door. I want to talk to you before we leave.'

George is nodding. A little unsure, but willing to do what he's told. Walking along the corridor and round the corner to the lifts. Thinking that something like this was inevitable. You get pushed to do more important work, and you become involved in a more important fuck-up. Inevitable. The police will be all over this soon. Amazing that they're not already. Distracted by bigger things, perhaps. They'll open a murder inquiry. That'll make his life impossible, because they know he was first on the scene. He's shaking his head as the lift carries him down.

As soon as George is out of sight, Calum's turning to his mother. Getting off his chair and crouching down in front of her. Holding both her hands and looking her in the eyes.

'Listen to me Ma. I need you to listen, and hear what I'm saying. I don't want you to say anything, because I know you won't believe a lot of what I tell you. You won't want to believe it. But it's all true. It's my fault that William's dead. They did that to punish him for helping me. I was working for some bad people. Real bad people. I was important to them. They found out that I wanted to get away. Get out from working for them. Get out of Glasgow. They didn't like that. People aren't allowed to walk out on them, but I was trying. I couldn't do it alone, though. I needed someone to help me. I needed William to help me, and he did. He did it because he's my big brother and he loves me. And because of that, they killed him. Whatever they say about William, I want you to remember that he did it for me. That he lost his life because of me. Because he was such a good brother. Okay?'

He can see the confusion in her. He can see the hurt. But it's going to get worse. He has to tell her what's going to happen next, and that's going to be even harder for her to take. But the first priority is making sure she doesn't believe anything she hears about William. The police will uncover stuff he's done. Handling stolen vehicles and parts. They'll link him to organized crime; make him sound like he was much more involved than he was. She mustn't believe the bullshit.

'Listen, Ma, I have to go. I don't just mean for now. I mean forever. I have to leave the city. Get out of the country. If they find me, they'll want to kill me too.' Now she's opening her mouth to say something. Say anything that'll keep her last son in the city. 'I have to go, Ma,' he's saying. Interrupt her, before she says anything he can't handle hearing. 'I don't have a choice. If I stay, they'll kill me too. Talk to the police. Tell them everything. I love you,' he's saying, the first time he's said it since he was a child. Leaning forward and kissing her on the forehead.

He's standing up, lifting the bag with his belongings over his shoulder, turning and walking away from her. Walking along the white corridor to the corner. Stopping and looking back. She's still sitting exactly as she was. Staring slightly downwards. Hasn't moved. Her shoulders are moving up and down. She's not strong. Their father died a few years ago – she has nobody now. Friends will rally round, but that won't help. One son murdered, another fleeing the city. She won't want to leave the house. Won't want to be seen. Worried that people are talking about her. Speaking badly of her two boys. The shame. It might destroy her. But there's no other way. The alternative is to stay in the city and end up another victim. Better to give her the glimmer of hope that comes from knowing that Calum's alive. She might not be able to see him, but he'll try to get in touch at some point. She can cling to that at least. It's all she'll have.

Calum doesn't do crying. Doesn't really do emotions. Can't remember the last time he was tearful. He goes cold instead. A form of controlled anger. And he's cold right now. Thinking with a clarity that only comes when you're under intense pressure. When you're doing a job, and you know you have to get every last detail of it right. Didn't have that ability when he started. Something you learn with time. With effort. One of the things that's made him so good at what he does. The lift doors are opening, and he's looking left and right as he comes out into the reception area. Plenty of people around, but none that stand out as suspicious. He can see George, standing at the double doors, looking nervous. You'd think he was an expectant father, the way he's chewing his thumbnail and walking back and forth.

Calum's walked across to him. They've made their way outside, into the car park. Quieter here, nobody to hear them talk.

'Listen to me, George,' Calum is saying. 'Things are going to change. You have to get out. The position they've put you in, the position I've put you in – you have to get out.'

'I can't just get out,' George is saying, and shaking his head. It's cold this morning. There's a little wind whipping around them.

'Yes, you can,' Calum is saying, 'but you only have one chance. Take that chance: get out and leave everything behind. I mean everything. I'm going to change things, George. You don't want to be here when it happens. They'll think you helped me. They'll blame you. If you stay, you're killing yourself.'

George is walking round in a circle, hands on his head. Maybe with planning you can run, but not like this. This isn't workable.

'You have an opportunity,' Calum's telling him. 'You have nobody to leave behind. Ditch everything. Go straight to the train station from here. Get on a train and go south. The police will be looking for you. So will Jamieson. You can't be here for either of them to find you. I'm going to do something that might change the business in this city. If you're still here in twenty-four hours, you could be swept away by it.'

George is looking at him now. 'Jesus, Calum, don't do anything stupid here.'

Calum's smiling. 'That ship is long gone. I'm only going to do what I have to do. You need to get out. Head south. Down to London. Hell, I might even see you there. Just . . . don't stay here. Go.' And he's sticking out a hand. George is shaking it. Calum's turning and walking across the car park, taking William's phone from his pocket.

# 39

Fisher doesn't have time for her. He'll have to make some. Deana Burke is a woman capable of making trouble. Capable of spoiling what's shaping up to be a damned good week. She called half an hour ago, said she wanted to talk to him. He tried to put her off, but she was having none of it. Deana Burke wants to talk; she's not the sort to wait. A lot of them are the same. Women who spend their lives on the fringes of the industry. They think they're as hard as their men. Think they have the right to behave any way they want. Bloody nightmare, the lot of them. Dealing with the family can be the worst part of an arrest. Not that Burke is family. She was Kenny's girlfriend, nothing more. But she might have information. Things are falling his way right now. She might actually have something worth listening to.

He got about four hours' sleep last night. Nipped home for it. Some people take a nap in the station, shower there. Not Fisher. It's necessary to get out of the building when you can. There's a temptation for a cop like him to turn it into a second home. Got to resist. Went home, slept, showered and got something to eat. Then back to the station. Not tired. Not even a bit. Reinvigorated. All of the weight that's been

279

building up on him in the last few months is falling away. Finishing line in sight. For now, a detour. Down the stairs and into the car park. Deana wants to meet – Fisher suggested her house. She said no. She even suggested the station. Fisher said no to that. Too many leaks. If Greig sees her here, then it means trouble. That little bastard would report to Shug. Greig's another problem that he'll soon resolve – he's been getting away with it for far too long. Not much longer.

They're meeting in some fancy coffee bar that she suggested when he refused the station. Fisher's never been here before. Doesn't much like the look of it. Quiet, but people coming and going. Never mind. It'll do. Little chance anyone here will report to Shug. The arrest will come soon. Oh, that's going to be sweet. Can't wait for that. Tomorrow, if he gets his own way. Some want to wait, suggesting they should take the time to gather more evidence. No way. That's just creating time for Jamieson to take the decision out of Fisher's hands. Time for Shug and MacArthur to hide evidence. Time for them to reduce the potential damage that the police can do. Maybe even run. Not MacArthur – that old bastard wouldn't shuffle away now. But then they probably won't get enough to arrest him anyway. Shug might run. Des Collins certainly would.

He can see Deana sitting at a table by herself. Dressed normally. Hair down. Has the look of a woman who's decided that a week is quite long enough to grieve. A woman ready to move on. She looks calm and composed, he's thinking to himself as he walks across to sit opposite her. And he's already suspicious. She's given up on mourning. A smart woman like her, ready to move on. Suddenly she gets in touch. What does that mean?

'Deana, how are you?' he's asking. The words sound concerned, but the tone doesn't.

'I'm okay. Dealing with things. How is your investigation?'

'Moving quickly,' he's telling her. 'Won't be long now, I can assure you. We've made a lot of progress in a short while. I'll have some big news for you very soon.'

She's nodding. Mixed feelings for Deana. She wants everyone involved in Kenny's killing to get a taste of their own medicine. A bullet for a bullet. Arrests just don't seem enough. But you take what you can get. And you let people like Peter Jamieson follow the path they think best.

She's listening to him. He's telling her some vague things about the investigation. No detail. Nothing that could identify who he plans to arrest. Or when he plans to make his move. She knows he doesn't trust her. Why should he? Opposite sides of the fence.

'I received some information,' she's saying.

Fisher's suddenly paying attention. His head rising sharply, watching her. 'Information? What information did you receive?'

'I was told a name for who shot Kenny. I think it's true.

Makes sense to me. Do you know of a man called Des Collins?'

'I do,' he's saying quietly. Nothing more.

'I was told that Collins did it. That he was working for Alex MacArthur. MacArthur has a deal with Shug Francis. They went after Kenny to send a message to Jamieson. And I think the job Kenny did that night was targeting MacArthur, not Shug.'

A collision of instincts, cynical at first. Sounded like she was telling him a story she'd carefully learned. It was too perfect. Naming Collins and MacArthur. Felt like a set-up. A set-up that pointed him in the correct direction, but he was still suspicious. Then that last sentence. That turned it all around. With that one sentence, trust. He had thought she was a plant. Telling him what Jamieson wanted him to hear. It seemed a little transparent. Then that – Jamieson would never let her give that sort of information away. Not to a cop. Not to anyone. Jamieson targeting Alex MacArthur is big news. Private news.

'What do you know about the job Kenny was doing that night?' he's asking her. Asked her before, and she said she knew nothing. Let's see what she's learned since.

'I've been told that it was a job against MacArthur. Nothing big. Just setting something up, or sending a message, something like that. Kenny dropped off the person doing the job with him. Between then and getting home, they got him.'

There's almost no point at all in asking. But he will. Has to. It's his job, after all. They pay him to ask. She's too smart to be offended by the question. Too smart to make a scene.

'And where did you get all this information?'

She's looking at him and she's smiling. 'From a friend. Someone in the business. Someone who knows. I can't say more than that.'

He's nodding. 'I can't do anything with that information if I don't know it's credible. You know that. I need to know where it came from.'

She's smiling. She knew he would say it. And she knows that he doesn't expect an answer. Just going through the routine.

She's getting up and walking out, leaving him behind. He's glancing round to watch her go. Much more confident than any of their previous encounters. Something's changed. Only been a week, but she seems like a different person. Confident, relaxed. Someone's responsible. Jesus, they don't take long to move on. Shouldn't judge her. You live her life, and you have to be able to move on quickly. You have a life with someone in the criminal business, and there's a chance it can all come crashing down in a heartbeat. There's something admirable about her. The strength it takes to move on. Fisher was married. Divorced. Life moved on, but it left a scar. Takes real strength to shrug it off and move straight along. Looking for your next opportunity. Ready for the chance to put the past behind you. Must be nice to live that way. To be able to. The past walks beside Fisher, walks beside most people.

If Deana Burke is naming Des Collins, then it won't be long before others are. It'll become the talk on the street. People will wonder why the police aren't doing something about it. They need to get Collins. For the sake of publicity, they need Collins, but he doesn't really matter. Not to Fisher. You put Collins away for fifteen, and someone else steps up to replace him. It might scare a few people around MacArthur, but time will quell that. The one who matters is Shug. He can get Shug. Will get him. Has to make it just right. Don't overreach. Don't charge him with things you can't be certain of. Play safe. Get him sent down. And when he's stewing away inside, you have all the time you need to nail down the other charges. Many people have fallen by the wayside in the last few months. People connected to Shug and Peter Jamieson. Lewis Winter was murdered because of his work in the drug trade. Glen Davidson too. Tommy Scott. Andy McClure. Maybe even Frank MacLeod. Must be possible to find the evidence for one or two of those.

# 40

It was a long night. Feels like it's going to be a long day. Young's been searching for info from just about every contact he has and keeps coming up short. Nobody knows. Hard to ask the right questions. They can't give anything away. Can't let people know that Calum's running, and that they're running after him. Once word gets out, people will begin to question Jamieson. Question the grip he has over his own people. Doesn't matter what he does to Shug. People will shrug it off. So what, you took down Shug, but you can't even hold on to the people you've got. What kind of leader does that make you? So Young's asking vague questions. Mostly trying to find George Daly. Find him, and he finds Calum. He's phoned George repeatedly through the night, but his phone's switched off.

He's almost convinced now that George is helping Calum. Either that or he's been killed by him. Helping seems more likely. Should have done it the other way round. He knows that now. Send George to deliver the beating, and Hutton to watch Calum. Too late. Young was just so pissed off with the brother. And he trusted George so little. Didn't think George would deliver much of a punishment. Still doesn't think so, but doesn't care any more. The brother was never the priority. Shouldn't have been the priority anyway. Should have focused on Calum. That's what Jamieson is thinking. Young knows it. Spoke to him on the phone about an hour ago. Told him he was still trying to find information. Jamieson was short with him. Didn't say anything aggressive; nothing that would let Young know how annoyed he is. But Young knows from the tone. The subtle change. The exasperation.

He spoke to Greig. Couldn't find Higgins. Either asleep or at work. Greig will have to do. Asked him if he knew anything about George Daly. Whether he was arrested in the night. 'Didn't hear about it, if he was. Whole station's gearing up for a raid on Shug Francis. Fisher's close. Going after him and Des Collins. Didn't hear about anyone else.'

So George hasn't been arrested. His name didn't show up on any hospital checks, either. Now Young's making his way back into the office at the club. Jamieson's sitting behind his desk, looking up at Young walking into the room. Eyebrows raised.

'Nothing,' Young's saying. Slumping into the couch at the side of the room. Jamieson won't say anything. Doesn't need to. This has been a balls-up. Young knows it, and nobody's going to be harder on him than himself.

He doesn't make many mistakes. Any mistake at this level is a big mistake. They can all come back to haunt you. It's about how well you clean up after it. And, of course, making sure you never repeat it. These are areas where Young's record is exemplary. Always cleans up well, never repeats a mistake. Except this time. This time he's not cleaning up well. He's lost sight of the target, and the man tracking the target. That's a double failure. Could turn it around. Jamieson expects that he will. They'll sort this out, and they'll nail Shug, and things will work out in the end. That's what he thinks will happen. But there will still be consequences. People will know that Calum nearly slipped through their fingers. That George helped him. Most of all, they'll know that Jamieson and Young had two men working for them who unsettled their entire operation. That'll make them look weak. Which means having to do something strong in response. Strong and fast.

'We need to accelerate moves against MacArthur,' Jamieson's saying. 'As soon as the Shug thing is done, we make a move.' MacArthur still seems to think that their deal to isolate and destroy Shug is genuine. That Jamieson will live up to his end of the bargain. Nope. Being able to connect MacArthur to Shug gives Jamieson the false justification he needs to go after MacArthur next.

Young's nodding. Grateful for the chance to talk about something that isn't Calum. 'I'm hearing that they'll be arresting Shug in the next day or two. If we want to make the Fizzy angle work for us, you need to call Shug up real soon. Try to get him aboard. We probably have less than twenty-four hours for that. Still, worst-case scenario, he gets locked up and we can use Fizzy to muscle in on the car-ring.'

Jamieson's nodding. The car-ring doesn't matter much to him. Getting rid of Shug matters. Having Shug as an excuse to attack MacArthur – that matters. Makes MacArthur look bad. MacArthur had a connection with Shug, and must be punished for it. Gives Jamieson the chance to look strong. Something his instincts tell him he needs right now.

Young's phone is ringing. He's looking at the screen, frowning slightly. 'It's Greig,' he's saying. Not long since he spoke to the cop. Not thrilled about an unexpected phone call. He's answering it there in the office. Nothing to hide from Jamieson. 'Hello.'

'Hi, John, listen, is now a good time to talk?' Sounding so casual. Sounding like he's Young's best mate.

'Now's fine. What's up?'

'I know you're looking for George Daly. I heard something when I got to the station a wee while ago.'

'Go on.'

'Last night there was a report of a guy called William MacLean being battered in the garage he owns. He was taken to hospital. Died early this morning.'

Jamieson's only hearing half the conversation, but he can see the grimace that's just spread over Young's face. This isn't good news. Must be something to do with Calum. Couldn't reasonably be anything else. Jamieson's sitting in silence, tapping his forefinger on the top of his desk. Watching and listening. Wondering what's happened now that could make matters any worse. It's that grimace from Young. So unlike him. Usually so reserved, so confident in everything he does. That's because he's usually in control. There's an uncomfortable feeling spreading through Peter Jamieson. All his working life he's had John Young at his side, and Young's never let him down. Always had the skill for it. Always had the organizational nous. Maybe things have got too big for Young. Maybe the organization is outgrowing him.

'You're sure?' Young's asking.

'Yeah, certain,' Greig's saying. 'Listen. There were two people with MacLean at the hospital. The detective who went there spoke to them. One was MacLean's brother, Calum. The other one was George Daly. They had nothing interesting to say. Just that they found him and called the ambulance. Said they had no idea what the beating was all about.'

'Okay, fine,' Young's saying. His tone suggests that it's not fine, but there you go – people say these things. Just trying to wrap up the phone call so he can work out where this puts them.

'Listen, there's something else,' Greig's saying. 'When word went round about William MacLean dying, well, most people didn't care. Hadn't heard of him. Just another investigation. Then Fisher heard about it. He's adding it to his investigations. Says it's connected. Wants to find the brother, Calum. Seems to think he might be connected to you.'

Young's grimacing again. Not a good look. 'Does anyone know where they are now?' he's asking Greig.

'No. They sent someone to the hospital. The two witnesses were gone. Just found the dead boy's mother. Said that her other son was gone and that he wasn't coming back. She wasn't making a lot of sense, apparently. Traumatized, I suppose.' Greig's beginning to sound rather bored. He's done his bit, reporting this to Young. It's up to Young to try and rescue whatever crisis this is.

'How close is Fisher to making arrests?' Young's demanding.

'I don't know,' Greig's saying with a sigh, 'I'm not in on the investigation. He keeps me at arm's length. Won't be today. He's being held back by people above him. Probably tomorrow. Evening would be my guess. I don't know, though – just a guess. Usually a guy who takes his time with these things, wants to get it just right. Seems like he's trying to rush this one, though, so, you know, might be sooner than expected.'

Young's hanging up the phone. Looking down at the screen, taking his time before he talks to Jamieson, picking the right words. Hard to come up with any version of events that isn't his fault, though. He sent Hutton to do the beating. A gunman to do muscle-work. Like most people who encounter Shaun Hutton professionally, William MacLean has ended up dead. Hutton will take some of the blame. He was warned not to kill the boy. But it's ultimately Young's responsibility. Should have seen this coming.

'William MacLean is dead,' Young's saying quietly. Leaning forward on the couch, phone still in his hands, looking down at the floor.

'Dead?' Jamieson's saying. 'How can he be dead?'

A little sigh. 'I sent Hutton to do the beating. He went too far, obviously.'

'Hutton? Why did you send Hutton after the brother?' Then a dismissive swipe of the hand. 'Never mind. What do the police know?'

The possible saving grace. 'They don't know where Calum and George are. They spoke to both of them at the hospital,' Young's saying.

'Both of them?'

'George was there with Calum. I don't know why. I can guess, but I don't know. Police spoke to them, didn't think anything of it. It was only when Fisher found out that William had died; he put two and two together. He knows who Calum is. Or thinks he does. They'll be searching for Calum and George. Calum especially. So, we have to find them first.' Looking over at Jamieson, waiting for a reaction. He can see the anger boiling in his friend. Jamieson's about to say something when Young's phone rings again. Young's looking at the screen. 'It's George,' he's saying, as he answers.

'Hello?' It's a cautious hello from Young. Unsure what to expect from a man he doesn't trust.

'Hello, John, it's me, George.' Whispering, sounding breathless. 'I can't speak for long. Just to report in. Listen, I picked up Calum when he left his brother's house yesterday. Took him to his brother's garage. Found the brother dying. So I had to go to the hospital, stay with him, keep up the pretence. He's left the hospital now. William died this morning. You were right. He's running. Leaving the city. But I don't know what he's going to do now. Now that his brother's dead. I think he's looking for someone. He's armed, John, he's armed. I'm following him. On foot. Can't let him catch me, because I can't explain it if he does.' Then a pause, just the sound of someone walking, George breathing. 'Jesus,' he's whispering. 'Shit!' And the phone's gone dead.

# 41

The first and last thing he needs is a gun. He hoped it wouldn't come to this. Hoped that the last time he had held a gun would be the last time he held a gun. When he killed Kenny. That would have been the case, if all had gone well. All has not gone well, Calum's reflecting. A change in strategy. The dream of a smooth departure dead. The fake ID useless. Other things matter now. Like making people pay a high price for their actions. He's sitting in the back of a taxi, being driven through the city. He knows which taxi firms can be trusted and which can't. Some are very close to the criminal business. You have to avoid the ones that might report your journey. He knows which are clean. Or thinks he does, anyway. These things change quickly and often. Doesn't matter a whole lot. Calum's going to move fast now.

The taxi's pulling up outside the address Calum gave the driver.

'Wait here,' he's saying. Getting out of the back of the car and glancing left and right. No other cars on the street. Nobody watching him. Walking in through the front garden and up to the front door. It's his usual supplier. He thought about going to someone else. Someone who wouldn't recognize him. If word's been going round for the last twelve hours that Calum's wanted by Jamieson, then the supplier might know. Might report Calum as soon as he leaves the house. Go to someone who doesn't know you – they have nothing to report. All they know is your name, not your face. But going to someone you don't know brings its own risks. No guarantee that they won't recognize him. No guarantee that they're reliable. No guarantee that they'll be willing to do business. His own supplier might not have heard that Calum's *persona non grata*. Might not care if he is. People in the gun trade are good at keeping their mouths shut.

A whole industry built on the principles of a blind eye and a deaf ear. Calum's relying on that now. People for whom silence is intuitive. Ringing the doorbell and waiting. There's a routine to this. Do nothing that upsets that routine. This will go somewhat beyond the routine. Nine days since he was last here, buying the gun he used to kill Hardy and Kenny. The dealer will have expected that gun to be returned. Calum's a returner – that's the routine. Not this time. He chucked that gun. Thought he would never need another one. And now he's back on the doorstep, looking for another gun. So soon after the last job. Paying the going rate. Cash in his bag. The door opening. The seller looking at him. A short little man in his later years. Nodding for Calum to come in. Nothing to say, not yet.

Inside the house. Warm in here. The seller won't mention the previous gun. The fact that it wasn't returned. Fine by him. Means he gets to keep the whole fee. Calum's a reliable client. He knows he can rely on the boy to say nothing about it. To expect no money back, if he's not able to return the weapon. Some people do make a fuss. Clients who somehow think they're special. Think they can get some of their money back without returning the gun. Morons – they're the ones who never last. The ones who think they can rewrite the rule book to suit themselves. The reliable ones, like Calum, are the good clients. They last because they understand. Shape themselves to fit the business, not the other way round.

'Single piece, small?' the old man's asking him.

'Single piece, small,' Calum's nodding. And that's all they'll say to one another.

The old man's gone upstairs. Going to his loft to get the gun for Calum. Leaving the younger man standing by himself just inside the front door. Old man could be doing anything. Gone up there to call Peter Jamieson and tell him to get someone round here quick. Would he do that? It would end his career if people found out he'd been so disloyal to a client. You have to be able to trust your supplier. That's rule one. Maybe he would call Jamieson if he thought nobody would ever find out. Everyone, no matter how experienced, is capable of convincing themselves that they can get away with things other people can't. Everyone likes to believe they're special. But honest or not, he's a businessman, so he will sell the gun. Never refuse a sale. So he'll go and get the gun. And he'll sell it to Calum, and he'll take the risk that comes from that. It could be the gun used to attack Jamieson or Young. That's the risk you run as a dealer.

He's back downstairs. A small handgun, wrapped in a cloth and placed in a thick plastic bag. Handing it across to Calum. Calum reaching into his pocket and paying the man. Seems like the right thing to do. He'll never be back. What's going to happen next means that he'll never need another gun from this man again. He knows this. He could just walk out. Tell the old man to stick his money. Nothing the old man could do about it. But he's not going to do that. The old man's always played straight with Calum, so Calum's going to play straight with him. He's paying the man. Taking the wad of cash from his pocket, paying up. The old man nodding and opening the door for his client, as he always does. Calum's nodding goodbye and walking out.

The old man closing the door, pausing for a few seconds. You survive in this business by knowing who to ingratiate yourself with. Not always an easy thing to get right. He got a call about half an hour ago from John Young. Young knew that this was Calum's usual supplier. Called to ask if Calum had picked up a new gun recently. The dealer told him that Calum picked one up about ten days ago, never returned it. Young cursed under his breath. Didn't seem to be good news. Young was thinking that he might have used that gun on George. That he might ditch it and replace it. Told the supplier to let Young know if he saw Calum at any point in the next couple of days. The old man's making his way back upstairs. Doesn't matter that Calum's loyal. Doesn't matter that other clients would be spooked if they found out about his grassing Calum. The most important thing always is surviving. You can't do that if you piss off people like Peter Jamieson. The old man's redialling the number that called earlier.

'Yes?'

'Mr Young, this is Roy Bowles. I just sold another gun to Calum MacLean. He just left my house in a taxi.'

Calum's given the driver the next address. He's always liked his supplier. Trusted him to do his job properly. But let's not mistake Calum for a blundering idiot here. He knows his business. He knows what doing his job properly means to an old survivor like Roy Bowles. It means keeping the big people happy. Backing the biggest, most dangerous bloody horse in the race. If he knows about Calum being on the run, then he'll call it in. Of course he will. That's his job. It's what Calum would do if the roles were reversed. Doesn't matter. They don't know where he's going next. He'll pay this taxi off when they reach their destination, and when he needs to move again, he'll call a different one. All a question of judgement. Relying on people like his dealer to be a grass. Relying on them all to be unreliable. As long as you trust them all to be untrustworthy, they'll never let you down.

They're stopping outside a small corner shop. Should be the right sort of place. The taxi's waiting outside. Calum walking in. Dingy place. Darker than a corner shop should be. Not very inviting. Along to the short aisle that sells cleaning products. On a bottom shelf he can see the familiar blue box, about the size of a tissue box. Thin gloves for cleaning with. Taking them to the counter. The young woman behind the counter is a study in boredom. Not interested in this young man coming in to buy gloves and nothing else. Not interested in looking him in the eye. Running the box over the scanner, telling him how much he owes. Taking the money, giving the change. Within ten seconds of him leaving the store she won't remember even vaguely what he looked like or what he was wearing. There'll be a security camera somewhere. That does her thinking for her. It'll remember the detail she won't, Calum's thinking, as he walks back out to the taxi. They're pulling away from the shop, on to the next address.

Paying the driver and getting out of the taxi. Starting to walk the wrong way, until he's sure he's out of sight. If the dealer reported him to Jamieson, then he might have taken the number of the taxi as well. They'll track it down; demand to know where the driver dropped him off, which way Calum was going when he got out, that sort of thing. The driver's the next link in the chain. The driver won't know anything. He's dropped Calum off twenty minutes away from Calum's actual destination. Keep taking precautions until the job is done. They can still get to you if you're sloppy. Walking the long walk to the house. A large detached house in a good area. Along the side and round the back. Nobody's seen him so far. The key's under the plant pot beside the shed. In the back door, to the big, empty, cold house.

This is where Jamieson and Young put him after he killed Glen Davidson. Their safe house. Swanky place, but mostly devoid of furniture. It's somewhere to hide out. Might even have to stay the night. Looking at his watch: it's into the late afternoon now. The timing of what happens next isn't in his own hands. Relying on other people to be able and willing to do their part. He knows they'll be willing. Able is another question. He can force the issue. He's dialling a number on his mobile. Standing in the big airy living room, asking the woman to put him through to his target. She's putting him through. The phone ringing and ringing. Calum scuffing his foot along the bare wooden floors. Sounds loud in here. Everything does. The phone eventually answered by the wrong person. Telling him the person he's looking for is out. Probably won't be back for a few hours. Couldn't say when.

'That's fine,' Calum's saying. 'As long as they're in tomorrow morning, I'll call again then.' Looking at his watch. Get some sleep. Tomorrow's going to be long and difficult. The last day.

299

# 42

They'll have to do this in a hurry. Anything they get from this is a bonus anyway. They've done the most important part of setting Shug up. MacArthur's been in contact this morning to let Jamieson know he's made the call. Ditched Shug. But that doesn't mean you stop working. As long as there's an angle, you work it. Jamieson's behind his desk in the office. Young's sitting on the couch at the side of the room. Jamieson has the phone number in his hand, but hasn't started dialling yet. It's early evening. Might not get through. Hell, he might be ringing a phone that'll never be answered again. People run. Some stay because they don't want to look weak. Or because they can't believe they'll ever be brought down. But the ones with sense run. Jamieson would. He wouldn't admit it, but push comes to shove and he's out of here. So long, life of crime. Nice knowing you. Not hanging around for the consequences.

Dialling the number. The man could be pissed out of his skull by this hour. Jamieson would be, if he were up excrement creek without a means of propulsion. It's ringing. Almost a surprise. He thought Shug might have pulled the phone from the wall. Cut himself off from the world before he gets his shit together and gets out of town. He has a wife and kids. He must be doing something to protect them, if not himself.

'Hello?' Shug's voice. Well, a man's voice – Jamieson's guessing Shug. Sounds miserable.

'Hello, is this Shug Francis?'

'It is,' he's saying, 'how may I help?'

Yep, he's drunk. You can hear the thickness in his voice. A drunk man making too much effort to sound sober. Trying to be polite. 'Shug, this is Peter Jamieson. I think things have got to the point where you and me need to have a proper conversation.'

There's silence. Jamieson waiting to hear Shug hanging up. That's what he would do. Shug has to see that he's in a no-win situation here. There's no chance of getting out of the trap he's walked into. Jamieson would know it. He'd rather take the destruction than be manipulated and humiliated one last time. There's a chance with Shug. A chance that he doesn't know the business well enough. A chance that he'll reach out and grasp at any consolation he can get.

'You think so?' Shug's asking him.

'I do.' Jamieson's relieved. Just by answering back, Shug's letting the conversation run. Giving Jamieson a chance. He usually only needs one. 'Things have gone in a strange direction for both of us. You tried to step on my toes, and I didn't like that. Fine, it's business. I'm willing to let that slide, given recent events. Someone hit one of my men. Someone hit your moneyman. I think we both know who was behind it. I think we both know we're being played here.'

More silence. It's not really a question of what Shug believes. More what he wants to believe. Poor little bugger's been knocked around from pillar to post. Right now, he'll be most pissed off with Alex MacArthur. That, Jamieson hopes, is where his greatest sense of betrayal lies. The man who just abandoned him.

'You think MacArthur's been playing you, too?'

'He told me he was looking to make peace with me,' Jamieson's saying. Happy, because of the word 'too'. Shug's already blaming MacArthur, doesn't need to be pushed. 'Told me that he was making moves against you. Fine, I said. I'll leave you to it, I said. If he wants to solve my problems for me, so be it. Then he hits my man. That was when I knew I'd been made a sucker by the fucker. Killed my man, right under my nose. Made me look like I can't protect my own. You know what that does for my credibility? Fuck-all, that's what it does. So now, I want to strike back. I want to make sure MacArthur doesn't get what he wants. He works this hard to play you and me, he's doing that for a reason. To take your business and make me look weak. I'm his next target. I say we don't let him play us. I say we protect your business, make me look strong and make him look like a total idiot.'

You see, this is the problem in having a conversation

with a drunk man. They're prone to bouts of silence, while they try to compose the next sentence. They don't realize it. They think they're being fluid. Just being careful about what they say. So Jamieson's waiting. And waiting. Not that he blames Shug for taking his time. This is worth thinking about. Even if he were sober, Jamieson would allow him a little time to consider it.

'You have an offer?' Shug's asking. Wanting to know what's in it for him.

'I do,' Jamieson's saying. 'I'm suggesting that you sell me a half-share in your company. Call it forty-nine per cent. You still get to run it. I'll be buying the legit business. A legit deal. And a promise that I won't try and take the rest from you, either. See, MacArthur wants it all. Whatever he offers, he wants it all. I'm guaranteeing you a deal that leaves you still making money. No matter what happens, your family gets provided for if you go down. Gives you something to come out to.'

Nobody likes hearing that they have to make plans for a prison sentence. But Shug's going to get one. Even he has to see that, drunk or not.

'You might have a point. What do I have to lose?' he's saying with a snort. The kind of self-pitying bullshit that Jamieson's been expecting. 'I've got nothing else. I'm going to lose it all. Shit! I've lost it all. Yeah, the fuck, I'll do a deal.' A pause, signalling a slightly more careful consideration of his position. 'Not tonight. Not right now. I'll meet you. Tomorrow.'

Jamieson's turn to pause. Shug might not have a tomorrow. If Fisher's moving at the speed suggested, an appointment for tomorrow could be a waste of time. But if he pushes Shug, he'll lose the deal anyway.

'Okay. Tomorrow. Come round to the club tomorrow morning. You can bring someone with you. One person. Unarmed, obviously. Your mate, what's his name – Fizzy, Fuzzy, whatever. Poor bastard, we've heard what he's been going through, too.'

'What d'you mean?' Shug's asking. A little more quickly this time.

Play it careful. Don't overdo it. 'Oh, well, I don't know if it's true. If he hasn't told you, then it might not be right. I just heard that he was a target for MacArthur. Heard that he had to go to ground. You know, off the radar. I don't know, though – it's just the word that was going round at street level. Talk of Shaun Hutton working for MacArthur, going after Fizzy. If you haven't heard it, then it might not be true. If it is true, then we can offer him protection. You know, if he doesn't go down, too.'

A pause. 'No, well, I don't know,' Shug's saying. So unsure now. 'Maybe.'

'Listen,' Jamieson's saying, moving to end the conversation, 'we can get this done, Shug. We can make sure that MacArthur doesn't get things all his own way.'

Young's smiling. Looks like the little bonus might just pay off. Shug on his own. Paranoid and scared. Knowing that the end of his miserable race is probably round the next corner. Willing to take whatever deal is in front of him. Anything that lets him think he's getting one over on the people who've screwed him. The chance to get off the hook with Fizzy, by blaming it on MacArthur. That sense of revenge – no matter how flimsy – is powerful.

'I think we got him,' Jamieson's saying. 'He was pissed, though. Might have a whole different story to tell when he sobers up.'

'No,' Young's saying, shaking his head confidently. 'He might sober up, but he'll still be in a corner on his own. And he'll still be mighty pissed off with Alex MacArthur. He'll do the deal. Just to screw with MacArthur. Doesn't mean he won't change his mind later on and start trying to make trouble, mind you. But I don't think that'll be a problem. Not with Fizzy on board to run the business for us. That neuters Shug.' Saying it with just a little bit of smugness.

That annoys Jamieson. It's a rookie mistake to wallow in small victories when there's a big problem looming over you. All this Shug stuff could mean nothing until they know where Calum is. What he's up to. They sent someone to the hospital, but he found nothing. Tracked down the taxi driver who took Calum away from his dealer's house, but he was useless. Told them where he dropped Calum off. Obviously a false location. Nowhere nearby Calum could use. Calum probably called another taxi from there. He's a smart runner. Can't find George, either. He's just disappeared since that phone call. Could be lying dead in an alleyway somewhere. In a canal. God only knows.

'Call Fizzy yourself, tell him to answer the next call he gets from Shug. And tell him the story is that he's been hiding from MacArthur and Hutton, not Shug. Make sure he has the same lie we do.' Saying it with no great enthusiasm. 'And when you're done, let's get our focus back on what matters.'

# 43

It was a cold night in a strange bed. Hardly ideal preparation, but that doesn't matter. Calum's up and checking his gun. Still there, loaded and ready for use. Washing now. Cold water, a sliver of soap, no toothpaste. He's not going to smell great by the time today ends. Stinking won't be the worst thing that happens, though. Going through the kitchen cupboards, trying to find something to eat. Nope. They fill the kitchen only when they know they're going to be hiding someone here. Obviously haven't used the place for ages. Maybe not since Calum was last here. He'll get something to eat on the way. Find a cafe or sandwich shop. First thing he needs to do is get away from this house.

It was a fitful sleep. All the while thinking about someone turning up at the house. Worrying that Young or Jamieson might work out where he's gone. They haven't, because they don't know him well enough. Don't understand how isolated he's chosen to be. They don't understand how few options he has. Leaving by the back door. Locking it, putting the key back under the flowerpot. The habit of cleaning up after yourself. Leaving no trace. Calling a taxi from the back garden. Using a different firm this time. Waiting ten minutes until he hears a car blowing its horn out on the road. Along the side of the house, looking carefully along the street. No sign of anything out of place. Just the taxi idling in the middle of the road. Calum dropping into the back of it.

'Cowcaddens, is it, mate?' the driver's asking.

'Aye, that's right,' Calum's nodding.

Sitting in the back of the car, watching the city drift by. Early morning. People getting to work, getting kids to school. A few streets he recognizes. Knows he's getting close. It's a strange feeling, looking out the window at his city. Born and raised here. Yet it means so little to him now. Just bricks and mortar. Only one person left alive in the city that he cares about, and he's destroyed her life. You live a life that isolates you from others, isolates you from the place itself – it stops meaning anything to you. A city, it's just a place. A place of work, a place to sleep. There's no emotional connection. Nothing to make him regret saying goodbye. People tell false tales about their connection to a certain place, Calum's sure of that. It's not the place you're connected to. It's the people, the time, the events that happen there. Or it's yourself. A misinterpreted love of the self. No chance of that here.

'Pull up here on the right,' Calum's telling the driver. Paying him and getting out next to a sandwich shop. He's only a street away from where he wants to end up. Doesn't matter. He's minutes away from being out of Jamieson's reach. Into the shop and buying a sandwich and an orange juice. Eating on the go. Across the street and round the corner. He can see the building he's aiming for. Plenty of activity around it. That's fine, just means his target is probably there. Walking along to a bin and placing the empty bottle and sandwich wrapper inside. Stopping to look up and down the street. It's busy. Plenty of people around, and any one of them could be dangerous. Any one of them could be ready to approach him. Monday morning, lots of glum faces. Calum's touching his chest, feeling the gun in the pocket. Inside left pocket of his coat, where he always keeps it.

It's not his gun he's taking out of his pocket first. It's his phone. Dialling the same number he tried last night. A different woman saying hello. Calum asking her to put him through to the same person. He's standing across the road from the building, waiting. The phone's ringing. He's letting it go on. This could be another missed call. Beginning to look like a potential problem. He doesn't have a plan B. Shouldn't need one. But this bastard is proving hard to get a hold of. Doesn't matter how busy he is, he will have time for this.

'Yes?' A terse voice. The phone answered by someone with better things to do.

'Is this Detective Inspector Michael Fisher?'

'It is.'

'This is Calum MacLean. I believe you've been looking for me. I want to talk to you. Get to your car alone, bring a recording device and I'll give you further instructions.'

MacLean's hung up. Fisher's standing in the busy office, phone in hand. Glancing around. Everyone getting ready. They're going to move against Shug today. They have a team chasing down Des Collins. Should get him soon. Everything working out nicely, and now this. Calum MacLean. Definitely important, if he is who he says he is. This could be a trap. They're bound to try something. This could be a set-up. Fisher's spent months keeping an eye open for MacLean, for any information about what he does. He's in the business, that's for sure. And he ran away from his flat around the time Glen Davidson went missing. Now his brother's lying in the morgue, waiting for an autopsy and funeral arrangements to be made. A mother in shock, giving them no information they can use. Calum and his pal George Daly missing. Daly a known thug for Peter Jamieson. Calum probably an employee of Jamieson, too. And now Calum phoning him up, telling him to get to his car.

You go with your gut, because there isn't enough clear info to judge. Common sense tells him that he shouldn't go anywhere near this. The risk is far too high. Someone wanting to silence him. Procedure says you stay away. But MacLean's brother just died. Nothing to do with the police, something to do with the industry. If MacLean's pissed off at anyone right now, it'll be someone in his own line of work. If there's one time that MacLean might just be willing and able to give him info, it's now. Besides, everything's falling his way. He's heard people say it. You get waves of good luck, so ride them. It'll all come crashing down at some point.

'I'm going out, don't know for how long,' he's saying to DC Davies. Davies is looking at him, puzzled. 'Just got a call from someone who might be Calum MacLean. Might have info on his brother's killer. This could help.'

'That's a risk. You want someone to come with you?' Davies is asking, praying his senior officer doesn't say yes.

'No. I'll go alone. If I'm not in touch in a couple of hours, start getting nervous.'

If DCI Reid finds out about this, then he will give Fisher an absolute bollocking. Worth it. The chance of big information. This William MacLean death feels big to Fisher. More than just some dodgy garage owner getting the shit kicked out of him over money. The connection to his brother is too important. No coincidence. Fisher's pulling his coat on and grabbing a small MP3 player as he goes down the stairs. Out into the car park. Could this be all they want? Get him out of the building, take a shot at him and speed away. Nah, that sort of thing doesn't happen round here. Far too risky. The big players are too smart to play that sort of game. You shoot one cop and you get every other cop in the city looking to take you down. Looking to crush you. Any means necessary. He's out in the bright morning, walking slowly across to his car. Pausing. The young man on the phone said get to your car and you'll get further instructions. How can he give further instructions? He doesn't have Fisher's mobile number or he wouldn't have called the office line. Shit, they just want him outside.

'Detective.'

A male voice. Fisher's spinning round and glaring at the man. He's been standing back against the wall, down towards the entrance to the car park. Fisher recognizes him as he's getting closer. Calum MacLean. He looks like shit, to be honest. Pale and tired. Looks like a man who's been through a lot and isn't finished with the drama just yet.

'My name's Calum MacLean. Whether you realize it or not, you've been looking for me for a long time now. I think it's time we had a detailed discussion. I have a lot to tell you.'

Doesn't sound threatening. Doesn't look it. Seems genuine. 'Okay. Why don't we go inside and we can talk about it there?'

Calum's smiling. A knowing smile. 'No, I'd rather not. Let's go for a drive. I'll talk, and when we're done we can decide where we both stand.'

It would be easy enough to rush into the station, get officers to grab MacLean. Hell, there's two uniformed cops making their way over to a car just now, looking across at Fisher and his companion as they go. Just call them across and bring the boy in. Then what happens? Nothing. He clams up, because he's not getting his own way. Or you go in the car with him, and take your chances. Common sense versus gut feeling, round two.

'Is this about your brother?' Fisher's asking him. Rules say he must be allowed one question.

'Yes,' Calum's saying with a sad nod of the head. 'But it's more than just William. There's a lot I want to tell you. About stuff that goes much further back. But it's what happened to William that brought me here. He died because of me. And I need to make amends.'

# 44

He finally got through to Fizzy late last night. It wasn't an easy conversation. Lots of apologies on both sides. Shug cried a little, but managed to hide it well during the call. Fizzy kept telling him not to worry about the argument they had. Kept saying that he understood it all. He admitted that he'd been hiding for days. Running scared of MacArthur. Heard MacArthur wanted to kill him.

'I didn't even know he was after you,' Shug said.

'Nobody did – that was the point, I suppose. I think he was trying to get rid of anyone that was close to you. Probably thought it would make it easier to get control of your business.' Didn't sound convincing to Fizzy when he said it, but Shug was too highly strung and pissed to notice.

'Yeah,' Shug said. If that's what Fizzy wants to believe about the man trying to kill him, then so be it. He's lost everything else; this is a chance to salvage a friendship. 'Listen, I'm going down. I know it. I'll get a good stretch, probably. I need someone to run the business while I'm away. I want you to do that for me.'

'Shug, I could be going down, too.'

'Nah. You might get a short sentence, but nothing more

than that. Your fingerprints aren't on any of the really bad stuff.'

Now it's morning, and they're sitting in Shug's office. Just the two of them. So much like the old days. Atmosphere's not the same. Can't pretend it is. Things have changed. Partly because of the falling-out; it casts a cloud. Fizzy will never forget that Shug ordered a man to kill him. He'll smile and joke and play along, but the old friendship is gone. Dead. This is just business now. There's also an atmosphere because they know what's going to happen next. You can't carry on as normal when you know your world is going to come crashing down.

'Maybe you could run,' Fizzy's suggesting.

'No,' Shug's saying with certainty. 'I can't do that. Not with Elaine and the kids. I have to accept it. I went for something big and I botched it. Now I have to handle the fallout. That's my punishment. Fair enough, I'll take it, handle it. But I need people I can trust on the outside. That's why I want you at this meeting.'

Fizzy's playing a difficult game. Trying to sound like he's unsure of the Jamieson deal. He is unsure. He hasn't suddenly learned to trust Peter Jamieson after everything that's gone on. But he can't let Shug know that he's been part of a deception. Sound unsure, but don't change his mind. If Shug backs out of this, Fizzy is a dead man. This deal is life now.

Piss off Jamieson and he's dead. Keep Jamieson happy and he's rich and powerful.

'Fine,' Fizzy's saying, putting reluctant acceptance into his voice. 'I'll accept whatever you and Jamieson come up with. But you have to remember, if I go down, then I won't be there to run anything. And if Jamieson decides to try to take your share when you're behind bars, then I'll have to fight against that. Have to do it under my own steam.' Disingenuous bullshit, but convincingly said.

Shug's smiling – first time since Fizzy came here this morning – smiling at his friend, and his determination to do what's right for them and for the business. 'That's fine by me,' Shug's saying.

The car journey to the club was quiet. Not a lot to say. A week ago they were doing a deal to hand over a chunk of the business to MacArthur. Now it's Jamieson. Interchangeable bastards. This one's a little bit different. With MacArthur, it was a share of the car-ring. It was all more vague, all about getting a deal in place. That's because MacArthur never had any intention of honouring a proper agreement. Just get his feet in the door and then take the lot. Different with Jamieson. More detail. Legally binding, because it's built around the legit business. Okay, he could still stab them in the back, but it seems unlikely. The legit business matters more to him, because he's trying to build something. Something large, something that makes a lot of clean money.

MacArthur's built everything he's ever going to build. Every-thing he really needs. Shug knows what matters most to Jamieson about this, and it's not the business. It's the chance to piss off MacArthur. That's the next great battle. Jamieson and MacArthur. This is an opening shot in that, which is why Jamieson has to honour the deal. Make himself the man that others want to deal with.

They're in through the front door and making their way up the stairs. Fizzy tripping and nearly falling forward. Cursing imaginatively at the offending step, drawing a smile from Shug. Through the snooker room and along the corridor to Jamieson's office. Led by a surly-looking barman. He's knock-ing on the door and holding it open for them. Jamieson's behind his desk, standing as they come in. Young getting up from a couch at the side of the room. Young coming over, introducing himself, shaking hands. Now shaking hands with Jamieson. There's a coldness. An atmosphere hanging unpleasantly in the room. Shug assumes it's because of every-thing that's gone between them in the past. A reasonable assumption. Wrong, but reasonable. There are two chairs in front of the desk, which Shug and Fizzy are sitting in.

'I'm glad we're doing this,' Jamieson is saying. 'Not just for the obvious reasons, either. The last few months, what's happened between us, it was a mistake. We should have found a way of sorting it out much sooner. I take the blame for that. I've been around long enough to see it and do something about it. But I'll tell you something, Shug: there isn't a man in this business who's got rich from looking backwards. Not one. We need to look at what we can do for each other going forward. There's a neat fit here. You have a legit business that we currently have no role in. Your business doesn't clash with ours at all. Complements it, in fact. And we can offer you a lot of things that are going to help you going forward. Police contacts, for one thing. Try to make sure we can reduce charges against you. Or evidence against you, anyway. Protection's another thing. For you and your family. For all the people that matter to you.'

All the things Shug wants to hear. No point in Jamieson pretending he can keep Shug out of jail. They both know that's not true. Don't promise miracles. Be honest about your limitations. Offer him only the things he knows you can deliver. Make him trust you. Shug's nodding. He didn't expect more than he's being offered.

'And MacArthur?' he's asking. 'How do you handle him?'

Jamieson's smiling. 'We have things on him. As soon as we knew he was moving against us, we started to defend ourselves. We can handle him. Won't be easy. Going to be messy,' he's saying, leaning back in his chair. 'I won't bullshit you here; I can't guarantee that he's not going to do me some harm. And I can guess that he'll target your business because of this. But I'll give you the best protection you can get anywhere in this city.'

It all adds up to the best offer Shug's going to get. A man about to be sent down. A man with a business under attack from Alex MacArthur. Losing 49 per cent of that business is a small price. He doesn't trust Jamieson. Why should he? But in a battle of honesty between Jamieson and MacArthur, there's a clear winner. He might not feel the same way if he understood the games being played between those two men, but Shug can only work with the information he has available. Besides, there's an issue beyond trust. If he wants to come out of jail with anything at all in his possession, he needs to pick the winner in the next fight. The last fight was Shug and Jamieson, and Jamieson won. The next winner will be Jamieson or MacArthur. One or the other. Pick your fighter; pray he doesn't get knocked out. Which man has the talent to make it to the end of the fight? Shug's backing Jamieson. Knows that backing him makes Jamieson stronger, gives him more credibility. Gives Shug the chance to come out to something that at least resembles his old life.

'I want you to know that when I come out, I'll only be focusing on the car-ring and the garages,' Shug's saying. 'After what's gone on, no more of anything else. And I think it would be better if you didn't involve the car business in your own . . . enterprises.'

Jamieson's nodding along. He has no intention of using the car business for drugs anyway. Better to keep it separate, let it earn its own money without becoming a target. That was Shug's mistake from the beginning. Taking a profitable and safe business and turning it into a target for people in the drugs business. He's learned his lesson. All this talk is the song of the repentant sinner. Just what Jamieson expected. Just what he's heard so many times before.

'I fully intend to keep it separate. There'll be no crossover whatsoever with my businesses. Truth is, we do that already with a lot of stuff. Better to keep them separate, raises fewer eyebrows. Stops them becoming a target.'

It never felt like a friendly meeting. Never felt like Jamieson was happy with the discussion. Which seems strange to Shug, because Jamieson's the one making a killing here. He's the one who comes out of this battle between the pair with half of Shug's business. Comes out with an enhanced reputation. An opportunity to strike against MacArthur. What more does he want? Yet he seemed distracted. Shug and Fizzy are making their way back down to the car. Fizzy scarcely said a thing throughout. When Shug and Jamieson agreed that Fizzy should take control of the business, he nodded, but said nothing. Seems depressed by the whole thing.

'Did you think there was something weird with Jamieson and Young?' Shug's asking.

'Weird?'

'Like a bad atmosphere.'

Fizzy's shrugging. 'Weird atmosphere, maybe. They know what's about to happen.'

And that kills the conversation between these two. They know what's about to happen. The police are about to start making their moves.

# 45

It was Calum's choice of location. Close to the river. Private, of course, but not so far from people that Fisher might get nervous. Fisher, bless his heart, still thinks he's in control of this situation. Sitting in the driver's seat, literally and figuratively. They've driven in silence, Calum telling the cop where to go. Fisher sneaking an occasional glance at the young man beside him. He's noticed the clear gloves Calum's wearing. A little concern at that, but let's not overreact just yet. Seen his picture, been in his flat, tried to work out who he was and what he was up to. Didn't learn much. Not enough. Now the chance to find out everything. Won't let this one slip through his fingers. The car's coming to a halt in a small car park. Surrounded by overgrown weeds, a large wooden fence and the back wall of a storage unit. There are a couple of people working round the side of the building, paying them no attention. They can see the river off to their left. Ahead of them weeds, to the right the fence. Fisher's switching off the engine.

'I'm going to tell you a lot,' Calum's saying, staring straight ahead, 'so you might want to record this.'

Fisher's taking his small recorder from his pocket.

Switching it on and placing it on the centre console between the seats. 'Can you introduce yourself, please?' Fisher's asking.

'My name's Calum MacLean. I've worked for Peter Jamieson for about six months.' Why stop at the introduction? He knows what he wants to say. He's not here to be questioned by Fisher – that'll only lead to conflict. There are certain things Calum wants to say, certain things to avoid. Just get on with the story. 'It was his right-hand man, John Young, that got in touch with me first. I went into the club and met Jamieson and Young in the office there. They told me they wanted Lewis Winter dead. That was my job. To kill him.'

A quick glance at Fisher, who's glaring back at him. Opening his mouth to say something. Calum's carrying on. Don't let the questions begin, or the story will never be told. Going through the details of the Winter hit and the aftermath. Throwing a few names at Fisher, but never stopping to gauge the reaction. If he takes one glance sideways, that will serve as an invite for Fisher to start the questions. Give Fisher the story he needs to hear about Winter – that was Fisher's case, and he got no one. He needs to know why. Names. They're easy to throw around. Jamieson and Young. Shug and Fizzy. Winter and Davidson. Easy. Easy to hold back the ones he doesn't want to share. George. He'll keep George's involvement a secret. Dates are harder to remember. You work as a gunman, it means you live an isolated life. You don't have a memory of events by which to remember times. Long periods of nothing. So he can't provide dates, but Fisher can piece them together himself. So he's giving as much as he can.

Calum's pausing. Not deliberately. It's just that this is very uncomfortable. Not because he's telling it to a cop, but because he's telling it to anyone. You live your life with big secrets and they come to define you. Suddenly giving them away to anyone is unnerving. Carry on; you pause, and you might never get started again. Talking about the safe house, the new flat, the late-night call. No mention of Emma. If anyone deserves to be left out of this . . .

Calum can sense a little movement from Fisher when he mentions Frank. Rattle through it. Tommy Scott and Andy McClure. Two more names to throw into the conversation. Explaining the circumstances of that night. A lot to explain. Then Frank. That's a lot to talk about. Hard to say, hard for Fisher to hear. A few pauses there, but Fisher never interrupts. He needs to hear this. Needs to hear the detail. And he can tell how hard it is for Calum to say. He hates what he's hearing, but he respects the difficulty of the tale. Respects it because he can hear the honesty. And now Calum's reached Kenny and Hardy.

'Jamieson knew that Kenny was talking to you. Got it from one of his contacts in your station. I don't know who. He wanted to get rid of Kenny, punish him. Wanted rid of Hardy too, knew it would harm Shug Francis. People were talking about Jamieson and Shug. Couldn't understand why Jamieson was taking so long to deal with Shug. Jamieson also had Alex MacArthur on board for this. See, Shug's operation was leaking like a sieve at this point. As soon as Shug tried to set up a meeting with MacArthur, Jamieson knew about it. So he called MacArthur and they did a deal. They were going to screw Shug over. But Jamieson had plans. As soon as he was done with Shug, he was going after old MacArthur. He was going to use the Shug connection to make MacArthur a target. MacArthur's fake deal with Shug was supposed to justify it. So me and Kenny went and picked up Hardy. Killed him. Kenny was digging the grave when I killed Kenny, too.

'I knew maybe two months ago that I was going to get out. Get out of the business. Get out of the city. I was giving up too much to be good at what I did. So I decided to use those killings as an escape route. Jamieson and Young wouldn't expect to hear from me for a week, maybe more. That gave me time to get everything I needed and get out. I needed help from someone I could trust. So I turned to my brother, William. He was happy to help. He'd wanted me to get out of the business for ages. He went and picked up the fake ID I was going to use, from a man called Barry Fairly. Must have been Fairly who grassed us up to Jamieson. I wanted them to think that maybe I'd been killed that night. The night I killed

Hardy and Kenny. I wanted them to be unsure. Fairly ruined that. So Jamieson sent a man called Shaun Hutton to attack my brother. Hutton killed him.'

Calum's stopped, and now he's looking Fisher square in the face. Fisher isn't saying anything. Sitting there looking back at him. A little puzzled. A little shocked. Not sure how much of this he can trust. Usually he would trust nothing. A man turns up and starts telling stories about the people he thinks are responsible for his brother's death and you can ignore most of it. People blurt out all sorts of bullshit in the quest for revenge. This is different. What Calum's said about himself makes this much more credible. Nobody offers that much incriminating evidence as part of a yarn. And a lot of what he's said fits in with Fisher's suspicions. Someone dying in Calum's flat, for one thing. Calum disappeared and the place was deep-cleaned. Fisher knew something had happened there that was worth a meticulous cover-up.

'What about before Jamieson?' Fisher's asking. Surprising himself with that question. It shouldn't be the first. Focus on what's right in front of you. But he feels a need to know more about this young man.

'Before Jamieson I worked,' Calum's saying with a shrug. 'But I haven't come here to talk about before Jamieson. I've come here to talk about Jamieson.'

'I have evidence that says Shug ordered the hit on Kenneth McBride and Richard Hardy.'

'Your evidence is planted,' Calum's telling him. 'They can manipulate all sorts of stuff to point you the wrong way. Phone records. Suggestions to coppers from contacts. They've been doing it for a while. I think that's what kept me off your radar. You didn't know I was the man you were looking for. Didn't even know that it was someone working for Jamieson you should be chasing. They're careful. Always plotting. Always playing the game.'

Fisher's rubbing his forehead. He knows he shouldn't let the conversation halt, but there's too much to think about. He needs more detail – that's a start. 'The murder weapons—' he's starting, before Calum interrupts him.

'All gone. Long gone. I always got my guns from a man called Roy Bowles,' he's saying. Fairly grassed, so he was grassed in turn. Now it's the old man's turn. 'He's an old pro, been in the business for years. I don't have any of the weapons I got from him. I don't know where they are.'

Fisher's nodding. That makes sense. About the only thing that does. Taking another look at Calum. He's just lost his brother, sure, so that makes him unpredictable. But this? A long-term gunman, low on the radar and successful, confessing and throwing names around. This doesn't quite make sense. Not even if the boy was emotional, which he's not. Told the whole thing with a cold voice. Like it was no big deal.

# 46

Hutton's arrived at the club. Been parked across the street from the entrance for about five minutes. Pretending to check messages on his phone. Doing no such thing. Gathering his nerves. Got the call from Young about half an hour ago. Shouldn't be nervous. This will be the job against Calum. Punished the brother, now it's finally time to move against the man who matters. This is what Hutton's good at. There's a part of him that's looking forward to it – the part that wants to feel comfortable with his work again. So far, the crossover and a job he hasn't liked. They must know that he hasn't liked being muscle for them. He's not being paranoid here, but he's convinced they're unhappy with the work he's done. This will turn it around. They hired him as a gunman, and a good performance against a well-regarded target like Calum MacLean overshadows all past poor performances.

He's across the street and heading to the entrance. Stopping as he sees John Young coming along the street. Young seems to be giving him a dirty look. That's not good. Hutton's nodding a hello.

'Come on,' Young's saying, leading him into the club.

They're going up the stairs without saying a word. Young going faster than Hutton because he's used to them.

'Is this about Calum?' Hutton's asking. There's nobody around. No reason not to ask that Hutton can see. Yet the question's getting a dirty glance from Young.

'You could say that.' That's all he's saying, pushing open the doors to the snooker room. You don't ask a business question anywhere other than the office. Certainly not on the stairs of the club, where anyone can come and go. But his annoyance runs deeper. Hutton made Young look bad. Hutton's incompetence made Young's judgement seem suspect. There are few worse mistakes for an employee to make.

They're walking through the snooker room. Hutton knowing enough to know that he should walk behind. Along the corridor and knocking on the office. Inside, taking seats. They're in their usual places. Young on the couch to the side, Jamieson behind the desk. Hutton's sitting on the chair in front of Jamieson, stewing. The atmosphere is wrong. If this is a call for a job, then the mood should be different. There should be tension, of course, but it should be excited tension. There should be a sense of people being busy. People wanting to get you in and out quickly. Don't ever be seen with the gunman.

Not this time. Languid and angry. A strange atmosphere, that doesn't bode well. Jamieson's sitting opposite, looking sulky. Not even glancing at Young. The atmosphere between those two is what worries Hutton. A bad feeling towards himself is scary, sure. Means they're not happy with his performance and he has to step up his game. A bad feeling between Jamieson and Young could mean serious problems for the business. Could have consequences for everyone who works for them.

'William MacLean's dead,' Jamieson's saying to Hutton. Looking at him accusingly. It's taking Shaun Hutton a few seconds to remember the name.

'Oh,' he's saying. Then saying nothing else, because what else do you say? Jamieson's just told him that he botched a job. Worst kind of botch. Brought a murder investigation to their doorstep. Anything he says now will only antagonize.

'Oh? Is that it? Oh? And that explains why you kicked the bugger to death, does it?'

Apparently saying nothing antagonizes as well. 'I didn't think I gave him that much of a kicking. I went, I isolated him, I did the job I was given. I didn't mean for him to die. Look, that was muscle-work. I never said I knew muscle-work.' Now he's stopping, because his brain is catching up with his mouth. Brain isn't happy with mouth's performance. He's just suggested that Young made the mistake by sending him to do the job. Just admitted that he can't be trusted with muscle-work.

Jamieson's glancing across at Young. He can see Young bristle, but Young won't say anything. He'll stick to protocol.

Jamieson won't. Not today. He has things he has to say. Dereliction of duty if he doesn't. And he needs to vent.

'So it's someone else's fault, because you don't know how to kick the shit out of someone without killing them? Is that it?'

'That's not—' Hutton's starting, before being silenced by Jamieson's growing rage.

'It was a rhetorical question.' He's standing up now. 'You fucked up. Badly. Worse than badly. You killed the wrong fucking brother. Now Calum's out there somewhere, walking round with a grudge. How do you think that's going to work out? That's rhetorical, too,' Jamieson's shouting before anyone can open their mouth. 'You had a very simple job to do. You failed, and failed badly. You're finished with us.'

Hutton knows what that means. His name is about to become poison. He's about to become unemployable in this city. Even as a freelancer, he'll struggle for work. Might have to move away, but even that might not be all of it. He could become a target. The man who knows too much. He's opening his mouth to say something, but Young's beaten him to it.

'Peter, come on.' Looking across at Jamieson. Trying to talk him down, but knowing he may be wasting his breath. Jamieson's anger isn't out of control. On the contrary. He's thought about this. He knows what he's doing here. The cold anger. Seems like he's lashing out, but he's not. He's plotted this, and is now delivering the message. It's one that Young doesn't think should be delivered to the guilty party. You don't tell a man that he's a potential target.

'Get out,' Jamieson's saying to Hutton. 'Come on. Get up and get out. Don't show your face here again. We're done, you and me. Finished. Go on, piss off!'

Hutton's getting slowly to his feet. Looking across at Young. Young's giving him a little nod. A nod that tells him to do as he's told. Leave, but Young will try to work on this. Might not be as bad as it looks. That's what Hutton's thinking. Hoping. Making his way to the door and out of the office. Praying that this is an elaborate warning. Good cop, bad cop. The boss fires you; his right-hand man calls you up a few hours later and tells you you're back in the organization. Just keep your nose clean and standards high from now on. Makes sense to Hutton. The right-hand man's the one you deal with most often. The one you need to like. Fear the boss, like his deputy. And Hutton can change things. There's something he can do. First he needs a drink to kill his nerves. As he's making his way down the stairs, he's telling himself that this isn't over. It just feels like it.

As soon as Hutton's closed the door, Young's turning on Jamieson. 'That was stupid. Even if you want him out, you don't tell him. There's nobody else, for Christ's sake. You get rid of him and we have no cover at all.'

'Yeah,' Jamieson's saying quietly, 'and whose fault is that?' Letting it hang.

Young's taking a deep breath. 'Not my fault that Frank turned out the way he did. Not my fault that Calum wasn't committed. He was Frank's recommendation. Maybe Hutton isn't the best choice, but he served us well in the past. He could serve us again. Look, we sort out this Calum thing . . .'

'Hah, and how's that coming along, John? Tell me. Have you solved that wee problem?'

Now he's looking to create an argument. Young knows it. 'I'm not going to fight with you, Peter. We'll find Calum. This is a bump in the road.'

Jamieson's reaching into his drawer, taking out a bottle and a small glass. 'Yeah. A bump. Don't come back until you're over the bump. Now get out of my sight.'

# 47

'I'm sorry about your brother,' Fisher's saying. It maybe sounds like he doesn't mean it, but he does. Fisher comes across people like William MacLean all the time. People who aren't heavily involved. Fringe players. Sometimes people who aren't involved in criminal activity at all. But they're related to someone who is. Or they're a friend of someone who is. And they end up carrying the can for someone else's behaviour. Truth is, Fisher's sick of seeing people like William MacLean. Sick of seeing people who've done little wrong end up on the slab because some thug thinks he can justify it to himself. Peter Jamieson. Shaun Hutton. Thugs that Fisher has to stop.

'Thank you,' Calum's saying. Doesn't sound like he believes it. Doesn't need to. He's not here for sympathy. 'I want to say something about my brother,' Calum's continuing. 'He wasn't involved in anything. Not really. He helped me, but only because it was me. He wouldn't have done it for anyone else. Maybe he occasionally did little things that he shouldn't have in the garage, just to make a bit of extra dough. But it was nothing serious. Never was. He didn't deserve what happened to him, and he doesn't deserve to be trashed now. I know people will want to trash him, because he's dead. I know you'll look to trash him, because he's my brother. But he doesn't deserve that. He deserves to be treated with respect. That's who he was. A good guy. Not some criminal. Not some thug. A good guy.'

Fisher's nodding. 'We won't trash your brother. I know he wasn't involved.' He won't deny that they destroy the reputations of people, because it happens. Sometimes it's necessary to tell the unpleasant truth about someone. Not in William's case. Not now.

Is this all about getting a good obituary for his brother? Revenge too, obviously. But to throw himself at a cop like this? That's unheard of. Might be grief, Fisher's guessing. Calum's not thinking straight, and that's what's causing him to tell the truth. Grief can do funny things to people. Although he doesn't seem grief-stricken. A bit depressed perhaps.

'Is that all you want to tell me?' Fisher's asking. Calum's told his story, fallen silent. Time for Fisher to take back control of events.

'That's it.'

'And what do you think is going to happen now?' There's a little irony in Fisher's voice. Like it doesn't matter what Calum thinks will happen next, because he doesn't get to choose.

'I think you're going to get out of the car and I'm going to drive it away,' Calum's saying. 'And I think we're never going to see each other again.'

Fisher's about to laugh. Say something a little derisive, but not aggressive. This is still a dangerous man he's dealing with. Now he's silent. Silent because he can see Calum reaching into his inside coat pocket, and Fisher thinks he knows what that means. Odd thing is, even as he sees the gun emerge, he doesn't fear for his life. A killer in a car with a cop, and the cop isn't afraid. Why tell that long story just to kill the man you told it to? He'll let Fisher go, but he's showing how dangerous he is. Holding the gun low on his lap, pointing it at Fisher. Not saying anything. The gun does the talking for him.

'Okay,' Fisher's saying quietly. 'Just promise me that you're not going to go out and use that thing. You said you wanted your last job to be your last job. I think I know why you've told me this. I think I know what you're doing. That's fine. Just don't use that thing, okay?'

Calum's turning and looking at him. A sharp look. 'I'm almost gone,' he's saying.

Fisher's opening the car door and stepping out. Walking slowly round to the front of the car. Clutching the recorder. It's still recording, incidentally. Recording the noise of Calum starting the car. It better have bloody worked. Fisher's watching, thinking. How much of this can he even use? Hardly a reliable witness. Now a disappearing witness. They'll chase after him, of course, but Fisher has a feeling about that boy. Cold and sharp. The type who'll know how to disappear. How to stay off the radar. There aren't many like him. Few enough that those you do meet stand out. He might just have delivered Jamieson and Young. Shug was already at the end of the rope, but there was mention of MacArthur in this, too. It's not so much the detail Calum MacLean gave about who did what to whom; the most important thing was clearing up the relationships. Who's working with whom. Who's working against whom. It makes sense of a complicated picture. Tells Fisher what he needs to do next.

Calum's sliding across into the driver's seat. Watching Fisher go round to the front of the car. Fisher's smart. Not an accident where he's standing – away from the doors of the car. Making a show of the fact that he's not going to get in the way. Not going to try to stop Calum. Reversing the car and turning. Moving alongside the storage unit, looking back in the mirror. Fisher's still standing there, watching the car go. Not doing anything. He won't until the car is out of sight. Once Calum's out of view, he'll be into his pocket for his mobile. Good for him. Won't make any difference. Calum will be ditching this car at the first safe location. Fisher will get it back unharmed. So long as they weren't followed. So long as there aren't half a dozen cops waiting for him when Calum emerges at the front of this building and into the street.

There aren't. He's out onto the street, and driving away.

As soon as the red Renault is out of view, Fisher's reaching into his pocket. Pulling out his mobile. Stopping, remembering the little MP3 player in his other hand. Still recording, the tiny screen says. Been recording for seventy-four minutes. Now his mind's running off in another direction. How does he justify bringing charges on the basis of what's on the recorder? He can't. But he can use this info to direct him to better evidence that he *can* use. All the ducks are lined up now. Winter was working for Shug, so Jamieson had him removed. Shug hired Glen Davidson to kill Calum. Scott and McClure were killed on Jamieson's orders, as was Frank MacLeod. Kenny McBride and Richard Hardy as well. Seems like Jamieson's been a busy little beaver. Fisher's smiling, and then remembering that he's stuck here, car-less.

Calling the station, straight through to his own desk. They must be waiting for him back at the station. Wondering where he is. Worrying about him. By God, they better be. The phone's ringing and ringing. Maybe there's nobody in the office. All out looking for him? Not bloody likely. If someone's decided to take it upon themselves to lead the arrest against Shug and Fizzy in his absence, Fisher will raise hell when he gets back to the office. Or maybe they just don't want to answer his phone. He did tell them not to in the past. Doesn't like other cops dealing with his business, even if it's just to take a message. But he's letting it ring so long now that someone has to answer it.

'Hello, DI Fisher's desk, DC Davies speaking.' Sounding nervous and a little excited. Like he knows he's not supposed to answer, but wants to.

'Davies, it's Fisher here. Come and pick me up.'

'Okay, where are you?'

Silence.

Fisher's had to go out onto the street and down to the corner to find a road sign. He's telling Davies that he's on the corner of the street.

'What corner?'

'Just go from one end of the bloody street to the other – you'll find me.' Fisher's getting annoyed now. Annoyed at not having his car. Annoyed at the time that's going to be lost waiting for Davies to collect him and take him back to the station. That was probably part of MacLean's plan. Smart little bastard. Helpful as he's been, he still has to be a target. Tempting to let him have a head start. He's not the most important person here. Jamieson's the biggest target now available. But Calum MacLean is a killer, and Fisher is going to hunt him down.

Standing on the corner, waiting for Davies, has given him time to think. How he's going to play this. Go get Shug now. Such a strong temptation to go and arrest Jamieson first. But no. There are leaks in the station. Play it the way Jamieson expects you to play it. Shug and his people first. Then, when Jamieson thinks he's won his little battle, you swoop on him.

Has to play this one close to his chest. Looking at his watch: after eleven. They can have Shug in custody by, let's say, half-one. Then Jamieson. Going to need a lot of manpower, but he has to move fast. He has Calum's story. The quicker he puts it to others, the better chance he has that he can trip them up. They must know that Calum's running from them. Christ's sake, they killed his brother. They can't be stupid enough to think he won't move against them. It's a funny thing, though, Fisher's thinking as he watches Davies approach at last. A lot of these criminals just don't think of the police when it comes to internal business. They don't imagine that one of their own would go to the police. They're probably thinking that Calum will come after them with his gun. They won't be expecting Fisher at all.

# 48

They've been sitting in the den since they got back to the house. Having a beer and a sandwich and talking about old times. The last meal before the gallows. Shug doesn't seem nervous. He must know that he's looking at years. He's drinking and laughing and enjoying this moment. That's how it seems to Fizzy, but Fizzy doesn't know what's going on inside Shug's head. There's bitterness there. Not towards Fizzy. Not even towards Peter Jamieson. A little towards Alex MacArthur, but he's not the main target. The main target is himself. This – sitting here, laughing and having fun – used to be normal. Not that long ago this would have seemed pretty damned ordinary. They'd be talking about cars. Only a little about the business. Seems weird to look back and remember how little they actually talked shop. There was so little to talk about. It was just that easy. And he threw it away.

They're both being careful with their conversation. Every subject is one that pre-dates this failure. Nothing from Shug that might hint about Hutton. Nothing from Fizzy that hints that he already knows. Nothing that hints at what's going to happen next. Just enjoy this, because it isn't going to happen again for a while. There were three phone calls this morning.

All from Greig. All ignored. That bastard's been playing too many games. Trying to work every side. Well, he can find someone else to play with him. He's burned his bridges with Shug. What could Shug get? If they nail him for the Hardy murder, he could be looking at twelve, fifteen, maybe more. Shug blames MacArthur. That worries Fizzy, but he won't mention that, either. Start naming MacArthur for everything and you become a major target for MacArthur. In jail, you're a sitting duck. Maybe they're both targets already. Maybe MacArthur's already making moves against Shug. Ah, hell, too many maybes. Enjoy the beer and the conversation. Face the future with whatever guts you have, but don't spend the present worrying about it. It'll be here soon enough, no matter how you approach it. Fizzy has protection from Jamieson, which has to be worth something. And if Shug does get hit in jail, who gets to run the business permanently? Fizzy.

Ten past one is when the ugly future arrives. They're hearing the doorbell. Hearing Elaine answering it. You can just make out voices if you strain yourself, but you can't hear what they're saying. Neither Shug nor Fizzy has got up. Why bother? The cops will come crashing in and demand they get up anyway. Let them have their fun, arresting the big bad criminals. People moving along the corridor. Sounds like there's a lot of them. Shug's grateful that his kids are at school. The door's opening and two detectives are walking in. There are two uniformed officers hanging around in the corridor; you can just see them over the chubby detective's shoulder. They look embarrassingly useless.

'My name's Detective Inspector Michael Fisher, this is Detective Constable Ian Davies,' the slimmer one's saying. Fisher looks older than Shug expected. Looks worn out, actually. Shug can sympathize with that.

'I know why you're here,' Shug's saying. Getting to his feet. 'I want you to know that I had absolutely nothing to do with the death of Richard Hardy. I liked that man. He was a good man, and I wouldn't do anything to harm him.'

'Hugh Francis?' Fisher's asking. A nod in response. 'So you must be David Waters,' he's saying to Fizzy. He looks like he's in his element. Arresting people. Arresting people who don't know what they're being arrested for. 'Okay. Well, as it happens, I believe you. I'm not here to arrest you over Richard Hardy's death. I'm sure we can talk about the documentation relating to your business that we found in his office, but that's for a later date. I am arresting both of you in connection with the death of Glen Davidson. I'm also arresting you both for your involvement in the distribution of class-A drugs. I'm sure you don't mind coming to the station to discuss this, do you?'

The cops are loving this, Shug can see. The joy of confusing your prey. Glen Davidson. Shit! He'd thought that was all in the past. Buried and forgotten. It's not as though he killed Davidson. Or ordered his killing. He sent Davidson to do a job

343

and the big lump fucked up. But he sent Davidson to kill a man. This is something he is guilty of. Suddenly he feels much more nervous. He was resigned to being charged over Richard Hardy. But he wasn't scared of it, because he knows he's innocent on that one. Not this one, though. Indisputably guilty of sending Davidson to kill Calum MacLean. That was an almighty cock-up from start to finish. Just didn't realize that this was going to be the finish. He's glancing round at Fizzy. Fizzy drove Davidson that night. Suddenly it looks worse for him. But there's nothing he can say, because the uniformed cops are coming forward to cuff him.

They're marching him out of the office and along the corridor of his house, stopping beside the front door. Shug's wife, Elaine, is standing there. Watching them. About to tell her husband that she'll call their lawyer. That she'll pick up the kids from school. That she'll do something. Not able to say anything, because Fisher's speaking first.

'Elaine Francis. I think you should come down to the station with us as well. I believe you may have information that will prove valuable to our investigation. Don't need to cuff her,' he's saying as an aside to one of the uniformed cops. Shug's about to say something, but there's no point. She does know some things that the police would find useful. Not a lot of detail, but she knows when Shug was at home. Knows when people came to visit the house. She's smart. She can handle this.

There are three cars parked out at the front of the house. Only one of them a marked police car. Shug's being put into the marked car, the two uniformed officers getting in with him. It's only as he sits in the back of the car and looks over his shoulder that he sees there's a driver sitting in each of the other two cars. So two detectives and four other cops, just to arrest him, Fizzy and Elaine. Seems like a farce. He still thinks of himself as harmless. It's a joke to send six cops to arrest him. And then he thinks about what he's been arrested for. Sending Davidson to kill MacLean. Trying to force his way into the drug trade. You think about that, and you think that maybe they should have sent more than six. He can see the DC getting into the back of a car with a cuffed Fizzy. And he can see Fisher getting into the back of another car with Elaine.

A silent journey to the station. The two young cops aren't saying a word to Shug. Probably a good thing that Greig isn't here. Shug wouldn't trust his temper around that treacherous bastard. They're pulling into the station car park. All traipsing into the building.

'Put him in interview one,' Fisher's saying to the uniformed cops, 'put the other two in cells.' They're leading Shug along a corridor and into an interview room. The two cops sitting him down. One turning to the other.

'You can handle him; I'm going for a piss.' Now Shug and one young cop. They look excited, the two younger ones. This is probably a big deal for them, Shug's thinking. How big a deal? They're after him for Davidson. They could nail him for that, but what evidence do they have? Taken them long enough to arrest him. Might be nothing. And there's a silver lining. Fisher believes he wasn't involved in the Hardy hit. So they must be onto MacArthur.

The young uniformed cop is back in the room, just before Fisher gets there. He has the chubby detective in tow. A nod to the two cops and they're leaving. Fisher's sitting opposite Shug. Looking at him. Judging him.

'Your lawyer will be here in a few minutes,' he's saying. 'You don't have to wait for him to get here, if there's anything you'd like to say first.'

Shug knows what this is. The recorder hasn't been switched on, there's no lawyer present: this is the one opportunity to say something off the record. A hint that any help given now will play well later. Shug's weighing it up. 'Elaine knew nothing,' he's saying. 'I kept her out. And Fizzy didn't know a lot.'

Fisher's nodding his head. 'I can be persuaded about your wife, not so much about your mate. But I need to be persuaded.'

'I know things,' Shug's saying. 'Things you'll be interested in.'

Fisher doesn't want to hear it right now. Too much else to do. He wants Shug to commit to telling him; the actual telling will have to wait until later. If Fisher gets bogged down in that now, then the main business of the day is pushed back, possibly by hours. Can't have that. They have to move before Jamieson has the chance to find out. That means now. He's told them all to be waiting for him in the incident room. Waiting for instructions. He and Davies are making their way in, the four plods and a couple of new arrivals standing there.

'Right. We're going to arrest Peter Jamieson and John Young. We know to arrest Jamieson at the nightclub he owns. He's the priority. Young we're not so sure about. We think he's on the streets. Right now we focus on Peter Jamieson. We need to move fast. We can't give him any opportunity to get away. This is once-in-a-lifetime stuff.'

# 49

Young's driving. Been to see a contact, who turned out to be more useful than expected. The way things are going, Young expects everyone to be hopeless. Not this woman. Works for a taxi firm. A clean one – they have nothing to do with the criminal industry. She works in the office, takes calls, that sort of thing. Her brother is involved at a low level with Angus Lafferty, Jamieson's biggest importer. Lafferty must have mentioned Calum to the brother, the brother mentioned him to the sister and she contacted Young. She told him that they had a pick-up this morning. Young man, fits the description. As soon as she told him the house he was collected from, he knew they were on the right track. The little bastard! Probably thought it was hilarious to spend the night in a house owned by Jamieson. It's a joke you only get to make once. The driver dropped Calum off in Cowcaddens. Doesn't mean anything to Young, but it's the next location to check.

Now his phone's ringing. He's ignoring it until he sees somewhere he can park. He's a pro. Not going to be pulled over for driving whilst using a phone. Then you get your name on the police radar and they start harassing you every chance they get. Already ignored one call this morning. That was from Greig. That lying bastard can burn in the fire he's created, snuggling up to Shug.

He's found somewhere to stop. Pulling over and taking his phone from the dashboard. Still ringing. A number on the screen, not a name. Vague recognition of the number, but he can't quite place it.

'Hello?'

'Hello, John,' the young man on the other end is saying. Now Young remembers. PC Joseph Higgins. Higgins used to get in touch with Young on an old pay-as-you-go mobile that only Higgins knew the number to. Not now. This is a busy time, and Higgins is a man with important information, so he has Young's regular mobile number. Allowed to call to make sure he gets straight through. When this is done, and Higgins goes back to being just another contact, he'll return to the dedicated mobile. Less convenient, but safer. Now he's making a hushed call, whispering into his phone.

'What's up, Joseph?' Young's asking. Instinctively thinking that the young cop's probably overreacting to something.

'They've arrested Shug. They have him at the station,' Higgins is saying. Talking fast and quiet. 'I was there when they arrested him. Something's changed. They didn't arrest him over Hardy. They arrested him over Glen Davidson. Fisher went out in the morning and came back at lunchtime. Something changed. I think Fisher might be looking past Shug now.' And he's hung up. He's given Young fair warning, and now he's going back to his job. Leaving Young sitting in his car at the side of the road, trying to digest what he's just heard. Something's changed. Well, Jesus, that's just vague enough to mean anything at all. But the kid wouldn't ring if it was good news. Good news is no news at all. Things have changed for the worse. Looking past Shug? Looking at who? It's when he remembers the mention of Glen Davidson that things start to fall into place.

But it's not the mention of Davidson that clinches it. It's that mention of Fisher. He left the station in the morning, came back at lunchtime. After that meeting something changed. The station is in Cowcaddens. There's a cold feeling in Young's stomach. Calum going after them all. Looking to bring them all down. Fisher's arrested Shug, sure, because Calum gave him detail that implicated Shug. But you can bet he's looking past Shug. Way past that gullible, snivelling little bastard. Much bigger targets lined up behind him. Never mind the rules of the road, Young needs to move. He's pulling out and racing along the street. Got to get back to the club. He's calling Jamieson as he drives, but there's no answer. Calling the office, but nothing. Damn it all! He knows Jamieson's there. Why the hell isn't he picking up? Oh God, don't say Calum's got there first. This is all unravelling. Come on, hurry up!

Screeching to a halt outside the club. Lucky he wasn't pulled over by a cop car on the way. He'll certainly get done by a camera, but that's the last of his worries now. Half-surprised, half-relieved that there isn't an ambulance and a bunch of cop cars outside the club already. Up the stairs and through the snooker room. The usual handful of daytime drinkers at the bar. They look as if nothing has penetrated the perpetual gloom of their lives, which is a good sign. Along the corridor, relaxing a little. Not bothering to knock on the door, just barging in. And stopping in his tracks. Jamieson on the couch, glass in hand. Deana Burke beside him. Smiling at Jamieson. Keeping her sweet? Nope, Young's patience doesn't stretch to this.

'This is why you didn't answer your fucking phone?' he's shouting, slamming the door shut behind him. 'This silly bitch is why you ignored me twice. We're in serious trouble here, Peter, and you're fumbling around with this tart. Jesus, it's hardly a week since we put Kenny in the ground.' Well, that'll end a romance.

Jamieson's standing up. That cold anger he gets. Usually means trouble. 'What the fuck are you talking about?' he's demanding.

'I'm talking about Calum going to Fisher this morning and spilling his guts. I'm talking about the police probably being on their way here as we speak. They arrested Shug for Glen Davidson, not for Hardy. If they know about Davidson, then they know about every fucking thing.'

Deana's standing beside Jamieson, but she's irrelevant to

him now. Professionalism overwhelms every other feeling. Jamieson's staring at Young. The anger has gone, wiped out by uncertainty. Calum going to Fisher. If he talked about Davidson, talked about his killings, then he must be in custody. Must have turned himself in. Oh, shit! He's thrown himself on the fire in revenge for his brother. Slitting his own throat in the hope of drowning them all in his blood.

A moment of silence. A deep breath. 'Call the lawyer. Get them on this straight away. Anything that can be moved out of Fisher's reach, do it. Now! Lockdown, everything hidden. And let's all just calm down a wee bit, okay.' Saying that to Young.

Deana is now a non-person. Just a body in the room who happens to be hearing their conversation. If you have nothing to contribute to this, then you are nothing.

'If all they have is Calum's evidence, then they don't have much. We kept him at arm's length. He doesn't know shit. His word in a court is worth nothing. Nothing. So let's just keep cool.' Looking at Young with a meaningful expression. It's been a long time since they talked about what they would say and do if the police turn up. Used to talk about it a lot in the early days. The better you get at this, the more remote the possibility feels. So they haven't talked about it recently, but they both know the standard they have to set in an interview room. The evasive tactics required.

'What did he say about Kenny?' Deana's asking quietly.

She half-knew. Let's be honest here – deep down she had her suspicions. She wanted to believe it was MacArthur. It felt better to think that it was some distant enemy rather than Kenny's own boss. And Jamieson was nice. He was offering her an opportunity to move on with her life. But she can't ignore what Young just said. Certainly not after hearing Jamieson's assessment. He's in trouble, it's obvious. She doesn't want to be around him if his world is about to collapse. Jamieson's looking at her, but she's moving towards the door. She's heard enough to know that she doesn't want to be here. Young's reaching out to stop her, but Jamieson's shaking his head. She doesn't know anything. Jamieson is nobody's fool. He's said nothing in front of her that he can't easily deny. Said nothing she can hope to prove.

Deana's down the stairs, heading for the front door. Out onto the street and stopping dead. Timing is everything. If she'd left two minutes earlier, she'd be gone. Instead she's standing three feet away from DI Fisher as he gets out of the passenger seat of an unmarked police car.

'Well, Deana, this is a surprise,' he's saying with a knowing smile. Not two days ago she was telling him that Alex MacArthur and Des Collins were behind Kenny's murder. Now she's leaving the office of the man responsible. In Fisher's eyes, she's either been badly deceived or she's a lying bitch. Fisher's guessing the latter, but either way she might be useful. 'Matheson,' he's saying to one of the plods getting out of a marked car, 'find Miss Burke a seat in the back of your car and stay with her.' Matheson's groaning. He gets to sit with this cow while the rest of them get to go inside and arrest Peter Jamieson. Life just isn't fair sometimes.

They're into the building, moving up the stairs. One of the plods – Fisher doesn't know his name – trips. Falling forward, scratching his hand. Other cops are laughing. Fisher's going to let them. He's in that good a mood. He knows where the office is, found that out ages ago. Wanted to know, just in case this day came. Ignoring the old boozers who are gawping at them. Marching through the snooker room and along the corridor.

'Check these rooms,' Fisher's saying to anyone who happens to be walking behind him. He knows the office is the last door at the far end. Still sensible to check for people hiding in other rooms. He can hear doors opening behind him. A couple of calls of 'Clear'. Walking to the office door, not slowing for an instant. Don't let the other cops see your nerves. Arrests like this make your legend. Let history think you were nerveless.

Jamieson's sitting behind his desk. Young's sitting on the couch to the side of the room. They're both looking at the door. Both standing up. They obviously saw the cars arrive; the office windows look down onto the street. They've been sitting here. Waiting patiently.

'Detective Inspector Fisher,' Jamieson's saying, trying to

take the initiative. 'What can we do to help you? Anything at all – you name it.' Said with a cheeky smile. Trying to write his own little legend. The guy who was as cool as ice when the cops turned up. The guy who knew he could beat any charge they threw at him. It'll sound brilliant, but only if it turns out to be true.

'You can join my colleagues and me at the station and have a little chat. You think you can both manage that?'

See how quickly the cheeky smile fades. Not because of the arrest, Jamieson knew that was coming. It's because Fisher's picked up Jamieson's tone and has thrown it back in his face.

'Am I being arrested?' Jamieson's asking.

'Yes, you are,' Fisher's telling him, and going through the procedure. Enjoying it, sure, but that isn't what counts. You can arrest anyone, any time; doesn't mean you're going to make the charge stick. The arrest means little. The conviction means everything. Fisher's reeling off the list of names. Watching Jamieson closely as he does. Lewis Winter. Thomas Scott. Andrew McClure. Frank MacLeod. Richard Hardy. Kenneth McBride. William MacLean. No reaction to any of them. Jamieson standing there and watching Fisher. No expression this time. It's serious now. Accusations of drug dealing and money-laundering thrown in for good measure. No reaction to those, either.

Jamieson's mind is working at a swift pace. Working out

what he can deny and what he can't. Confident that he can beat every serious charge on the sheet. Confident, but only just. Not confident about what this is going to do for him. Everyone on the street will know he's been taken in. They'll know Fisher was correct with all those accusations. Even if Jamieson doesn't get a long stretch, he's now hanging on by his fingernails.

Fisher's read the same list to Young. Young saying nothing, just glaring at the cops. He's spotted Higgins, but he'll say nothing. A good police contact is more valuable now than ever. Higgins is the last person Young or Jamieson will throw overboard. Both men cuffed. Now Fisher has the joy of walking them out through their own club in chains. Shame only the afternoon drinkers are in. Would be much better if it was night and the place was full. Still, those grizzly, whiskey-sodden losers will tell the story of the arrest to anyone who'll listen. There's nothing those sad bastards love more than telling a story about another's misfortune. They're moving down the stairs. Near-silence. Just the scuffing of shoes. Everyone focused, everyone careful. Out onto the street and putting them each into a car. Fisher sitting in the back with Jamieson. Jamieson won't say a word, not until he's been briefed by his lawyer. Doesn't matter. Fisher just wants to savour the moment.

# 50

They've all been in their cells for a couple of hours. They've all spoken to their lawyers. Fisher's been waiting impatiently, but he'll stretch his patience a little further. Tempting to get into an interview room with Peter Jamieson first, because he's the biggest fish. But that's not always the most profitable approach. Go for the little guys first. See what you can get them to cough up about the big guy. Get every possible piece of ammunition you can gather before you take on the big fellow. Fisher and DC Davies are going into the interview room. Shug and his lawyer, sitting at the table, ready. He's a good lawyer, this one. Fisher doesn't like him. The higher up the scumbag chain you go, the better the lawyers. Inevitable – greed follows money. Davies will do as he's told, which is nothing. Sit there and keep his trap shut, let Fisher ask the questions.

Fisher's informing Shug that the tape recorder and camera are being switched on. Now he's introducing himself and Davies, naming the lawyer and Shug. Shug knows the drill. Deliver something useful and his wife walks. No charges against her. Deliver something sparkling, and he might just do himself a few favours. The lawyer knows it, too. He'll have advised accordingly.

'You know why you're here,' Fisher's saying. 'Is there anything you'd like to say?'

A nod from the lawyer, and Shug's leaning forward. 'I know I've made a few mistakes in my life, but I've never killed anyone, or asked for anyone to be killed,' he's saying. Disappointing that he's denying the whole Davidson thing, but hardly a surprise. Means Fisher's going to have to build a case. 'But I have done silly things. Not of my own accord. I was guided . . . pushed into it by Alex MacArthur.'

Jackpot! Hard to suppress a smile. 'Go on,' Fisher's saying.

Shug's pausing. Weighing his words carefully. 'I have a chain of garages. We handle a lot of vehicles, obviously. We help to move some around. MacArthur thought he saw a chance to profit from that. He got in touch with us, through his right-hand man, Don Park. I admit that I was blinded by the money I could make, but I was also afraid. Everyone knows the price of crossing Alex MacArthur. I had to do as I was told.' Saying it all with contrition. Knowing that the only person who'll contradict him is MacArthur, and he's even less believable than Shug. Fizzy won't.

'You're willing to stand up in court and say that MacArthur pushed the deal between you and him?' Fisher's asking.

'Yes. That's the truth. I'll tell the truth.'

Lashing out against the old lag he thinks was responsible for his downfall. Fisher knows different. Well, slightly different. Shug's right that MacArthur screwed him over, but he thinks he has a friend in Jamieson. He thinks wrong. Calum spilled the beans that should open Shug's mouth on Jamieson.

'Tell me about your relationship with Peter Jamieson,' Fisher's saying.

Shug's pausing. Shrugging slightly. 'I know who you mean. He's a businessman. We've been negotiating an agreement on investment. All legal. I know people have said Jamieson isn't entirely above board, but, I don't know, he seems decent enough. A straightforward guy.'

'Uh-huh,' Fisher's saying. Sitting back in his chair. Comfortable in every way. 'You say that, but that's not the information I have. The information I have says that Peter Jamieson and Alex MacArthur had an agreement in place some time ago to set you up. The two of them got together. Plotted against you. Came up with the idea of making you look guilty in the disappearance of Richard Hardy. MacArthur leaves you high and dry and gets your business. Jamieson gets rid of a rival.'

Shug's saying nothing. Staring at the top of the table. Trying to look expressionless, ends up looking pained.

'I don't know what you're talking about,' Shug's saying now. Standard response from people who just got bad news in this room.

'You know,' Fisher's saying. 'You thought you had a deal

with Jamieson. You thought MacArthur was the one who played you. Well, he did, but Jamieson was playing you, too. They both set you up. They wanted you to go down for a long stretch. Tried to set you up on the Hardy and McBride killings. But it was Jamieson who carried those out. MacArthur knew about it, sure, but he didn't do it. Jamieson's been playing you for rather a long time. Now, I'll ask you again to tell me about your relationship with Peter Jamieson.'

More staring at the table. Pained turning to angry. That's good. The first thing anger attacks is common sense. 'One of the guys who was working for me,' Shug's saying, and pausing. Has to maintain his lie. Make MacArthur seem largely responsible. 'There was a guy called Lewis Winter. I think he was a drug dealer. Not my kind of guy. But MacArthur's kind. Jamieson had Winter killed for stepping on his toes. There was another guy. Replaced Winter, I guess. Tommy Scott. Jamieson killed him, too. You say Jamieson killed Richard Hardy. You might be right, I don't know. I know I had nothing to do with it. I liked Richard. A good man.'

Fisher's letting the conversation rest for a few seconds. Shug might be angry, but he's still careful. Trying to avoid anything that implicates himself. Trying to implicate MacArthur instead, and obviously lying to do so. MacArthur wasn't involved with Lewis Winter. That was all about Shug and Jamieson – Calum made that clear. MacArthur's a late arrival to this party. Shug being too careful to be useful. But he's provided ammo.

One last question for now. 'Tell me about your relationship with PC Paul Greig,' Fisher's saying. Shug looking up sharply. Davies is stirring in his seat. First time in years he's shown any signs of life in an interview.

Shug's scoffing. 'Relationship! Yeah. He's another one. Another crook and a liar. Everyone knows that bastard's bent. Everyone. Even you do, I bet. Course you do, it's why you're asking. He screwed me over.' The lawyer touching his arm, but it's making no difference. 'Was supposed to be a friend. Was supposed to be helping me out. Help keep me out of trouble. What a laugh! He was never a friend of mine. He was a friend of Don Park, I can tell you that. You ask Park about him. I bet he has a few stories to tell.'

'But Greig took money from you in exchange for help? For information?'

'Didn't get a lot of help from him,' Shug's saying with a bitter laugh. 'Was supposed to, but didn't. Information, though. Yeah, some of that. You bet he took money.'

Fisher's out into the corridor. There'll be much longer interviews with Shug to come. The details, rather than the overview he's getting now. Won't be hard to nail him on a number of charges. One victory in the bag, and it feels good. DCI Reid is coming out of interview room two. He has John Young in there. The senior officer sticking his nose in, now that the work's done. Fine, whatever. Everyone knows who made this happen. At least Reid has the grace to leave Peter Jamieson for Fisher.

'Anything?' Fisher's asking.

'Nothing,' Reid's saying with a shake of the head. 'Clammed up. A lot of "No comments". Won't get anything from him, either. Too sharp. Too much of a professional at this. Told him we know they must have falsified phone records to set up Francis and Collins. Nothing. We've got someone contacting the phone companies. That should give us someone else to aim at. You?'

'Francis is singing,' Fisher's saying with a smile. 'There's more to get out of him on Jamieson, but he's so busy trying to make himself look innocent it's hard to get much that's honest.' Pausing in silence as a uniformed officer walks past. Fisher wants to keep all this between himself and Reid, for now. 'He's talking about other things, though. MacArthur.'

Reid's eyes are lighting up. There have been moments in the last few months when he's wondered about Fisher. Always thought he was a good cop, but when a man stops delivering, you have to worry. He's delivered Shug Francis. That'll be a conviction. He might deliver Peter Jamieson. That would be a huge victory. Throw in Alex MacArthur, and you have the sort of once-in-a-generation score that's long spoken about.

'He'll go in the box?' Reid's asking. Meaning the witness box, rather than a coffin, which might be more apt.

'Says he will. Might change his mind, but we have him on camera talking about MacArthur. Talking about the deal they had. We can put MacArthur before a jury with what we have from Shug. If we can get anything more from Young or Jamieson . . .' he's saying, and trailing off wistfully. That's wishful thinking, but it's been a day of wishes coming true.

'They found your car, by the way,' Reid's saying. 'Dumped in a car park not that far from where you spoke to MacLean. They found his gun in the glove box; they don't think it's been used.'

Fisher's nodding. Relief. Calum MacLean didn't go looking for people to shoot with that gun. Had it just so that he could get away from the cop he confessed his sins to. All premeditated. It wasn't emotion that drove that boy to Fisher, it was pragmatism. He wanted out of the city. Couldn't get out from under Jamieson. Now Jamieson's in the station, his organization is up in the air and MacLean can run.

'We're looking for the boy,' Reid's saying, 'but no luck so far.'

Fisher's nodding. 'I doubt he's even in the city any more. He's too smart not to take his chance. There's a bunch of other people to round up,' Fisher's saying. 'We'll need to move fast. The rats will run when they hear Jamieson's in.'

DCI Reid's about to answer when another detective comes along the corridor. It's that fat guy. Fisher's trying to remember his name. Nope, still nothing.

'DC Baird, how can I help?' Reid's asking. That's what separates Fisher from the top of the pile: remembering people's names.

'We just got a call from the phone company, sir. We had them watch out for William MacLean's mobile. He used it to call a taxi, went east. Switched it off. Then on again a couple of minutes ago. It was just switched on for a few seconds, then switched off. It was just on long enough to pick up the signal, then off.'

Both senior cops are looking at him with frowns. Failure to give the important information first. 'Where?' Reid's demanding to know.

'East end, sir. Take them a little longer to be precise.'

Reid's looking at Fisher. Fisher's staring at the ceiling. East – it hits him. The sort of thing the cheeky bastard would do. 'Send a couple of cars to his brother's garage,' Fisher's saying quickly. Reid's nodding. Baird's running off down the corridor.

'Looks like we might have MacLean. If we can get MacArthur and Jamieson locked up, too,' Reid's saying, 'God, what a boost that would be.'

It'll be hard to get convictions that put them both away for long, Fisher knows that. Might not matter. Even without a conviction, they could end the career of an old man like MacArthur. You make a man that age look weak and vulnerable and he doesn't have time to recover. Jamieson will be more difficult to destroy without a long stretch. But still possible.

'There is one other thing, sir,' Fisher's saying, even remembering his 'sirs', such is his mood. 'Shug Francis is also accusing PC Paul Greig of taking money from him in exchange for favours. Information, it mostly seems to be. But offering other help, too. He's accused Greig of being a friend of Donald Park, one of MacArthur's right-hand men.'

Now Reid doesn't look so happy. He doesn't want this. An allegation of corruption to take the shine off an otherwise perfect day. It'll make the force look bad. 'That's a damn shame. Are we sure that it's not just mud-slinging?'

'I'm sure,' Fisher's saying. 'I've suspected for a while. I even followed Greig to Shug's house on Friday morning. He's been helping them, sir. Helping them all.'

'Shit!' Reid's muttering. They all had suspicions, but Greig's always been so useful. You don't throw away useful unless you really have to. 'He called me, hour and a half ago,' Reid's saying quietly. 'I put him off. Didn't have time, not with all this. He must have wanted to get his excuses in first.'

A loud sigh. 'There are people who won't like this,' Reid's saying ominously.

'I don't like it, sir,' Fisher's saying, and almost sounding genuine. 'Doesn't stop it being true.'

'Fine. Well. So long as it's isolated to Greig.'

Fisher's pausing. Nodding, with a little bit of a shrug. He can't commit to that. Reid's frowning. Fisher can't stop thinking about what Calum said. Young found out about Kenny talking from a contact in the station. Who knew? Reid. Davies. Higgins. Can't think of anyone else. Not Greig. 'I think it might be worth looking a little deeper, that's all,' Fisher's saying.

He's left Reid muttering to himself in the corridor. Fisher's joining Davies in the interview room containing Peter Jamieson and his fabulously wealthy lawyer. Jamieson's glancing at him as he comes in. Nothing more than that. The lawyer beside him, looking ready for a challenge. Fisher going through the routine introductions.

'I know what this is,' Jamieson's saying.

'Do you?'

'Yes, I do. You've been set up. I know that you don't have Calum MacLean in custody,' he's saying, glancing across at his lawyer, who is obviously in possession of some irritating facts. 'I know he came to you. A disgruntled former employee, making up stories. Trying to hijack his own brother's death to use it against me. Sickening, I'd say. I know you have no evidence of wrongdoing against me. You've been played.'

And Fisher's smiling. He can make a charge stick. Something – anything. He can. And yeah, he's been played by Calum MacLean. They're all playing the game. Just might be that, this time, it's Fisher's turn to win.

# 51

Calum dumped the car in the first small car park he drove past. Small and quiet, not the sort of place that'll have a security camera nearby. The car's far too hot to use. Every cop in the city will have their eyes open for it. Safer to go on foot. Sometimes you can walk right past a cop and they don't know you're the man they're supposed to be looking for. Not that he'll push his luck. Not this close to the exit. Take no stupid risk. You get this close to the end, think the hard work's over and you take it easy. Then you trip up. There's still one more trick to pull before he can get out. He thought about keeping the gun. Decided there was no point. If the police catch up with him, then he won't use it. You never use it against the police. Just guaranteeing that they pour every resource into arresting you. Delaying the inevitable.

He would use it against anyone Jamieson sent to get him, though. That's where the real threat probably lies. But who do they use? The police are chasing Hutton now that they have his name. God knows where George has gone. Calum trusts him, though. George allowed himself to be backed into a corner. He let Calum do that. Now he can't go back to Jamieson and Young. Doesn't leave them with much. Nobody that Calum fears. Nobody Calum thinks is competent enough to catch him. Wait; don't get complacent. Could easily be some little scruff with no talent who takes you down. Could be the only useful thing they ever do in their lives, and you could be the victim of it. You never forget that. Never. But he's still leaving the gun. If he can't get out of here without using it, then he can't get out. Shoving it in the glove box, so nobody will see it. Tucking the keys under the visor and getting out.

Full paranoia-mode. Trust nobody. Speak to nobody. Anybody approaches, assume the worst. Plot a careful course. He's not too far from where he needs to be. Another reason why he chose the meeting place he did. The first part he can do on foot without straying into any busy areas. Won't be the case for most of it. And busy streets mean cameras. Cameras that may well be looking for him. Assume they are. He's passed three people already and crossed to the next street at a junction. Still quiet. People happily ignoring him. Calum happy to be ignored. Very little traffic. A van going down the street behind him. Accelerating more than seems necessary. Calum turning to look, ready to react. The van driving past. Just someone rushing to his work.

Okay, can't keep this up for long. Too slow. Too high-risk. Reaching the corner and stopping. How long would he have to wait for a taxi to go past? Too long, probably, but he doesn't want to call one. Police might already be alert to people calling a cab. Nope; been standing here for nearly five minutes and not one taxi has gone past. Using William's phone to call for one. They're bound to be looking out for the phone. Too bad. Still too close to where he left the car. Damn it all! This is now luck and timing. If Fisher goes back to the station, gets all his troops out looking for Calum, out looking for the car, then this call could be a big mistake. If he goes back to the station and starts running around after Peter Jamieson, then Calum becomes a minor point. The car becomes an afterthought. If this has worked at all, then Calum should have created chaos among everyone interested in him. Pray that's correct. Calling the taxi, telling them where to pick him up. Giving them a drop-off point some distance from where he actually wants to go. That's not a problem. He can picture in his head a clear path to his final destination.

First hurdle over. He doesn't recognize the taxi driver. Now they're making their way through the streets, Calum paying close attention. If this car takes one wrong turn, this is going to become nasty. It would be an easy set-up. Taxi picks him up, delivers him to his enemies. It's happened to others before. The driver is talkative. Annoying, but reassuring. Dropping him off at the correct point, Calum paying. Waiting until the car's out of sight before he moves one way or the other. Checking up and down the street. No sign he's being followed. Walking briskly now. His nerves are bothering him. Too many people looking for him. This whole thing going on too long. The consequences costing more than the reward. Pretend that this is all for William. Keep pretending. Walking through back streets – industrial area. People around, but all working. Along another alleyway. Looking at his watch. Five past one. Been walking for longer than he thought. He's there now.

Along the back street. Reaching the back door and pausing. Listening. No sound of anyone around. Calum's prepared to break in if he has to, but he's taking a chance. Trying the handle. It's opening. Calum's sighing. It's opening because of what happened. William was here yesterday morning. He'll have unlocked the doors; going out the back, out the front, checking cars; getting out of the house to calm his nerves. Then Shaun Hutton turned up. Obviously nobody thought to lock the doors since. The police will have been all over the garage. A chance they might still have someone there. Closing the door behind him. Quiet in here. Dark, too. The front doors pulled all the way shut. Calum's walking silently into the main garage, alert and ready to bolt. Glancing back at the office. Nobody there. Checking every part of the garage. Clear.

Stopping on the left-hand side. This is where they found him. There are signs of that. Markings on the floor that the police have made. A couple of blood-stains ringed in yellow spray-paint. Calum's stopping and staring down. Remembering William. Being here yesterday and finding him. Knowing that it's all his own fault. How does what he's doing now make up for that? Don't think about it, he's telling himself. There's work to do. Into the office. Here's where his knowledge of William's work pays off. Calum knows where all the keys are. There's no car inside the garage now, the police moved them out, but there'll be several outside. Into the bottom drawer of the battered desk. Taking the key from the back of it. Using that key to open the locked drawer at the top of the desk. Six sets of car keys, carefully lined up. Ignoring the BMW keys. Take nothing fancy. Nothing recognizable. Taking a set with the Ford badge and closing the drawer.

Down to the front door. Carefully pulling it open, just a little. Peeking out like a frightened schoolboy. Nobody there. No cops, that's the main thing. No CCTV, either. William always laughed at the idea of this street getting security cameras. Cameras would be worth more than the buildings they'd be guarding. Pushing open the doors all the way and moving along the line of cars parked at the side of the road. Pressing the unlock button on the key at the first Ford he stands beside. Nothing. There's another Focus parked across the road. Over to that and pressing the button. The indicators blinking and the doors unlocking. Calum reversing the car back into the garage, right up to the back. Out and closing the doors behind him. Switching a light on. Across to the metal shelving on the side wall. Going through all the number plates there, trying to find two that match. Find two that aren't much too old for the Focus. Easy to change the plates, and he just needs the ruse to last until he gets south. London, probably. Disappear amongst the biggest crowd. Work out his future from there.

He's walking towards the garage doors when they open from the outside. Just a little. Enough for one person get in. Stumble in, to be more accurate. Shaun Hutton. Notably drunk, pulling the doors shut before he even notices Calum. Hutton's pulling a knife from his coat pocket.

'I knew it,' Hutton's saying with a grin. 'Cos I think like you. I knew it. You'll run. Where do you get a car? Cos you ain't using public transport, are you?'

Calum's standing still and silent. Trying to work out what the hell this is. Not organized, that's obvious.

'I had a job to do here,' Hutton's saying. 'I did it wrong. I'm sorry, okay. But now I got to do the second part. Business. You know.'

And Calum does know. He's smiling a little. Hutton botched it when he killed William. Jamieson will be furious. This is Hutton trying to fix what he broke. A piss-poor attempt.

'You're wasting your time,' Calum's saying quietly. 'Jamieson's been arrested. Young, too. They're finished. So are you, with them.'

Hutton's actually taken a step back. The result of shock mixed with drunkenness. Now would be the moment. What is it with big guys, thinking they can get away with using a knife. As drunk as he is, Hutton's useless. Calum could get to him. Get the knife. Kill him. Here and now. In the same place Hutton killed William. Poetic, almost. But Calum's letting the moment pass. Not for himself. For William. Sure, William would want to see Hutton suffer, but in jail. The last thing he would want is Calum using his death as an excuse to kill again. No more blood.

'You're lying,' Hutton's saying.

An idea. Calum's taking William's phone from his pocket. Switching it on. Making sure there's a signal. Tossing the phone across to Hutton. 'Call him. A cop will answer.'

Hutton's caught the phone. An achievement itself. Glancing at the screen. Throwing it on the floor. Shouting something Calum can't understand.

Hutton's mumbling. Stumbling across to a workbench at the side of the room and sitting down. Calum's walking to the doors. Pushing them wide open. Hutton's just sitting there, staring at the floor. He made his choice, and it was the wrong one. Calum can identify with that. There was a day, not long ago, when he might have felt sorry for Hutton. Instead he's focusing all his energy on resisting killing him. The last temptation. A test he will pass. Once he's out of here, there'll never be people like Hutton in his life again. Just people he can trust. People he can like. That's a warm thought. He's walking slowly to the car. Watching Hutton all the time. Two gunmen without a gun between them.

Pulling out onto the street. Looking left and right. No sign of the police yet, but they can't be far away. Glancing at the clock on the dashboard. Twelve minutes to two. Fisher's had enough time to round up some of his targets. Things will be happening in the city. Happening to the people who ought to be looking for Calum. They won't be looking for a plain black Focus. Not until someone reports it stolen from the garage, or the police work it out. That could be hours. They should track the phone signal to the garage, but they won't spot the car gone. When they do spot it, they'll report the number plate it's supposed to have. With any luck, this car gets him across the border. He'll abandon it quickly. He won't burn it. A burnt-out car is reported as soon as it's spotted. A nice clean car left sitting in a car park can be ignored for weeks. Would have been nice to get to London with this car, but he can't risk that now. Not since he's alerted them to him using the garage.

There's traffic, but all normal. Nothing suspicious. No sign of a tail. Beginning to relax.

Looking at the clock again as he pulls onto the motorway. Quarter past two on a Monday afternoon. Driving south in a nondescript car. Doesn't feel like the right way to leave the city. Hell, any way is the right way. He's starting to smile as he thinks of the chaos he's leaving behind. Thinking about Peter Jamieson and John Young. They believed they could get the better of him. Thought it would be so simple. He beat them; beat them at their own game. The smile's getting wider. Now fading. The price of victory. William – he's told himself that everything he's done is revenge for William. Told himself again and again. Fisher knew the truth. He said before he got out of the car that he knew why Calum was doing this. He thought Calum was doing this to provide himself with a chance to escape. It was that transparent.

Calum's tapping the steering wheel as he accelerates further away from his city. Causing all this chaos, not for his brother, but for himself. Is he that selfish? Scoffing at himself for bothering to ask. Fine, this was for himself, and it worked. But stealing this car is his last crime. Now he has to pay William back. Now he has to become the person his brother always wanted him to be.

# EPILOGUE

Been on remand for three and a half weeks. Sitting in a prison cell, bored out of his skull. They're holding Jamieson in a separate wing from anyone they know worked for him. Keeping him in a different prison from John Young. So be it. Jamieson knows how to live on his own. Not that he's on his own. There are people in the wing looking out for him. As soon as those on the outside knew where he was, moves were made. Calls to inmates. Look out for this guy – he'll make it worth your while. So he's protected. Has people helping him out, getting him things. You have to assume the opposite is also the case. That there are people watching him on behalf of others. People who don't have his best interests at heart. You would think there must be, but Jamieson hasn't found them yet. That'll be because of the chaos going on out there. Chaos he should be taking advantage of.

He hears everything. Information flows freely, and Jamieson has to piece together the bits that matter. That's where he's going just now. A meeting with his lawyer. Led along the corridor, into the meeting room. His lawyer across the table. Standing up to shake his hand. The prison officer stepping outside and closing the door. A good lawyer is important.

'How are you, Peter?' the lawyer's asking.

'Same old. What's the news?' No pleasantries, down to business.

'Spoke to Kevin Currie yesterday,' the lawyer's saying, sitting down. 'He's got his side of things under control for now, but he's worried. People are sniffing around.'

'Any attacks?'

The lawyer's shaking his head.

He's a chubby fellow, Jamieson's lawyer. Charles Simpson, his name is. Good at his job. Likes the life. There's a moral sacrifice in helping Peter Jamieson, but the rewards are good. Let's face it, if he didn't do it, someone else would. The world loses nothing from Simpson helping Jamieson. That's how he sees it.

'Did you speak to Lafferty?'

Simpson's nodding. 'Took a while. I think he was avoiding me. Maybe he didn't know who I was.'

'He knew.'

'I called him a few times. Got a call back this morning. He said nothing's changed. He's been approached by all manner of people, but nobody serious.'

Jamieson's nodding. Makes sense. The big players aren't moving yet. The little guys trying to take advantage, but getting nowhere.

Chaos. That's the news Simpson's been bringing him. That's what the other prisoners are hearing. Fisher's name being mentioned a lot. Bastard's having a field day. Arresting all manner of people. Jamieson the biggest: that's the catch. But Fisher's working his way down the chain. Arresting gun suppliers and counterfeiters. Chasing Alex MacArthur. They say he's pushing MacArthur closer to the devil than he's ever been. Coughing and wheezing and struggling. MacArthur's operation is struggling all of a sudden. People are saying it's about damn time that Don Park took over from him. That's good news and bad. MacArthur's looking inwards, which means he isn't able to move against the Jamieson organization. But if Park takes over, he'll have to be seen to make a move. The easiest big first impression would be sweeping up the remains of Jamieson's businesses. The other big players are all sitting back. Watching and waiting. Nobody's going to rush in. Foolish to rush in, if Jamieson is out of prison in a fortnight's time. Better to wait and see what he gets. If he goes down, the vultures will move.

And he is going down. He knows it. Simpson knows it. It's not whether he gets a custodial sentence, it's how long he gets. Simpson's confident he can beat the hard accusations. Confident they won't even make it to court. Essentially, it's Calum MacLean's word against Peter Jamieson's. Calum MacLean is nowhere to be seen. It's not that a jury would automatically believe Jamieson over Calum, but Calum has to be there to make the accusations. Fisher's been looking for him. A car went south. Abandoned just across the border.

Must have taken a train, wherever he went from there. They won't find Calum. He's gone. Gone for good. Smart enough to stay disappeared. Even Jamieson probably won't try to look.

Hutton's kept his mouth shut. That's important. He's looking at a long stretch. Murdering William MacLean. He's denying it, but that won't get him far. He's screwed. They got him at William's garage. Just sitting there. Drunk as a lord, so they say. They found William's phone lying on the floor of the garage. Hutton wouldn't tell them anything. Didn't say if Calum had been there. Didn't tell them why he had the phone. There's a story there somewhere, Jamieson's sure, but Hutton isn't telling.

Deana Burke is silent. Has to be. Only way she can beat her charge of withholding evidence. Young's kept his mouth shut, too. The good thing about having a close right-hand man – there's nothing he can accuse you of that doesn't implicate himself. He's looking at time, too.

Someone's blabbed. Talked about drugs. Could have come from anyone. Someone has given the police the evidence that's going to put both Jamieson and Young away. Simpson reckons two years, two and a half maybe. Depends on the judge. Depends a little on how much evidence finds its way into court. That's the challenge now. Using contacts to bribe, intimidate and generally make evidence disappear. Three years max. First offence, you see. Dealing, but they can't prove the scale. Can't prove enough. But three years is enough to give Fisher what he wants. Even two would be enough, if he can get rid of Young as well. Jamieson and Young were the organization. Put both of them away and there's a very good chance that everything they've left behind falls apart.

Jamieson thinks about that a lot. Two years inside. What's left after that? Usually, fuck-all. Most organizations can't survive that long without leadership. There are good people out there, looking after their bits of the organization for Jamieson. But even they can't make it last two years. Opportunities will come along for the likes of Currie and Lafferty. Chances to stab Jamieson in the back. They'll take those chances.

But there's another thought. The one that claws away at the back of Jamieson's mind. Young's going down, too. But Simpson's spoken to his lawyer. Won't be any more than eighteen months. First offence. Not in charge. The evidence is that Young facilitated crimes. The evidence can't place him at the scene or in charge. So he'll be out first. Maybe with more than a year's head start. That's what bothers Jamieson more than anything: Young getting out first. He takes charge of whatever's left of the organization; Jamieson comes out a year later. Then what?

Simpson's telling him a few more things. PC Paul Greig has quit the force. He won't be prosecuted, because quitting spares them a lot of embarrassment. Protecting their own. Fisher's furious about that, so the story goes. Only thing that's gone against him recently. No sign of Calum. No sign of George Daly. They buried William MacLean five days ago. Took a long time to release the body because of the murder charge. Lots of people at the funeral. Not Calum, though.

'Any message you want me to deliver?' Simpson's asking him as he gets up to leave. Jamieson's spoken to his wife. Does regularly. Easy to get a phone. Simpson wants to know if he should say anything to the world at large. The industry. John Young in particular.

'Just make sure everyone knows what they need to do. Let them know that I'm still organizing. That I won't accept any change in behaviour from people just because I'm in here.'

'Okay. And for Mr Young?'

Jamieson's pausing. 'Nothing.' And there will be nothing. Young, with all he knows, getting out first, has leaped from best friend to biggest threat. Jamieson knows how to deal with threats.

## Acknowledgements

There are more people that deserve acknowledgement than I care to mention, so to everyone who's helped and supported me, and everyone who's helped this trilogy reach its conclusion, thank you.

# PROLOGUE

He ended up unconscious and broken on the floor of a ware-house, penniless and alone. He was two weeks in hospital, unemployable thereafter, but that didn't matter. What mattered was that, for a few weeks beforehand, he had money. Not just a little money, but enough to show off with, and that was the impression that stuck.

It had been a while since they'd seen him. Months, probably. They were heading back from the jobcentre having made a typically fruitless effort at sniffing out employment. They went in, they searched the touchscreen computer near the door, and they left. Two friends, officially unemployed since the day they left school together a year before, both willing to do unofficial work if that was available. They bumped into Ewan Drummond as they walked back up towards Peterkinney's grandfather's flat.

'All right lads,' Drummond said, grinning at them, 'need a lift anywhere?' He was as big and gormless as ever, but the suggestion of transport was new.

'Lift? From you?' Glass asked.

'Yeah, me. Got myself a motor these days. Got to have one in my line of work, you know.' He said it to provoke questions that would allow him to trot out boastful answers.

Glass and Peterkinney looked at each other before they looked at Drummond. There wasn't a lot of work among their circle of friends. The kind of work that let a man like Drummond make enough money to buy a car was unheard of. They could guess what was involved in the work, but they wanted to hear it.

'Yeah, we'll take a lift,' Peterkinney nodded.

They followed Drummond back down to where his car was parked. Turned out to be a very respectable-looking saloon, not some old banger or boy racer's toy.

'Well, yeah, got to keep up appearances you see.'

Glass dropped into the passenger seat, Peterkinney the back. They were in no hurry to get anywhere, but this was too intriguing to pass on.

'Come on then, big man,' Glass said with a mischievous smile, 'what's this big job you got?'

'Well, uh, I can't really tell you much. Shouldn't tell you much, I mean. Hush-hush, you know.'

By this point Peterkinney was leaning over from the back seat, crowding Drummond, knowing he couldn't keep quiet for long. Drummond's mouth and brain had always been loosely acquainted, so things he shouldn't say frequently slipped out.

'I mean, I suppose I can tell you a bit, but you got to keep it quiet, right.'

'Sure,' they answered together.

'I'm working for Potty Cruickshank. I'm one of his boys.' He said it with such pride, such force, that they both assumed it meant something. Then they thought about it.

'Who?' Glass asked.

'One of his boys? The hell does that mean?' Peterkinney asked warily.

'Nah, nothing like that. He's, like, a debt collector. I go round and pick up money that people owe him. It's all legit. Well, sort of, financial services, that sort of thing. Good money, real good money. You know how much I made last week alone?'

'Isn't that dangerous?' Peterkinney asked.

'Not really, no. Well, now and again, but you got to be tough to make a living these days, guys, that's how it is. How else you going to make good money?' Said with wisdom he presumed but didn't possess. 'So come on, guess what I made last week.' He was desperate to tell them by this point and unwilling to wait for a guess that might be accurate enough to take the wind out of his sails. 'Six-fifty I made last week. Worked four days, couple of hours a day. Six-fifty. I'm telling you, it's the life.'

They didn't say much more to Drummond; just let him rumble on about how much money he was making until he dropped them off. They walked up to the flat Peterkinney shared with his grandfather, a poky little place you would only invite a real friend back to. They went silently into Peterkinney's small bedroom, a cramped room with nothing in the way of luxuries. There was only one subject of conversation.

'Six-fifty a week he's making. Him,' Glass said. 'He's making ten times what we make on Job Seeker's.'

'Come on, it ain't six-fifty a week. It was six-fifty in one week, but that doesn't mean he'll get it every week. And look what he has to do for it. How long you think it's going to be before someone kicks the living shit out of him? His teeth will be down his throat and his money will be up the wall.'

Glass sighed. 'All right, yeah, fine, but look at the money. He's making good money. Even if it's short-term, right, it's still money. And he's got to do some shitty stuff for it, but, come on, you think we're going to get a job that pays us that for non-shitty work?'

'I don't think we're going to get a job at all,' Peterkinney sighed, and slumped back on his bed.

A sentence he was tired of uttering. Glass sat on the chair in the room and tilted his head back, thinking about Ewan Drummond. No smarter than either him or Peterkinney, probably less so. No tougher when push came to shove, although he was bigger than them, which helped. He was no better connected than they were, which was to say that he hadn't been connected to the criminal industry at all as far as Glass knew. Must have gotten his foot in the door without realizing where he was stepping. All of which suggested that employment in the business, and six hundred and fifty quid a week, was within their grasp.

Glass didn't say any of this to Peterkinney because he knew what the reaction would be. Peterkinney would pour scorn on it; tell him he needed to get real. Peterkinney was all about getting whatever job he could, no daydreaming attached. That was fine by Glass; how his best friend had always been. A realist. They left school under-qualified and stumbled together into a job market that had no room for them or interest in them. So they struggled along together, and were still struggling.

Glass couldn't stop thinking about it, and that was really the point. People like Ewan Drummond were useful both in the work they did and the people they encouraged. None too bright and loaded with cash. He was a walking billboard for employers like Potty Cruickshank. A debt collector like Potty had a high turnover of staff, so that positive PR was worth its weight. Glass saw Drummond and knew he was at least as capable. Six-fifty a week, four days a week, a couple of hours a day. Think about it. The money, the cars, the women, the parties. Him and Peterkinney, lounging around doing fuck-all, waiting for some god-awful nine-to-five that would pay them buttons and last six months if they were lucky. No, what Drummond was doing, that was real work.

It wouldn't have mattered if Glass had known. Even if he'd

seen Drummond lying on that warehouse floor two weeks later, it would have made no impact. He would have spent the previous two weeks thinking of nothing but the money Drummond was making, and working out how he and Peterkinney could do the same. Nothing, no matter how grim, was going to change his mind. That was the way to make good money. That was the best option.

'I'll ask the old man if he's heard of anything going,' Peterkinney said quietly. 'We can go back down the job-centre again in a couple of days.' His grandfather was going to have a word with a friend at a packaging factory on their behalf sometime today, although that would lead nowhere as usual. Their names on a list for future reference.

'Yeah,' Glass said. But he wasn't thinking about the job-centre. Wasn't thinking about any sort of work that was going to be advertised. He was thinking of the world Drummond now inhabited. He was thinking of the money. He was thinking of the life.

# 1

Start with a kick to the door. He got a crack out of it, and the plain door shuddered in the frame. Didn't open though. Still staring back at them. Try again. Not a boot this time. Give it a shoulder. A short run-up and a collision with the door. A bigger crack and the door caves in, buckled on the hinges and smashed around the lock. Alex Glass stumbles in with it.

'Shit.' A mutter under his breath. Embarrassed by his ungainly entrance. Embarrassment pushed aside by an attempt at professionalism. He's taking the lead here. Older by six months. His accomplice, Oliver Peterkinney, is still only nineteen. Anyway, this is Glass's job. He set it up. He found the target.

They're searching downstairs, through the kitchen, through the living room. It's a small house, which helps. Tidy as well, everything where it should be. No rubbish for someone to leap out from behind. Flicking lights on and off as they check each room. No attempt at subtlety, not after that entrance. To the bottom of the stairs. If he's here, he's heard them by now. He's had time enough to get a weapon. They didn't plan for that. What if he keeps a weapon by his bed?

Something else to put on the long list of things they didn't plan for.

A light comes on at the top of the stairs. Glass and Peterkinney look at each other. Never been here before. Never been in this situation. If they had to make a split-second decision, they would be too late. A man has emerged at the top of the stairs. Older than these two by ten years. Fatter by three stone. Wearing nothing but his boxer shorts. That makes up their minds for them.

They're looking up the stairs, necks craned. Suddenly feeling confident. The amateurs just got lucky, as all amateurs need to in this business. Peterkinney moves up one step.

'All right, Holmes,' he's saying. Because it is Jim Holmes, the target. He doesn't need clothes to look like his picture. Big and broad, with a thick head of dark hair and a dimpled chin. 'We can sort this out nice and quiet. No need for trouble.' Peterkinney's smart enough to know how dumb that sounds. You smash your way into a guy's house and tell him there's no need for trouble. This isn't how Peterkinney would have played it.

Holmes had his hands in the air, but they're falling now. Who did he think he was going to find at the bottom of the stairs? Maybe the police. Probably the police. Would be about fucking time. He'd raise his hands to them; try to make a good impression. Could have been worse than the police. Could have been a real tough guy. He knows Marty Jones is looking for him. Wants to send a strong message. Marty's big on sending messages. Marty is under the protection of Peter Jamieson. That could get him the use of a man like Nate Colgan. Now there's a man you raise your hands to, no matter how tough you are. But these two? These are just kids. The one coming up the stairs doesn't even look like he's started shaving.

'The fuck are you pair?' Holmes is growling. Going for his best tough-guy voice, which is pretty good by general standards. He's had plenty of practice. Being a tough guy is his job. It's how he makes his living. Marty lends money to people. That money gathers interest at a mathematically improbable rate. Men like Holmes collect the debt. But Holmes got a little tired of handing all that nice money over to a smarmy prick like Marty. Holmes did the hard work, deserved more of the reward. So he started keeping a bigger share for himself. Took Marty an awful long time to work that out, for a guy who figures himself as sharp as a razor. But he was always going to work it out eventually. Marty's no mug.

'We're here for Marty,' Glass is saying. Saying it like it means something.

Peterkinney, three steps up, is looking back at him. Scowling. Shouldn't have said Marty. Should have said Jamieson. That would have carried more weight. Common sense says you exaggerate the power you have behind you.

'*Pft.*' A snort of derision. Not aimed at Marty. Holmes isn't stupid either; he knows how dangerous Marty can be. A well-connected guy with a big ego and a short temper? Those are always dangerous. 'He sending kids to do his fighting for him now?' There's a smile in his eyes. Marty actually has sent kids. There are other debt collectors he could have sent. Tough guys. They'd have done it too, for the right price, even though they know Holmes. Plenty of general muscle he could have hired for the job. But Marty sent the cheap option. A couple of kids looking to make a good first impression.

'Look, we can sort this out,' Glass is saying from the bottom of the stairs. Still trying to lure him down. Trying to fool a man who does this for a living. Still hoping this can be easy. It was never going to be that easy.

Peterkinney isn't waiting. Holmes won't be won round. Once he has it in his head that they're kids, he's going to treat them that way until they change his mind. Only way to change his mind is to do what they came here to do. And the clock is ticking. You don't think the neighbours heard them smash the door in? You don't think they'll be calling the police right now?

Glass is about to open his mouth to say something else when Peterkinney moves. Jumping two steps at a time, getting to Holmes and making a grab for him. So what if he's older? So what if he's tougher, has a reputation for bad things? He's nearly naked. There are two of them. They came here to send a message for Marty. They can't leave until they've tried and they need to leave soon. So you do some-thing, don't you?

Holmes has seen him coming. Leaning his weight for-wards on the balls of his feet. Shoulders down, ready. Peterkinney is two steps from the top and reaching out for a grab. It looks like a wild attempt. A throw of the arms in the general direction of the target. An amateur lunging at a pro. That's what Holmes thinks. It's what he thinks when he throws his weight directly at Peterkinney. He thinks he's going to knock the kid back down the way he came.

That's not what Peterkinney's thinking. He's thrown his arms out there, but he's not watching where he's throwing. He's watching Holmes's feet. Waiting for that reactive lurch forwards. And now it's coming, and Peterkinney's moving his feet, pushing himself backwards against the stair wall with a thud. Watching as Holmes goes sailing past. Holmes's shoul-der catches him, but it's glancing, no impact. Holmes is falling onto the stairs, shouting something loud that doesn't involve words. But Holmes has experience of falling over at other people's insistence. This is standard for him. He's man-aged to push out and wedge himself in the stairs, three steps down from the top.

But that isn't enough to make him safe. Not nearly enough, and Holmes knows it. You can't be on your back in this situation. You're either on your feet or you're out of the fight. You can rely on them being kids, but you can't rely on them being stupid. Before Holmes can struggle to his feet, Peterkinney's got his first kick in.

Knocking Holmes down a couple of steps with the first kick. Holmes shouting, but this fight is over. All Holmes has left is noise. Peterkinney jumping downward, kicking into Holmes with both feet. Peterkinney's landing on his arse, it's jarring but worth it. Holmes is bouncing down the stairs now. Glass had been moving up the stairs to help, now jumping down the last three to get out of the way. A grunting ball of flesh crashing down after him. Holmes has rolled to the bottom. Lying there. Not moving. Groaning, but not moving.

Glass is watching, doing nothing. Standing beside Holmes, looking up at Peterkinney. As far as Glass is concerned, this is over. Peterkinney's quickly down the stairs, standing beside Glass now. Looking down at Holmes. Taking a step back and kicking him hard in his ample guts.

'Try and knock me down the fucking stairs,' Peterkinney's saying. Speaking low, a little spit on his lips. 'That's for Marty. You remember that. That's what happens.' An intensity conjured from a place Glass didn't know his friend possessed.

Glass is pulling at Peterkinney's arm. The job is more than done, time to go. A second person has emerged at the top of the stairs. A thickset woman, glaring down at them. The woman who keeps this house organized and tidy.

'Get out,' she's shouting at them. 'Go on, get out.' She's

starting to march down the stairs towards them. Wrapped up in a thick dressing gown, hair tied back, slippers too big for her making an unsettling slapping noise as she walks. Scowling like she was born that way. Moving towards her partner at the bottom of the stairs. He's groaning on the floor, rolling slightly. Trying to twist into a position that relieves the pain. Trying to turn his back on them, so they can't kick him in the stomach again. Facing the striped wallpaper, hoping this is over. Peterkinney's given him one last kick in the small of the back, he and Glass turning for the door.

The woman's still shouting something, but it's inaudible and entirely her own business. They're out into the night, across the small front garden with no fence and moving down the street. Trying not to run, but walking fast enough to draw attention. The neighbours will have heard the door being broken. They'll hear the shouting. People will be looking out of windows.

'We should have brought balaclavas,' Glass is saying.

'We should have brought a lot of things.' Peterkinney's thinking of all the things they did wrong in this job. More than he realizes. Their first job. Thrown into it by Marty Jones. Someone with experience, a professional, would have done it differently. They did the best that amateurs could.

'First thing I'm spending money on is a car,' Glass is saying. They're still walking too fast, but they're putting distance between themselves and the house. Looking backwards half the time. Nobody following. But then, nobody would need to. You can see their guilt from a distance.

Peterkinney isn't saying anything. Glass wanted this. He's in charge, so let him do the talking. He's his best mate, and you don't puncture your best mate's balloon. But this has been a shambles. They didn't think about it beforehand. Marty gave Glass the job. Their first chance to make a good impression. They rushed out to do it, knowing the prize that will be waiting for them. Next time will be different. Next time they'll make an effort to plan it. Having a vehicle to get away in will be a good start. Neither of them owns a car. Peterkinney doesn't even have a licence.

They've reached the bottom of the street, round the corner. A little relief. They're out of view of the scene of the crime. Walking faster, almost jogging. Anyone looks out a window and they see two guilty-looking young men running past. The kind of guilty young men you remember. Maybe mention to the police if they knock on your door looking for information.

'We did it though,' Glass is saying. 'We fucking did it.'

'Yeah,' Peterkinney's nodding, and he's smiling despite himself. 'We fucking did.'

extracts reading groups

competitions books new

discounts extracts

extracts discounts

competitions

books

new events

extracts books

new titles reading groups

interviews

events extracts

discounts

new books events

events new

discounts extracts discounts

**www.panmacmillan.com**

extracts events reading groups

competitions books extracts new

reading groups events

books

books

reading groups